LEWIS CARROLL

Alice's Adventures in Wonderland

AND

Through the Looking-Glass

and What Alice Found There

THE CENTENARY EDITION

Edited with an Introduction and Notes by

HUGH HAUGHTON

PENGUIN BOOKS

PENGUIN BOOKS

Published by the Penguin Group
Penguin Books Ltd, 27 Wrights Lane, London W8 5TZ, England
Penguin Putnam Inc., 375 Hudson Street, New York, New York 10014, USA
Penguin Books Australia Ltd, Ringwood, Victoria, Australia
Penguin Books Canada Ltd, 10 Alcorn Avenue, Toronto, Ontario, Canada M4V 3B2
Penguin Books (NZ) Ltd, Private Bag 102902, NSMC, Auckland, New Zealand

Penguin Books Ltd, Registered Offices: Harmondsworth, Middlesex, England

Alice's Adventures in Wonderland first published 1865
Through the Looking-Glass first published 1872
Alice's Adventures under Ground first published in facsimile edition 1895 and
reproduced by permission of the British Library (Add Ms 46.700)

Published in Penguin Classics 1998

5 7 9 10 8 6

Set in 10/12.5 pt PostScript Monotype Bembo
Designed in QuarkXpress on an Apple Macintosh
Printed in England by Clays Ltd, St Ives plc

ALICE'S ADVENTURES IN WONDERLAND

AND

THROUGH THE LOOKING-GLASS

AND WHAT ALICE FOUND THERE

LEWIS CARROLL was the pen-name of the Revd Charles Lutwidge Dodgson. Born in 1832, he was educated at Rugby School and Christ Church, Oxford, where he was appointed lecturer in mathematics in 1855, and where he spent the rest of his life. He wrote numerous satirical pamphlets on Oxford politics, including *Notes by an Oxford Chiel* (1874), and works on logic such as *Euclid and His Modern Rivals* and *Symbolic Logic* (1896). He also became a pioneering amateur portrait photographer, specializing in Victorian celebrities and children. Though Dodgson never married, children were the main interest of his life. After the publication of *Alice's Adventures in Wonderland* (1865) and *Through the Looking-Glass* (1871), both of which were originally written for Alice Liddell, the daughter of the dean of his college, he became the most famous children's writer of the day. In addition to his two nonsense classics, he also published several books of nonsense verse, including *Phantasmagoria and Other Poems* (1896), *The Hunting of the Snark* (1876) and *Rhyme? And Reason?* (1882); numerous books of puzzles and games such as *The Game of Logic* (1887); and towards the close of his life, a long children's novel in two parts, *Sylvie and Bruno* (1889, 1893). He died in 1898.

HUGH HAUGHTON is a senior lecturer at the University of York. He has edited Gustav Janouch's *Conversations with Kafka* (1985), *The Chatto Book of Nonsense Poetry* (1988), Rudyard Kipling's *Wee Willie Winkie* (1988) and co-edited, with Adam Phillips, *John Clare in Context* (1994).

CONTENTS

ACKNOWLEDGEMENTS vii
INTRODUCTION ix
FURTHER READING lxvi
A NOTE ON THE TEXT lxx
A NOTE ON TENNIEL lxxv

Alice's Adventures in Wonderland

CONTENTS 7
I DOWN THE RABBIT-HOLE 9
II THE POOL OF TEARS 16
III A CAUCUS-RACE AND A LONG TALE 24
IV THE RABBIT SENDS IN A LITTLE BILL 31
V ADVICE FROM A CATERPILLAR 40
VI PIG AND PEPPER 50
VII A MAD TEA-PARTY 60
VIII THE QUEEN'S CROQUET-GROUND 69
IX THE MOCK TURTLE'S STORY 78
X THE LOBSTER-QUADRILLE 87
XI WHO STOLE THE TARTS? 95
XII ALICE'S EVIDENCE 102

Through the Looking-Glass, and What Alice Found There

CONTENTS 119
I LOOKING-GLASS HOUSE 121
II THE GARDEN OF LIVE FLOWERS 135

III LOOKING-GLASS INSECTS 145
IV TWEEDLEDUM AND TWEEDLEDEE 156
V WOOL AND WATER 170
VI HUMPTY DUMPTY 181
VII THE LION AND THE UNICORN 194
VIII "IT'S MY OWN INVENTION" 205
IX QUEEN ALICE 220
X SHAKING 235
XI WAKING 237
XII WHICH DREAMED IT? 238

INTRODUCTION: ALICE'S ADVENTURES UNDER GROUND 243
ALICE'S ADVENTURES UNDER GROUND 249

'"ALICE" ON THE STAGE' 293

NOTES TO ALICE'S ADVENTURES IN WONDERLAND 299
NOTES TO THROUGH THE LOOKING-GLASS 324
APPENDIX I: PREFACE TO THE EIGHTY-SIXTH THOUSAND 6/- EDITION OF ALICE'S ADVENTURES IN WONDERLAND 356
APPENDIX II: PREFACE TO THE SIXTY-FIRST THOUSAND EDITION OF THROUGH THE LOOKING-GLASS 357

ACKNOWLEDGEMENTS

Too many people have played their part in the production of this edition to be named here. The critical and editorial history of the Alice books involves a large cast of players, a fact which has inspired and inhibited me at the same time. The annotation in this edition is more indebted to my editorial predecessors than I can acknowledge in detail, in particular to editions by Martin Gardner, Douglas Gray and R. L. Green, and the trailblazing essay of the great poet critic William Empson.

My thanks to the staff of Cambridge and York University Libraries and all those who have helped me personally in producing this edition, in particular Tony Fothergill, Kenneth Fuller of Marchpane Books, David Haughton, Karen Hodder, Hermione Lee, Jacqueline Rose, the late Geoffrey Summerfield and Marina Warner. Special thanks go to my patient and inspiring editor at Penguin, Paul Keegan, who commissioned it and bore with me during its long adventures underground, to Adam Phillips whose conversations have helped make sense of it all, and to Fiona Shaw who has gone the whole distance with me.

The edition is dedicated to my daughters Eliza and Jesse with love.

INTRODUCTION

"No! No! The adventures first," said the Gryphon in an impatient tone: "explanations take such a dreadful time." ('The Lobster-Quadrille')

"Even a joke should have some meaning – and a child's more important than a joke, I hope." ('Queen Alice')[1]

1: The Child, Nonsense and Meaning

'"The adventures first"', says Carroll's Gryphon, with his dread of 'explanations', and all readers know this is the right order. Yet introductions inevitably come before adventures and introductions tend to mean explanations. Lots of things happen the wrong way round in these texts – '"Sentence first – verdict afterwards"', shouts the Queen of Hearts[2] – so readers who share the Gryphon's priorities can always read the introduction after the stories, or not at all. You simply follow the instructions of the King of Hearts: '"Begin at the beginning . . . and go on till you come to the end: then stop"'.[3]

Yet Carroll's heroine, at the heart of these adventures, is very much concerned with questions of meaning. When she dreamily finds her way to the other side of the looking-glass, one of the first things she encounters is a poem called 'Jabberwocky'. After reading it, Alice remarks '"It seems very pretty . . . but it's rather hard to understand!"' '"Somehow it fills my head with ideas"', she reflects, '"only I don't exactly know what they are!"'[4]

In this respect, the nonsensical mirror-poem 'Jabberwocky' stands as a mirror of the classic literary double-act of which it is part. All readers of *Alice's Adventures in Wonderland* and *Through the Looking-Glass*, those undisputed classics of nonsense literature, find themselves in much the same predicament as the heroine. The stories fill our heads with ideas, but we don't know what they are.

All the same, readers tend to divide between those who are content to find the stories 'pretty' – as Alice somewhat incongruously finds that monstrous travesty of a heroic monster-slaying saga 'Jabberwocky' 'pretty' – and those who want to know what those obscure 'ideas' Alice intimates really are. Of the verses read out in the court-room scene at the close of *Alice's Adventures in Wonderland*, Alice declares '"I don't believe there's an atom of meaning in it"', which prompts the King to reflect:

"If there's no meaning in it," said the King, "that saves a world of trouble, you know, as we needn't try to find any. And yet I don't know," he went on, spreading out the verses on his knee, and looking at them with one eye; "I seem to see some meaning in them after all. '*—said I could not swim—*' you ca'n't swim, can you?" he added, turning to the knave.[5]

To read the Alice books is to plunge into a world of narrative distortions and nonsensical explanations, and the reader is perpetually caught between the two contradictory positions adopted by Alice and the King, of finding no meaning in it, as she does, or attempting to decode 'some meaning' from it all, like the King. Finding meaning, like losing meaning, involves pleasure as well as pain. But then losing meaning, like finding it, does too, as the best nonsense reminds us.

In *Through the Looking-Glass*, Alice brings her comparable puzzlement about the 'Jabberwocky' poem to Humpty Dumpty. '"You seem very clever at explaining words, Sir"', she says, '"Would you kindly tell me the meaning of the poem called 'Jabberwocky'?"'[6] Humpty Dumpty, an egghead absolutely obsessed with meaning, duly obliges, with an intellectual confidence rare even among critics of poetry: '"I can explain all the poems that ever were invented – and a good many that haven't been invented yet"'. He goes on to interpret 'Jabberwocky' according to whimsical fiat on the one hand ('"'*Brillig*' means four o'clock in the afternoon"') and a theory of 'portmanteau words' on the other hand: this enables him to unpack the different meanings he sees packed into one nonsense word (so that 'slithy', for example, can be decoded as an amalgam of 'lithe' and 'slimy'). Though authoritative, and even seductive, as a piece of off-the-cuff philological commentary upon 'Jabberwocky', Humpty Dumpty's 'explanation' of the nonsense idiom of the poem is as nonsensical as his definition earlier of 'glory' as a 'knock-me-down argument'. It is as much a parody of philosophical and linguistic authority as an instance of it, and, as the familiar nursery rhyme warns Alice he will do, this hubristic nonsense commentator comes to a sticky end.

If the problem of meaning – of what Alice's adventures and what she finds in them means – haunts the text and its heroine, it has also, since the date of its first publication, haunted its readers. Though many readers share the 'adventures first' view of the Gryphon that 'explanations' are a waste of time, others adopt the viewpoint of the Red Queen that '"Even a joke should have a meaning—and a child's more important than a joke"'. In fact, we could classify readers of the books as either Gryphons or Queens. Those in the first camp simply wish to enjoy the story as a story, as they think appropriate for a book originally written for children, and rebuff all efforts to interpret it. Those in the second, contrariwise, insist that it is meaning and not meaninglessness which makes Carroll's nonsense expressive, and that all readings of the Alice books are necessarily interpretative. Why should meaningless jokes or meaningless stories be more interesting than meaningful ones?

Historically, the Carrollian editor and biographer R. L. Green falls into the first camp and stands as the prime spokesperson for Gryphonism.[7] The poet and critic William Empson stands at the forefront of the latter or Red Queen's camp, with his ground-breaking essay on 'The Child as Swain' setting the agenda for all subsequent Freudian and historical interpretations of Lewis Carroll's work.[8] The editor Martin Gardner, a mathematician and logician like Carroll, is the ultimate exponent of the Red Queen school of thought and in his masterfully Dumptyan *The Annotated Alice* explains the Alice books with reference to the whole intellectual universe before and since – and the whole intellectual universe by reference to the Alice books.[9]

These divergent approaches to reading the Alice books reflect something of the enigmatic or hybrid nature of the text itself. These are sophisticated 'fairy tales' on the one hand, as Carroll announces in the prefatory poem to *Wonderland*, and they abound in the spontaneous enigmatic coinings of dreams, slips of the tongue, jokes and improvisatory free-association. On the other hand they are also riddling, aesthetically highly wrought products of a child-haunted adult, obsessed by questions of meaning, and have something of the eerie perfection of the literary sphinx about them, of Wildean contrivance as well as the vertiginous spontaneity of improvisation. On the one hand, these are two of the few widely acknowledged classics of children's literature which helped in themselves to redefine the possibilities of writing for children. On the other hand, they are two of the most original, experimental works of literary fiction in the nineteenth century and have had a huge impact on subsequent fiction and culture. Translated by Nabokov into Russian, adopted by the Surrealists as proto-surrealist dream books in France, taken up by T. S. Eliot, Virginia Woolf, James Joyce, W. H. Auden and more recently Peter Ackroyd as models, the Alice books have been taken to prefigure modernism at its most experimental as well as children's writing at its most elemental.[10] This double fate may embarrass some readers but is surely inherent in the stories Carroll wove around his heroine Alice, and surely part of their challenge and appeal to all readers, young and old.

In a sense this dispute represents a reaction to something beyond the Alice books themselves. It represents a dispute about the meaning of children's literature (whatever that is), about childhood and literary representations of childhood, about the relation between books for children and books for adults, about 'nonsense' as a genre and classification, about dreams, and of course about reading.[11] *Alice's Adventures in Wonderland* originated as a children's story and was marketed as a book for children, yet since the day of its first publication it has always appealed to adults too and, with the Bible and Shakespeare, is reputed to be the most quoted of English texts. Carroll's two dream books about a seven-year-old middle-class Victorian girl offer themselves as absurd and riddling parables of narrative and linguistic innocence, but they are also allegories of experience: incarnations of philosophical sophistication and perverse intellectual wit, constructed around the adventures of a child.

What is ultimately at stake in disagreements about the 'innocence' of such children's classics as the Alice books is, I suspect, a debate about the relationship between adulthood and childhood – and where in that complex, troubled and mesmerizing relationship the interest of 'innocence' is to be found and in whose interest. Talking about Carroll, W. H. Auden wrote that 'there are good books which are only for adults, because their comprehension presupposes adult experiences, but there are no good books which are only for children'.[12] In this sense, it is natural for children's books to become adult books if they are any good; since all adults have been children, books for and about children are always potentially for and about adults too. William Empson has said that the Alice books are about 'growing up', which is certainly true.[13] They are also, perhaps more surprisingly, about grown-ups. Alice, after all, is, apart from a fleeting baby (who turns into a pig) and those stuffed archetypal schoolboys Tweedledum and Tweedledee, the only child in the books at all. Like Henry James's *What Maisie Knew*, the stories give us not so much an adult's view of childhood as a child's view of adulthood. Seen through the lens of Alice, the world of adulthood is as dismayingly bizarre and perverse as those of Dickens and James.

Virginia Woolf resolves the question of readership in a different way. 'The two *Alices* are not books for children', she wrote in 1939, 'they are the only books in which we become children'.[14] According to Woolf, his childhood, 'lodged whole and entire' inside Dodgson, forming 'an impediment at the centre of his being' which 'starved the mature man of nourishment' but enabled him in fiction to 'do what no one else has ever been able to do . . . return to that world' and 'recreate it . . . so that we too become children again'. This is a large claim and magically dissolves the barrier between adult and child. In *Jacob's Room*, *To the Lighthouse* and *The Waves* Woolf herself tried to 'recreate' that childhood world too, so her tribute to Carroll is born out of a sense of affinity. Carroll should be placed with the modernist novelists Proust, Joyce and Woolf, as well as the Oedipal father of modern childhood, the psychoanalyst Freud, as part of a cultural movement placing the child's story at the heart of adult culture.

The Alice books are children's literature, but also, as much as Dickens's *Great Expectations*, Emily Brontë's *Wuthering Heights* or Henry James's *What Maisie Knew*, part of the nineteenth century's expanding literature about childhood. In foregrounding problems of language and meaning, they are as formally disorienting and psychologically searching representations of childhood subjectivity as Joyce's *A Portrait of the Artist* or Woolf's *To the Lighthouse*. 'Adventures' and 'Wonderland' suggest 'fairy tale' and 'romance', but Alice's most parlous adventures underground and through the mirror are intellectual and social rather than physical, dialectical rather than folkloric. The Gryphon, Monstrous Crow and Jabberwocky are comparatively harmless antagonists compared to all the querulous logicians and niggling philosophers of meaning she meets on her travels, all ready to pounce like vultures on any phrase or idiom, however 'normal', that can be wrested into the discomforting abnormality of 'nonsense'. The author of the Alice books was an Oxford logician, and at every turn of her looking-glass quest, Alice's conversations bring her into close encounters not only with figures from games of cards and chess like the Queen of Hearts and the White Knight, or from the traditional repertoire of nursery rhymes like Humpty Dumpty and the Unicorn, but with the persistent puzzles, paradoxes and riddles which haunt the apparently stable mirror theories of language which have dominated the philosophy of the West.[15]

The question of the meaning of nonsense haunts Alice and many of her interlocutors. '"It's really dreadful"', Alice reflects at one point, '"the way all the creatures argue. It's enough to drive one crazy!"'[16] Many of these maddening arguments concern the questions of meaning, identity, names, logic and the philosophy of language which have vexed philosophers since Plato. The seven-year-old Alice is caught up in a series of bad-tempered dialectical duets which call in question or put into play the conceptual foundations of her world. It is no wonder that the relation between children, jokes and meaning raised by the Red Queen should haunt readers of Lewis Carroll's story.

2: *Biographical*

One familiar – and familiarizing – way of re-framing the riddle of the Alice books is biographical, to look to the life of the author for clues to the meaning of his dream texts. One answer to Alice's last question in *Through the Looking-Glass*, as to 'who it was that dreamed it all?' is 'Lewis Carroll'.[17]

'Lewis Carroll' was the pseudonym of the Reverend C. L. Dodgson. And if during his lifetime, as Virginia Woolf said, 'The Rev. C. L. Dodgson had no life',[18] since his death he has been subjected to innumerable posthumous Lives, starting with his nephew Stuart Dodgson Collingwood's *The Life and Letters of Lewis Carroll*, published in 1898, the year of his death.[19] Unfortunately the Dodgson that emerges from the densely documented pages of these Lives is almost as enigmatic and controversial a figure as Alice.

Charles Lutwidge Dodgson was born in 1832, the year of the Reform Act, into a rural parsonage in Daresbury, Cheshire. He was the third of eleven children and the eldest son. His father, a High Churchman in the mould of his friend Pusey, was a graduate of Christ Church, Oxford, where he took a First in classics and mathematics. Though his son rarely mentions him in letters or diaries, his father and Christ Church were to cast a long shadow over his entire life. The Reverend Charles Dodgson had married his cousin, Frances Jane Lutwidge (about whom we know dismayingly little beyond the family's image of her as ideal Victorian Mother), and six years after he left Oxford, they settled in the remote parish of Daresbury, where he was appointed curate (it was in the gift of Christ Church). The first eleven years of young Charles Dodgson's life were spent in this crowded rural parsonage, dominated by his father's strong intellectual personality and the rituals of Anglican piety and family games. During these first years of what his nephew called 'complete seclusion from the world',[20] young Charles, his seven sisters and two brothers were educated at home by their mother, and subjected to a heavy daily dose of High Church Christianity from their father.

Though Stuart Dodgson Collingwood retails family anecdotes about his climbing trees and making friends with snails and toads or encouraging 'civilised warfare among earthworms',[21] modern biographers have little to go on when trying to imagine Dodgson's formative years in this formative place. His child friend Isa Bowman called him 'the man who above all others has understood childhood'[22] and Virginia

Woolf thought that 'childhood remained in him entire' all his life, persisting as an 'impediment in the centre of his being'.[23] He said himself that children were 'three-fourths' of his 'life',[24] and the cult of childhood was clearly central to his entire adult life. This makes it the more surprising that, apart from in a couple of early poems, Dodgson never talked about his own childhood, his family, early games or reading. In 'Faces in the Fire', written in 1860, he evokes 'the happy place where I was born', 'an island farm' amid 'broad seas of corn',[25] and in 'Solitude' (the first poem to bear the signature of 'Lewis Carroll', written when he was twenty-one) he invokes 'the golden hours of Life's young spring/Of innocence, of love and truth', affirming he would give all his adult wealth 'To be once more a little child/For one bright summer-day'. These are surprising sentiments for a twenty-one-year-old student perhaps, but not for the period.[26] They tell us more about the post-Wordsworthian romance of childhood than about Dodgson's own early life.

In 1843, the Reverend Charles Dodgson, who by then had completed an edition of Tertullian commissioned by Pusey in addition to running his quiet Cheshire parish, acquired the larger, altogether less secluded parish of Croft on Tees in North Yorkshire, thanks to Bishop Longley's intervention with the Prime Minister, Robert Peel. The vicarage at Croft was much grander, set in a big well-tended garden, close to the newly built railway and industrial Darlington. The family grew larger too, since before long Mrs Dodgson gave birth to another son. Thereafter the eleven Dodgson children seemed to thrive in the new rectory, with its greater space and access to the wider world. They were to remain a close-knit family throughout their long lives. One of their odder shared characteristics was a chronic stammer. Charles himself had to battle with a stammer all his life (he had regular speech therapy as an adult), and six of his seven sisters were stammerers too. The 'Dodo' of *Wonderland* represents the first syllables of his stammered surname – 'Do-Do-Dodgson' – and it may be that his fine ear for linguistic nonsense, and for semantic and logical impediments of all kinds, had some relation to his speech impediment.

In 1844 Charles's school education began, setting up the rhythm that shaped the rest of his life. Henceforward, there was to be an oscillation between serious all-male academic life on the one hand and the company of young children – mainly girls – on the other. He went first as a boarder to Richmond School, ten miles from home, where his headmaster noticed 'an uncommon share of genius' and what was to become a highly characteristic inability to 'rest satisfied without a most exact solution of whatever seems to him most obscure'. Two years later the fourteen-year-old Dodgson found himself further from home and from happiness in that archetypal nineteenth-century public school, Rugby, where he arrived shortly after the death of Thomas Arnold. This was the period of *Tom Brown's Schooldays*, but Dodgson was no Tom Brown. 'I cannot say I look back on my life at a Public School with any sensations of pleasure', he wrote later in the privacy of his diary of 1855 in a rare moment of class disloyalty, 'or that any earthly considerations would induce me to go through my three years again.'[27]

However uncongenial he found the all-male, sport-dominated culture of public school, he typically won prizes in almost every subject, and soon found himself, under the patronage of his father's mentor Dr Pusey, at his father's college, Christ Church, Oxford, where he took up residence in 1851. Dr Pusey wrote to his father, commending his 'uniform, steady and good conduct', and young Charles continued to follow in his father's footsteps. He read classics and mathematics like him, like him emerged with a First in mathematics (falling short of his father's Double First), and like him ended up with a studentship at Christ Church with the expectation of going on into the Church. Though young Charles was eventually ordained in 1861, after some soul-searching, he didn't go on, like his father, to a parish and family of his own. Christ Church was not to be a stepping-stone but his home for the rest of his life.

His childhood was over, but the idea of it lived on. Nothing could be much less like the Brontës' childhood in that other Yorkshire parsonage than the Dodgsons' at Croft, but as for the Brontës at Haworth, the children's home-made writing culture helped shape Charles's future career. As Donald Thomas notes, 'the most impressive and durable memorial of Croft was the succession of magazines for the younger children that Charles wrote, edited and produced'.[28] A far cry from the Brontës' chronicles of Angria, these largely comic productions were full of spoofs, parodies and jokes. They included the ironically entitled 'Useful and Instructive Poetry' written for Wilfred and Louisa in about 1845 and 'The Rectory Magazine' of 1848, culminating in 'The Rectory Umbrella', christened after the giant yew tree in the garden, which Charles wrote and illustrated on his own for a year and a half before going up to Oxford.[29] There is a sense in which these occasional performances established the pattern he was to follow for the rest of his life. In the closed environment of the God-fearing, conservative vicarage of his childhood, Charles discovered a quasi-magical role as children's entertainer in contrast to that of preacher like his father. Though he did eventually become a clergyman and a reluctant preacher, he remained a comic writer, puzzle-maker and spellbinder, whose inventive gifts were largely directed towards an audience of children (or, in the Oxford squibs and pamphlets, his fellow dons at Christ Church). 'The Rectory Umbrella' seems an inspired umbrella title for all the comic household magazines devised in the school holidays, in the margins of his serious, prize-laden academic career in Rugby. The frontispiece of 'The Rectory Umbrella' shows a figure sheltering below an umbrella of Jokes, Riddles, Fun, Poetry and Tales, taking refuge from the stones slung at him by the demons of woe, crossness, ennui and spite. Dodgson's long career as a solo entertainer was lived out under sheltering familial umbrellas – first that of the parental rectory at Croft, then that of Christ Church, Oxford, which in 1851 became his permanent home. In both places, the comic art of this most defensive personality clearly functioned as a defence against anxieties that could not be held at bay even there.

In his diary for 1855, which he calls 'the most eventful year of his life', Dodgson notes that he had begun it 'as a poor bachelor student', and ended it as 'a master and tutor in Ch. Ch., with an income of more than £300 a year, and the course of mathematical tuition marked out by God's providence, for at least some years to come'.[30] In fact, providence ordained that Dodgson would be a mathematics lecturer for twenty-five years and persist in the even tenor of his way at Christ Church until his death in 1898, nearly half a century later. His subsequent career as a bachelor clergyman and successful children's writer, living at the heart of the academic and social establishment as a Christ

Church don, was, like his childhood, an impeccably conventional one in almost all respects – but it had one deep-rooted anomaly at its heart: a dream of childhood, focused on the figure of a beautiful young girl.

It was in 1853, in his third year at Oxford, and after the death of his mother, that Dodgson wrote 'Solitude', in which he evoked an infant sobbing itself asleep 'Upon a mother's breast', recalling 'the golden hours of Life's young Spring', before declaring he would give everything 'to be once more a little child/ For one bright summer's day.'[31] This anomalous cult of the child was to bring him fame through the Alice books and a certain social cachet through his camera, but in its wake it also woke shadowy rumours of scandal as a result of his increasingly obsessive fascination with girls before puberty, and his growing preoccupation with photographing them in as scantily clad a state as possible, in bathing drawers for example, or, preferably, in the nude. 'A girl of about twelve is my ideal beauty of form', he wrote in 1893, and 'one hardly sees why the lovely forms of girls should *ever* be covered up.'[32]

The anomaly's first name and incarnation was Alice Liddell, and it was in the shadow of Alice's name and the pseudonym of Lewis Carroll, author of the Alice books, that Dodgson lived his later life. The Liddell children first entered the young mathematics tutor's life in 1856, the year after their father Henry Liddell – previously head of Westminster School, co-author of the famous Greek lexicon and a high-profile reformer – was, to the conservative Dodgson's alarm, appointed Dean of Christ Church. It was Harry Liddell he met first ('the handsomest boy I ever saw'),[33] then Lorina. In April, however, the twenty-four-year-old Dodgson, then very much a novice at what was called the 'black art' of photography, tried to photograph the new Dean's three small daughters, including the three-year-old Alice, in the Deanery Gardens.[34] It wasn't a success aesthetically (they wouldn't keep still), but this first of innumerable attempts to photograph Alice and her sisters established him at the Deanery: 'The three girls were in the garden most of the time, and we became excellent friends', he wrote in his diary.[35] In June he took the ten-year-old Harry Liddell rowing with him on the river, and soon afterwards the unchaperoned seven-year-old Lorina on another river trip. He noted that day in his diary with a 'white stone' (as he marked all special days).[36] During the next few years there were many such days and Dodgson, despite his political differences with the Dean on many college issues, became a regular intimate of the Dean's family, taking pictures, playing cards and croquet, telling jokes and stories, and messing about on the river. While he was by most accounts a rather dreary college tutor for undergraduates, he seems to have been in his element with the Deanery children, who clearly put him in touch with his familiar role as family entertainer under the Rectory Umbrella at Croft. During these years his intimacy with Alice grew, as the series of haunting, yet subliminally creepy photographs of her and her sisters show. As Michael Bakewell says, these 'pictures tell us, if nothing else, he was in love with Alice.'[37]

But they don't tell the whole story, and there is a frustrating gap in the written records just at this crucial point. Dodgson began keeping a diary in his third year in Oxford and went on doing so until his death. The thirteen volumes of these were available to his first biographer, but the two volumes that cover the years from April 1858 to May 1862, during which Dodgson's intimacy with Alice was maturing, have disappeared (either lost, as the family subsequently maintained, or, more likely, destroyed).[38] Furthermore, though they fortunately resume just in time to record the weeks leading up to the genesis of *Wonderland* and the famous river expedition that June, the diaries are interrupted once again for the three days in late June 1863 when Dodgson's intimacy with Alice and the other Liddells was abruptly terminated for ever by her mother, the formidable, socially ambitious Lorina Liddell. Mrs Liddell also destroyed all his letters to Alice.[39] It is one of the great ironies of Dodgson's life that by the time *Wonderland* was published in 1865, making her about the most famous seven-year-old girl in history and him the most famous children's writer, their relationship was a thing of the past and Dodgson was banned from the Deanery. We don't know why the kissing had to stop, or what brought to an end the stories, photos and river expeditions which provide the frame for *Wonderland*, but stop they did. When he saw the Liddell children again the following December, the diary records 'I held myself aloof from them, as I have done all this term.'[40]

There were family rumours that Dodgson proposed to Alice, but was rejected – either because she was too young, or that he in his thirties was too old, or that this obscure young mathematics don didn't match Mrs Liddell's notoriously snobbish expectations for her daughters (she liked hobnobbing with royalty and is probably parodied in the references to 'Kingfishers' in Dodgson's skit on the Dean's architectural taste, 'The Vision of the 3 T's').[41] Romance with teenagers, like stuttering, was evidently something to which the Dodgson boys were prone, for at about the same time Dodgson was head over heels in love with Alice, his younger brother Wilfred fell in love with another teenage Alice, the fourteen-year-old Alice Donkin. Unlike Charles, however, Wilfred went on, after a decent interval, to marry her (in 1862 Charles had photographed her prophetically as a teenage bride in a bizarrely composed photo 'The Elopement'). In a diary entry in 1866 Dodgson describes a conversation about Wilfred and 'A.L.' (presumably, Alice Liddell) as 'a very anxious subject'. It was such an 'anxious subject' for everyone concerned that none of the interested parties ever discussed it again in public. Recalling her memories of Wonderland seventy years later, Alice Hargreaves (as she then was) steers well away from any mention of her or the celebrated author's feelings, and though Dodgson spoke later of Alice as his 'ideal child friend',[42] he never explained the nature of their friendship or the dramatic rift that separated them.

By the time he published *Through the Looking-Glass* in 1872, he was writing 'as if she was dead'.[43] Its opening verses ('Child of the pure unclouded brow') speak of Alice and the author being 'half a life asunder', while the closing poem ('A boat beneath a sunny sky') reads like an elegy for Alice, though it was written when she was still in her teens. In fact the coda to her adventures through the mirror is almost Hardyesque in its wintry words and lyric attenuations: 'Long has paled that sunny sky:/ Echoes fade and memories die:/ Autumn frosts have slain July./ Still she haunts me phantomwise/ Alice moving under skies/ Never seen by waking eyes.' Alice has become a figure in his dream.

The nature of Dodgson's love of Alice remains a subject of speculation. On the evidence of his surviving letters and diaries, Dodgson, though a most self-conscious writer, was not a man with a very intense self-consciousness or interest in his own motives or feelings. Dodgson the photographer 'had a horror' of being photographed himself.[44] Similarly while his diaries and letters diligently record his daily visits, meetings, and journeys, including his rendezvous with children, they tell us remarkably little about his feelings – in complete contrast to the diaries of his younger contemporary Kilvert with their vivid insights into that other bachelor cleric's voyeuristic interest in young girls. In his diaries Dodgson regularly commemorates his meetings with Alice and the other Liddells during their years of close contact (he was obviously half in love with the whole family) by marking the days in his diary by a 'white stone', his usual code for a day of exceptional pleasure. After the boating expedition in 1856 with Harry and Ina Liddell, for example, he wrote 'Mark this day, annalist, not only with a white stone, but as altogether, 'Dies mirabilis'.[45] Another entry, for 26 June 1857, goes:

> Spent the day at the Deanery, photographing, with very slender success. Though I am disappointed in missing this last opportunity of getting good pictures of the party, it was not withstanding one of the pleasantest days I have ever spent there. I had Alice and Edith with me till 12; then Harry and Ina till the early dinner at 2, which I joined; and all four children all afternoon. The photographing was accordingly plentifully interspersed with swinging, backgammon, etc. I mark this day most specially with a white stone.[46]

This is as close as the diary ever comes to telling us what the children meant to him, but it conceals as much as it reveals. The 'annalist' is no analyst. The cryptically jubilant sign-post of the 'white stone' is also a burial stone, a symbol of what his contemporary Matthew Arnold called 'The Buried Life'. When we look for evidence of Carroll's 'inner life', what kinds of experience might lie buried behind the rigidly 'externalized' record of the diaries and letters, the pamphlets and memoirs, this is what meets us: a white stone.

A number of 'serious' poems dating from these years and published later in *The Three Sunsets* (1898) suggest a preoccupation with sexual guilt, contrasted with visions of childlike innocence: 'The Valley of the Shadow of Death', 'Beatrice', 'Stolen Waters', 'Only a Woman's Hair'. They may tell us something of Dodgson's mysterious paedophile sexuality. The watery guilt scenario played out in 'Stolen Waters' of 1862, for example, though largely stolen from Coleridge and Keats's exercises in the Gothic ballad form, invokes a 'happy, innocent child' (apparently five years old), and this 'sainted, ethereal maid' is threatened by 'a grim wild beast', a 'savage heart' in 'human guise'.[47] During the same period, Dodgson's diaries are particularly racked with conventionally pious expressions of guilt and resolutions to change his life, as his best recent biographer, Morton N. Cohen, notes.[48] Such entries occur overwhelmingly in the decade 1862 to 1872, his great creative decade, most intensively in the years from 1862 to 1867, culminating in 1863, the year of the break with the Liddells and the time of the genesis of the Alice books. Some time later, his friend Lord Salisbury wrote, 'They say Dodgson has gone out of his mind in consequence of having been refused by the real Alice (Liddell)', adding that 'It certainly looks like it.'[49] Dodgson himself, while noting the fact of his banishment from the Liddells, says nothing of this – or anything else about his state of mind at the great watershed in his life represented by the publication of *Alice's Adventures in Wonderland* in 1866 and the break with its only begetter, Alice Liddell.

There's a telling moment in *Through the Looking-Glass* which bears on Dodgson's resistance to autobiography. '"The horror of that moment"', the King cries after Alice has put the little royal chess piece down, '"I shall never, *never* forget!"' Advised by the Queen to make a note of this in his memorandum book, he starts to do so, only to have Alice force his hand and write '*The White Knight is sliding down the poker. He balances very badly*'. Reading it, the Queen exclaims, '"That's not a memorandum of *your* feelings!"' The same holds true not only of Dodgson's diaries but Carrollian nonsense: they hold both 'horror' and 'desire' at bay. In fact nonsense can convert the disorderly world of unbalanced feeling into externalized absurdity.[50] Much of the obsessional inventiveness of Dodgson's life, in particular his imaginative life – his investment in inventing games, puzzles, ingenious gadgets like his Nictograph for night-writing, his lists and catalogues – can be seen as a defensive construction against not only anxiety but his own subjectivity, and its potential for disorder. In the Preface to the revealingly entitled *Pillow Problems* (1893), Part II of the less revealingly entitled *Curiosa Mathematica*, he recommended his mathematical puzzles and exercises as a way of diverting people's minds from troubling thoughts and disturbing feelings:

> There are sceptical thoughts, which seem for the moment to uproot the firmest faith; there are blasphemous thoughts, which dart unbidden into the most reverent souls; there are unholy thoughts, which torture with their hateful presence, the fancy that would fain be pure. Against all these some real mental work is a most helpful ally.[51]

This tells us something about his thoughts, as well as his thoughts about how to divert and disperse them by 'mental work'. His taste for mathematical problems, such as those in *A Tangled Tale*, for new word games such as Doublets and Syzgies, for logical puzzles such as are described in *The Game of Logic*, obviously provided him with harmless, obsessional activity which deflected him from the dangerous world of subjective feeling. This must have been one of the attractions of nonsense too, with its systematic, playful derangements of sense, its experiments in disorder from within an unshaken framework of orderliness. Yet in the nonsense of the Alice books, as nowhere else, Dodgson found a licence to explore not only his identifications with his child heroine, but the disorienting, 'sceptical' dimension of his own intelligence, which most of his life he had to hold at bay.

Dodgson by all accounts was profoundly preoccupied by balance, orderliness and control. As Isa Bowman noted, 'all the minutiae of life received an extreme attention at his hands' and his hands always 'wore a pair of grey cotton gloves'.[52] There were two sides to this. It made him a stickler for detail, principle, rules and regulations when it came to running the college, which led to regular altercations with the Dean, college servants, and fellow dons when he was Curator of the Common Room. 'Except to little girls, he was not an alluring personage', wrote William Tuckwell of New College. Tuckwell characterized him as 'austere, shy, precise, absorbed in mathematical reverie, watchfully tenacious of his dignity, stiffly conservative in political, theological, social theory, his life mapped out in squares like Alice's landscape.[53] Yet to girls he clearly *was* an alluring personage, as many of them testified later, and his rooms in Tom Quad appeared to Isa Bowman as 'a fairy-land for children.'[54] If so, it was a fairy-land which, like the squares in

Alice's landscape, was precisely mapped out. As *Through the Looking-Glass*, *The Game of Logic* and his popularizing works on logic all show, Dodgson remained a Euclidean even at play.

At the heart of the Alice books is Dodgson's dream identification with his child heroine. The writer sees through Alice's eyes. In his later work he never attained this kind of identification again. In his other literary and pictorial representations of children, they remain very much objects of adult manipulation. They are viewed through the sentimentalist's or the voyeur's lens, as idealized fictional innocents like the protagonists of *Sylvie and Bruno* or as the carefully staged beauties, captured clothed, partially clothed or unclothed in the huge archive of his photographs of child models. The newly invented camera was Dodgson's passport to respectable middle-class and artistic homes, allowing him to gratify his passion for capturing the famous social, literary and artistic 'lions' of the day on the one hand – Tennyson, the Rossettis, Millais, George MacDonald, Ellen Terry, Prince Leopold and other Oxonian and national celebrities – and little girls on the other. The girls might be dressed as themselves or in theatrical costume, or in what came to be his 'favourite costume', wearing nothing at all. Alice Liddell was his passport to Wonderland – and *Alice in Wonderland* became his passport to Fame, a fame that, for all his notorious touchiness about his incognito (he would return letters addressed to 'Lewis Carroll'), was central to his relationship to the host of little girls who succeeded Alice. Writing to her in 1885, he wrote that his 'mental picture' of his 'ideal child friend' was as 'vivid as ever'. He had had 'scores of child friends' since her time, he said, 'but they have been quite a different thing'.[55]

Dodgson's life, with the exception of his unlikely trip to Moscow in 1867, was lived at the heart of upper-middle-class England, anchored to Christ Church, Oxford. From this base, he kept an eye on his many unmarried, stuttering siblings, who went to settle in Guildford after their father's death, and took long seaside holidays, first on the Isle of Wight, then at the more respectable Eastbourne, where he could indulge his passion for other people's young daughters. During the rest of the year, he took regular trips to London, to photograph the famous, visit family and friends, and pursue his main cultural interests by visiting theatres and galleries. As with photography, however, his cultural interests too revolved almost exclusively around little girls. He enjoyed their company, and regularly took them to plays and pantomimes, art galleries and exhibitions, where he was particularly interested in viewing other girls on stage or in the picture frame. His taste in theatre was largely determined by his taste for child actresses – like Ellen Terry – and by the real or imagined taste of his child friends. He disapproved of music-hall and in Podsnappish vein told Marianne Richards, 'I have a dream of Bowdlerising Bowdler', that is 'editing a Shakespeare that shall be absolutely fit for *girls*'.[56] He disapproved of Isa Bowman when she played morally questionable roles, and was a ceaseless campaigner to keep theatre free of any remote sexual innuendo or whiff of 'irreverence'.[57] Much the same can be said of the visual arts. Though he was a keen admirer of the Pre-Raphaelites, the views on art recorded in his diaries are largely confined to remarks about the beauty or otherwise of the children represented there. It was fortunate for him, in this respect, that Victorian painting catered so generously for his particular tastes – had he been born in the heyday of Cubism or Abstract Expressionism, he would not have fared so well. Year by year, his diaries scrupulously record not only these visits to studios, galleries and theatres, but the list of child conquests made on trains, beaches and in other places of public amusement. Dodgson was the Casanova of the Victorian nursery. In 1863, he listed in his diary the names of 108 children (all girls) that were 'Photographed or to be Photographed', arranging them alphabetically (there were five Alices, five Beatrices, six Constances and so on). His diaries year by year are a roll-call of conquests. Eastbourne 1877 was a particularly good year for cruising at the seaside ('I could, if I liked, make friends with a new set of nice children every day!' he wrote in August) and when he set off for Guildford in late September, he listed thirty-four children's names in his diary, all female.[58] He was writing *Euclid and His Modern Rivals* at the time. In 1879 he told the twelve-year-old Kathleen Eschwege, one of the many girls he met on trains: 'I am fond of children (except boys) and have more child friends than I could possibly count on my fingers, even if I were a centipede (by the way have they fingers? I'm afraid they're only feet, but, of course, they use them for the same purpose and that is why no other insects, *except centipedes*, ever succeed in doing *Long Multipli-*

cation)'.[59] Dodgson's particular variation on Long Multiplication with little girls earned him Jean Cocteau's title of 'Impuni Don Juan des naïves amours'.[60]

With the exception of his anomalous pursuit of this endless sequence of little girls, he led a thoroughly conventional, industrious and parochial life as a don in Oxford, and, after his father's death in 1868, as head of the largely unmarried Dodgson family (he had six unmarried sisters), now housed at Guildford. In addition to his children's books and comic verse, he published over 200 books and pamphlets, as Warren Weaver calculated.[61] These include over sixty popularizing works on mathematics and logic, from *Euclid and His Modern Rivals* (1879) to *Symbolic Logic* (1896); thirty or so devoted to games and puzzles, from *Croquet Castles*, devised for the Liddells in 1863, to *Lawn Tennis Tournaments: The True Way of Assigning Prizes* (1883) and his own *Game of Logic* (1886); a further fifty, taking part in quarrels and contentions at Christ Church, mostly revolving around disputes with the two reformers Jowett and Liddell (the most important of these being collected in *Notes by an Oxford Chiel* in 1874); and a further fifty or so on miscellaneous public subjects ranging from proportional representation, antivivisectionism (*Some Popular Fallacies about Vivisection*, 1875), to *The Stage and the Spirit of Reverence* (1888) – one of the perennial bees in his clerical bonnet – and a belated pamphlet, 'Resident Women Students' (1896), finally endorsing the principle of higher education for women, not at Oxford itself but in a separate women-only university.[62] Many of these ephemeral works cast some light on the mind-set which gave the world the Alice stories and are important for that reason, but it is doubtful that they would be read today were it not for the enduring appeal of the Alice books and *The Hunting of the Snark*.

Dodgson's great period was from 1862 to 1876, when he published his dark parodic nonsense epic, *The Hunting of the Snark*. 'Had he died in his mid-forties', one of his biographers reminds us, 'posterity would have lost much of C. L. Dodgson and little of Lewis Carroll.'[63] Even the ultimately misconceived *Sylvie and Bruno* was originally conceived between the two Alice stories. Dodgson resigned his mathematics lectureship in 1881, but stayed on as a Senior Student of his college, preferring to give occasional lectures on logic at girls' schools than teach undergraduates. After retirement, he published his most ambitious book on logic, *Symbolic Logic*, in 1896; his one collection of serious poems, *Three Sunsets* (1893); and his most ambitious children's books, the two parts of *Sylvie and Bruno*, in 1889 and 1893. These were intended, he said, to combine the 'innocent merriment' of childhood, with 'thoughts . . . not wholly out of harmony with the graver cadences of Life.'[64] Though *Sylvie and Bruno* has its place in the donnish tradition of romance-oriented children's writing that leads from George MacDonald to C. S. Lewis, it's largely unreadable and unread. Despite its dizzying experiments with time and interlocking narrative, the intrusive adult viewpoint of the narrative and the increasingly didactic preoccupations of the narrator prevent the huge contraption taking off. At its close, 'not Sylvie's but an angel's voice was whispering "IT IS LOVE".'[65] Here, as throughout his last years, the graver cadences have taken over.

Dodgson became increasingly reclusive, 'lonely', and moralistic, and, though he liked to dub himself the 'agèd agèd man' (after the character in the song from *Through the Looking-Glass*) his work rate never slackened. Nor, despite his increasingly moralizing public persona, did his taste for the company of young girls, as can be seen in a characteristic letter of 1892:

> For my old age I have begun to set 'Mrs Grundy' entirely at defiance, and to have girlfriends to brighten, one at a time, my lonely life by the sea: of all ages from ten to twenty-four. Friends ask, in astonishment, 'did you hear of any *other* elderly clergyman having young lady-guests in this way?' and I am obliged to confess I never *did*: but really I don't see why they shouldn't. It is, I think, one of the *great* advantages of being an old man, that one can do many pleasant things, which are, quite properly, forbidden to a younger man.[66]

In fact, he had been setting Mrs Grundy at defiance for years, and even as a much younger man doing just these things which he suggests are 'properly' forbidden. He had given up nude photography in 1880, soon after Mr and Mrs Owen began to 'condemn' this (to him) innocent pastime.[67] Once more the pages of the diary that record this crisis have been torn out.[68] In 1885, however, undeterred, he took up sketching young girls in the nude in the studio, and to commission pictures of them from his artist friend Gertrude Thomson. Many of his late letters concern these interests in nude children, and in a letter to his sister Mary of 1893 he had to defend himself against 'a good deal of utter misrepresentation' about all this. Rumours had continued to circulate. In another letter of 1893 he calls himself a 'sentimental old fogey',[69] but quite how all this related to the Christian vision of Love in his sermons and at the close of *Sylvie and Bruno* is an open question. Nowadays, no doubt, the police and the Social Services would have become involved, but in general the families of his child friends appeared to raise no objections. He died in January 1898 in Guildford, working to the end on the proofs of *The Three Sunsets* and the second part of *Symbolic Logic*. After a small-scale family funeral, he was buried in a modest tomb in the churchyard there.

However we understand it, Dodgson's intense fascination with young girls is the prismatic anomaly at the heart of his life – and his two unparalleled masterpieces, the Alice books. Though he never matched their art or popularity again, they transformed his life, and the rest of it was lived in their shadow. Dodgson continued to take an obsessional interest in their fate until he died. He not only went on revising the lay-out and punctuation of the twin Alice books until 1897, when he produced his final corrected text, but he also published the MS facsimile of *Alice's Adventures under Ground* in 1886, marketing the cheaper 'People's Edition' in 1887 to reach a wider audience, producing the embarrassingly awful shorter 'Nursery Alice' for younger children in 1890, kept an eye on translations into European languages, fostered stage adaptations, coached actresses who played Alice in the theatre, wrote '"Alice" on the Stage' for *The Theatre* in 1887, and revelled in a series of commercial spin-offs like Alice biscuit tins and umbrellas. Part of the reason for this was no doubt commercial – Dodgson was a shrewd business man – part of it was aesthetic – he loved to supervise and control every stage of the production of his works, and make them as near perfect as possible. More than this, however, I would guess that such activity linked him to his most creative moment, his literary birth as an author, his ever-multiplying audience of children, and the story's first listener and heroine, Alice Liddell.

3: *The Genesis of Alice*

The story of the composition of Carroll's *Alice's Adventures in Wonderland* is almost as well known as the book. Indeed it forms part of the story itself. If the character of the author has an intimate bearing on the book, so does the character of its first listeners, its setting and its heroine.

Most of the protagonists have left accounts of the origin and development of *Alice's Adventures*, but the most prominent of them is condensed in the opening poem of the book itself. The verse prelude or 'frame' poem anchors the text in the 'golden afternoon' when he first improvised it for three children in a boat on a river:

> Thus grew the tale of Wonderland:
> Thus slowly, one by one,
> Its quaint events were hammered out—
> And now the tale is done,
> And home we steer, a merry crew,
> Beneath the setting sun.

On this model the whole 'tale', though growing 'slowly', was hammered out on that one golden afternoon and was finished by the journey home that evening.

When they came to record their recollections of Dodgson after his death, two of the other passengers on the boat confirmed this miraculous tale of the tale. Canon Duckworth told his first biographer:

I was very closely associated with him in the production and publication of 'Alice in Wonderland'. I rowed *stroke* and he rowed *bow* in the famous Long Vacation voyage to Godstow, when the three Liddells were our passengers, and the story was composed and spoken *over my shoulder* for the benefit of Alice Liddell, who was acting 'cox' of our gig. I remember turning round and saying, 'Dodgson, is this an extempore romance of yours?' And he replied, 'Yes, I'm inventing it as we go along.' I also well remember how, when we had conducted the three children back to the Deanery, Alice said, as she bade us good night, 'Oh Mr Dodgson, I wish you would write out Alice's adventures for me.' He said he should try, and he afterwards told me that he sat up nearly the whole night, committing to a MS book his recollections of the drolleries with which he had enlivened the afternoon. He added illustrations of his own, and presented the volume, which used often to be seen on the drawing-room table of the Deanery.[70]

According to Duckworth's miraculously condensed account, Dodgson narrated the story one afternoon, wrote it all up that evening at a sitting, and presented it to the Deanery soon after.

Alice herself left two accounts, confirming the golden-afternoon story but also modifying it. She told Dodgson's first biographer:

I believe the beginning of "Alice" was told one summer afternoon when the sun was so burning that we had landed in the meadows down the river, deserting the boat to take refuge in the only bit of shade to be found, which was under a new-made hayrick. Here from all three came the old petition of 'Tell us a story', and so began the ever-delightful tale. Sometimes to tease us – and perhaps being really tired – Mr Dodgson would stop suddenly and say, 'And that's all till next time.' 'Ah, but it is next time', would be the exclamation from all three; and after some persuasion the story would start afresh. Another day, perhaps, the story would begin in the boat, and Mr Dodgson, in the middle of telling a thrilling adventure, would pretend to go fast asleep, to our great dismay.[71]

She elaborated on this in an article written with her son in the *Cornhill* during the centenary year of Dodgson's birth:

Nearly all of *Alice's Adventures under Ground* was told on that blazing summer afternoon with the heat shimmering over the meadows where the party landed to shelter for awhile in the shadow cast by the haycocks near Godstow. I think the stories he told us that afternoon must have been better than usual, because I have such a distinct recollection of the expedition, and also, on the next day I started to pester him to write down the story for me, which I had never done before. It was due to my 'going on and on' and importunity that, after saying he would think about it, he eventually gave the hesitating promise which started him writing it down at all. This he referred to in a letter written in 1883 in which he writes of me as the 'one without whose infant patronage I might possibly never have written at all.'[72]

She acknowledges, however, that both the poem and the Canon telescope the time of composition more than a little:

The result was that for several years, when he went away on vacation, he took the little black book about with him, writing the manuscript in his own peculiar script, and drawing the illustrations. Finally the book was finished and given to me. But in the meantime, friends who had seen and heard bits of it while he was at work on it, were so thrilled that they persuaded him to publish it.[73]

Alice Liddell (Alice Hargreaves by then), looking back nearly seventy years later, extends the timescale of writing but also of oral composition. On her account, the 'golden afternoon' was only one of a series:

As it is, I think many of my earlier adventures must be irretrievably lost to posterity, because Mr Dodgson told us many, many stories before the famous trip up the river to Godstow. No doubt he added some of the earlier adventures to make up the difference between *Alice in Wonderland* and *Alice's Adventures under Ground*, which latter was nearly all told on that one afternoon. Much of *Through the Looking-Glass* is made up of them too, particularly the ones to do with chessmen, which are dated by the period when we were excitedly learning chess.[74]

Though we are bound to be a little sceptical about Canon Duckworth's turning his walk-on part into a starring role, there can be no question about Alice's role as heroine, audience and patron. Nevertheless, like most of the other accounts, Alice's plays up her participation in the production of the whole thing, in this case also attributing most of the second book to stories improvised for herself and her sisters.

In '"Alice" on the Stage', written in 1887, over twenty years after the event, Dodgson gives his own fullest account of the story:

Many a day had we rowed together on that quiet stream – the three little maidens and I – and many a fairy tale had been extemporised for their benefit – whether it were at times when the narrator was "'i' the vein,'" and fancies unsought came crowding thick upon him, or at times when the jaded Muse was goaded into action, and plodded meekly on, more because she had to say something than that she had something to say – yet none of these many tales got written down: they lived and died, like summer midges, each in its own golden afternoon until there came a day when, as it chanced, one of my little listeners petitioned that the tale might be written out for her. That was many a year ago, but I distinctly remember, now as I write, how, in a desperate attempt to strike out some new line of fairy-lore, I had sent my heroine straight down a rabbit-hole, to begin with, without the least idea what was to happen afterwards. And so, to please a child I loved (I don't remember any other motive), I printed in manuscript, and illustrated with my own crude designs – designs that rebelled against every law of Anatomy or Art (for I had never had a lesson in drawing) – the book which I have just had published in facsimile. In writing it out, I added many fresh ideas which seemed to grow of themselves upon the original stock; and many more added themselves when, years afterwards, I wrote it all over again for publication: but (this may interest some readers of 'Alice' to know) every such idea and nearly every word of the dialogue, *came of itself*.[75]

What is striking about Dodgson's account is his insistence on the automatism of it all, a founding state of dissociation comparable to psychoanalytic or Surrealistic 'free association'. The story and the ideas 'came of themselves', he insists, without his conscious intervention or control. Though Dodgson reinforces the myth of the 'golden afternoon' of its origin, he identifies two other stages in its composition: firstly the manuscript stage completed for Alice soon afterwards and secondly ('years afterwards') the stage of writing up for publication. In all three stages, however, the narrative material is self-generating.

If we turn from these public and retrospective accounts of the genesis of *Alice's Adventures* to the evidence of Dodgson's diaries and letters of the time, we get a more detailed sense of its progress from improvised open-air children's story to published book. The 1862 diary entry for the day in question sets the scene but curiously doesn't mention storytelling at all:

July 4. (F). Atkinson brought over to my rooms some friends of his, a Mrs. and Miss Peters, of whom I took photographs, and who afterwards looked over my album and stayed to lunch. They then went off to the Museum, and Duckworth and I made an expedition *up* the river to Godstow with the three

Liddells: we had tea on the bank there, and did not reach Christ Church again till quarter past eight, when we took them on to my rooms to see my collection of micro-photographs, and restored them to the Deanery just before nine.[76]

It was only the following February he annotated this on the opposite page:

On which occasion I told them the fairy-tale of *Alice's Adventures under Ground*, which I undertook to write out for Alice, and which is now finished (as to the text) though the pictures are not yet nearly done.[77]

On this evidence, the first written text of the *Adventures* was completed six months after the day the oral story was pulled spontaneously out of Dodgson's hat like the white rabbit with which it begins.

Dodgson's diaries record other incidents from before and after the 'golden afternoon', which find their way into the final text – such as the visit to Nuneham on 17 June where Duckworth, Dodgson and the three girls got drenched (this resurfaces in the Pool of Tears episode, in which Duckworth and Dodgson feature as the Duck and Dodo and everyone gets soaked), and the game of croquet at the Deanery on 3 July which must have contributed to the Queen's croquet party in Wonderland. The story continued to evolve and grow after 4 July. On 1 August he mentions going to hear the children sing the song 'Beautiful Star', which is the source of the soupy parody 'Turtle Soup'.[78] On 6 August, a month after the 'golden afternoon', on another river trip to Godstow he records he 'had to go on with my interminable fairy-tale of *Alice's Adventures*'.[79]

It was not until 13 November, in fact, that he records the strictly literary genesis of the tale, the day after an embarrassingly frosty encounter with Mrs Liddell – he had been 'out of her good graces' since the hushed-up showdown in June:

Began writing the fairy-tale for Alice, which I told them July 4, going to Godstow – I hope to finish it by Christmas.[80]

In the diary, as in other accounts, Dodgson makes it clear the story was written for Alice, but there were other influences. In May he expressed his pleasure in Christina Rossetti's *Goblin Market* and on 9 July he records a meeting with George MacDonald 'on his way to a publisher with the MS of his fairy-tale "The Light Princess" in which he showed me some exquisite drawings by Hughes'.[81] These contemporary precedents must have encouraged Dodgson to think in terms of working up his own story for publication. If Alice eventually prompted him to think of writing it four months after the golden afternoon, the diaries offer a much less telescoped account of the shift from oral tale to writing than either Duckworth or Alice. They also suggest Dodgson was ripe for the suggestion.

According to the diaries he finished the MS of *Alice's Adventures under Ground* on 10 February 1863 and his illustrations for it on 13 September of the following year. He finally sent the book to Alice herself in November 1864. However, by this stage Dodgson was no longer thinking of the manuscript version as the end of Alice's adventures. By then he had fallen out with Mrs Liddell and was in very strained professional relations with the Dean. In fact after 25 June 1863 he was to see very little of Alice or her sisters[82] and when he encountered her in Christ Church quadrangle in May 1865, he noted 'Alice seems changed a good deal, and hardly for the better – probably going through the usual awkward stage of transition'.[83] This was clearly a personally difficult period for Dodgson too. As his dearest 'child-friend' began to undergo the 'awkward' changes associated with puberty, he himself began to undergo their awkward effects upon himself – and the aftermath of the break with the Liddells. By the time the MS was completed, Alice was already a figure from his past. Everyone had moved on a long way from the golden afternoon.

In October 1863 he met the future publisher of *Alice*, Alexander Macmillan, to arrange for some of Blake's *Songs of Innocence* to be printed for him. Soon, in December 1863, he was writing to Tom Taylor for an introduction to Tenniel:

> Do you know Mr Tenniel enough to be able to say whether he could undertake such a thing as drawing a dozen wood-cuts to illustrate a child's book, and if so, could you put me into communication with him? The reasons for which I ask . . . are that I have written such a tale for a young friend, and illustrated

it in pen and ink. It has been read and liked by so many children, and I have been so often asked to publish it, that I have decided on doing so.[84]

Greville MacDonald remembers his father George MacDonald being one of those Dodgson consulted and remembers himself, aged six, exclaiming 'there ought to be sixty thousand volumes of it'. 'It was our enthusiasm', he wrote, 'that persuaded our Uncle Dodgson . . . to present the English-speaking world with one of its future classics'.[85]

Dodgson was confident enough by late 1863 to pursue publication at his own expense and to apply to one of the foremost cartoonists of the day to illustrate it. As illustrations had played an integral part in his conception of the book from the start – even in the MS, the story begins with Alice asking 'where is the use of a book . . . without pictures or conversations?' – and as he had no confidence in his own draughtsmanship, he needed a pictorial collaborator. Tom Taylor having cleared the way, Dodgson met Tenniel in January and heard from him on 5 April 1864 that he consented to 'draw the pictures for *Alice's Adventures under Ground*'.[86] The stage was set for a classic double-act. Though there have subsequently been numerous brilliant illustrators of the Alice books – including Rackham, Peake, Dali and Steadman – none have dislodged Tenniel's foursquare Victorian embodiments of Carroll's dream text.

Dodgson sent Tenniel the first slip for *Alice's Adventures* in May 1864, and one reason for the close bond between text and image is the tight control he exerted over the production of the book. Throughout the next year there was a close, often tense collaboration between writer and illustrator, until the appearance in June 1865 of 2,000 copies of the finished book printed by Clarendon Press for publication by Macmillan and Company. A special presentation copy was sent to Alice Liddell on 4 July, exactly three years after the legendary boat trip to Godstow. Soon afterwards, however, Tenniel expressed himself 'entirely dissatisfied with the printing of the pictures', and Dodgson decided to scrap it, ordering a total reprint and sending off the unbound sheets to D. Appleton and Company, New York, who issued the book in America in 1866. If he was dismayed by the cancellation of the first edition and what it cost him to withdraw it from circulation, he was more than satisfied by the second. Dated 1866 but actually published in November 1865, this second edition he found 'very *far* superior to the old, and in fact a perfect piece of artistic printing'.[87] It is an ironic token of Dodgson's perfectionism that what was effectively the first edition of his classic was in fact a second edition.

Reviews were not long in coming and, though mixed, were mainly highly favourable. The *Reader* on 18 November described it as 'a glorious artistic treasure', 'an antidote to a fit of the blues' and thought it 'sure to be run after as one of the most popular of its class'. On 16 December, the *Athenaeum*, however, wrote it off as a 'stiff, overwrought story' and the *Illustrated Times* as 'too extravagantly absurd to produce more diversion than disappointment and irritation'. It was not long, however, before the public were won over to Dodgson's book and Macmillan undertook the first of many republications during the author's lifetime.

By 1867, Dodgson was engaged in arrangements for French and German translations and by as early as August 1866 he was telling his publishers he had 'a floating idea of writing a sort of sequel to *Alice*'.[88] Alice had well and truly entered the public domain, but in a sense her adventures there had only just begun.

Through the Looking-Glass does not advertise its own origins in the same way as the first book. The prefatory poem harks back to 'the tale begun in other days', that is the moment *Alice's Adventures* was conceived rather than the new book. By representing the relationship with Alice so firmly in the past it hints at the break with the Liddells as well as establishing a new wintry tone to the story.

In February 1867, six months after first mooting the idea, Dodgson wrote to Macmillan saying he was 'hoping before long to complete another book about Alice'.[89] In '"Alice" on the Stage', Carroll claimed that both the Alice books were 'made up of bits and scraps, single ideas that came of themselves'. Nevertheless the essay confirms that the plot of *Wonderland* came to him on the trip to Godstow and became the magnet which attracted the 'bits and scraps' he subsequently added. *Through the Looking-Glass* had no such single narrative genesis; its twin structural ideas of the chess game and mirror journey appear to have come from different sources. Reminiscing from the distance of 1932,

Alice Liddell claimed the second book, like the enlarged *Wonderland*, was made up of the 'many, many stories' he had told them 'before the famous trip up the river to Godstow', 'particularly the ones to do with chessmen, which are dated by the period when we were excitedly learning chess.'[90] In that same year (1932) Dodgson's cousin Alice Raikes, also a child-friend from the 1860s, provided a rival account. She claimed it was she who had provided the inspiration for the idea of the mirror. While visiting his family in Onslow Square, where she also lived, Dodgson apparently called her over, saying 'You are another Alice. I'm fond of Alices. Would you like to come and see something which is rather puzzling?' She then followed him into his house and 'into a room full of furniture with a tall mirror standing across one corner'.

> 'Now', he said, giving me an orange, 'first tell me which hand you have got that in.' 'The right', I said. 'Now', he said, 'go and stand before that glass, and tell me which hand the girl you see there has got the orange in.' After some perplexed consternation, I said, 'The left hand.' 'Exactly', he said. 'And how do you explain that?' I couldn't explain it, but seeing that some solution was expected, I ventured, 'If I was on the *other* side of the glass, wouldn't the orange still be in my right hand?' I can remember his laugh. 'Well done, little Alice', he said. 'The best answer I've had yet.'
>
> I heard no more then, but in after years was told that he said that this had given him his first idea for *Alice Through the Looking-Glass*, a copy of which, together with each of his other books, he regularly sent me.[91]

There is no record in his diary of Carroll meeting Alice Raikes before June 1871, by when the text was completed. As reported, his remark that hers was 'the best answer' he'd heard 'yet' suggests the mirror-game was a standard trick of Dodgson's and he never credited her directly with being his inspiration, even in her inscribed copy of the book. Incidentally, another correspondent to *The Times* in February the same year claimed *she* had furnished Carroll with the idea of the Red Queen turning into 'the Black Kitten' at the close.[92]

The three rival accounts of child friends' contributions to *Through the Looking-Glass* are now all part of the legend that has grown up around the composition of *Alice*. Though they have all come to acquire gospel status in the Carrollian literature, it is worth bearing in mind that they all date from the year of the Carroll centenary over fifty years after its publication and need to be treated with a grain of salt. What is certain is that Alice Liddell, if not the 'onlie begetter' of the stories, remained their heroine – and inspiration. Though no longer in communication with her in person, Dodgson made arrangements to send her a presentation copy of *Through the Looking-Glass* 'with an oval looking-glass let into the cover'.[93] Behind the figure in the mirror of Tenniel's Alice, or in front of it in this case, stands the face of Alice Liddell.

The letters and diaries of the time tell us nothing about the details of composition, only glimpses of the timetable between conception and completion. By January 1868, after working on it in Ripon, he is asking Macmillan whether he can print a page or two of the new volume 'in *reverse*', which suggests that both 'Jabberwocky' and the idea of the looking-glass are settled.[94] In his diary for 8 April he refers to it as *Looking-Glass House* and on 1 November he confirms that he has finally signed up his reluctant illustrator. 'The second volume of *Alice* will after all be illustrated by Tenniel, who has reluctantly consented, as his hands are full: I have tried Noel Paton and Proctor in vain.'[95] By December the same year he is able to inform Macmillan that he will 'have a lot of MS ready'[96] to set up in proof for the new volume, and he tells a child correspondent that he hopes Tenniel will have the pictures done by the following Christmas. In fact, three more years were to pass before Tenniel, whose hands were indeed full, had completed the pictures and the book was ready for publication. In January 1869, he refers to it as *Behind the Looking-Glass and What Alice Found There*, and it was not until March 1870 that Macmillan confirms the final title, endorsing '*Through*' as 'just the word'.[97] On 4 January 1871, he noted in his diary that he had 'finished the MS of *Through the Looking-Glass*' and on 13 January that 'nothing remains to be printed but the verses at the end', adding that 'the volume has cost me, I think, more trouble than the first, and *ought* to be equal to it in every way'.[98] In April, he records it 'lingers on though the text is ready'. The first copy of the finished book arrived on 6 December and on 8 December he was finally able to send copies to the Deanery and to await its reception in the wider world.

The success was instantaneous. There were over 7,000 advance orders and by the end of January 1872 it had sold 15,000 copies. Henry Kingsley wrote that 'it is the finest thing we have had since *Martin Chuzzlewit*', and, when he compared it to the earlier book, called it 'a more excellent song than the other'.[99] The *Examiner* found the sequel 'hardly as good' as the original, but praised its 'wit and humour' and found it 'quite good enough to delight every sensible reader of any age'. The *Illustrated London News* of 16 December described it as 'quite as rich in humorous whims of fancy, quite as laughable in its queer incidents, as lovable for its pleasant spirit and graceful manner as the wondrous tale of Alice's former adventures underground'.

If *Through the Looking-Glass* never won quite the same popularity as the earlier book and never attained quite the same place in most readers' hearts, it is none the less one of the most successful sequels in literary history. *The Hunting of the Snark* followed soon after and thereafter Carroll, though he continued to write for another twenty-five years, was never to produce anything of comparable inventiveness or resonance. What he found in Wonderland and through the Looking-Glass during the 1860s he was never to find again.

4: *Alice's Identity*

"'Who in the world am I?' That's the great puzzle!"

In the opening chapter of *Alice's Adventures in Wonderland* we are told Alice is 'fond of pretending to be two people', but early in her shape-changing adventures she fears 'there's hardly enough of me left to make one comfortable person'. Wondering if she'd been changed in the night, she asks, '"Who in the world am I?"' In a book humming with puzzles, this is probably the greatest puzzle of all for Alice.

It is the question that the best novels and children's stories return to again and again. If the heroine is at one level the straight guy in a series of bizarre comic turns, at another her adventures compose a miniature *Bildungsroman* in nonsensical form. It is as if what Harold Bloom called 'the internalization of the Quest Romance' in Romantic poetry, with its obsession with questions of identity, were rewritten as a utopian comedy of manners – a combination of Shelley's *Alastor* and Jane Austen's *Pride and Prejudice*. The queerness of nonsense language and the bizarre rules and regulations the creatures try to impose on Alice tell us much about the terrifying arbitrariness of the world she has to operate in, but also about who she is. One of the great appeals of the Alice books is that, like Kafka's *The Trial* and *The Castle*, they dramatize the puzzling nature of identity in a world dominated by rules and rulers that remain obstinately unpredictable and indecipherable. In one of the early shape-changing scenes in *Wonderland*, Alice goes to a table to 'measure herself by it'. There is a sense in which this is what is happening all through both narratives.

In fact, when Alice worries about her identity, she reveals herself to be very much a child of her time and class. In this she is like Alice Liddell, the daughter of the Dean of Christ Church, born into the heart of the English establishment, a well-educated upper-middle-class Oxonian girl, versed in good manners, good verse, and the rules of chess, cards and croquet.[100] Christ Church was the smartest Oxbridge college, where the Prince of Wales became an undergraduate in 1859, and Queen Victoria visited the Liddells in the Deanery in 1860. Not long after *Through the Looking-Glass*, Alice was briefly involved with Prince Leopold (who'd attended her sister Lorina's wedding in 1874 and had been photographed by Dodgson), so that the royal scenario that pervades both stories reflects on her own social status, as well as on the romance conventions of fairy tales and the games of cards and chess she is caught up in. The fictional Alice measures herself by her superior knowledge and social status: '"I'm sure I ca'n't be Mabel, for I know all sorts of things, and she, oh, she knows such a very little! Besides, *she's* she, and *I'm* I, and—oh dear, how puzzling it all is!"' Her adventures test her sense of identity to the full. Her worries have something in common with those Elizabeth Bishop dramatizes in her searching autobiographical poem 'In the Waiting Room' about a young girl exactly Alice's age, who, looking into the mirror of other people, reflects on who she is herself. 'Why should I be my aunt,/or me, or anyone?' she asks:

I said to myself: three days
And you'll be seven years old.
I was saying it to stop
the sensation of falling off
the round, turning world
into a cold, blue-black space.
But I felt: you are an *I*,
you are an *Elizabeth*,
you are one of *them*.[101]

Alice's fall down the rabbit-hole induces a comparable identity crisis. The descent into the 'deep well' shakes all the assumptions of her waking self. When she tries to re-establish her poise by reciting the improving verses of Isaac Watts's 'How doth the little busy bee', the admirably industrious bee turns into a predatory crocodile with 'gently smiling Jaws.' Having travestied the pious hymn, she fears she must be Mabel after all: '"I shall have to go and live in that poky little house, and have next to no toys to play with, and, oh, ever so many lessons to learn! No, I've made up my mind about it: if I'm Mabel, I'll stay down here!"'

When the White Rabbit takes her for a 'housemaid' soon afterwards, Alice exclaims, '"How surprised he'll be when he finds out who I am."' Whoever she is, she couldn't be one of the servant classes in a 'poky little house'. Hers is a world of governesses, school-rooms, middle-class etiquette, tea-parties, croquet lawns, visiting royalty, and querulous pedants – just like Alice Liddell's (and Dodgson's own). By and large those she meets in her adventures are upper and middle class too; with the exception of the Rabbit's stage-Irish gardener, Hattan and Haigha and a few other bit-part players with vaguely cockneyfied voices, the creatures generally speak what Alice calls 'good English'. As I hope the notes to this edition show, Dodgson constructed Alice's dream worlds out of the details of Alice Liddell's actual environment, and did so with something of the meticulous literalism of contemporary paintings such as Ford Maddox Brown's *Work*, Frith's *Derby Day*, or the domestic genre scenes of painters admired by Dodgson, such as Arthur Hughes and Millais. Tenniel therefore proved an inspired choice of illustrator for Alice and her world. His graphic idiom, however fantastic and allegorically grotesque, is as pedantically referential as an exhibition catalogue of Victorian social types, settings, furniture and costume – just like Dodgson's own. When Alice travels underground and through the glass, it is not only her unconscious dream world that she finds – but Victorian England, and the world of the Oxford establishment she shared with Dodgson.

Alice's unconscious parody of Watts's hymn about the busy bee invokes not Protestant industry and moral purposiveness, but a crocodile's 'jaws' and 'claws', and William Empson has pointed out how high a proportion of the jokes, poems and parodies in the Alice books hinge upon death and eating. The secure domestic order of Alice's moral universe is exposed to reveal terror and appetite. 'Wonderland' sounds Edenic, as do many of Dodgson's accounts of childhood, but the world of the stories is grim as well as comic. There's a 'lovely garden' there but also a 'pool of tears'; nature in Wonderland is more akin to Tennyson's 'Nature red in tooth and claw' than Wordsworth's 'fair seed-bed'; it's overshadowed by the fear of death and extinction (think of the Dodo), and reverberations of the Darwinian debate about evolution that had taken place in Oxford in 1859–60. The Wonderland garden is no childhood Eden, but a life-and-death croquet match presided over by a homicidal Queen shouting 'Off with their heads' every second minute. Faced with all this random violence and competitiveness, Alice notes '"they're dreadfully fond of beheading people here"', '"the great wonder is there's anyone left alive"'. Even Alice herself, when she gets to the 'lovely garden' is taken to be a marauding snake (a 'serpent') by the outraged maternal Pigeon of Wonderland, not a 'human child' (she inspires comparable terror in the fawn of *Looking-Glass* as soon as they leave the wood of no names). '"We're all mad here"', says the grinning Cheshire Cat; the Carrollian grin, like the crocodile's, reveals a disconcerting madness and violence at the heart of its order – both the 'natural' order of the garden, and the legal order of the Trial, with its travesty of justice. In all this, Alice emerges as the book's nonsensometer (she dismisses the court's verdict as 'stuff and nonsense') and, as much as any Jane Austen heroine, its intellectual conscience. Sense-making is imperative in this world, but it's a lonely business.

In the tonally bleaker, more elegiac *Through the Looking-Glass*, the winter sequel to the Maytime trip to Wonderland, Alice's sense of self hardens in the colder, more political climate she finds six months later behind the glass. The air grows cold in the region of mirrors. The looking-glass, like Keats's 'magic casement', leads into the world of Victorian medievalism and the 'dark wood' of Spenserean Romance, albeit in a comically warped form. It is a world where modern railways, newspapers and postal systems interlock with Quixotic knights, lions and unicorns. It is dominated by political battling – the competing Kings and Queens, the battling Tweedle brothers, the Lion and Unicorn, the White and Red Knights, and the political images of Gladstone and Disraeli in the railway carriage. In the carriage, as in the shop, wood and palace, Alice's attempts to decipher the world around her become more critical and anxious. Even the garden of live flowers offers a pricklier, colder pastoral than that of Wonderland, as can be seen in the less than rosy world-view of the Rose Alice chats to:

> "You're beginning to fade, you know—and then one ca'n't help one's petals getting a little untidy."
>
> Alice didn't like this idea at all: so, to change the subject, she asked "Does she ever come out here?"
>
> "I daresay you'll see her soon," said the Rose. "She's one of the kind that has nine spikes, you know."
>
> "Where does she wear them?" Alice asked with some curiosity.
>
> "Why, all round her head, of course," the Rose replied. "I was wondering *you* hadn't got some too. I thought it was the regular rule."[102]

Against the cruel pathos of seeing the seven-and-a-half-year-old Alice as a fading flower, the Rose presents adulthood with a certain grim realism. She is referring to the Red Queen with her spiky chess crown ('the essence of all Governesses', as Dodgson called her),[103] and the Queens as representatives of the queenliness Ruskin ascribed to all women, are at best a grisly duo – the one all bossiness and bile, the other all slovenliness and resignation, the one manically over-assertive (like Humpty Dumpty and the Tweedles), the other ineffectually depressive (like the gnat and Knight). In the chess world of *Through the Looking-Glass* it seems to be the regular rule that creatures (even the two bona fide children, the Tweedles) protect themselves by a rather acerbic style of conversational prickliness; though they tend to be sticklers for their own rules and regulations, their style is domineering and their order profoundly irrational.

Despite this, Alice, who starts out as a pawn in the game, 'would like to be a Queen best'. These Queens are not like the idealized stereotypes envisaged by Ruskin in his tract on women's education, 'Of Queens' Gardens', but studies in power and powerlessness. However well-mannered Alice may be, she aspires to be a Queen too, and a powerful one, and as the story draws towards a close, she aspires towards an impressive vision of feminine autonomy in the face of the bullying she faces on all sides.

When Tweedledum says she is only part of the Red King's dream and isn't real, Alice retorts '"I am real!"' and begins to cry. Though she succumbs to tears, she is able to argue her corner ('"If I wasn't real ... I shouldn't be able to cry"') and attempts to dismiss the disconcerting Berkleyan idealism of the Tweedles as 'nonsense'. Still, faced by the dark wood, the battling philosophical twins and the monstrous crow, she keeps her composure as best she can. When she meets that arrogant egghead Humpty Dumpty, who murderously advises her to 'Leave off at seven', she comes out with one of the great defiant lines of nineteenth-century childhood literature (not unlike Oliver Twist's 'I want some more'): '"I never ask advice about growing"'. After the battle between the Lion and Unicorn, she says, '"I do hope it's *my* dream"', '"I don't like belonging to another person's."' Later, after the shambolic battle between the two knights which the White Knight calls a 'glorious victory', she affirms her freedom with characteristic defiance, '"I don't want to be anybody's prisoner. I want to be a Queen."' Having shown admirable kindness and good humour towards the absent-minded quixotic Knight, she eventually gets her crown, but this isn't the end of her subjection to the bossiness endemic in Carrollian nonsense. She immediately finds herself peppered with regal advice by the other Looking-Glass Queens and finds she really doesn't like 'being found fault with so much'. Eventually, when she rises to give a speech at her coronation banquet, and the tediously formal dinner-party breaks up into pandemonium, she cries out with her most powerful blast of self-assertion, '"I can't stand this any longer!"' – thus freeing herself from the game, the dream and the mirror. Though she 'wins' her crown and the game, it seems she outgrows both at the very moment when the dream of being a Queen is realized and found to be as nightmarish as her time as a child and pawn.

Though Dodgson inherits the first generation of Romantic poets' sense of childhood (Humpty Dumpty's 'glory' recalls Wordsworth's as does the opening poem of *Looking-Glass*) and the second generation's interest in romance and dreams, his own 'dream-child' pursues her quest through a world which is as profoundly social as that of Jane Austen. In the frame poems of each book, and in the account he gives in '"Alice" on the Stage', the author writes as if Alice travels to some fairyland of pastoral childish innocence. As Isa Bowman noticed, however, Dodgson himself 'cared for neither flowers nor animals',[104] and the language of *Wonderland* is a product of culture, not nature. In it Alice is confronted by grave travesties of most of the institutions which govern her and her author's life – the monarchy, the rule of law, education, grammar and social etiquette. So, after the fall and bodily metamorphoses of the opening chapters of *Wonderland*, Alice is caught up first with a Caucus Race with wild animals (a parody of competitive 'natural selection' and democratic procedure), then the fussy domestic life of a fastidious bachelor rabbit (complete with maid and gardener). Having discussed growth and reproduction with a caterpillar and pigeon, and madness with a brainy disembodied cat, Alice finds herself in the more complex rituals of Wonderland society – first the endlessly rotating Mad Tea Party, with its parodies of a parlour-song recital, children's story (as told by the dormouse) and tea-time etiquette; then the shambolic royal Croquet Game with the Queen, her courtiers and minions all flaunting the rules of that popular new middle-class game (regularly played by the Liddells on the Deanery lawn) and playing havoc with the garden; then, to cap it all, the Mock Turtle and Gryphon's nostalgic Old Boys' duet about their schooldays. The Mock Turtle and Gryphon are two highly artificial creatures, fathered not by biology but language, and their mournfully punning chronicle of distant school-days recollected in tranquillity parodies not only the established curriculum of private education in the public schools of the day, but the entire educational system based on 'reeling and writhing'. There's a particular pungency in the allusions to classical 'Laughing and Grief' (Latin and Greek, but also the classical genres of comedy and tragedy), since these were intimately associated with Alice's father, Dean Liddell, co-author of the famous Greek lexicon used in schools. '"How the creatures order one about, and make one repeat lessons"', Alice observes, '"I might just as well be at school at once"'. The Gryphon and Mock Turtle are parodic products of the education system they romanticize so tearfully, just as their performance of 'The Lobster Quadrille' is a galumphing parody of fashionable ballroom dancing (an institution that played a positively Darwinian role in the struggle of nineteenth-century girls for suitable husbands). Nonsense thrives on travestying authority, and Alice's last view of Wonderland is the absurd court scene, where the Knave of Hearts is accused of stealing tarts, and tried before a court dominated by an incompetent King, tyrannical Queen and abject jury. The nonsense theatre of Wonderland, with its haywire kings and queens, comes to a climactic finale in this finely tuned satire on the social order. It offers a deadpan comedy of (bad) manners.

The social world of *Through the Looking-Glass* is dominated by the nominal kings and queens of chess, and is, if anything, more systematically constricting than that of the earlier book. It begins in an untidy Janus-faced version of the *haute bourgeoisie* drawing-room of Alice's home, peopled by quarrelling kings and queens, but soon moves into another garden, a caricature of the lush flower garden evoked by the disappointed lover in Tennyson's *Maud* and part of a wider landscape which is modelled, not on any natural or picturesque order, but on a geometrically mapped out chessboard. This may seem less anarchic than *Wonderland* but it's no less threatening as a mirror of modernity. 'It's all a great game of chess that's being played – all over the world', we are told, where 'it takes all the running you can do to keep in the same place' as the Red Queen says, and where people in the railway-carriage think (in chorus) that 'time is worth a thousand pounds a minute', land 'a thousand pounds an inch' and language 'a thousand pounds a word'. In the 'Looking-Glass Insects' episode where she takes the train, Alice is caught up as a cypher in the communication networks of Victorian England. She has to produce a ticket to validate her travel, but is told she could as well be sent by luggage, telegraph or post (since, like a stamp, she 'had a head on her') and gets classified in terms of ticket-offices, alphabets and (in a chapter about names) her name. Throughout all this, she is confronted by two imposing male figures who in Tenniel's drawing look suspiciously like the two politicians who dominated parliamentary politics at this time, William Gladstone and Benjamin Disraeli (the latter appropriately dressed in paper and reading a newspaper). She is also subjected to aggressive public scrutiny.

All this time the Guard was looking at her, first through a telescope, then through a microscope, and then through an opera-glass. At last he said "You're traveling the wrong way," and shut up the window, and went away.

Alice's progress, as befitting a pawn in the game of chess, is made through a series of bewilderingly abrupt and involuntary jumps from place to place and from time to time. Despite the projections of the modern political order of Victorian Britain that shape so much of the looking-glass world, and those archetypal modern settings, the train and the shop, *Looking-Glass* is haunted by the past – in disconcertingly parodic nonsensical forms. 'Jabberwocky', the first poem Alice encounters, is a telegrammatic *reductio* of a dragon-slaying northern epic, and after her railway journey Alice finds herself in the wood of no names – an eerie place where she loses her own name ('"and who am I?"' she wonders) and, during her brief Pan-like communion with the Fawn, her identity as a 'human child'. Though she recovers her name, she isn't out of the wood yet. The bulk of the rest of her journey is set against the backdrop of a dark forest that is a legacy of both Spenserean romance and German fairy tales. It is there that she meets a series of characters from traditional nursery rhymes[105] – Tweedledum and Tweedledee, the Lion and the Unicorn and Humpty Dumpty – and the White Knight, a sad quixotic figure who is both an eccentric inventor (like Dodgson) and a travesty of the heroic Pre-Raphaelite medievalism of Rossetti, Morris and the Laureate's *Idylls of the King* (Tenniel's frontispiece illustration of the White Knight guys the lumbering pictorial medievalizing of *Sir Isumbras at the Ford* in the same vein). *Through the Looking-Glass* has some affinity with the Gothic revivalism of Pugin's Houses of Parliament and, nearer home for Dodgson, the fake antique frescos recently designed for the Oxford Union, but revels in its own nonsensical anachronism. Even as the book takes us through the iconography of the chivalric and royal past – Humpty Dumpty characteristically assumes Alice has read about him in a 'History of England' and the Lion and the Unicorn survive in the royal coat of arms – its conversational style, manners and tone are unmistakably modern. In *Through the Looking-Glass*, Tenniel dresses Alice in the newly fashionable hair-band and striped stockings of her time, and the author always presents her as a thoroughly contemporary girl. Though the story veers back and forth between past and present as dizzily as Twain's *Connecticut Yankee*, Alice's final coronation banquet is clearly represented in the text and illustrations as a Victorian dinner party, complete with decanters and soup tureens. The text ends with a *Dunciad*-like apocalypse of that hierarchical social world, as the story dissolves in Alice's final impatient gesture of revolt.

"I ca'n't stand this any longer!" she cried, as she jumped up and seized the tablecloth with both hands: one good pull, and plates, dishes, guests, and candles came crashing down together in a heap on the floor.

Alice's protest is against the irrational nonsense of the mad chess game she has dreamed she is part of – with its comic, but potentially threatening, dream logic. To re-establish her own identity and her faith in the real world of social conduct, she has to reject the awful travesty of proper social life played out by the Queens, Kings and subjects of the Looking-Glass world. Despite his subsequent canonization by the Surrealists, Dodgson was a Euclidean logician, a pious Christian and a political conservative, whose life was fanatically devoted to tidiness and order. Alice mirrors him in this. Nevertheless, it is possible to read her dream adventures as a protest against the world of governesses, teachers, bullies and pedagogues, and all the social rituals they impose on her. The hall-of-mirrors discovered in the Looking-Glass inevitably reflects back on the world of the Victorian drawing-room, school-room and play-room, and the ordinary assumptions of a comfortable middle-class childhood this side of the mirror.

'Who dreamed it?' asks the last chapter, and the book's dream realism is clearly a reflection of the fictional Alice's waking world. It can also be read as a reflection of the real Alice Liddell's domestic universe, as I've suggested earlier. Beyond that, however, we can read the two books as reflexes of their author, Charles Dodgson, also of Christ Church. He appears to have so closely identified with his dream heroine that his problems of identity, of establishing coherent selfhood in the face of the violent changes inherent in human life and the disorder at the heart of the order, seem mirrored in hers.

Looking-Glass is much preoccupied by passing time, violence, ageing and death, as well as the potential for linguistic aberration and disorder discovered in *Wonderland*. The obsessively tidy Dodgson was acutely concerned by contemporary debates which threatened the established order. The dreams of Alice, that Oxford child, and her author abut on to the universe of mid nineteenth-century Oxford, a place that considered itself with good reason to be at the centre of British intellectual life at the time. In *An Oxford Chiel*, published in 1874, only four years after *Through the Looking-Glass*, Dodgson published a series of highly political satirical squibs on university issues written over the previous nine years – about the new belfry commissioned by Liddell for Christ Church, the defeat of Gladstone as MP for Oxford, the salary and status of the Liberal Jowett (who was Professor of Greek and a notoriously 'heretical' contributor to the *Essays and Reviews* of 1861), the terms of Max Müller's professorship of comparative philology, among other burning issues of the time. Though Dodgson disclaimed making any such topical or political allusions in the Alice books, controversy is the very air breathed by the embattled creatures in both; Humpty Dumpty is the most belligerently radical of the many philosophers of language who haunt their pages, but the majority of the creatures Alice meets are comparably argumentative, and constitutionally prone to wrangle about the interpretation of words, names, rules and logic. We should remember that in between the two Alice books in 1869, Dodgson published one of his own most sustained exercises in academic controversy, *Euclid and His Modern Rivals*, a work intended to champion and popularize Euclidean geometry for a modern audience. It's a dramatic dialogue, featuring the ghost of Euclid, in which a modern mathematics lecturer (ominously called Minos) and his antagonist Professor Niemand (the German for 'Nobody'), sit in judgement over thirteen rival theorists who challenge the secure order of Euclidean geometry which Dodgson wished to defend. In the disputatious world of *Wonderland* it is possible to hear echoes of such controversies, as well as the more stirring controversies aroused by the Oxford Movement, the Darwinian debate of the 1860s, Ruskinian aesthetics, Max Müller's brand of comparative philology and Arnold's *Culture and Anarchy* (1869). In one of his Popean satires of the time, Dodgson ironically takes the Liberal side, warning readers to 'shun Conservatism's evil star', and affirm 'the march of Mind' against Oxford's 'wisely slow' traditional order, in which intellectual values were tempered by moral and Christian ones:

> Neglect the heart and cultivate the brain –
> Then this shall be the burden of our song,
> 'All change is good – whatever is, is wrong –'
> Then Intellect's proud flag shall be unfurled,
> And Brain and Brain alone, shall rule the world![106]

Possible ripples and aftershocks of these ideological contests may be detected playing over and under the elusively nonsensical surface of the two children's books the conservative Dodgson wrote for the daughter of the Dean of Christ Church he christened 'the relentless reformer' Liddell.[107]

But if there are echoes of such contemporary debates, they are muted and indirect. The main focus of the two books is Alice's own consciousness, as she struggles to make sense of a world through the looking-glass that is more unstable, changeable and radically nonsensical than her author could acknowledge elsewhere. The 'innocent' language of nonsense associated with Alice, 'the child of [his] dreams',[108] gives expression to more things than are dreamed of in Dodgson's conscious philosophy – or his culture's dream of order.

5: Decoding Nonsense, Decoding the Child

When the Red Queen, in one of the book's many 'knock-me-down arguments', makes the typically grand claim '"*I* could show you hills in comparison with which you'd call that a valley"', Alice contradicts her: '"a hill *ca'n't* be a valley, you know. That would be nonsense."' Not to be put down so easily, the Queen trumps her with, '"*I've* heard nonsense, compared with which that would be as sensible as a dictionary!"'

Alice rarely speaks nonsense – and rarely enjoys it when it's served up to her; if the readers laugh, the heroine almost never even smiles. Yet what Freud calls 'the pleasure in nonsense',[109] for Dodgson was part of the repertoire of childhood – or at least part of the repertoire of tricks, puzzles, games and jokes with which he amused and amazed his child friends. Freud associates the pleasure in nonsense with other infantile pleasures – with word-play, punning, oral thrills of all kinds – and it may be that there is a developmental logic in all this, whereby 'nonsense' signifies 'innocent' ways of thinking and feeling that are left behind when adulthood is attained. Yet Dodgson's interest in little girls is of questionable 'innocence', and the dream-worlds he devises for Alice, though free from obvious sexual feeling, are often highly disturbing, as many children and adults alike feel.

To see how Dodgson used nonsense in his relations with children, but not with adults, we could look at a group of letters, written in 1870, the year he completed *Through the Looking-Glass*. Two are to his sister Mary about her son's christening, written in his role as brother and clergyman. They show Dodgson at his most familial and serious. They are interspersed, however, with two very different letters to one of his little girlfriends, Edith Jebb, written in his role of children's entertainer. They neatly illustrate the split between the sensible and nonsensical selves of the author, a split that in almost diagrammatic fashion reproduces the more fundamental cultural split between adulthood and childhood.

First a note to his sister, written on 13 January:

My dearest Mary,
I must write one line to *yourself*, if only to say – God bless you and the little one now entrusted to you – and may you be to him what our own dear mother was to *her* eldest son! I can hardly utter for your boy a better wish than that!
Your loving brother,
C. L. Dodgson.[110]

This is a dutiful brotherly note, blessing the arrival of his nephew (and eventual biographer), little more. We might notice, however, the way Dodgson envisages the love of mother and son as a mirror image of his own relationship to his mother, and the way the letter (as such letters often do) foregrounds itself as a speech act: 'I must *write*', 'if only to *say*', 'I can hardly *utter*'. The nonsensical letter he writes to little Edith a few days later is very different, as you would expect – though it's in some ways more sophisticated:

My Dear Edith,
Did you happen to notice that curious-looking gentleman who was in the railway-carriage with me, when I left Doncaster? I mean the one with a nose in this shape –  (I don't know any name for that sort of nose) and eyes like this –  He was peeping with one eye out of the window, just when I was leaning out to whisper 'good-bye' into your ear (only I forgot where your ear was exactly, and somehow fancied it was just above your chin), and when the train moved off he said, 'She seems to be VS. Y?' Of course I knew he meant 'Very sorry. Why?' So I said, 'She was sorry because I had said I meant to come again.' He rubbed his hands together for half an hour or so, and grinned from ear to ear (I don't mean from one ear to the other, but from one ear round again to the same) and at last he said, 'SSSS.' I thought at first he was only hissing like a snake, so I took no notice – but at last it crossed my mind that he meant 'She shows some sense,' so I smiled and replied, 'SSS' (meaning of course 'Sensibly said, Sir') but he didn't understand me, and said in a rather cross tone, 'Don't hiss at me like that! Are you a cat or a steam-engine? SS.' I saw that this meant 'Silence, stupid!' and replied, 'S', by which you will guess at once that I meant to say 'Sertainly.' All he said after that was,

'Your head is MT,' and as I couldn't make out what he meant, I didn't say anything. But I thought I had better tell you all about it at once, that you might tell the police, or do anything else you thought ought to be done. I believe his name was 'HTIDE BBEJ' (isn't it a curious name?).
Yours affectionately,
Lewis Carroll[111]

In contrast to the letter to his sister signed 'C. L. Dodgson', over the signature of 'Lewis Carroll' the writer engages in the kind of extravagant but weirdly perverse nonsense that characterizes so many of his letters to his child friends.

Like so much of Dodgson's nonsense, however, this is not only a nonsense letter but a letter *about* nonsense. The gags depend on questions of naming and intending, and involve implausible acts of encoding and decoding. It begins with a joke about a nameless sort of nose, and then an innuendo-style allusion to Dodgson's kissing another orifice – this time renamed – the girl's mouth, which is here represented in code by the whispered good-bye into an 'ear' which is 'just above [her] chin'. What follows is an absurd dialogue between the two men about what the girl's behaviour means, conducted entirely in terms of single letters which are presumed to stand for unsaid, but implicitly understood, sentences. The comedy turns on verbs of construing and interpreting: 'I know he meant', 'meaning of course', 'I couldn't make out what he meant' and so on. Dodgson turns his farewell to the girl on the train into a kind of everyday hermeneutic farce based on the idea of imputed, concealed and deciphered meanings, meanings that are attributed to the hissing sound (or letter) 'S'. We are close here to the strange idea Dodgson expresses elsewhere of an innocent conversation in ordinary English which might mean something 'horrendous' in another language.[112] The crotchety tone of the interlocutor ('HTIDE BBEJ') is reminiscent of the querulous creatures Alice encounters on her adventures, and what is satirized here is the confidence of both parties that they know what the other means. The letter writer is told his head is 'MT', but whether this language is 'empty' or 'full' of significance remains in question. The joke about telling 'the police' at the end declares this is all innocent fun but also tellingly invokes the idea of guilt and the law. What fascinates Dodgson in all this is the idea of nonsense as a code, a secret language which in the letter is that which he shares with his reader Edith Jebb, but which depends on meanings which they cannot fully share and which remain indecipherable, held in brackets as it were, like the interpretations of the code offered by the writer of the letter.

This is to make heavy weather of some light-hearted playing about but the joke letter makes light of some complicated interpretative manoeuvres and shows us something on which the Alice books depend: Dodgson's assumption that children are interested in the comedy of meaning itself.

Having sent off another letter to his sister, praying for 'present and future blessings' for her son at his baptism, he writes a second note to Edith, addressing her as 'My poor dear puzzled child'.

> I won't write you such a hard letter another time. And can't you really guess what the gentleman meant when he said, 'Your head is MT'? Suppose I were to say to you, 'Edith my dear! My cup is MT. Will u B so kind as 2 fill it with T?' Shouldn't you understand what I meant? Read it loud and try again.[113]

We all switch linguistic registers and degrees of seriousness in our conversation and letters, especially when we shift between addressing adults and children. Nevertheless the switch in Dodgson's case is marked to an unusual degree and plays a structural role in the way he organized his life – and writings. In his letters to his sister we hear the don and clergyman, in those to Edith and other child friends we hear the author of *Alice*, the puzzling creator of games and dreams for a 'dear puzzled child'.

'The cup is MT' is relatively easy to decode, but the 'sense' of the apparently empty letters has to be deciphered on quite different lines to those required to decode 'SSSS' in the earlier letter; they aren't a phonetic pun but a series of initial letters which the letter writer construes as abbreviations for utterly disparate terms. At the end, after some jokes about the exchange of letters between them, Dodgson asks Edith for her other names, so that he will make a monograph for her 'for writing all the initials at once' – another play on isolating initial letters and devising new patterns for them. This, of course, is one of

Dodgson's specialities, as his many acrostic verses on the names of child friends illustrate – not least, the final poem of *Through the Looking-Glass*, where the initial letters of each line spell the full name of Alice Pleasance Liddell. The letter is partly about letter writing in the usual sense – a subject that preoccupied Dodgson who later published 'Eight or Nine Wise Words About Letter Writing' to accompany the Wonderland Stamp-case in 1888[114] – it is largely taken up with the writing of alphabetical letters (such as 'MT') as a code for other things. Such empty play is obviously full of meaning for the figure who signs himself in one letter 'Yours affectionately, Lewis Carroll', and in the other, with another abbreviation, 'Ever yours afftely, C. L. Dodgson'.

My reading of the letter is undoubtedly pedantic, but so was Dodgson, as Oxford don and children's writer too. Making a 'dear child' puzzled was a central thread in Dodgson's puzzling relationships with children, and clearly this is central to the Alice stories. It is Alice's combination of curiosity ('curiouser and curiouser' indeed) and puzzlement which offers the reader a mirror through which to read the nonsense she encounters. Quite as much as Maisie in Henry James's *What Maisie Knew*, Alice is engaged in a quest to interpret and master the complex and strange phenomena of the largely adult world she encounters – there are no other *children* in her dream. What Alice knows, and how she interprets it, holds centre stage, giving her a paradoxical intellectual authority. In his letter to Edith Jebb, as apparently in many of his relationships with children, Dodgson engineers a semantic equivalent of a sado-masochistic relationship between himself as powerful adult creator of puzzles and the 'poor dear puzzled girl' who encounters them. Yet in the books, where variations of the same scenario occur in every episode, the same psychic economy produces a different psychological (and literary) effect. The adults in the stories – the March Hare, the Duchess, Humpty Dumpty and the Red Queen – are, for all their bossiness and superiority, shown up as perverse and childish weirdos, recognizable contemporaries of Dickens's Quilp, Scrooge, Miss Havisham and Mr Dick. In creating Alice's dream, and making it the centre of the books, Dodgson found not only a fertile channel for his genius for nonsense, but transformed the ways it might be meaningful. Alice, even as a seven-year-old, emerges as more than equal to her intellectual as well as social adventures, more than equal too to bullying interlocutors such as Humpty Dumpty, the first bona fide philosopher of nonsense. His presumptuous boast '"When I use a word . . . it means just what I choose it to mean"' provokes Alice's retort, '"The question is whether you *can* make words mean so many different things."' Not to be fazed, Dumpty replies, '"The question is . . . which is to be master – that's all."'

The Alice books mean 'many different things', as the huge critical literature they have inspired makes clear, but Alice's struggle for mastery and meaning is at their centre. This is clear from the vertiginous start of *Wonderland*, where Alice, inspired by her curiosity (that key word in the book), follows the rabbit underground. During the fall down the 'deep well' Alice sees cupboards and bookshelves flash by, maps and pictures hung up on pegs, and neatly labelled jars (one marked 'ORANGE MARMALADE'). As she falls, she calls up snippets learned in geography 'lessons in the school-room', and enjoys the consolations of 'nice grand words to say' like 'Latitude or Longitude'. At the end of the dreamily time-suspended fall, she comes to earth with a 'thump' on a 'heap of sticks and dry leaves'. Maps, pictures, labels, words: Alice's free fall takes her through the models of linguistic order she has learned at home and in the school-room. In her dream adventures, such tools cease to offer stability yet they are never lost sight of, and the world she travels through is always composed of language. Comically transfigured, it is nevertheless built out of the familiar, educational and social world of a middle-class child of her time. The playing-cards and chess-pieces which provide the narrative coherence for her dreams have no supernatural or magical dimension: they are part of familiar rule-bound household games (despite the label 'fairy tale', there are no fairies or supernatural powers in the Alice books, such as you find in the children's fiction of those other religious dons, George MacDonald and C. S. Lewis). Alice clings on to her received codes even as they are put under pressure from all sides; she keeps her composure as best she can, as she travels through the discomposed linguistic halls of mirrors which are her dreams. As she says to the discouragingly moralistic Ugly Duchess, '"I've a right to think"'.

Dodgson was a logician with a taste for children, and he brings his professional thinking about questions of meaning to bear upon his fascination with childhood. The result is a 'fairy tale' about a seven-year-old which is not only an adventure story but a philosophical joke-book, a mixture of genially grotesque pantomime and surreal Socratic dialogue. Despite the mind-bending series of jokes about language and logic, however, this is not a philosophical *divertissement* disguised as a children's book, and if Alice is subjected to perverse logical jokes, the joke is never on Alice. '"You shouldn't make jokes"', Alice tells the gnat, '"if they make you so unhappy"', and the jokes other creatures tell – she makes none herself and she doesn't generally seem to find other people's very funny – don't make her happy either. They do, however, enlarge her, and our, sense of the possible ways the world and words have meaning. Dodgson's genius was to make the construction of meaning an intrinsic part of the narrative of the child's dream experience. Like later books, such as *The Game of Logic* in its different way, they assume that the idea of meaning is meaningful to children.

The publication of the Alice books marks a watershed in the literature about childhood as well as children's literature. For all their originality, they are a product of a culture with a huge and developing investment in the idea of childhood. Childhood had begun to play an increasing role in adult fiction of the period. Charlotte Brontë's *Jane Eyre*, Emily Brontë's *Wuthering Heights*, and Charles Dickens's *Oliver Twist* (1837), *Dombey and Son* (1848), *David Copperfield* (1850) and *Great Expectations* (1861) all played a large part in colonizing modern childhood for literary representation. During the same period a new literature for children rapidly developed. In the 1820s Taylor's translation of the Grimm brothers' *Household Tales* acted as an 'open sesame', and Lewis Carroll's thoroughly 'modern' transformation of the traditional 'fairy tale' in the Alice books is part of a much broader development of writing specifically directed at children in the Victorian period, much of it associated with the major writers of the time. Edward Lear's *Book of Nonsense* had appeared in 1846, Dickens's *A Christmas Carol* in 1843 and Thackeray's pastiche fairy tale *The Rose and the Ring* in 1854, all of which helped clear the way for Carrollian nonsense.[115] Dodgson gave the Liddell girls a copy of Catherine Sinclair's *Holiday House* for Christmas in 1861, read Christina Rossetti's *Goblin Market* when it came out in 1862 and the MS of his friend George MacDonald's 'exquisite' 'Light Princess' in the same year, while 1863 was the year *The Water-Babies* of Charles Kingsley appeared (Dodgson met him in 1869). MacDonald's *At the Back of the North Wind* (1871) appeared the same year as *Through the Looking-Glass*, and *The Princess and the Goblin* the following year. By the end of his life, Dodgson had collected a series of other books on the Alice model, as he notes in his diary:

Got *Mabel in Rhymeland*, by Edward Holland, as part of the collection I intend making of books of the *Alice* type. Besides this, I have *From Nowhere to the North Pole* by young Tom Hood; *Elsie's Expedition* by F. E. Weatherly, and *A Trip to Blunderland*, by Jambon; and *Wanted – A King* by Maggie Browne. One more book I have added, *The Story of a Nursery Rhyme*.[116]

By the end of the century Twain, Frances Hodgson Burnett, Stevenson and Kipling had extended the scope of children's literature further, but Dodgson had every reason to be conscious of the importance of his own work in this development. The Alice books combine modern and 'romance' elements, psychology and comedy, in a highly original, liberating way that was at home with the real world of Victorian childhood on the one hand, and the kinds of meaning coded in fantastic fairy tales on the other, and had no truck with the ugly didacticism associated with the Ugly Duchess's 'Everything's got a moral, if only you can find it.'

This brings us back to the altercation between Alice and the Red Queen with which we began:

"I'm sure I didn't mean"—Alice was beginning, but the Red Queen interrupted her impatiently.

"That's just what I complain of! You *should* have meant! What do you suppose is the use of a child without any meaning? Even a joke should have some meaning—and a child's more important than a joke, I hope. You couldn't deny that, even if you tried with both hands."

The nonsense jokes, and the jokes about meaning in particular, get their resonance in the end because of the importance of the child's experience of the contestation of meanings in which she is caught up. Dodgson was frightened of the best sources of jokes – sex and religion – and worked hard to keep his writings untainted by even the faintest humorous allusions to either; nevertheless the jokes the child Alice encounters make free with the most 'important' issues in her world – food and the food-chain, growing and ageing, manners and madness, childhood and adulthood, freedom and rules, authority and identity.

It was only in the twinned Alice books, and in *The Hunting of the Snark* of the same period, that Dodgson found a medium to explore his puzzling temperament, with its anomalous investment in young girls and questions of meaning. In these works he transformed his perverse imagination into works of art that have not only survived their moment, but have gone on to generate new meanings with every generation of readers, enlarging the possibilities not only of children's literature but all literature. As the countless subsequent interpretations, translations and adaptations show, Alice's adventures continue and are 'to be continued'.

Notes

1 'The Lobster-Quadrille', *Alice's Adventures in Wonderland*, chapter 10; 'Queen Alice', *Through the Looking-Glass*, chapter 9.
2 *AAIW*, chapter 12.
3 *AAIW*, chapter 12.
4 *TLG*, chapter 1.
5 *AAIW*, chapter 12.
6 *TLG*, chapter 6.
7 R. L. Green, Introduction, *Alice's Adventures in Wonderland* and *Through the Looking-Glass*, Oxford, 1982.
8 William Empson, 'Alice in Wonderland: The Child as Swain', *Some Versions of Pastoral*, London, 1935.
9 Martin Gardner ed. *The Annotated Alice*, with an introduction and notes by Martin Gardner, Harmondsworth, 1965/1970.
10 On this, see Hugh Haughton, Introduction, *Chatto Book of Nonsense Poetry*, London, 1988; J. S. Atherton, 'Carroll: The Unforeseen Precursor', *The Books at the Wake*, New York, 1960; Michael Holquist, 'What is a Boojum? Nonsense and Modernism', *Yale French Studies*, vol XLIII, 1970; Elizabeth Sewell, 'Lewis Carroll and T. S. Eliot as Nonsense Poets' in Neville Braybrooke ed. *T. S. Eliot*,

New York, 1958; Jeffrey Stern, 'Lewis Carroll the Surrealist' in Edward Guiliano ed. *Lewis Carroll Observed*, New York, 1976.

11 See Jacqueline Rose, *The Case of Peter Pan: or the Impossibility of Children's Fiction*, London, 1984.

12 'Today's wonder-world needs Alice', *The New York Times Magazine*, 1 July 1962; reprinted in W. H. Auden, *Forewords and Afterwords*, ed Edward Mendelson, 1973, p. 291.

13 'The books are so frankly about growing up that there is no great discovery in translating them into Freudian terms; it seems only the proper exegesis of a classic even when it would be a shock to the author'. Empson, 'The Child as Swain', *Some Versions of Pastoral*, p. 203.

14 Virginia Woolf, 'Lewis Carroll', *The Collected Essays*, ed. Leonard Woolf, vol 1, London, 1966, pp. 254ff.

15 See Richard Rorty, *Philosophy and the Mirror of Nature*, Princeton, 1979, for an historical account of the dominance of the mirror as a philosophical paradigm of truth. See also George Pitcher, 'Wittgenstein, Nonsense, and Lewis Carroll', *The Massachusetts Review*, VI (1965) for a discussion of Wittgenstein's reading of Carroll; Peter Heath ed, *The Philosopher's Alice*, London, 1974; Jean-Jacques Lecercle, *The Philosophy of Nonsense: The Intuitions of Victorian Nonsense Literature*, London, 1994.

16 'Pig and Pepper', *AAIW*, chapter 6.

17 'Queen Alice', *TLG*, chapter 9.

18 Virginia Woolf, 'Lewis Carroll', *The Moment and Other Essays*, London, 1952.

19 Stuart Dodgson Collingwood, *The Life and Letters of Lewis Carroll*, London, 1898. For a selection of the many Lives of Dodgson, see under Biographical in Further Reading.

20 Collingwood, *Life*, p. 11.

21 Collingwood, *Life*, p. 11.

22 Isa Bowman, *Lewis Carroll as I Knew Him*, London, 1899. Reprinted, New York, 1972, p. 3.

23 Virginia Woolf, 'Lewis Carroll', *Collected Essays*, vol 1.

24 Quoted in Bowman, *Lewis Carroll as I Knew Him*, p. 60.

25 'Faces in the Fire', *Three Sunsets and Other Poems* (1898), *The Complete Works*, ed. Alexander Woollcott, London, 1939, reprinted Harmondsworth, 1988, p. 875.

26 'Solitude', *Three Sunsets and Other Poems*, *Complete Works*, p. 861.

27 Quoted in Collingwood, *Life*, p. 30.

28 Donald Thomas, *Lewis Carroll: A Portrait with Background*, London, 1996, p. 60.

29 For an account of the 'Rectory Umbrella', see Collingwood, *Life*, chapter 1. For reproductions of these family magazines, see Lewis Carroll, *The Rectory Umbrella and Mischmasch*, ed. Florence Milner, London, 1932; and the facsimile *The Rectory Magazine edited by Lewis Carroll*, Austin, 1975.
30 *The Diaries of Lewis Carroll*, 2 vols, ed. R. L. Green, London, 1953, vol 1, p. 70.
31 'Solitude', *Complete Works*, p. 860.
32 *The Letters of Lewis Carroll*, 2 vols, ed. Morton N. Cohen, with the assistance of R. L. Green, London, 1979, vol 2, p. 947.
33 *Diaries*, vol 1, p. 79.
34 Entry for 25 April 1856. *Diaries*, vol 1, p. 83.
35 *Diaries*, vol 1, p. 83.
36 Entry of 5 June. *Diaries*, vol 1, p. 86.
37 Michael Bakewell, *Lewis Carroll: A Biography*, London, 1996, p. 104.
38 Stuart Dodgson Collingwood quotes from the missing diaries frequently in Chapters 2 and 3 of his *Life*. The editor of the Diaries, R. L. Green, gives the family's account of their loss on pp. xi–xiii of vol. 1. Cohen discusses this in *Lewis Carroll: A Biography*, London, 1995, pp. 46–7 and p. 100.
39 Diary entries for 27, 28 and 29 June, have been torn out. See Cohen, *Lewis Carroll: A Biography*, p. 100.
40 Entry for 5 December 1866. *Diaries*, vol 1, p. 208.
41 *Complete Works*, p. 1038.
42 Letter to Alice (Liddell) Hargreaves, 1 March 1885. *Letters*, vol 1, p. 561.
43 Thomas, *Lewis Carroll: A Portrait*, p. 149.
44 'Of being photographed he had a horror.' Bowman, *Lewis Carroll as I Knew Him*, p. 14.
45 *Diaries*, vol 1, p. 86.
46 *Diaries*, vol 1, p. 13.
47 *Complete Works*, pp. 861–3.
48 Cohen, *Lewis Carroll: A Biography*, pp. 203–5.
49 Letter to Lady John Manners of August 1878, quoted in Cohen, *Lewis Carroll: A Biography*, p. 101.
50 Elizabeth Sewell argues that true nonsense depends on playful detachment from feeling ('insulation against emotion and dream'), and that when 'the heart is affected', as in Lear's lyrics and Carroll's *Hunting of the Snark*, the genre collapses, *The Field of Nonsense*, London, 1952, p. 135 and pp. 149–62. This is highly suggestive, but confuses method and function.
51 Introduction to *Pillow Problems Thought Out During Sleepless Nights*, 1893. Quoted in Florence Becker Lennon, *The Life of Lewis Carroll*, New York, 1972, pp. 108–9.

52 Bowman, *Lewis Carroll as I Knew Him*, p. 37, p. 9.
53 William Tuckwell, *Reminiscences of Oxford*, Oxford, 1900, pp. 161–2.
54. Bowman, *Lewis Carroll as I Knew Him*, p. 21. See also the numerous recollections by other children in Morton N. Cohen ed. *Lewis Carroll: Interviews and Recollections*, London, 1989.
55 *Letters*, vol 1, p. 561.
56 *Letters*, vol 1, p. 457.
57 See for example 'The Stage and the Spirit of Reverence', *The Theatre*, June 1888. This is reprinted in *The Complete Works*, pp. 1102–10.
58 Entries for 20 August, 27 September 1877. *Diaries*, vol 1, pp. 365–6.
59 Letter to Kathleen Eschwege, 24 October 1879. *Letters*, vol 1, p. 351.
60 Quoted in Bakewell, *Lewis Carroll: A Biography*, p. 345.
61 Warren Weaver, quoted in Thomas *Lewis Carroll: A Portrait*, p. 212.
62 See the 'Miscellany' section of *The Complete Works* for these, pp. 1009 ff.
63 Thomas, *Lewis Carroll: A Portrait*, p. 223.
64 Preface to *Sylvie and Bruno*, *Complete Works*, p. 257.
65 *Sylvie and Bruno Concluded*, *Complete Works*, p. 674.
66 *Letters*, vol 2, p. 887.
67 For a fuller discussion, see Cohen, *Lewis Carroll: A Biography*, p. 188.
68 Thomas, *Lewis Carroll: A Portrait*, p. 352.
69 *Letters*, vol 2, p. 983.
70 From a letter from Canon Duckworth to Stuart Dodgson Collingwood, quoted in *The Lewis Carroll Picture Book*, ed. Stuart Dodgson Collingwood, London, 1889, pp. 358–60.
71 Collingwood, *Life*, p. 96.
72 'Alice's Recollections of Carrollian Days, as Told to her Son', *Cornhill Magazine*, 73, July 1932, 1–12, reprinted in Cohen, *Interviews and Recollections*, pp. 86–7.
73 Cohen, *Interviews and Recollections*, pp. 86–7.
74 Cohen, *Interviews and Recollections*, p. 84.
75 '"Alice" on the Stage', *The Theatre*, 1887. See pp. 293–8.
76 *Diaries*, vol 1, p. 181.
77 Entry dated 10 February 1863, quoted in *Diaries*, vol 1, pp. 181–2.
78 *Diaries*, vol 1, p. 185.
79 *Diaries*, vol 1, pp. 185–6.
80 *Diaries*, vol 1, p. 188.
81 *Diaries*, vol 1, pp. 176 and 184.
82 *Diaries*, vol 1, p. 208.
83 *Diaries*, vol 1, pp. 230–31.
84 *Letters*, vol 1, p. 62.

85 Quoted in Cohen, *Interviews and Recollections*, pp. 149–50.
86 *Diaries*, vol 1, p. 212.
87 *Diaries*, vol 1, p. 236.
88 *Lewis Carroll and the House of Macmillan*, ed. Morton N. Cohen and Anita Gandolfo, Cambridge, 1987, p. 44.
89 *Lewis Carroll and the House of Macmillan*, p. 48.
90 'Alice's Recollections of Carrollian Days', in Cohen, *Interviews and Recollections*, p. 84.
91 From a letter to *The Times*, 15 January 1932, in Cohen, *Interviews and Recollections*, pp. 196–7.
92 Cohen, *Interviews and Recollections*, pp. 197–8.
93 *Lewis Carroll and the House of Macmillan*, p. 84.
94 Letter of 24 January 1868, *Lewis Carroll and the House of Macmillan*, p. 58.
95 *Diaries*, vol 1, p. 275.
96 Letter of 9 December 1868, *Lewis Carroll and the House of Macmillan*, p. 73.
97 *Lewis Carroll and the House of Macmillan*, p. 85.
98 *Diaries*, vol 2, pp. 294–5.
99 Quoted in Collingwood, *Life*, pp. 142–3.
100 For a fuller account of Alice Liddell, see Anne Clark, *The Real Alice: Lewis Carroll's Dream Child*, London, 1981, and Colin Gordon, *Beyond the Looking-Glass: Reflections of Alice and her Family*, London, 1982.
101 Elizabeth Bishop, 'In The Waiting Room', *The Complete Poems 1927–1979*, London, 1983.
102 'The Garden of Live Flowers', *TLG*, chapter 2.
103 In '"Alice" on the Stage'. See p. 296.
104 Bowman, *Lewis Carroll as I Knew Him*, p. 73.
105 J. O. Halliwell, collector of *Popular Rhymes & Nursery Tales of England* (1849), a book owned by Dodgson, calls his prefatory essay 'Nursery Antiquities'. He argues there that 'the humble chap-book is found to be descended from medieval romance, but also not infrequently from the more ancient mythology, whilst some of our simplest children's rhymes are chanted to this day by children of Germany, Denmark and Sweden, a fact strikingly exhibiting their great antiquity and remote origin' (p. 1).
106 'The Elections to the Hebdomadal Council', 1866–8, *The Lewis Carroll Picture Book*, pp. 88–9.
107 *The Works of Lewis Carroll*, ed. R. L. Green, Feltham, 1965, p. 950.
108 '"Alice" on the Stage'.
109 'Since the pleasure from jokes has the same origin – a core of verbal pleasure and pleasure from nonsense, and a causing of pleasure in the lifting of inhibitions or in the relief of psychical expenditure – this similar relation to

inhibition explains the internal kinship between the naive and jokes.' Freud, *Jokes and Their Relation to the Unconscious* (1905), trans. James Strachey, London, 1960, p. 185.

110 *Letters*, vol 1, p. 146.

111 *Letters*, vol 1, pp. 146–7.

112 'No word has a meaning *inseparably* attached to it; a word means what the speaker means by it, and what the hearer understands by it, and that is all. I meet a friend and say 'Good morning!' Harmless words enough, one would think. Yet possibly, in some language he and I have never heard, these words may convey horrid and loathsome ideas. But are we responsible for this?' 'The Stage and the Spirit of Reverence' (1887), *Works of Lewis Carroll*, p. 1105.

113 *Letters*, vol 1, p. 147.

114 *Works of Lewis Carroll*, p. 1075 ff.

115 Dodgson never refers to his fellow nonsense writer Edward Lear, but it is hard to think he was unaware of him, when literary acquaintances like Tennyson and Ruskin admired the children's writing of both.

116 11 September 1891, *Diaries*, vol 2, p. 486.

FURTHER READING

Works of Lewis Carroll

The Diaries of Lewis Carroll, ed. Roger Lancelyn Green, London: Cassell & Co., 1953. 2 vols.

The Letters of Lewis Carroll, ed. Morton N. Cohen, with the assistance of Roger Lancelyn Green, London: Macmillan, 1979. 2 vols.

Lewis Carroll and the House of Macmillan, ed. Morton N. Cohen and Anita Gandolfo, Cambridge: Cambridge University Press, 1987.

The Complete Works, ed. Alexander Woollcott, London: The Nonesuch Press, 1939. Reprinted, Harmondsworth: Penguin Books, 1988.

The Annotated Alice, ed. Martin Gardner, Harmondsworth: Penguin, 1965. Revised edition, 1970.

Lewis Carroll, *Oeuvres*, ed. Jean Gattégno, with Véronique Béghain, Alexander Révérend and Jean-Pierre Richard, and translations by Philippe Blanchard, Fanny Deleuze, Jean Gattégno, Henri Parisot, Alexander Révérend and Jean-Pierre Richard, Paris: Gallimard, 1990. 2 vols.

Donald J. Gray ed., *Alice in Wonderland: Authoritative Texts, Backgrounds, Essays in Criticism*, New York: W.W. Norton, 1971.

Roger Lancelyn Green ed., *Alice's Adventures in Wonderland* and *Through the Looking-Glass*, Oxford: The World's Classics, 1982.

Alice's Adventures under Ground. Facsimile of the author's manuscript book, with a new Introduction by Martin Gardner, New York: Dover Publications, 1965.

Alice's Adventures under Ground, Foreword by Mary Jean St Clair, London: Pavilion Books in association with the British Library, 1995.

Martin Gardner ed., *Lewis Carroll: The Wasp in a Wig: A 'Suppressed' Episode of Through the Looking-Glass*, with a Preface, Introduction and Notes by Martin Gardner. London: Macmillan, 1977.

The Lewis Carroll Picture Book, Diversions and Digressions of Lewis Carroll, ed. Stuart Dodgson Collingwood, London: T. Fisher Unwin, 1899. Reprinted as *The Unknown Lewis Carroll: Eight Major Works and Many Minor Works*. New York: Dover, 1961.

William Warren Bartley, III ed., *Lewis Carroll's Symbolic Logic*, Brighton: Harvester Press, 1977.

The Rectory Magazine, edited by Lewis Carroll, Austin & London: University of Texas Press, 1975. A facsimile of one of the private Dodgson family magazines.

Biographical

Michael Bakewell, *Lewis Carroll: A Biography*, London: Heinemann, 1996.

Isa Bowman, *The Story of Lewis Carroll*, London: J. H. Dent & Co, 1899. Reprinted as *Lewis Carroll as I Knew Him*, with a new introduction by Morton N. Cohen, New York: Dover, 1972.

Anne Clark, *The Real Alice: Lewis Carroll's Dream Child*, London: Michael Joseph, 1981.

Anne Clark, *Lewis Carroll: A Biography*, London: J.M. Dent & Sons, 1979.

Morton N. Cohen, *Lewis Carroll: A Biography,* London: Macmillan, 1995.

Morton N. Cohen ed., *Lewis Carroll: Interviews and Recollections*, Basingstoke: Macmillan, 1989.

Stuart Dodgson Collingwood, *The Life and Letters of Lewis Carroll*, London: T. Fisher Unwin, 1898.

Rodney Engen, *Sir John Tenniel: Alice's White Knight*, Aldershot: Scholar Press, 1991.

Helmut Gernsheim, *Lewis Carroll: Photographer*, New York: Chanticleer Press, 1949. Reprinted, New York: Dover, 1969.

Colin Gordon, *Beyond the Looking-Glass: Reflections of Alice and her Family*, London: Hodder and Stoughton, 1982.

Derek Hudson, *Lewis Carroll*, London: Constable, 1954. Revised edn.

— *Lewis Carroll: An Illustrated Biography*, London: Book Club Associates, 1976.

Florence Becker Lennon, *Victoria through the Looking-Glass*, 1945. Revised and enlarged as *The Life of Lewis Carroll*, New York, 1962. Reprinted, New York: Dover, 1972.

A. L. Taylor, *The White Knight: A Study of C. L. Dodgson*, Edinburgh: Oliver & Boyd, 1952.

Donald Thomas, *Lewis Carroll: A Portrait with Background*, London: John Murray, 1996.

Critical

Peter Alexander, 'Logic and the Humour of Lewis Carroll', *Proceedings of the Leeds Philosophical and Literary Society*, 6, 1951.

James Atherton, 'Carroll: The Unforeseen Precursor', *The Books at the Wake: A Study of Literary Allusions in James Joyce's Finnegans Wake*, London: Faber and Faber, 1960.

Nina Auerbach, 'Alice and Wonderland: A Curious Child', *Victorian Studies* 17, September 1973; 'Falling Alice, Fallen Women and Victorian Dream Children', *English Language Notes* 20, no. 2, December 1982.

Harold Bloom, ed., *Modern Critical Views: Lewis Carroll*, New York: Chelsea House, 1987.

William Empson, '*Alice in Wonderland,* The Child as Swain', *Some Versions of Pastoral*, London: Chatto & Windus, 1935. Reprinted, Harmondsworth: Penguin, 1966, 1995.

Edward Guiliano, ed., *Lewis Carroll: A Celebration: Essays on the Occasion of the 150th Anniversary of the Birth of Charles Lutwidge Dodgson*, New York: Clarkson N. Potter, 1982.

Edward Guiliano, ed., *Lewis Carroll Observed: A Collection of Unpublished Photographs, Drawings, Poetry, and New Essays*, New York: Potter/Crown, 1976.

Edward Guiliano & James R. Kincaid eds., *Soaring with the Dodo: Essays on Lewis Carroll's Life and Art*, Charlottesville: University of Virginia Press, 1982.

Michael Hancher, *The Tenniel Illustrations to the 'Alice' Books*, Columbus: Ohio State University Press, 1986.

Michael Holquist, 'What is a Boojum? Nonsense and Modernism', *Yale French Studies*, 43, 1969.

James R. Kincaid, 'Alice's Invasion of Wonderland', *PMLA*, 88, January 1973.

Jean-Jacques Lecercle, *The Philosophy of Nonsense: The Intuitions of Victorian Nonsense Literature*, London: Routledge, 1994.

Anne K. Mellor, 'Fear and Trembling: From Lewis Carroll to Existentialism', *English Romantic Irony*, Cambridge, Massachusetts: Harvard University Press, 1980.

Robert Phillips, ed., *Aspects of Alice: Lewis Carroll's Dreamchild as seen through the Critics' Looking-Glasses 1865–1971*, London: Victor Gollancz, 1972. Reprinted: Harmondsworth: Penguin, 1974.

Donald Rackin, *Alice's Adventures in Wonderland* and *Through the Looking-Glass: Nonsense, Sense and Meaning*, New York: Twayne Publishers, 1991

Elizabeth Sewell, *The Field of Nonsense*, London: Chatto & Windus, 1952.

Warren Weaver, *Alice in Many Tongues: The Translations of Alice in Wonderland*, Madison: University of Wisconsin Press, 1964.

Sidney Herbert Williams and Falconer Madan, revised and augmented by Roger Lancelyn Green, now further revised by Denis Crutch, *The Lewis Carroll Handbook*, Folkestone: Dawson, Anchor Books, 1974. First published as *A Handbook of the Literature of the Rev. C. L. Dodgson*, Oxford, 1931.

Edmund Wilson, 'C. L. Dodgson: The Poet Logician', *The Shores of Light*, New York: Farrar, Strauss & Giroux, 1952.

A NOTE ON THE TEXT

There are numerous textual variants in the various editions of the two Alice books published in Carroll's lifetime and since his death, but Carroll's final revision of both texts for the 1897 edition remains the most authoritative in the view of most Carroll scholars. This, with a few modifications, is the text used here.

The textual history has been exhaustively dealt with by Selwyn Goodacre – and others. In a series of articles in *Jabberwocky* (the journal of the Lewis Carroll Society) and elsewhere, Selwyn Goodacre has itemized and analysed the numerous changes and typographical errors corrected and introduced in the various editions supervised by Carroll during his lifetime. In general, when Carroll revised his text – in 1866, and in 1897, in particular – he left the details and phraseology of the story almost wholly intact, but fiddled with its punctuation and presentation. In revising the published texts, he seems almost exclusively concerned with the placing of dots, dashes and commas; he was not interested in improving or reshaping the literary material itself, only with polishing its presentation and buttoning up his already fastidious conventions regarding quotation, italicization and hyphenation. Carroll was always fussy about the representation of speech in the texts – as in the stage versions – and much of his worrying about punctuation stems from this. His particular bugbear concerned the punctuation of the sentences in inverted commas quoted within the text – where to put the stops and commas – and the fidgeting over italics is related to this concern with the relationship between the textual and the oral, the written and the spoken text. Hyphenation was a particular hobby-horse of his. Though the latest text of the books is probably the fussiest as regards punctuation, Carroll was always one of the prissiest of all English writers and the pedantic elaboration of his textual presentation contributes to his peculiar brand of impeccable and deadpan surrealism.

Lewis Carroll rejected the first edition of *Alice's Adventures in Wonderland* in 1865 in large part because of Tenniel's dissatisfaction with the quality of the printed illustrations. Having withdrawn the edition from circulation, he brought out a second edition the following year in 1866. In his account of the reasons for this drastic action, W. H. Bond records that 'a collation of the text shows seventy points of difference, most of them relatively insignificant', of which fifty-nine 'may represent the author's revisions'.[1] Putting the question of the illustrations aside, there is only 'one instance of real verbal revision', as Bond notes: in the incident where Alice is left holding the baby which turns into a pig; her remark that 'it would have *been* a dreadfully ugly child' becomes 'it would have *made* a dreadfully ugly child'. That apart, Carroll used the opportunity of another edition to tidy up the text here and there – adding and deleting commas, adding hyphens ('seashore' becomes 'sea-shore', 'flowerbeds' 'flower-beds'), and correcting the odd misprint (bringing the 'twinkle' back to 'twinkl', for example). Despite the drastic decision to recall that first 1865 book, there are very few obvious differences between it and the second edition.[2]

The popularity of *Alice* was such that in November 1866 Macmillan issued another 3,000 copies in a slightly smaller size, and for this reissue, as Selwyn Goodacre has documented, Carroll again revised the text.[3] This was another small-scale revision which was almost entirely confined to punctuation. As Goodacre notes, it showed 'the gradual implementation of the Carrollian fondness for hyphenated words' (the hole-in-one 'mousehole' for example, becomes a two-stroke 'mouse-hole') and 'the liberal addition of commas'. There are some spelling changes (such as 'toffy' to 'toffee', a change Carroll was to reverse in 1897) and a couple of grammatical twitches: 'She felt it ought to be treated with respect' becomes the more grammatically respectable 'she felt *that* it ought to be treated with respect', and the Hatter's rather knottedly colloquial 'I hadn't but just begun' becomes the plainer 'I hadn't begun'. Most of these changes were retained in later editions. In addition to the various verbal readjustments, two illustrations were moved from the gutter position to the outer side of the page – those of the card gardeners and Alice with the flamingo mallet. They remained there in all subsequent editions. *Alice's Adventures in Wonderland* was thereafter only thoroughly revised again, with *Looking-Glass*, in the final corrected edition of 1897.

Through the Looking-Glass was first published in December 1871, with the title page dated 1872, and was not fully revised until the sixty-first thousand. This was published in December 1896 but dated 1897, and was effectively, as Denis Crutch notes, its second edition.[4] Until that date, with the exception of alterations to the preliminary and end matter, the text was to all intents identical, being printed from electrotypes made in 1871.

In September 1896, Carroll borrowed a bound-up copy of the two Alice books (*Wonderland*, 1882; *Looking-Glass*, 1880) from a former child friend May Barber (later Mrs Stretton) and made manuscript corrections and amendments for the editions of 1897, when the books were wholly reset in new type with a special preface dated Christmas 1896. The scale and importance of the 1897 revisions of Carroll's two classic texts were first documented by Stanley Godman in the late 1950s.[5] Godman's article records Carroll's corrections in detail and notes that 'a study of a representative selection of the editions which have appeared since his death shows ... that the author's final intentions, as represented by the corrections in Mrs Stretton's copies and the 1897 editions based on them, have rarely been respected in their entirety'. More recently, Selwyn Goodacre has provided a more complete record of the extensive alterations to the 1897 text of *Wonderland*.[6]

The 1897 revisions are generally along the same lines as the earlier revisions – adjustments to punctuation or spelling or hyphenation rather than additions or excisions of textual material. He changed 'can't' and 'won't' to the more laboriously accurate 'ca'n't' and 'wo'n't' throughout, and multiplied the already multiple instances of hyphenation that occur in each revision. So he gave instructions not only to convert a 'schoolroom' into a 'school-room' and 'kidgloves' into 'kid-gloves', which seem unexceptionable, but 'Cheshire Puss' into 'Cheshire-Puss', 'Multiplication Table' into 'Multiplication-Table' and even 'shepherd boy' into 'shepherd-boy', which seem almost bizarre in their pursuit of correctness. Carroll was obviously offended by nouns acting as adjectival qualifiers of other nouns, so committed himself to further oddities such as 'winter-day' and 'railway-station' too. He also at this stage came to insist that an exclamation mark finishes a sentence, so that 'Hush! hush!' became 'Hush! Hush!' and 'Alas! it was too late' became 'Alas! It was too late'. Some of the gendered terms that are applied to the creatures also got altered in this revision – so that the mouse's tail is changed from 'his tail' to 'its tail', the Dodo referred to as a 'he' rather than an 'it', and the dormouse changed from 'he' to 'it' throughout the tea-party (though he survives as a male in the trial scene). As to spelling, 'toffee' reverts back to the 'toffy' of the original manuscript.

Apart from this characteristic punctuational fidgeting towards correctness and consistency – never fully realized, since certain inconsistencies remained despite his best efforts – Carroll made a number of tiny additions to the narrative in this edition. Shakespeare is said to have 'stood' rather than 'sat' in the pictures of him, for example! The most significant changes are a few minute but telling touches added to the dialogue and stage directions of the trial scene in *Wonderland*. They include changing 'These were the verses the White Rabbit read:—' to 'There was dead silence in the court, whilst the White Rabbit read out these verses:—' and adding a couple of further interpretations of the evidence by the King ('*If she should push the matter on*'—that must be the Queen—'*What would become of you*—what, indeed!—'). Perhaps Carroll's sense of theatre had been sharpened by seeing the stories performed. The other significant addition was certainly a result of his theatrical experiences. On the proofs Carroll instructed the printers to take in ten extra lines into ''Tis the voice of the lobster' from 'The People's Edition' (originally written for 'Alice on the Stage') – though as Goodacre notes, they were already included in the 6*s*. editions after 1886.

This edition incorporated the two revisions to *TLG* marked in the revised copy-text Carroll sent the printers for the 1897 edition which Stanley Godman noted had not been incorporated into the final text. These are a peculiarly arresting comma after the first word in the penultimate stanza of 'Jabberwocky' ('And, hast thou slain the Jabberwock?') and a smoother final 'e' on 'smooth' in 'Queen Alice'

('Smoothe her hair—lend her your nightcap'). I have also silently modified a very small number of errors of punctuation (such as unclosed inverted commas), reinstated the 'Dramatis Personae' to *TLG* which formed part of the 1872 and other early editions but was omitted in 1897, and put the 1896 Christmas Prefaces to both books in the Appendices. Otherwise, the text is that of the last edition Carroll supervised through the press.

Notes

1 W. H. Bond, 'The Publication of *Alice's Adventures in Wonderland*', *Harvard Library Bulletin*, Autumn 1956.
2 For a fuller account see Selwyn Goodacre, 'The Textual Alterations to *Alice's Adventures in Wonderland* 1865–1866', *Jabberwocky*, vol 3, no 1, Winter 1973, pp. 17–20.
3 Selwyn Goodacre, 'The Textual Alterations to *Alice's Adventures in Wonderland* 1866–1867', *Jabberwocky*, vol 17, nos 1 and 2, Winter/Spring 1988, pp. 3–7.
4 Denis Crutch, 'The Writings of C. L. Dodgson', privately printed, London, 1974.
5 Stanley Godman, 'Lewis Carroll's Final Corrections to "Alice"', *TLS*, 2 May 1958, p. 248.
6 Selwyn Goodacre, 'Lewis Carroll's Alterations for the 1897 6s Edition of *Alice's Adventures in Wonderland*', *Jabberwocky*, vol 11, no. 3, Summer 1982.

A NOTE ON TENNIEL

Alice's adventures are propelled by her dissatisfaction with the book her sister is reading, which has 'no pictures or conversation in it'. Though Dodgson produced his own home-made illustrations for the original *Alice's Adventures under Ground*, when he decided to have it published, he was intent from the outset on hiring a first-rate illustrator to provide the 'pictures' accompanying his own 'conversations'. At the end of 1863, he wrote to his friend Tom Taylor, a *Punch* journalist and popular dramatist, to ask his advice on the matter:

> Do you know Mr Tenniel well enough to say whether he could undertake such a thing as drawing a dozen wood-cuts to illustrate a child's book, and if so, could you put me into communication with him? The reasons for which I ask ... are that I have written such a tale for a young friend, and illustrated it in pen and ink. It has been read and liked by so many children, and I have been asked so often to publish it, that I have decided on doing so. I have tried my hand at drawing on the wood, and come to the conclusion that it would take much more time than I can afford, and the result would not be satisfactory after all. I want some figure-pictures done in pure outline, or nearly so, and of all artists on wood, I should prefer Mr Tenniel. If he should be willing to undertake them, I would send him the book to look over, not that he should at all follow my pictures, but simply to give him an idea of the sort of thing I want. I should be very much obliged if you would find out for me what he thinks of it.[1]

Since 1850, John Tenniel (1820–1914) had been a principle cartoonist for *Punch* and was already a successful book illustrator, with contributions to numerous anthologies and story-books and complete illustrations to De La Motte Fouque's *Undine* (1845), *Aesop's Fables* (1848) and Thomas Moore's *Lalla Rookh* (1861). Dodgson finally got in touch with his preferred illustrator himself on 25 January 1864.

As Dodgson recorded in his diary, Tenniel 'seemed to think favourably of undertaking the pictures', but he wanted 'to see the book before deciding'.[2] He must have approved of what he saw, and on 5 April he agreed to do the pictures, despite the pressure of personal troubles (his mother was ill) and other commissions – he was not only producing his weekly copy for *Punch* but sixty pictures for R. H. Barham's *Ingoldsby Legends* (1864) and others for Dalziel's *Arabian Nights* (1865). Dodgson sent the first slips less than a mo`nth later in early May, and found Tenniel's slow progress immensely frustrating. It seems probable that Tenniel saw Dodgson's own illustrations, and as the text grew, Carroll sent him rough sketches and even occasional photographs of models, as well as suggesting numerous alterations and additions to Tenniel's first drafts. Given both men were obsessive perfectionists, with strong ideas of their own, it was a protracted and difficult as well as a productive collaborative process. Tenniel sent back the first twelve proofs complete in December (his first picture was for the Pool of Tears), while the last proofs did not arrive until June 1865.

When the book came back from the printers in July that year, Dodgson heard that Tenniel was 'dissatisfied' with the state of the pictures. It is a sign of the perfectionist Dodgson's commitment to the visual dimension of the book that this was enough to lead him to cancel the entire first edition and, at his own expense, order a complete reprint in August. The new impression won Tenniel's approval in November, and the book was published for Christmas 1865. Though the *Athenaeum* thought the illustrations 'square and grim, and uncouth', most reviewers and readers sided with *The Times*, which said he had illustrated the story 'with extraordinary grace'.

It was a measure of the success of this initial double-act, that when Dodgson finished the sequel, *Through the Looking-Glass*, a few years later, having first tried Richard Doyle ('Doyle isn't good enough', he told Mrs MacDonald) and then Noel Paton, he approached Tenniel once again, and after some initial reluctance to renew the troublesome collaboration with the finicky author of *Alice*, the illustrator was eventually persuaded in 1868 to do so, provided he could do them in his own time: 'The second volume of *Alice* will after all be illustrated by

Tenniel, who has reluctantly consented, as his hands are full'.[3] Henceforward, however various her subsequent reincarnations on page, stage and screen, the face and fate of Dodgson's heroine have been inextricably intertwined with Tenniel's original images. Unfortunately this particular collaboration between author and illustrator was never to be repeated, since Tenniel refused to have anything more to do with Dodgson after the experience of working on the Alice books with him and Dodgson had to look elsewhere for illustrators to *The Hunting of the Snark*, *Sylvie and Bruno* and his collections of verse. It took nearly three years for Tenniel to complete the fifty illustrations for *Through the Looking-Glass* – three years of delays, corrections and negotiations between author, artist and printers, in which Dodgson usually had the upper hand (though he accepted a number of suggestions by Tenniel, such as making the Walrus's companion a carpenter rather than a butterfly or baronet, and making Alice grab the goat's beard rather than an old lady's hair in the carriage scene). Though when the book was published in 1871, it was another triumph, one of the high points in the artist's career, Tenniel later wrote that: 'It is a curious fact that with *Through the Looking-Glass* the faculty of making drawings for book illustrations parted from me, and notwithstanding all sorts of tempting inducements, I have done nothing in that direction since'.[4] When Harry Furniss agreed to illustrate *Sylvie and Bruno*, Tenniel told him that 'Lewis Carroll is impossible'. Nevertheless, while it lasted, their partnership resulted in one of the most memorably successful combinations of image and text in the history of English book production.[5]

The Alice books were published during perhaps the most self-conscious and richly productive period of English printed book illustration.[6] Following in the wake of George Cruikshank's pioneering illustrations to the brothers Grimm's *Household Tales* and Charles Dickens's *Oliver Twist*, Hablot Browne (under the pseudonym of 'Phiz') provided densely detailed illustrations to over ten novels by Dickens and innumerable works by contemporaries, making book illustration integral to contemporary fiction as well as to the publication of anthologies of tales and poems, ancient and modern, in the period. This was the period of the great illustrators associated with *Punch* – not only Tenniel, but also Richard Doyle, John Leech, Charles Keene and

George du Maurier – and also the heyday of Pre-Raphaelitism, in which Arthur Hughes, Dante Gabriel Rossetti and Millais provided illustrations not only for earlier literature but for contemporary writers such as George MacDonald, Christina Rossetti, Trollope and Tennyson. Luckily for Alice, with her predilection for books with 'pictures' in them, text and image were probably more closely allied during the Victorian period than at any time since the Middle Ages. Dodgson was an enthusiastic follower of contemporary art – he photographed many of the foremost artists of the day, possessed the Pre-Raphaelite periodical the *Germ*, owned paintings by Rossetti and Arthur Hughes, photographed drawings of Burne-Jones and Rossetti, and his library indicates a developed taste for illustrated books of both the earlier generation of Gillray, Seymour and Cruikshank and contemporaries, such as Richard Doyle (illustrator of Ruskin's *The King of the Golden River*), Noel Paton (in particular, his Shakespeare illustrations) and the later work of children's artists such as Randolph Caldecott and T. Pym, an early imitator of Kate Greenaway.[7] In opting for John Tenniel as his illustrator for his story, he knew exactly what he was doing.

Tenniel's earlier book illustrations show the influence of German and English Victorian medievalism (as in *The Book of British Ballads*, 1842), as well as Gothic (in his versions of Poe's 'The Raven'), picturesque orientalism in his *Lallah Rookh* (1861) and the Dalziels's *Arabian Knights Entertainment* (1863), and probably the satirical anthropomorphism of the brilliant French cartoonist Grandville in his *Aesop's Fables*. As the principal political cartoonist for *Punch* from 1864 until his retirement in 1901, Tenniel was one of the most influential visual artists of the period, combining a satiric fantasy style with a solid circumstantial grasp of the social and political details of the Victorian world (these cartoons were collected in book form too, as in the four volumes of *Cartoons from Punch by John Tenniel*, 1864, 1864–70, 1871–81 and 1882–91, and *The Queen and Mr Punch*, 1897, and *Cartoons by Sir John Tenniel*, 1901). The combination of his crisply grotesque *Punch* style and the fashionable atmospheric medievalism of his 'serious' book illustrations, in addition to the meticulous anthropomorphism of his animal cartoons for *Aesop* and *Punch*, all contribute to the soberly fantastic idiom of the two Alice books. It is a strange irony that this talented and prolific graphic artist should be remembered now almost exclusively for his contributions to two children's books – but his pictures bear the imprint of his broad and solid experience in those other fields, enabling the illustrations, like the text, to infuse a fantastic tale for children with strangely representative status as an expression of the Victorian age.

Though there have been numerous brilliant illustrators of the Alice books in the twentieth century – by among others, Arthur Rackham, Mervyn Peake, Salvador Dali, the Walt Disney studio and Ralph Steadman – Carroll's text has remained indissolubly bound up with the original illustrations which appeared in all the texts published in his lifetime (with the exception of the 1886 facsimile of *Alice's Adventures under Ground*). Tenniel's illustrations form an inescapable complement and counterpart to Carroll's dream text and to the reader's sense of the squarely down-to-earth 'dream child' in her striped stockings and long brushed hair, as well as her various fabulous and incongruous interlocutors in Wonderland and beyond the mirror. If the books are, among other things, portrait galleries of nineteenth-century eccentrics à la Dickens, then this is in large part due to Tenniel. His portraits of the White Rabbit, the Queen of Hearts, the Mad Hatter, the Ugly Duchess, the Brothers Tweedle, the Walrus and the Carpenter, the White Knight (possibly a self-portrait) and Humpty Dumpty (based on a sketch by Dodgson) give solid, credible physiognomies and physical reality to speakers who have psychological and vocal individuality in Carroll's text but little of the specific visual identity Tenniel's designs confer. Tenniel has also fixed with memorable precision some of the more fantastic fauna of the Carrollian wonderlands – such as those phantasmal compound ghosts the Mock Turtle and Jabberwocky – and chronicled with admirable prosaic density the social scenes of the Mad Tea-Party, the Duchess's Kitchen, the courtroom where the Trial scene is held, the Oxonian shop where the sheep presides, the railway carriage, and the horribly convincing royal dinner party where Alice's coronation is finally celebrated. In depicting the cards, chess-pieces and animals around which the narratives revolve, Tenniel always manages to be true to their double-nature – as 'characters' and as non-humans, fantastical figures and social types. Above all, Tenniel's graphic idiom manages to create a visual equivalent of this most uncomfortable fantastic text's relationship to mid nineteenth-century Britain and to anchor it in the solid ground of the bourgeois public and domestic world and its comfortable self-representations.

Tenniel's image of Alice feeling her way through the solid reflective surface of the looking-glass into the world of dizzying instabilities and grotesque metamorphoses beyond is a beautiful instance of his art at its most expressively attuned to Carroll's text. It can also stand as an expressive emblem of the illustrator's contribution to Alice's books of 'pictures and conversations'.

Notes

1 20 December 1863, *Letters*, vol 1, p. 62.
2 *Diaries*, vol 1, p. 210.
3 *Diaries*, vol 1, p. 275.
4 Quoted in Anne Clark, *Lewis Carroll: A Biography*, London, 1979, p. 169.
5 On this, see Edward Hodnett, *Image and Text, Studies in the Illustration of English Literature*, Aldershot, 1986. For a fuller account of the collaboration between Carroll and Tenniel, see Rodney Engen, *Sir John Tenniel: Alice's White Knight*, Aldershot, 1991.
6 For a detailed account of this, see Forrest Reid, *Illustrators of the Sixties*, London, 1928, and Percy Muir, *Victorian Illustrated Books*, London, 1991.
7 For further details of Carroll and contemporary artistic taste, see Jeffrey Stern, 'Lewis Carroll and the Pre-Raphaelites', in *Lewis Carroll Observed*, ed. Edward Guiliano, New York, 1976.

Alice's Adventures in Wonderland

ALICE'S ADVENTURES IN WONDERLAND

BY

LEWIS CARROLL

WITH FORTY-TWO ILLUSTRATIONS BY JOHN TENNIEL

EIGHTY-SEVENTH THOUSAND

PRICE SIX SHILLINGS

London

MACMILLAN AND CO., LIMITED

NEW YORK : THE MACMILLAN COMPANY

1898

All in the golden afternoon[1]
Full leisurely we glide;
For both our oars, with little skill,
By little arms are plied,
While little hands make vain pretence
Our wanderings to guide.

Ah, cruel Three! In such an hour,
Beneath such dreamy weather,
To beg a tale of breath too weak
To stir the tiniest feather!
Yet what can one poor voice avail
Against three tongues together?

Imperious Prima flashes forth
Her edict "to begin it":
In gentler tones Secunda hopes
"There will be nonsense in it!"
While Tertia interrupts the tale
Not *more* than once a minute.

Anon, to sudden silence won,
In fancy they pursue
The dream-child moving through a land
Of wonders wild and new,
In friendly chat with bird or beast—
And half believe it true.

And ever, as the story drained
   The wells of fancy dry,
And faintly strove that weary one
   To put the subject by,
"The rest next time—" "It *is* next time!"
   The happy voices cry.

Thus grew the tale of Wonderland:
   Thus slowly, one by one,
Its quaint events were hammered out—
   And now the tale is done,
And home we steer, a merry crew,
   Beneath the setting sun.

Alice! A childish story take,
   And, with a gentle hand,
Lay it where Childhood's dreams are twined
   In Memory's mystic band,
Like pilgrim's wither'd wreath of flowers
   Pluck'd in a far-off land.[2]

CONTENTS

Chapter		Page
I	DOWN THE RABBIT-HOLE	9
II	THE POOL OF TEARS	16
III	A CAUCUS-RACE AND A LONG TALE	24
IV	THE RABBIT SENDS IN A LITTLE BILL	31
V	ADVICE FROM A CATERPILLAR	40
VI	PIG AND PEPPER	50
VII	A MAD TEA-PARTY	60
VIII	THE QUEEN'S CROQUET-GROUND	69
IX	THE MOCK TURTLE'S STORY	78
X	THE LOBSTER-QUADRILLE	87
XI	WHO STOLE THE TARTS?	95
XII	ALICE'S EVIDENCE	102

CHAPTER I

DOWN THE RABBIT-HOLE

Alice was beginning to get very tired of sitting by her sister on the bank, and of having nothing to do: once or twice she had peeped into the book her sister was reading, but it had no pictures or conversations in it, "and what is the use of a book," thought Alice, "without pictures or conversations?"[1]

So she was considering, in her own mind (as well as she could, for the hot day made her feel very sleepy and stupid), whether the pleasure of making a daisy-chain would be worth the trouble of getting up and picking the daisies, when suddenly a White Rabbit with pink eyes ran close by her.

There was nothing so *very* remarkable in that; nor did Alice think it so *very* much out of the way to hear the Rabbit say to itself "Oh dear! Oh dear! I shall be too late!" (when she thought it over afterwards, it occurred to her that she ought to have wondered at this, but at the time it all seemed quite natural); but, when the Rabbit actually *took a watch out of its waistcoat-pocket,* and looked at it, and then hurried on, Alice started to her feet, for it flashed across her mind that she had never before seen a rabbit with either a waistcoat-pocket, or a watch to take out of it, and, burning with curiosity, she ran across the field after it, and was just in time to see it pop down a large rabbit-hole under the hedge.

In another moment down went Alice after it, never once considering how in the world she was to get out again.

The rabbit-hole went straight on like a tunnel for some way, and then dipped suddenly down, so suddenly that Alice had not a moment to think about stopping herself before she found herself falling down what seemed to be a very deep well.

Either the well was very deep, or she fell very slowly, for she had plenty of time as she went down to look about her, and to wonder what was going to happen next. First, she tried to look down and make out what she was coming to, but it was too dark to see anything: then she looked at the sides of the well, and noticed that they were filled with cupboards and book-shelves: here and there she saw maps and pictures hung upon pegs. She took down a jar from one of the shelves as she passed: it was labeled "ORANGE MARMALADE," but to her great disappointment it was empty: she did not like to drop the jar, for fear of killing somebody underneath, so managed to put it into one of the cupboards as she fell past it.

"Well!" thought Alice to herself. "After such a fall as this, I shall think nothing of tumbling down-stairs! How brave they'll all think me at home! Why, I wouldn't say anything about it, even if I fell off the top of the house!" (Which was very likely true.)

Down, down, down. Would the fall *never* come to an end? "I wonder how many miles I've fallen by this time?" she said aloud. "I must be getting somewhere near the centre of the earth.[2] Let me see: that would be four thousand miles down, I think—" (for, you see, Alice had learnt several things of this sort in her lessons in the school-room, and though this was not a *very* good opportunity for showing off her knowledge, as there was no one to listen to her, still it was good practice to say it over) "—yes, that's about the right distance—but then I wonder what Latitude or Longitude I've got to?" (Alice had not the slightest idea what Latitude was, or Longitude either, but she thought they were nice grand words to say.)

Presently she began again. "I wonder if I shall fall right *through* the earth! How funny it'll seem to come out among the people that walk with their heads downwards! The antipathies, I think—" (she was rather glad there *was* no one listening, this time, as it didn't sound at all the right word) "—but I shall have to ask them what the name of the country is, you know. Please, Ma'am, is this New Zealand? Or Australia?" (and she tried to curtsey as she spoke—fancy, *curtseying* as you're falling through the air! Do you think you could manage it?) "And what an ignorant little girl she'll think me for asking! No, it'll never do to ask: perhaps I shall see it written up somewhere."

Down, down, down. There was nothing else to do, so Alice soon began talking again. "Dinah'll miss me very much to-night, I should think!" (Dinah was the cat.)[3] "I hope they'll remember her saucer of milk at tea-time. Dinah, my dear! I wish you were down here with me! There are no mice in the air, I'm afraid, but you might catch a bat, and that's very like a mouse, you know. But do cats eat bats, I wonder?" And here Alice began to get rather sleepy, and went on saying to herself, in a dreamy sort of way, "Do cats eat bats? Do cats eat bats?" and sometimes "Do bats eat cats?", for, you see, as she couldn't answer either question, it didn't much matter which way she put it. She felt that she was dozing off, and had just begun to dream that she was walking hand in hand with Dinah, and was saying to her, very earnestly, "Now, Dinah, tell me the truth: did you ever eat a bat?", when suddenly, thump! thump! down she came upon a heap of sticks and dry leaves, and the fall was over.

Alice was not a bit hurt, and she jumped up on to her feet in a moment: she looked up, but it was all dark overhead: before her was another long passage, and the White Rabbit was still in sight, hurrying down it. There was not a moment to be lost: away went Alice like the wind, and was just in time to hear it say, as it turned a corner, "Oh my ears and whiskers, how late it's getting!" She was close behind it when she turned the corner, but the Rabbit was no longer to be seen: she found herself in a long, low hall, which was lit up by a row of lamps hanging from the roof.

There were doors all round the hall, but they were all locked; and when Alice had been all the way down one side and up the other, trying every door, she walked sadly down the middle, wondering how she was ever to get out again.

Suddenly she came upon a little three-legged table, all made of solid glass: there was nothing on it but a tiny golden key,[4] and Alice's first idea was that this might belong to one of the doors of the hall; but, alas! either the locks were too large, or the key was too small, but at any rate it would not open any of them. However, on the second time round, she came upon a low curtain she had not noticed before, and behind it was a little door about fifteen inches high: she tried the little golden key in the lock, and to her great delight it fitted!

Alice opened the door and found that it led into a small passage, not much larger than a rat-hole: she knelt down and looked along the passage into the loveliest garden you ever saw. How she longed to get out of that dark hall, and wander about among those beds of bright flowers and those cool fountains,[5] but she could not even get her head through the doorway; "and even if my head *would* go through," thought poor

Alice, "it would be of very little use without my shoulders. Oh, how I wish I could shut up like a telescope! I think I could, if I only knew how to begin." For, you see, so many out-of-the-way things had happened lately, that Alice had begun to think that very few things indeed were really impossible.

There seemed to be no use in waiting by the little door, so she went back to the table, half hoping she might find another key on it, or at any rate a book of rules for shutting people up like telescopes: this time she found a little bottle on it ("which certainly was not here before," said Alice), and tied round the neck of the bottle was a paper label, with the words "DRINK ME" beautifully printed on it in large letters.

It was all very well to say "Drink me," but the wise little Alice was not going to do *that* in a hurry. "No, I'll look first," she said, "and see whether it's marked '*poison*' or not"; for she had read several nice little stories[6] about children who had got burnt, and eaten up by wild beasts, and other unpleasant things, all because they *would* not remember the simple rules their friends had taught them: such as, that a red-hot poker will burn you if you hold it too long; and that, if you cut your finger *very* deeply with a knife, it usually bleeds; and she had never forgotten that, if you drink much from a bottle marked "poison," it is almost certain to disagree with you, sooner or later.

However, this bottle was *not* marked "poison," so Alice ventured to taste it, and, finding it very nice (it had, in fact, a sort of mixed flavour of cherry-tart, custard, pine-apple, roast turkey, toffy, and hot buttered toast), she very soon finished it off.

*   *   *   *
  *   *   *
*   *   *   *

"What a curious feeling!" said Alice. "I must be shutting up like a telescope!"

And so it was indeed: she was now only ten inches high, and her face brightened up at the thought that she was now the right size for going through the little door into that lovely garden. First, however, she waited for a few minutes to see if she was going to shrink any further: she felt a little nervous about this; "for it might end, you know," said Alice to herself, "in my going out altogether, like a candle. I wonder what I should be like then?" And she tried to fancy what the flame of a candle looks like after the candle is blown out, for she could not remember ever having seen such a thing.

After a while, finding that nothing more happened, she decided on going into the garden at once; but, alas for poor Alice! when she got to the door, she found she had forgotten the little golden key, and when she went back to the table for it, she found she could not possibly reach it: she could see it quite plainly through the glass, and she tried her best to climb up one of the legs of the table, but it was too slippery; and when she had tired herself out with trying, the poor little thing sat down and cried.

"Come, there's no use in crying like that!" said Alice to herself rather sharply. "I advise you to leave off this minute!" She generally gave herself very good advice (though she very seldom followed it), and sometimes she scolded herself so severely as to bring tears into her eyes; and once she remembered trying to box her own ears for having cheated herself in a game of croquet she was playing against herself, for this curious child was very fond of pretending to be two people. "But it's no use now," thought poor Alice, "to pretend to be two people! Why, there's hardly enough of me left to make *one* respectable person!"

Soon her eye fell on a little glass box that was lying under the table: she opened it, and found in it a very small cake, on which the words "EAT ME"[7] were beautifully marked in currants. "Well, I'll eat it," said Alice, "and if it makes me grow larger, I can reach the key; and if it makes me grow smaller, I can creep under the door: so either way I'll get into the garden, and I don't care which happens!"

She ate a little bit, and said anxiously to herself "Which way? Which way?", holding her hand on the top of her head to feel which way it was growing; and she was quite surprised to find that she remained the same size. To be sure, this is what generally happens when one eats cake; but Alice had got so much into the way of expecting nothing but out-of-the-way things to happen, that it seemed quite dull and stupid for life to go on in the common way.

So she set to work, and very soon finished off the cake.

* * * *

* * *

* * * *

CHAPTER II

THE POOL OF TEARS

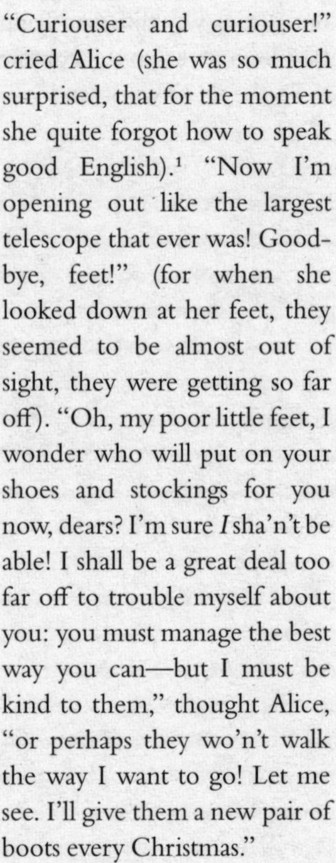

"Curiouser and curiouser!" cried Alice (she was so much surprised, that for the moment she quite forgot how to speak good English).[1] "Now I'm opening out like the largest telescope that ever was! Good-bye, feet!" (for when she looked down at her feet, they seemed to be almost out of sight, they were getting so far off). "Oh, my poor little feet, I wonder who will put on your shoes and stockings for you now, dears? I'm sure *I* sha'n't be able! I shall be a great deal too far off to trouble myself about you: you must manage the best way you can—but I must be kind to them," thought Alice, "or perhaps they wo'n't walk the way I want to go! Let me see. I'll give them a new pair of boots every Christmas."

And she went on planning to herself how she would manage it. "They must go by the carrier," she thought; "and how funny it'll seem, sending presents to one's own feet! And how odd the directions will look!

Alice's Right Foot, Esq.
Hearthrug,
near the Fender,
(with Alice's love).

Oh dear, what nonsense I'm talking!"[2]

Just at this moment her head struck against the roof of the hall: in fact she was now rather more than nine feet high, and she at once took up the little golden key and hurried off to the garden door.

Poor Alice! It was as much as she could do, lying down on one side, to look through into the garden with one eye; but to get through was more hopeless than ever: she sat down and began to cry again.

"You ought to be ashamed of yourself," said Alice, "a great girl like you," (she might well say this), "to go on crying in this way! Stop this moment, I tell you!" But she went on all the same, shedding gallons of tears, until there was a large pool all round her, about four inches deep, and reaching half down the hall.

After a time she heard a little pattering of feet in the distance, and she hastily dried her eyes to see what was coming. It was the White Rabbit returning, splendidly dressed, with a pair of white kid-gloves in one hand and a large fan in the other:[3] he came trotting along in a great hurry, muttering to himself, as he came, "Oh! The Duchess, the Duchess! Oh! *Wo'n't* she be savage if I've kept her waiting!" Alice felt so desperate that she was ready to ask help of any one: so, when the Rabbit came near her, she began, in a low, timid voice, "If you please, Sir——" The Rabbit started violently, dropped the white kid-gloves and the fan, and skurried away into the darkness as hard as he could go.

Alice took up the fan and gloves, and, as the hall was very hot, she kept fanning herself all the time she went on talking. "Dear, dear! How queer everything is to-day! And yesterday things went on just as usual. I wonder if I've been changed in the night? Let me think: *was* I the same when I got up this morning? I almost think I can remember feeling a little different. But if I'm not the same, the next question is 'Who

in the world am I?' Ah, *that's* the great puzzle!" And she began thinking over all the children she knew that were of the same age as herself, to see if she could have been changed for any of them.

"I'm sure I'm not Ada," she said, "for her hair goes in such long ringlets, and mine doesn't go in ringlets at all; and I'm sure I ca'n't be Mabel,[4] for I know all sorts of things, and she, oh, she knows such a very little! Besides, *she's* she, and *I'm* I, and—oh dear, how puzzling it all is! I'll try if I know all the things I used to know. Let me see: four times five is twelve, and four times six is thirteen, and four times seven is—oh dear! I shall never get to twenty at that rate![5] However, the Multiplication-Table doesn't signify: let's try Geography. London is the capital of Paris, and Paris is the capital of Rome, and Rome—no, *that's* all wrong, I'm certain! I must have been changed for Mabel! I'll try and say '*How doth the little*—'," and she crossed her hands on her lap, as if she were saying lessons, and began to repeat it, but her voice sounded hoarse and strange, and the words did not come the same as they used to do:—

"How doth the little crocodile[6]
Improve his shining tail,
And pour the waters of the Nile
On every golden scale!

"How cheerfully he seems to grin,
How neatly spreads his claws,
And welcomes little fishes in,
With gently smiling jaws!"

"I'm sure those are not the right words," said poor Alice, and her eyes filled with tears again as she went on, "I must be Mabel after all, and I shall have to go and live in that poky little house, and have next to no toys to play with, and oh, ever so many lessons to learn! No, I've made up my mind about it: if I'm Mabel, I'll stay down here! It'll be no use their putting their heads down and saying 'Come up again, dear!' I shall only look up and say 'Who am I, then? Tell me that first, and then, if I like being that person, I'll come up: if not, I'll stay down here till I'm somebody else'—but, oh dear!" cried Alice, with a sudden burst of tears, "I do wish they *would* put their heads down! I am so *very* tired of being all alone here!"

As she said this she looked down at her hands, and was surprised to see that she had put on one of the Rabbit's little white kid-gloves while she was talking. "How *can* I have done that?" she thought. "I must be growing small again." She got up and went to the table to measure herself by it, and found that, as nearly as she could guess, she was now about two feet high, and was going on shrinking rapidly: she soon found out that the cause of this was the fan she was holding, and she dropped it hastily, just in time to save herself from shrinking away altogether.

"That *was* a narrow escape!" said Alice, a good deal frightened at the sudden change, but very glad to find herself still in existence. "And now for the garden!" And she ran with all speed back to the little door; but, alas! the little door was shut again, and the little golden key was lying on the glass table as before, "and things are worse than ever," thought the poor child, "for I never was so small as this before, never! And I declare it's too bad, that it is!"

As she said these words her foot slipped, and in another moment,

splash! she was up to her chin in salt-water. Her first idea was that she had somehow fallen into the sea, "and in that case I can go back by railway," she said to herself. (Alice had been to the seaside once in her life,[7] and had come to the general conclusion that, wherever you go to on the English coast, you find a number of bathing-machines in the sea, some children digging in the sand with wooden spades, then a row of lodging-houses, and behind them a railway-station.) However, she soon made out that she was in the pool of tears which she had wept when she was nine feet high.

"I wish I hadn't cried so much!" said Alice, as she swam about, trying to find her way out. "I shall be punished for it now, I suppose, by being drowned in my own tears! That *will* be a queer thing, to be sure! However, everything is queer to-day."

Just then she heard something splashing about in the pool a little way off, and she swam nearer to make out what it was: at first she thought it must be a walrus or hippopotamus, but then she remembered how small she was now, and she soon made out that it was only a mouse, that had slipped in like herself.

"Would it be of any use, now," thought Alice, "to speak to this mouse? Everything is so out-of-the-way down here, that I should think very likely it can talk: at any rate, there's no harm in trying." So she began: "O Mouse, do you know the way out of this pool? I am very tired of swimming about here, O Mouse!" (Alice thought this must be the right way of speaking to a mouse: she had never done such a thing before, but she remembered having seen, in her brother's Latin Grammar,[8] "A mouse—of a mouse—to a mouse—a mouse—O mouse!") The mouse looked at her rather inquisitively, and seemed to her to wink with one of its little eyes, but it said nothing.

"Perhaps it doesn't understand English," thought Alice. "I daresay it's a French mouse, come over with William the Conqueror." (For, with all her knowledge of history, Alice had no very clear notion how long ago anything had happened.) So she began again: "Où est ma chatte?", which was the first sentence in her French lesson-book.[9] The Mouse gave a sudden leap out of the water, and seemed to quiver all over with fright. "Oh, I beg your pardon!" cried Alice hastily, afraid that she had hurt the poor animal's feelings.[10] "I quite forgot you didn't like cats."

"Not like cats!" cried the Mouse in a shrill, passionate voice. "Would *you* like cats, if you were me?"

"Well, perhaps not," said Alice in a soothing tone: "don't be angry about it. And yet I wish I could show you our cat Dinah. I think you'd take a fancy to cats, if you could only see her. She is such a dear quiet thing," Alice went on, half to herself, as she swam lazily about in the pool, "and she sits purring so nicely by the fire, licking her paws and washing her face—and she is such a nice soft thing to nurse—and she's such a capital one for catching mice——oh, I beg your pardon!" cried Alice again, for this time the Mouse was bristling all over, and she felt certain it must be really offended. "We wo'n't talk about her any more, if you'd rather not."

"We, indeed!" cried the Mouse, who was trembling down to the end of its tail. "As if *I* would talk on such a subject! Our family always *hated* cats: nasty, low, vulgar things! Don't let me hear the name again!"

"I wo'n't indeed!" said Alice, in a great hurry to change the subject of conversation. "Are you—are you fond —of—of dogs?" The Mouse did not answer, so Alice went on eagerly: "There is such a nice little dog, near our house, I should like to show you! A little bright-eyed terrier, you know, with oh, such long curly brown hair! And it'll fetch things when you throw them, and it'll sit up and beg for its dinner, and all sorts of things—I ca'n't remember half of them—and it belongs to a farmer, you know, and he says it's so useful, it's worth a hundred pounds! He says it kills all the rats and—oh dear!" cried Alice in a sorrowful tone. "I'm afraid I've offended it again!" For the Mouse was swimming away from her as hard as it could go, and making quite a commotion in the pool as it went.

So she called softly after it, "Mouse dear! Do come back again, and we wo'n't talk about cats, or dogs either, if you don't like them!" When the Mouse heard this, it turned round and swam slowly back to her: its

face was quite pale (with passion, Alice thought), and it said, in a low trembling voice, "Let us get to the shore, and then I'll tell you my history, and you'll understand why it is I hate cats and dogs."

It was high time to go, for the pool was getting quite crowded with the birds and animals that had fallen into it: there was a Duck and a Dodo, a Lory and an Eaglet, and several other curious creatures.[11] Alice led the way, and the whole party swam to the shore.

CHAPTER III

A CAUCUS-RACE AND A LONG TALE

They were indeed a queer-looking party that assembled on the bank—the birds with draggled feathers, the animals with their fur clinging close to them, and all dripping wet, cross, and uncomfortable.

The first question of course was, how to get dry again: they had a consultation about this, and after a few minutes it seemed quite natural to Alice to find herself talking familiarly with them, as if she had known them all her life. Indeed, she had quite a long argument with the Lory, who at last turned sulky, and would only say "I'm older than you, and must know better." And this Alice would not allow, without knowing how old it was, and, as the Lory positively refused to tell its age, there was no more to be said.

At last the Mouse, who seemed to be a person of some authority among them, called out "Sit down, all of you, and listen to me! *I'll* soon make you dry enough!" They all sat down at once, in a large ring, with the Mouse in the middle. Alice kept her eyes anxiously fixed on it, for she felt sure she would catch a bad cold if she did not get dry very soon.

"Ahem!" said the Mouse with an important air. "Are you all ready? This is the driest thing I know. Silence all round, if you please! 'William the Conqueror, whose cause was favoured by the pope,[1] was soon submitted to by the English, who wanted leaders, and had been of late much accustomed to usurpation and conquest. Edwin and Morcar, the earls of Mercia and Northumbria——' "

"Ugh!" said the Lory, with a shiver.

"I beg your pardon!" said the Mouse, frowning, but very politely. "Did you speak?"

"Not I!" said the Lory, hastily.

"I thought you did," said the Mouse. "I proceed. 'Edwin and Morcar, the earls of Mercia and Northumbria, declared for him; and even Stigand, the patriotic archbishop of Canterbury, found it advisable——' "

"Found *what?*" said the Duck.

"Found *it,*" the Mouse replied rather crossly: "of course you know what 'it' means."

"I know what 'it' means well enough, when *I* find a thing," said the Duck: "it's generally a frog, or a worm. The question is, what did the archbishop find?"

The Mouse did not notice this question, but hurriedly went on, " '—found it advisable to go with Edgar Atheling to meet William and offer him the crown. William's conduct at first was moderate. But the insolence of his Normans——' How are you getting on now, my dear?" it continued, turning to Alice as it spoke.

"As wet as ever," said Alice in a melancholy tone: "it doesn't seem to dry me at all."

"In that case," said the Dodo solemnly, rising to its feet, "I move that the meeting adjourn, for the immediate adoption of more energetic remedies——"

"Speak English!"[2] said the Eaglet. "I don't know the meaning of half those long words, and, what's more, I don't believe you do either!" And the Eaglet bent down its head to hide a smile: some of the other birds tittered audibly.

"What I was going to say," said the Dodo in an offended tone, "was, that the best thing to get us dry would be a Caucus-race."[3]

"What *is* a Caucus-race?" said Alice; not that she much wanted to know, but the Dodo had paused as if it thought that *somebody* ought to speak, and no one else seemed inclined to say anything.

"Why," said the Dodo, "the best way to explain it is to do it." (And, as you might like to try the thing yourself, some winter-day, I will tell you how the Dodo managed it.)

First it marked out a race-course, in a sort of circle, ("the exact shape doesn't matter," it said,) and then all the party were placed along the course, here and there. There was no "One, two, three, and away!", but they began running when they liked, and left off when they liked, so that it was not easy to know when the race was over. However, when they had been running half an hour or so, and were quite dry again, the Dodo suddenly called out "The race is over!", and they all crowded round it, panting, and asking "But who has won?"

This question the Dodo could not answer without a great deal of thought, and it stood for a long time with one finger pressed upon its forehead (the position in which you usually see Shakespeare,[4] in the pictures of him), while the rest waited in silence. At last the Dodo said "*Everybody* has won, and *all* must have prizes."

"But who is to give the prizes?" quite a chorus of voices asked.

"Why, *she*, of course," said the Dodo, pointing to Alice with one finger; and the whole party at once crowded round her, calling out, in a confused way, "Prizes! Prizes!"

Alice had no idea what to do, and in despair she put her hand in her pocket, and pulled out a box of comfits (luckily the salt water had not got into it), and handed them round as prizes. There was exactly one a-piece, all round.

"But she must have a prize herself, you know," said the Mouse.

"Of course," the Dodo replied very gravely. "What else have you got in your pocket?" it went on, turning to Alice.

"Only a thimble," said Alice sadly.

"Hand it over here," said the Dodo.

Then they all crowded round her once more, while the Dodo solemnly presented the thimble, saying "We beg your acceptance of this elegant thimble"; and, when it had finished this short speech, they all cheered.

Alice thought the whole thing very absurd, but they all looked so grave that she did not dare to laugh; and, as she could not think of anything to say, she simply bowed, and took the thimble, looking as solemn as she could.

The next thing was to eat the comfits: this caused some noise and confusion, as the large birds complained that they could not taste theirs, and the small ones choked and had to be patted on the back. However, it was over at last, and they sat down again in a ring, and begged the Mouse to tell them something more.

"You promised to tell me your history, you know," said Alice, "and why it is you hate—C and D," she added in a whisper, half afraid that it would be offended again.

"Mine is a long and a sad tale!" said the Mouse, turning to Alice, and sighing.

"It *is* a long tail, certainly,"[5] said Alice, looking down with wonder at the Mouse's tail: "but why do you call it sad?" And she kept on puzzling about it while the Mouse was speaking, so that her idea of the tale was something like this:——

"Fury said to
a mouse,[6] That
he met in the
house, 'Let
us both go
to law: *I*
will prose-
cute *you*.—
Come, I'll
take no de-
nial: We
must have
the trial;
For really
this morn-
ing I've
nothing
to do.'
Said the
mouse to
the cur,
'Such a
trial, dear
sir, With
no jury
or judge,
would
be wast-
ing our
breath.'
'I'll be
judge,
I'll be
jury,'
said
cun-
ning
old
Fury:
'I'll
try
the
whole
cause,
and
con-
demn
you to
death'. "

"You are not attending!" said the Mouse to Alice, severely. "What are you thinking of?"

"I beg your pardon," said Alice very humbly: "you had got to the fifth bend, I think?"

"I had *not!*" cried the Mouse, sharply and very angrily.

"A knot!" said Alice, always ready to make herself useful, and looking anxiously about her. "Oh, do let me help to undo it!"

"I shall do nothing of the sort," said the Mouse, getting up and walking away. "You insult me by talking such nonsense!"

"I didn't mean it!" pleaded poor Alice. "But you're so easily offended, you know!"

The Mouse only growled in reply.

"Please come back, and finish your story!" Alice called after it. And the others all joined in chorus "Yes, please do!" But the Mouse only shook its head impatiently, and walked a little quicker.

"What a pity it wouldn't stay!" sighed the Lory, as soon as it was quite out of sight. And an old Crab took the opportunity of saying to her daughter "Ah, my dear! Let this be a lesson to you never to lose *your* temper!"

"Hold your tongue, Ma!" said the young Crab, a little snappishly. "You're enough to try the patience of an oyster!"

"I wish I had our Dinah here, I know I do!" said Alice aloud, addressing nobody in particular. "*She'd* soon fetch it back!"

"And who is Dinah, if I might venture to ask the question?" said the Lory.

Alice replied eagerly, for she was always ready to talk about her pet: "Dinah's our cat. And she's such a capital one for catching mice, you ca'n't think! And oh, I wish you could see her after the birds! Why, she'll eat a little bird as soon as look at it!"

This speech caused a remarkable sensation among the party. Some of the birds hurried off at once: one old Magpie began wrapping itself up very carefully, remarking "I really must be getting home: the night-air doesn't suit my throat!" And a Canary called out in a trembling voice, to its children, "Come away, my dears! It's high time you were all in bed!" On various pretexts they all moved off, and Alice was soon left alone.

"I wish I hadn't mentioned Dinah!" she said to herself in a melancholy tone. "Nobody seems to like her, down here, and I'm sure she's the best cat in the world! Oh, my dear Dinah! I wonder if I shall ever see you any more!" And here poor Alice began to cry again, for she felt very lonely and low-spirited. In a little while, however, she again heard a little pattering of footsteps in the distance, and she looked up eagerly, half hoping that the Mouse had changed his mind, and was coming back to finish his story.

CHAPTER IV

THE RABBIT SENDS IN A LITTLE BILL

It was the White Rabbit, trotting slowly back again, and looking anxiously about as it went, as if it had lost something; and she heard it muttering to itself, "The Duchess![1] The Duchess! Oh my dear paws! Oh my fur and whiskers! She'll get me executed, as sure as ferrets are ferrets! Where *can* I have dropped them, I wonder?" Alice guessed in a moment that it was looking for the fan and the pair of white kid-gloves, and she very good-naturedly began hunting about for them, but they were nowhere to be seen—everything seemed to have changed since her swim in the pool; and the great hall, with the glass table and the little door, had vanished completely.

Very soon the Rabbit noticed Alice, as she went hunting about, and called out to her, in an angry tone, "Why, Mary Ann, what *are* you doing out here? Run home this moment, and fetch me a pair of gloves and a fan! Quick, now!" And Alice was so much frightened that she ran off at once in the direction it pointed to, without trying to explain the mistake that it had made.

"He took me for his housemaid," she said to herself as she ran. "How surprised he'll be when he finds out who I am! But I'd better take him his fan and gloves—that is, if I can find them." As she said this, she came upon a neat little house, on the door of which was a bright brass plate with the name "W. RABBIT" engraved upon it. She went in without knocking, and hurried upstairs, in great fear lest she should meet the real Mary Ann, and be turned out of the house before she had found the fan and gloves.

"How queer it seems," Alice said to herself, "to be going messages for a rabbit! I suppose Dinah'll be sending me on messages next!" And she began fancying the sort of thing that would happen: "'Miss Alice! Come here directly, and get ready for your walk!' 'Coming in a minute, nurse! But I've got to watch this mouse-hole till Dinah comes back, and see that the mouse doesn't get out.' Only I don't think," Alice went on, "that they'd let Dinah stop in the house if it began ordering people about like that!"

By this time she had found her way into a tidy little room with a table in the window, and on it (as she had hoped) a fan and two or three pairs of tiny white kid-gloves: she took up the fan and a pair of the gloves, and was just going to leave the room, when her eye fell upon a little bottle that stood near the looking-glass. There was no label this time with the words "DRINK ME," but nevertheless she uncorked it and put it to her lips. "I know *something* interesting is sure to happen," she said to herself, "whenever I eat or drink anything: so I'll just see what this bottle does. I do hope it'll make me grow large again, for really I'm quite tired of being such a tiny little thing!"

It did so indeed, and much sooner than she had expected: before she had drunk half the bottle, she found her head pressing against the ceiling, and had to stoop to save her neck from being broken. She hastily put down the bottle, saying to herself "That's quite enough—I hope I sha'n't grow any more—As it is, I ca'n't get out at the door—I do wish I hadn't drunk quite so much!"

Alas! It was too late to wish that! She went on growing, and growing, and very soon had to kneel down on the floor: in another minute there was not even room for this, and she tried the effect of lying down with one elbow against the door, and the other arm curled round her head. Still she went on growing, and, as a last resource, she put one arm out of the window, and one foot up the chimney, and said to herself "Now I can do no more, whatever happens. What *will* become of me?"

Luckily for Alice, the little magic bottle had now had its full effect, and she grew no larger: still it was very uncomfortable, and, as there seemed to be no sort of chance of her ever getting out of the room again, no wonder she felt unhappy.

"It was much pleasanter at home," thought poor Alice, "when one wasn't always growing larger and smaller, and being ordered about by mice and rabbits. I almost wish I hadn't gone down that rabbit-hole—and yet—and yet—it's rather curious, you know, this sort of life! I do wonder what *can* have happened to me! When I used to read fairy

tales,[2] I fancied that kind of thing never happened, and now here I am in the middle of one! There ought to be a book written about me, that there ought! And when I grow up, I'll write one—but I'm grown up now," she added in a sorrowful tone: "at least there's no room to grow up any more *here*."

"But then," thought Alice, "shall I *never* get any older than I am now? That'll be a comfort, one way—never to be an old woman—but then—always to have lessons to learn! Oh, I shouldn't like *that!*"

"Oh, you foolish Alice!" she answered herself. "How can you learn lessons in here? Why, there's hardly room for *you*, and no room at all for any lesson-books!"

And so she went on, taking first one side and then the other, and making quite a conversation of it altogether; but after a few minutes she heard a voice outside, and stopped to listen.

"Mary Ann! Mary Ann!" said the voice. "Fetch me my gloves this moment!" Then came a little pattering of feet on the stairs. Alice knew it was the Rabbit coming to look for her, and she trembled till she shook the house, quite forgetting that she was now about a thousand times as large as the Rabbit, and had no reason to be afraid of it.

Presently the Rabbit came up to the door, and tried to open it; but, as the door opened inwards, and Alice's elbow was pressed hard against it, that attempt proved a failure. Alice heard it say to itself "Then I'll go round and get in at the window."

"*That* you wo'n't!" thought Alice, and, after waiting till she fancied she heard the Rabbit just under the window, she suddenly spread out her hand, and made a snatch in the air. She did not get hold of anything, but she heard a little shriek and a fall, and a crash of broken glass, from which she concluded that it was just possible it had fallen into a cucumber-frame, or something of the sort.

Next came an angry voice—the Rabbit's—"Pat! Pat! Where are you?" And then a voice she had never heard before, "Sure then I'm here! Digging for apples, yer honour!"[3]

"Digging for apples, indeed!" said the Rabbit angrily. "Here! Come and help me out of *this*!" (Sounds of more broken glass.)

"Now tell me, Pat, what's that in the window?"

"Sure, it's an arm, yer honour!" (He pronounced it "arrum.")

"An arm, you goose! Who ever saw one that size? Why, it fills the whole window!"

"Sure, it does, yer honour: but it's an arm for all that."

"Well, it's got no business there, at any rate: go and take it away!"

There was a long silence after this, and Alice could only hear whispers now and then; such as "Sure, I don't like it, yer honour, at all, at all!" "Do as I tell you, you coward!", and at last she spread out her hand again, and made another snatch in the air. This time there were *two* little shrieks, and more sounds of broken glass. "What a number of cucumber-frames there must be!" thought Alice. "I wonder what they'll do next! As for pulling me out of the window, I only wish they *could*! I'm sure *I* don't want to stay in here any longer!"

She waited for some time without hearing anything more: at last came a rumbling of little cart-wheels, and the sound of a good many voices all talking together: she made out the words: "Where's the other ladder?—Why, I hadn't to bring but one. Bill's got the other—Bill! Fetch it here, lad!—Here, put 'em up at this corner—No, tie 'em together first—they don't reach half high enough yet—Oh, they'll do well enough. Don't be particular—Here, Bill! Catch hold of this rope—Will the roof bear?—Mind that loose slate—Oh, it's coming down! Heads below!" (a loud crash)—"Now, who did that?—It was Bill, I fancy—Who's to go down the chimney?—Nay, *I* sha'n't! *You* do it!—*That* I wo'n't, then!—Bill's got to go down—Here, Bill! The master says you've got to go down the chimney!"

"Oh! So Bill's got to come down the chimney, has he?" said Alice to herself. "Why, they seem to put everything upon Bill! I wouldn't be in Bill's place for a good deal: this fireplace is narrow, to be sure; but I *think* I can kick a little!"

She drew her foot as far down the chimney as she could, and waited till she heard a little animal (she couldn't guess of what sort it was) scratching and scrambling about in the chimney close above her: then, saying to herself "This is Bill", she gave one sharp kick, and waited to see what would happen next.

The first thing she heard was a general chorus of "There goes Bill!" then the Rabbit's voice alone—"Catch him, you by the hedge!" then silence, and then another confusion of voices—"Hold up his head—Brandy now—Don't choke him—How was it, old fellow? What happened to you? Tell us all about it!"

Last came a little feeble, squeaking voice ("That's Bill," thought Alice), "Well, I hardly know—No more, thank ye; I'm better now—but I'm a deal too flustered to tell you—all I know is, something comes at me like a Jack-in-the-box, and up I goes like a sky-rocket!"

"So you did, old fellow!" said the others.

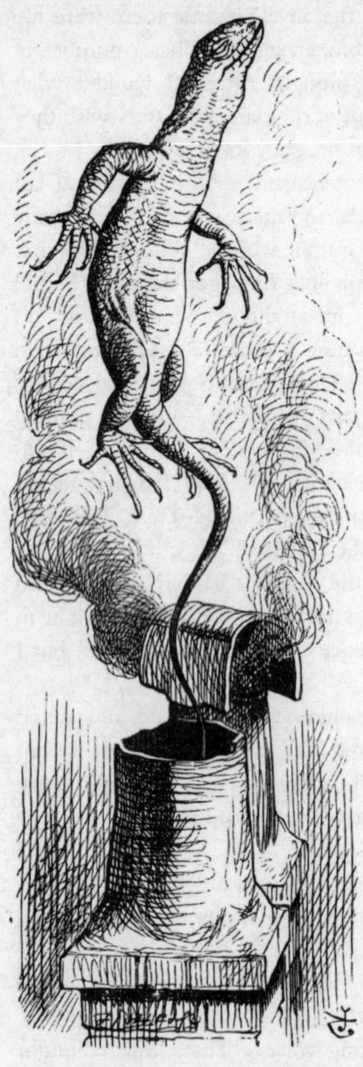

"We must burn the house down!" said the Rabbit's voice. And Alice called out, as loud as she could, "If you do, I'll set Dinah at you!"

There was a dead silence instantly, and Alice thought to herself "I wonder what they *will* do next! If they had any sense, they'd take the roof off." After a minute or two, they began moving about again, and Alice heard the Rabbit say "A barrowful will do, to begin with."

"A barrowful of *what*?" thought Alice. But she had not long to doubt, for the next moment a shower of little pebbles came rattling in at the window, and some of them hit her in the face. "I'll put a stop to this," she said to herself, and shouted out "You'd better not do that again!", which produced another dead silence.

Alice noticed, with some surprise, that the pebbles were all turning into little cakes as they lay on the floor, and a bright idea came into her head. "If I eat one of these cakes," she thought, "it's sure to make *some* change in my size; and, as it ca'n't possibly make me larger, it must make me smaller, I suppose."

So she swallowed one of the cakes, and was delighted to find that she began shrinking directly. As soon as she was small enough to get through the door, she ran out of the house, and found quite a crowd of little animals[4] and birds waiting outside. The poor little Lizard, Bill, was in the middle, being held up by two guinea-pigs, who were giving it something out of a bottle. They all made a rush at Alice the moment she appeared; but she ran off as hard as she could, and soon found herself safe in a thick wood.[5]

"The first thing I've got to do," said Alice to herself, as she wandered about in the wood, "is to grow to my right size again; and the second thing is to find my way into that lovely garden. I think that will be the best plan."

It sounded an excellent plan, no doubt, and very neatly and simply arranged: the only difficulty was, that she had not the smallest idea how to set about it; and, while she was peering about anxiously among the trees, a little sharp bark just over her head made her look up in a great hurry.

An enormous puppy was looking down at her with large round eyes, and feebly stretching out one paw, trying to touch her. "Poor little thing!" said Alice, in a coaxing tone, and she tried hard to whistle to it; but she was terribly frightened all the time at the thought that it might be hungry, in which case it would be very likely to eat her up in spite of all her coaxing.

Hardly knowing what she did, she picked up a little bit of stick, and held it out to the puppy: whereupon the puppy jumped into the air off all its feet at once, with a yelp of delight, and rushed at the stick, and made believe to worry it: then Alice dodged behind a great thistle, to keep herself from being run over; and, the moment she appeared on the other side, the puppy made another rush at the stick, and tumbled head over heels in its hurry to get hold of it: then Alice, thinking it was very like having a game of play with a cart-horse, and expecting every moment to be trampled under its feet, ran round the thistle again: then the puppy began a series of short charges at the stick, running a very little way forwards each time and a long way back, and barking hoarsely all the while, till at last it sat down a good way off, panting, with its tongue hanging out of its mouth, and its great eyes half shut.

This seemed to Alice a good opportunity for making her escape: so

she set off at once, and ran till she was quite tired and out of breath, and till the puppy's bark sounded quite faint in the distance.

"And yet what a dear little puppy it was!" said Alice, as she leant against a buttercup to rest herself, and fanned herself with one of the leaves. "I should have liked teaching it tricks very much, if—if I'd only been the right size to do it! Oh dear! I'd nearly forgotten that I've got to grow up again! Let me see—how *is* it to be managed? I suppose I ought to eat or drink something or other; but the great question is 'What?'"

The great question certainly was "What?". Alice looked all round her at the flowers and the blades of grass, but she could not see anything that looked like the right thing to eat or drink under the circumstances. There was a large mushroom growing near her, about the same height as herself; and, when she had looked under it, and on both sides of it, and behind it, it occurred to her that she might as well look and see what was on the top of it.

She stretched herself up on tiptoe, and peeped over the edge of the mushroom, and her eyes immediately met those of a large blue caterpillar, that was sitting on the top, with its arms folded, quietly smoking a long hookah, and taking not the smallest notice of her or of anything else.

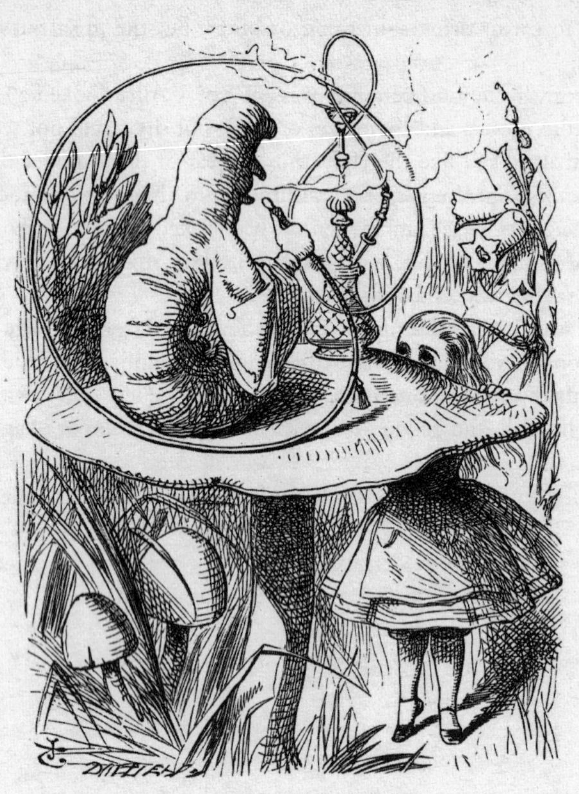

CHAPTER V

ADVICE FROM A CATERPILLAR

The Caterpillar and Alice looked at each other for some time in silence: at last the Caterpillar took the hookah out of its mouth, and addressed her in a languid, sleepy voice.

"Who are *you*?" said the Caterpillar.

This was not an encouraging opening for a conversation. Alice replied, rather shyly, "I—I hardly know, Sir, just at present—at least I know who I *was* when I got up this morning, but I think I must have been changed several times since then."

"What do you mean by that?" said the Caterpillar, sternly. "Explain yourself!"

"I ca'n't explain *myself*, I'm afraid, Sir," said Alice, "because I'm not myself, you see."

"I don't see," said the Caterpillar.

"I'm afraid I ca'n't put it more clearly," Alice replied, very politely, "for I ca'n't understand it myself, to begin with; and being so many different sizes in a day is very confusing."

"It isn't," said the Caterpillar.

"Well, perhaps you haven't found it so yet," said Alice; "but when you have to turn into a chrysalis—you will some day, you know—and then after that into a butterfly, I should think you'll feel it a little queer, wo'n't you?"

"Not a bit," said the Caterpillar.

"Well, perhaps *your* feelings may be different," said Alice: "all I know is, it would feel very queer to *me*."

"You!" said the Caterpillar contemptuously. "Who are *you*?"

Which brought them back again to the beginning of the conversation. Alice felt a little irritated at the Caterpillar's making such *very* short remarks, and she drew herself up and said, very gravely, "I think you ought to tell me who *you* are, first."

"Why?" said the Caterpillar.

Here was another puzzling question; and, as Alice could not think of any good reason, and the Caterpillar seemed to be in a *very* unpleasant state of mind, she turned away.

"Come back!" the Caterpillar called after her. "I've something important to say!"

This sounded promising, certainly. Alice turned and came back again.

"Keep your temper," said the Caterpillar.

"Is that all?" said Alice, swallowing down her anger as well as she could.

"No," said the Caterpillar.

Alice thought she might as well wait, as she had nothing else to do, and perhaps after all it might tell her something worth hearing. For some minutes it puffed away without speaking; but at last it unfolded its arms, took the hookah out of its mouth again, and said "So you think you're changed, do you?"

"I'm afraid I am, Sir," said Alice. "I ca'n't remember things as I used—and I don't keep the same size for ten minutes together!"

"Ca'n't remember *what* things?" said the Caterpillar.

"Well, I've tried to say '*How doth the little busy bee*,' but it all came different!" Alice replied in a very melancholy voice.

"Repeat '*You are old, Father William*,' "[1] said the Caterpillar.

Alice folded her hands, and began:—

"You are old, Father William," the young man said,
"And your hair has become very white;
And yet you incessantly stand on your head—
Do you think, at your age, it is right?"

"In my youth," Father William replied to his son,
"I feared it might injure the brain;
But, now that I'm perfectly sure I have none,
Why, I do it again and again."

"You are old," said the youth, "as I mentioned before,
And have grown most uncommonly fat;
Yet you turned a back-somersault in at the door—
Pray, what is the reason of that?"

"In my youth," said the sage, as he shook his grey locks,
"I kept all my limbs very supple
By the use of this ointment—one shilling the box—
Allow me to sell you a couple?"

"You are old," said the youth, "and your jaws are too weak
For anything tougher than suet;
Yet you finished the goose, with the bones and the beak—
Pray, how did you manage to do it?"

"In my youth," said his father, "I took to the law,
And argued each case with my wife;
And the muscular strength, which it gave to my jaw
Has lasted the rest of my life."

"You are old," said the youth, "one would hardly suppose
That your eye was as steady as ever;
Yet you balanced an eel on the end of your nose—
What made you so awfully clever?"

"I have answered three questions, and that is enough,"
Said his father. "Don't give yourself airs!
Do you think I can listen all day to such stuff?
Be off, or I'll kick you down-stairs!"

"That is not said right," said the Caterpillar.

"Not *quite* right, I'm afraid," said Alice, timidly: "some of the words have got altered."

"It is wrong from beginning to end," said the Caterpillar, decidedly; and there was silence for some minutes.

The Caterpillar was the first to speak.

"What size do you want to be?" it asked.

"Oh, I'm not particular as to size," Alice hastily replied; "only one doesn't like changing so often, you know."

"I *don't* know," said the Caterpillar.

Alice said nothing: she had never been so much contradicted in all her life before, and she felt that she was losing her temper.

"Are you content now?" said the Caterpillar.

"Well, I should like to be a *little* larger, Sir, if you wouldn't mind," said Alice: "three inches is such a wretched height to be."

"It is a very good height indeed!" said the Caterpillar angrily, rearing itself upright as it spoke (it was exactly three inches high).

"But I'm not used to it!" pleaded poor Alice in a piteous tone. And she thought to herself "I wish the creatures wouldn't be so easily offended!"

"You'll get used to it in time," said the Caterpillar; and it put the hookah into its mouth, and began smoking again.

This time Alice waited patiently until it chose to speak again. In a minute or two the Caterpillar took the hookah out of its mouth, and yawned once or twice, and shook itself. Then it got down off the mushroom, and crawled away into the grass, merely remarking, as it went, "One side will make you grow taller, and the other side[2] will make you grow shorter."

"One side of *what*? The other side of *what*?" thought Alice to herself.

"Of the mushroom," said the Caterpillar, just as if she had asked it aloud; and in another moment it was out of sight.

Alice remained looking thoughtfully at the mushroom for a minute, trying to make out which were the two sides of it; and, as it was perfectly round, she found this a very difficult question. However, at last she stretched her arms round it as far as they would go, and broke off a bit of the edge with each hand.

"And now which is which?" she said to herself, and nibbled a little of the right-hand bit to try the effect. The next moment she felt a violent blow underneath her chin: it had struck her foot!

She was a good deal frightened by this very sudden change, but she felt that there was no time to be lost, as she was shrinking rapidly: so she set to work at once to eat some of the other bit. Her chin was pressed so closely against her foot, that there was hardly room to open her mouth; but she did it at last, and managed to swallow a morsel of the left-hand bit.

* * * * *
* * * *
* * * * *

"Come, my head's free at last!" said Alice in a tone of delight, which changed into alarm in another moment, when she found that her shoulders were nowhere to be found: all she could see, when she looked down, was an immense length of neck, which seemed to rise like a stalk out of a sea of green leaves that lay far below her.

"What *can* all that green stuff be?" said Alice. "And where *have* my shoulders got to? And oh, my poor hands, how is it I ca'n't see you?" She was moving them about, as she spoke, but no result seemed to follow, except a little shaking among the distant green leaves.

As there seemed to be no chance of getting her hands up to her head, she tried to get her head down to *them*, and was delighted to find that her neck would bend about easily in any direction, like a serpent. She had just succeeded in curving it down into a graceful zigzag, and was going to dive in among the leaves, which she found to be nothing but the tops of the trees under which she had been wandering, when a sharp hiss made her draw back in a hurry: a large pigeon had flown into her face, and was beating her violently with its wings.

"Serpent!" screamed the Pigeon.

"I'm *not* a serpent!" said Alice indignantly. "Let me alone!"

"Serpent, I say again!" repeated the Pigeon, but in a more subdued tone, and added, with a kind of sob, "I've tried every way, but nothing seems to suit them!"

"I haven't the least idea what you're talking about," said Alice.

"I've tried the roots of trees, and I've tried banks, and I've tried hedges," the Pigeon went on, without attending to her; "but those serpents! There's no pleasing them!"

Alice was more and more puzzled, but she thought there was no use in saying anything more till the Pigeon had finished.

"As if it wasn't trouble enough hatching the eggs," said the Pigeon; "but I must be on the look-out for serpents, night and day! Why, I haven't had a wink of sleep these three weeks!"

"I'm very sorry you've been annoyed," said Alice, who was beginning to see its meaning.

"And just as I'd taken the highest tree in the wood," continued the Pigeon, raising its voice to a shriek, "and just as I was thinking I should be free of them at last, they must needs come wriggling down from the sky! Ugh, Serpent!"

"But I'm *not* a serpent, I tell you!" said Alice. "I'm a——I'm a——"

"Well! *What* are you?"[3] said the Pigeon. "I can see you're trying to invent something!"

"I—I'm a little girl," said Alice, rather doubtfully, as she remembered the number of changes she had gone through, that day.

"A likely story indeed!" said the Pigeon, in a tone of the deepest contempt. "I've seen a good many little girls in my time, but never *one* with such a neck as that! No, no! You're a serpent; and there's no use denying it. I suppose you'll be telling me next that you never tasted an egg!"

"I *have* tasted eggs, certainly," said Alice, who was a very truthful child; "but little girls eat eggs quite as much as serpents do, you know."

"I don't believe it," said the Pigeon; "but if they do, why, then they're a kind of serpent: that's all I can say."

This was such a new idea to Alice, that she was quite silent for a minute or two, which gave the Pigeon the opportunity of adding "You're looking for eggs, I know *that* well enough; and what does it matter to me whether you're a little girl or a serpent?"

"It matters a good deal to *me*," said Alice hastily; "but I'm not looking for eggs, as it happens; and, if I was, I shouldn't want *yours*: I don't like them raw."

"Well, be off, then!" said the Pigeon in a sulky tone, as it settled down again into its nest. Alice crouched down among the trees as well as she could, for her neck kept getting entangled among the branches, and every now and then she had to stop and untwist it. After a while she remembered that she still held the pieces of mushroom in her hands, and she set to work very carefully, nibbling first at one and then at the other, and growing sometimes taller, and sometimes shorter, until she had succeeded in bringing herself down to her usual height.

It was so long since she had been anything near the right size, that it felt quite strange at first; but she got used to it in a few minutes, and began talking to herself, as usual, "Come, there's half my plan done now! How puzzling all these changes are! I'm never sure what I'm going to be, from one minute to another! However, I've got back to my right size: the next thing is, to get into that beautiful garden—how *is* that to be done, I wonder?" As she said this,[4] she came suddenly upon an open place, with a little house in it about four feet high. "Whoever lives there," thought Alice, "it'll never do to come upon them *this* size: why, I should frighten them out of their wits!" So she began nibbling at the right-hand bit again, and did not venture to go near the house till she had brought herself down to nine inches high.

CHAPTER VI

PIG AND PEPPER

For a minute or two she stood looking at the house, and wondering what to do next, when suddenly a footman in livery came running out of the wood—(she considered him to be a footman because he was in livery: otherwise, judging by his face only, she would have called him a fish)—and rapped loudly at the door with his knuckles. It was opened by another footman in livery, with a round face, and large eyes like a frog; and both footmen, Alice noticed, had powdered hair that curled all over their heads. She felt very curious to know what it was all about, and crept a little way out of the wood to listen.

The Fish-Footman began by producing from under his arm a great letter, nearly as large as himself, and this he handed over to the other, saying, in a solemn tone, "For the Duchess. An invitation from the Queen to play croquet." The Frog-Footman[1] repeated, in the same solemn tone, only changing the order of the words a little, "From the Queen. An invitation for the Duchess to play croquet."

Then they both bowed low, and their curls got entangled together.

Alice laughed so much at this, that she had to run back into the wood for fear of their hearing her; and, when she next peeped out, the Fish-Footman was gone, and the other was sitting on the ground near the door, staring stupidly up into the sky.

Alice went timidly up to the door, and knocked.

"There's no sort of use in knocking," said the Footman, "and that for two reasons. First, because I'm on the same side of the door as you are: secondly, because they're making such a noise inside, no one could possibly hear you." And certainly there *was* a most extraordinary noise going on within—a constant howling and sneezing, and every now and then a great crash, as if a dish or kettle had been broken to pieces.

"Please, then," said Alice, "how am I to get in?"

"There might be some sense in your knocking," the Footman went on, without attending to her, "if we had the door between us. For instance, if you were *inside*, you might knock, and I could let you out, you know." He was looking up into the sky all the time he was speaking, and this Alice thought decidedly uncivil. "But perhaps he ca'n't help it," she said to herself; "his eyes are so *very* nearly at the top of his head. But at any rate he might answer questions.—How am I to get in?" she repeated, aloud.

"I shall sit here," the Footman remarked, "till to-morrow——"

At this moment the door of the house opened, and a large plate came skimming out, straight at the Footman's head: it just grazed his nose, and broke to pieces against one of the trees behind him.

"——or next day, maybe," the Footman continued in the same tone, exactly as if nothing had happened.

"How am I to get in?" asked Alice again, in a louder tone.

"*Are* you to get in at all?" said the Footman. "That's the first question, you know."

It was, no doubt: only Alice did not like to be told so. "It's really dreadful," she muttered to herself, "the way all the creatures argue. It's enough to drive one crazy!"

The Footman seemed to think this a good opportunity for repeating his remark, with variations. "I shall sit here," he said, "on and off, for days and days."

"But what am *I* to do?" said Alice.

"Anything you like," said the Footman, and began whistling.

"Oh, there's no use in talking to him," said Alice desperately: "he's perfectly idiotic!" And she opened the door and went in.

The door led right into a large kitchen, which was full of smoke from one end to the other: the Duchess was sitting[2] on a three-legged stool in the middle, nursing a baby: the cook was leaning over the fire, stirring a large cauldron which seemed to be full of soup.

"There's certainly too much pepper in that soup!" Alice said to herself, as well as she could for sneezing.

There was certainly too much of it in the *air*. Even the Duchess sneezed occasionally; and as for the baby, it was sneezing and howling alternately without a moment's pause. The only two creatures in the kitchen, that did *not* sneeze, were the cook, and a large cat, which was lying on the hearth and grinning from ear to ear.

"Please would you tell me," said Alice, a little timidly, for she was not quite sure whether it was good manners[3] for her to speak first, "why your cat grins like that?"

"It's a Cheshire-Cat,"[4] said the Duchess, "and that's why. Pig!"

She said the last word with such sudden violence that Alice quite jumped; but she saw in another moment that it was addressed to the baby, and not to her, so she took courage, and went on again:—

"I didn't know that Cheshire-Cats always grinned; in fact, I didn't know that cats *could* grin."

"They all can," said the Duchess; "and most of 'em do."

"I don't know of any that do," Alice said very politely, feeling quite pleased to have got into a conversation.

"You don't know much," said the Duchess; "and that's a fact."

Alice did not at all like the tone of this remark, and thought it would be as well to introduce some other subject of conversation. While she was trying to fix on one, the cook took the cauldron of soup off the fire, and at once set to work throwing everything within her reach at the Duchess and the baby—the fire-irons came first; then followed a shower of saucepans, plates, and dishes. The Duchess took no notice of them even when they hit her; and the baby was howling so much already, that it was quite impossible to say whether the blows hurt it or not.

"Oh, *please* mind what you're doing!" cried Alice, jumping up and down in an agony of terror. "Oh, there goes his *precious* nose!", as an unusually large saucepan flew close by it, and very nearly carried it off.

"If everybody minded their own business," the Duchess said, in a hoarse growl, "the world would go round a deal faster than it does."

"Which would *not* be an advantage," said Alice, who felt very glad to get an opportunity of showing off a little of her knowledge. "Just think what work it would make with the day and night! You see the earth takes twenty-four hours to turn round on its axis——"

"Talking of axes," said the Duchess, "chop off her head!"

Alice glanced rather anxiously at the cook, to see if she meant to take the hint; but the cook was busily stirring the soup, and seemed not to be listening, so she went on again: "Twenty-four hours, I *think*; or is it twelve? I——"

"Oh, don't bother *me*!" said the Duchess. "I never could abide figures!" And with that she began nursing her child again, singing a sort of lullaby to it as she did so, and giving it a violent shake at the end of every line:—

"Speak roughly to your little boy,[5]
And beat him when he sneezes:
He only does it to annoy,
Because he knows it teases."

CHORUS
(in which the cook and the baby joined):—
"Wow! wow! wow!"

While the Duchess sang the second verse of the song, she kept tossing the baby violently up and down, and the poor little thing howled so, that Alice could hardly hear the words:—

"I speak severely to my boy,
I beat him when he sneezes;
For he can thoroughly enjoy
The pepper when he pleases!"

CHORUS
"Wow! wow! wow!"

"Here! You may nurse it a bit, if you like!" the Duchess said to Alice, flinging the baby at her as she spoke. "I must go and get ready to play croquet with the Queen," and she hurried out of the room. The cook threw a frying-pan after her as she went, but it just missed her.

Alice caught the baby with some difficulty, as it was a queer-shaped little creature, and held out its arms and legs in all directions, "just like a star-fish," thought Alice. The poor little thing was snorting like a steam-engine when she caught it, and kept doubling itself up and straightening itself out again, so that altogether, for the first minute or two, it was as much as she could do to hold it.

As soon as she had made out the proper way of nursing it (which was to twist it up into a sort of knot, and then keep tight hold of its right ear and left foot, so as to prevent its undoing itself), she carried it out into the open air. "If I don't take this child away with me," thought Alice, "they're sure to kill it in a day or two. Wouldn't it be murder to leave it behind?" She said the last words out loud, and the little thing grunted in reply (it had left off sneezing by this time). "Don't grunt," said Alice; "that's not at all a proper way of expressing yourself."

The baby grunted again, and Alice looked very anxiously into its face to see what was the matter with it. There could be no doubt that it had a *very* turn-up nose, much more like a snout than a real nose: also its eyes were getting extremely small for a baby: altogether Alice did not like the look of the thing at all. "But perhaps it was only sobbing," she thought, and looked into its eyes again, to see if there were any tears.

No, there were no tears. "If you're going to turn into a pig, my dear," said Alice, seriously, "I'll have nothing more to do with you. Mind now!" The poor little thing sobbed again (or grunted, it was impossible to say which), and they went on for some while in silence.

Alice was just beginning to think to herself, "Now, what am I to do with this creature, when I get it home?" when it grunted again, so violently, that she looked down into its face in some alarm. This time there could be *no* mistake about it: it was neither more nor less than a pig,[6] and she felt that it would be quite absurd for her to carry it any further.

So she set the little creature down, and felt quite relieved to see it trot away quietly into the wood. "If it had grown up," she said to her-

self, "it would have made a dreadfully ugly child: but it makes rather a handsome pig, I think." And she began thinking over other children she knew, who might do very well as pigs, and was just saying to herself "if one only knew the right way to change them——" when she was a little startled by seeing the Cheshire-Cat sitting on a bough of a tree a few yards off.

The Cat only grinned when it saw Alice. It looked good-natured, she thought: still it had *very* long claws and a great many teeth, so she felt that it ought to be treated with respect.

"Cheshire-Puss," she began, rather timidly, as she did not at all know whether it would like the name: however, it only grinned a little wider. "Come, it's pleased so far," thought Alice, and she went on. "Would you tell me, please, which way I ought to go from here?"

"That depends a good deal on where you want to get to," said the Cat.

"I don't much care where——" said Alice.

"Then it doesn't matter which way you go," said the Cat.

"——so long as I get *somewhere*," Alice added as an explanation.

"Oh, you're sure to do that," said the Cat, "if only you walk long enough."

Alice felt that this could not be denied, so she tried another question. "What sort of people live about here?"

"In *that* direction," the Cat said, waving its right paw round, "lives a Hatter: and in *that* direction," waving the other paw, "lives a March

Hare. Visit either you like: they're both mad."[7]

"But I don't want to go among mad people," Alice remarked.

"Oh, you ca'n't help that," said the Cat: "we're all mad here.[8] I'm mad. You're mad."

"How do you know I'm mad?" said Alice.

"You must be," said the Cat, "or you wouldn't have come here."

Alice didn't think that proved it at all: however, she went on: "And how do you know that you're mad?"

"To begin with," said the Cat, "a dog's not mad. You grant that?"

"I suppose so," said Alice.

"Well, then," the Cat went on, "you see a dog growls when it's angry, and wags its tail when it's pleased. Now *I* growl when I'm pleased, and wag my tail when I'm angry. Therefore I'm mad."

"*I* call it purring, not growling," said Alice.

"Call it what you like," said the Cat. "Do you play croquet with the Queen to-day?"

"I should like it very much," said Alice, "but I haven't been invited yet."

"You'll see me there," said the Cat, and vanished.

Alice was not much surprised at this, she was getting so well used to queer things happening. While she was still looking at the place where it had been, it suddenly appeared again.

"By-the-bye, what became of the baby?" said the Cat. "I'd nearly forgotten to ask."

"It turned into a pig," Alice answered very quietly, just as if the Cat had come back in a natural way.

"I thought it would," said the Cat, and vanished again.

Alice waited a little, half expecting to see it again, but it did not appear, and after a minute or two she walked on in the direction in which the March Hare was said to live. "I've seen hatters before," she said to herself: "the March Hare will be much the most interesting, and perhaps, as this is May, it wo'n't be raving mad—at least not so mad as it was in March." As she said this, she looked up, and there was the Cat

again, sitting on a branch of a tree.

"Did you say 'pig', or 'fig'?" said the Cat.

"I said 'pig'," replied Alice; "and I wish you wouldn't keep appearing and vanishing so suddenly: you make one quite giddy!"

"All right," said the Cat; and this time it vanished quite slowly, beginning with the end of the tail, and ending with the grin, which remained some time after the rest of it had gone.

"Well! I've often seen a cat without a grin," thought Alice; "but a grin without a cat! It's the most curious thing I ever saw in all my life!"

She had not gone much farther before she came in sight of the house of the March Hare: she thought it must be the right house, because the chimneys were shaped like ears and the roof was thatched with fur. It was so large a house, that she did not like to go nearer till she had nibbled some more of the left-hand bit of mushroom, and raised herself to about two feet high: even then she walked up towards it rather timidly, saying to herself "Suppose it should be raving mad after all! I almost wish I'd gone to see the Hatter instead!"

CHAPTER VII

A MAD TEA-PARTY

There was a table set out under a tree in front of the house, and the March Hare and the Hatter[1] were having tea at it:[2] a Dormouse[3] was sitting between them, fast asleep, and the other two were using it as a cushion, resting their elbows on it, and talking over its head. "Very uncomfortable for the Dormouse," thought Alice; "only as it's asleep, I suppose it doesn't mind."

The table was a large one, but the three were all crowded together at one corner of it. "No room! No room!" they cried out when they saw Alice coming. "There's *plenty* of room!" said Alice indignantly, and she sat down in a large arm-chair at one end of the table.

"Have some wine," the March Hare said in an encouraging tone.

Alice looked all round the table, but there was nothing on it but tea. "I don't see any wine," she remarked.

"There isn't any," said the March Hare.

"Then it wasn't very civil of you to offer it," said Alice angrily.

"It wasn't very civil of you to sit down without being invited," said the March Hare.

"I didn't know it was *your* table," said Alice: "it's laid for a great many more than three."

"Your hair wants cutting," said the Hatter. He had been looking at Alice for some time with great curiosity, and this was his first speech.

"You should learn not to make personal remarks," Alice said with some severity: "it's very rude."

The Hatter opened his eyes very wide on hearing this; but all he *said* was "Why is a raven like a writing-desk?"[4]

"Come, we shall have some fun now!" thought Alice. "I'm glad they've begun asking riddles[5]—I believe I can guess that," she added aloud.

"Do you mean that you think you can find out the answer to it?" said the March Hare.

"Exactly so," said Alice.

"Then you should say what you mean," the March Hare went on.

"I do," Alice hastily replied; "at least—at least I mean what I say—that's the same thing, you know."

"Not the same thing a bit!" said the Hatter. "Why, you might just as well say that 'I see what I eat' is the same thing as 'I eat what I see'!"

"You might just as well say," added the March Hare, "that 'I like what I get' is the same thing as 'I get what I like'!"

"You might just as well say," added the Dormouse, which seemed to be talking in its sleep, "that 'I breathe when I sleep' is the same thing as 'I sleep when I breathe'!"

"It *is* the same thing with you," said the Hatter, and here the conversation dropped, and the party sat silent for a minute, while Alice thought over all she could remember about ravens and writing-desks, which wasn't much.

The Hatter was the first to break the silence. "What day of the month is it?" he said, turning to Alice: he had taken his watch out of his pocket, and was looking at it uneasily, shaking it every now and then, and holding it to his ear.

Alice considered a little, and then said "The fourth."[6]

"Two days wrong!"[7] sighed the Hatter. "I told you butter wouldn't suit the works!" he added, looking angrily at the March Hare.

"It was the *best* butter," the March Hare meekly replied.

"Yes, but some crumbs must have got in as well," the Hatter grumbled: "you shouldn't have put it in with the bread-knife."

The March Hare took the watch and looked at it gloomily: then he dipped it into his cup of tea, and looked at it again: but he could think of nothing better to say than his first remark, "It was the *best* butter, you know."

Alice had been looking over his shoulder with some curiosity. "What a funny watch!" she remarked. "It tells the day of the month, and doesn't tell what o'clock it is!"

"Why should it?" muttered the Hatter. "Does *your* watch tell you what year it is?"

"Of course not," Alice replied very readily: "but that's because it stays the same year for such a long time together."

"Which is just the case with *mine*," said the Hatter.

Alice felt dreadfully puzzled. The Hatter's remark seemed to her to have no sort of meaning in it, and yet it was certainly English. "I don't quite understand you," she said, as politely as she could.

"The Dormouse is asleep again," said the Hatter, and he poured a little hot tea upon its nose.

The Dormouse shook its head impatiently, and said, without opening its eyes, "Of course, of course: just what I was going to remark myself."

"Have you guessed the riddle yet?" the Hatter said, turning to Alice again.

"No, I give it up," Alice replied. "What's the answer?"

"I haven't the slightest idea," said the Hatter.

"Nor I," said the March Hare.

Alice sighed wearily. "I think you might do something better with the time," she said, "than wasting it in asking riddles that have no answers."

"If you knew Time as well as I do," said the Hatter, "you wouldn't talk about wasting *it*. It's *him*."

"I don't know what you mean," said Alice.

"Of course you don't!" the Hatter said, tossing his head contemptuously. "I dare say you never even spoke to Time!"

"Perhaps not," Alice cautiously replied; "but I know I have to beat time when I learn music."

"Ah! That accounts for it," said the Hatter. "He wo'n't stand beating. Now, if you only kept on good terms with him, he'd do almost anything you liked with the clock. For instance, suppose it were nine o'clock in the morning, just time to begin lessons: you'd only have to whisper a hint to Time, and round goes the clock in a twinkling! Half-past one, time for dinner!"

("I only wish it was," the March Hare said to itself in a whisper.)

"That would be grand, certainly," said Alice thoughtfully; "but then—I shouldn't be hungry for it, you know."

"Not at first, perhaps," said the Hatter: "but you could keep it to half-past one as long as you liked."

"Is that the way *you* manage?" Alice asked.

The Hatter shook his head mournfully. "Not I!" he replied. "We quarreled last March——just before *he* went mad, you know——" (pointing with his teaspoon at the March Hare,) "——it was at the great concert given by the Queen of Hearts, and I had to sing

'Twinkle, twinkle, little bat![8]
How I wonder what you're at!'

You know the song, perhaps?"

"I've heard something like it," said Alice.

"It goes on, you know," the Hatter continued, "in this way:—

'Up above the world you fly,
Like a tea-tray in the sky.
Twinkle, twinkle——'"

Here the Dormouse shook itself, and began singing in its sleep "*Twinkle, twinkle, twinkle, twinkle*——" and went on so long that they had to pinch it to make it stop.

"Well, I'd hardly finished the first verse," said the Hatter, "when the Queen bawled out 'He's murdering the time! Off with his head!' "

"How dreadfully savage!" exclaimed Alice.

"And ever since that," the Hatter went on in a mournful tone, "he wo'n't do a thing I ask! It's always six o'clock now."

A bright idea came into Alice's head, "Is that the reason so many tea-things are put out here?" she asked.

"Yes, that's it," said the Hatter with a sigh: "it's always tea-time,[9] and we've no time to wash the things between whiles."

"Then you keep moving round, I suppose?" said Alice.

"Exactly so," said the Hatter: "as the things get used up."

"But what happens when you come to the beginning again?" Alice ventured to ask.

"Suppose we change the subject," the March Hare interrupted, yawning. "I'm getting tired of this. I vote the young lady tells us a story."

"I'm afraid I don't know one," said Alice, rather alarmed at the proposal.

"Then the Dormouse shall!" they both cried. "Wake up, Dormouse!" And they pinched it on both sides at once.

The Dormouse slowly opened its eyes. "I wasn't asleep," it said in a hoarse, feeble voice, "I heard every word you fellows were saying."

"Tell us a story!" said the March Hare.

"Yes, please do!" pleaded Alice.

"And be quick about it," added the Hatter, "or you'll be asleep again before it's done."

"Once upon a time there were three little sisters,"[10] the Dormouse began in a great hurry: "and their names were Elsie, Lacie, and Tillie;[11] and they lived at the bottom of a well——"

"What did they live on?" said Alice, who always took a great interest in questions of eating and drinking.

"They lived on treacle," said the Dormouse, after thinking a minute or two.

"They couldn't have done that, you know," Alice gently remarked. "They'd have been ill."

"So they were," said the Dormouse; "*very* ill."

Alice tried a little to fancy to herself what such an extraordinary way of living would be like, but it puzzled her too much: so she went on: "But why did they live at the bottom of a well?"

"Take some more tea," the March Hare said to Alice, very earnestly.

"I've had nothing yet," Alice replied in an offended tone: "so I ca'n't take more."

"You mean you ca'n't take *less*," said the Hatter: "it's very easy to take *more* than nothing."

"Nobody asked *your* opinion," said Alice.

"Who's making personal remarks now?" the Hatter asked triumphantly.

Alice did not quite know what to say to this: so she helped herself to some tea and bread-and-butter, and then turned to the Dormouse, and repeated her question. "Why did they live at the bottom of a well?"

The Dormouse again took a minute or two to think about it, and then said "It was a treacle-well." [12]

"There's no such thing!" Alice was beginning very angrily, but the Hatter and the March Hare went "Sh! Sh!" and the Dormouse sulkily remarked "If you ca'n't be civil, you'd better finish the story for yourself."

"No, please go on!" Alice said very humbly. "I wo'n't interrupt you again. I dare say there may be *one*."

"One, indeed!" said the Dormouse indignantly. However, he consented to go on. "And so these three little sisters—they were learning to draw, you know——"

"What did they draw?" said Alice, quite forgetting her promise.

"Treacle," said the Dormouse, without considering at all, this time.

"I want a clean cup," interrupted the Hatter: "let's all move one place on."

He moved on as he spoke, and the Dormouse followed him: the March Hare moved into the Dormouse's place, and Alice rather unwillingly took the place of the March Hare. The Hatter was the only one who got any advantage from the change; and Alice was a good deal worse off than before, as the March Hare had just upset the milk-jug into his plate.

Alice did not wish to offend the Dormouse again, so she began very cautiously: "But I don't understand. Where did they draw the treacle from?"

"You can draw water out of a water-well," said the Hatter; "so I should think you could draw treacle out of a treacle-well—eh, stupid?"

"But they were *in* the well," Alice said to the Dormouse, not choosing to notice this last remark.

"Of course they were," said the Dormouse: "well in."

This answer so confused poor Alice, that she let the Dormouse go on for some time without interrupting it.

"They were learning to draw," the Dormouse went on, yawning and rubbing its eyes, for it was getting very sleepy; "and they drew all manner of things—everything that begins with an M——"

"Why with an M?" said Alice.

"Why not?" said the March Hare.

Alice was silent.

The Dormouse had closed its eyes by this time, and was going off into a doze; but, on being pinched by the Hatter, it woke up again with a little shriek, and went on: "——that begins with an M, such as mouse-traps, and the moon, and memory, and muchness—you know you say things are 'much of a muchness'[13]—did you ever see such a thing as a drawing of a muchness!"

"Really, now you ask me," said Alice, very much confused, "I don't think——"

"Then you shouldn't talk," said the Hatter.

This piece of rudeness was more than Alice could bear: she got up in great disgust, and walked off: the Dormouse fell asleep instantly, and neither of the others took the least notice of her going, though she looked back once or twice, half hoping that they would call after her: the last time she saw them, they were trying to put the Dormouse into the teapot.

"At any rate I'll never go *there* again!" said Alice, as she picked her way through the wood. "It's the stupidest tea-party I ever was at in all my life!"

Just as she said this,[14] she noticed that one of the trees had a door leading right into it. "That's very curious!" she thought. "But everything's curious to-day. I think I may as well go in at once." And in she went.

Once more she found herself in the long hall, and close to the little glass table. "Now, I'll manage better this time," she said to herself, and began by taking the little golden key, and unlocking the door that led into the garden. Then she set to work nibbling at the mushroom (she had kept a piece of it in her pocket) till she was about a foot high: then she walked down the little passage: and *then*—she found herself at last in the beautiful garden, among the bright flower-beds and the cool fountains.

CHAPTER VIII

THE QUEEN'S CROQUET-GROUND

A large rose-tree stood near the entrance of the garden: the roses growing on it were white, but there were three gardeners at it, busily painting them red. Alice thought this a very curious thing, and she went nearer to watch them, and, just as she came up to them, she heard one of them say "Look out now, Five! Don't go splashing paint over me like that!"

"I couldn't help it," said Five, in a sulky tone. "Seven jogged my elbow."

On which Seven looked up and said "That's right, Five! Always lay the blame on others!"

"*You'd* better not talk!" said Five. "I heard the Queen say only yesterday you deserved to be beheaded."

"What for?" said the one who had spoken first.

"That's none of *your* business, Two!" said Seven.

"Yes, it *is* his business!" said Five. "And I'll tell him—it was for bringing the cook tulip-roots instead of onions."

Seven flung down his brush, and had just begun "Well, of all the unjust things—" when his eye chanced to fall upon Alice, as she stood watching them, and he checked himself suddenly: the others looked round also, and all of them bowed low.

"Would you tell me, please," said Alice, a little timidly, "why you are painting those roses?"

Five and Seven said nothing, but looked at Two. Two began, in a low voice, "Why, the fact is, you see, Miss, this here ought to have been a *red* rose-tree, and we put a white one in by mistake; and, if the Queen was to find it out, we should all have our heads cut off, you know. So you see, Miss, we're doing our best, afore she comes, to—" At this moment, Five, who had been anxiously looking across the garden, called out "The Queen! The Queen!", and the three gardeners instantly threw themselves flat upon their faces. There was a sound of many footsteps, and Alice looked round, eager to see the Queen.

First came ten soldiers carrying clubs: these were all shaped like the three gardeners, oblong and flat, with their hands and feet at the corners: next the ten courtiers: these were ornamented all over with diamonds, and walked two and two, as the soldiers did. After these came the royal children: there were ten of them, and the little dears came jumping merrily along, hand in hand, in couples: they were all ornamented with hearts. Next came the guests, mostly Kings and Queens, and among them Alice recognised the White Rabbit: it was talking in a hurried nervous manner, smiling at everything that was said, and went by without noticing her. Then followed the Knave of Hearts, carrying the King's crown on a crimson velvet cushion; and, last of all this grand procession, came THE KING AND THE QUEEN OF HEARTS.[1]

Alice was rather doubtful[2] whether she ought not to lie down on her face like the three gardeners, but she could not remember ever having heard of such a rule at processions; "and besides, what would be the use of a procession," thought she, "if people had all to lie down on their faces, so that they couldn't see it?" So she stood where she was, and waited.

When the procession came opposite to Alice, they all stopped and looked at her, and the Queen said, severely, "Who is this?". She said it to the Knave of Hearts, who only bowed and smiled in reply.

"Idiot!" said the Queen, tossing her head impatiently; and, turning to Alice, she went on: "What's your name, child?"

"My name is Alice, so please your Majesty," said Alice very politely; but she added, to herself, "Why, they're only a pack of cards, after all. I needn't be afraid of them!"

"And who are *these*?" said the Queen, pointing to the three gardeners who were lying round the rose-tree; for, you see, as they were lying on their faces, and the pattern on their backs was the same as the

rest of the pack, she could not tell whether they were gardeners, or soldiers, or courtiers, or three of her own children.

"How should *I* know?" said Alice, surprised at her own courage. "It's no business of *mine*."

The Queen turned crimson with fury, and, after glaring at her for a moment like a wild beast, began screaming "Off with her head![3] Off with——"

"Nonsense!" said Alice, very loudly and decidedly, and the Queen was silent.

The King laid his hand upon her arm, and timidly said "Consider, my dear: she is only a child!"

The Queen turned angrily away from him, and said to the Knave "Turn them over!"

The Knave did so, very carefully, with one foot.

"Get up!" said the Queen in a shrill, loud voice, and the three gardeners instantly jumped up, and began bowing to the King, the Queen, the royal children, and everybody else.

"Leave off that!" screamed the Queen. "You make me giddy." And then, turning to the rose-tree, she went on "What *have* you been doing here?"

"May it please your Majesty," said Two, in a very humble tone, going down on one knee as he spoke, "we were trying—"

"*I* see!" said the Queen, who had meanwhile been examining the roses. "Off with their heads!" and the procession moved on, three of the soldiers remaining behind to execute the unfortunate gardeners, who ran to Alice for protection.

"You sha'n't be beheaded!" said Alice, and she put them into a large flower-pot that stood near. The three soldiers wandered about for a minute or two, looking for them, and then quietly marched off after the others.

"Are their heads off?" shouted the Queen.

"Their heads are gone, if it please your Majesty!" the soldiers shouted in reply.

"That's right!" shouted the Queen. "Can you play croquet?"[4]

The soldiers were silent, and looked at Alice, as the question was evidently meant for her.

"Yes!" shouted Alice.

"Come on, then!" roared the Queen, and Alice joined the procession, wondering very much what would happen next.

"It's—it's a very fine day!" said a timid voice at her side. She was walking by the White Rabbit, who was peeping anxiously into her face.

"Very," said Alice. "Where's the Duchess?"[5]

"Hush! Hush!" said the Rabbit in a low hurried tone. He looked anxiously over his shoulder as he spoke, and then raised himself upon tiptoe, put his mouth close to her ear, and whispered "She's under sentence of execution."

"What for?" said Alice.

"Did you say 'What a pity!'?" the Rabbit asked.

"No, I didn't," said Alice. "I don't think it's at all a pity. I said 'What for?' "

"She boxed the Queen's ears—" the Rabbit began. Alice gave a little scream of laughter. "Oh, hush!" the Rabbit whispered in a frightened tone. "The Queen will hear you! You see she came rather late, and the Queen said—"

"Get to your places!" shouted the Queen in a voice of thunder, and people began running about in all directions, tumbling up against each other: however, they got settled down in a minute or two, and the game began.

Alice thought she had never seen such a curious croquet-ground in her life: it was all ridges and furrows: the croquet balls were live hedgehogs, and the mallets live flamingoes,[6] and the soldiers had to double themselves up and stand on their hands and feet, to make the arches.

The chief difficulty Alice found at first was in managing her flamingo: she succeeded in getting its body tucked away, comfortably enough, under her arm, with its legs hanging down, but generally, just as she had got its neck nicely straightened out, and was going to give the hedgehog a blow with its head, it *would* twist itself round and look up in her face, with such a puzzled expression that she could not help bursting out laughing; and, when she had got its head down, and was going to begin again, it was very provoking to find that the hedgehog had unrolled itself, and was in the act of crawling away: besides all this,

there was generally a ridge or a furrow in the way wherever she wanted to send the hedgehog to, and, as the doubled-up soldiers were always getting up and walking off to other parts of the ground, Alice soon came to the conclusion that it was a very difficult game indeed.

The players all played at once, without waiting for turns, quarreling all the while, and fighting for the hedgehogs; and in a very short time the Queen was in a furious passion, and went stamping about, and shouting "Off with his head!" or "Off with her head!" about once in a minute.

Alice began to feel very uneasy:[7] to be sure, she had not as yet had any dispute with the Queen, but she knew that it might happen any minute, "and then," thought she, "what would become of me? They're dreadfully fond of beheading people here: the great wonder is, that there's anyone left alive!"

She was looking about for some way of escape, and wondering whether she could get away without being seen, when she noticed a curious appearance in the air: it puzzled her very much at first, but after watching it a minute or two she made it out to be a grin, and she said to herself "It's the Cheshire-Cat: now I shall have somebody to talk to."

"How are you getting on?" said the Cat, as soon as there was mouth enough for it to speak with.

Alice waited till the eyes appeared, and then nodded. "It's no use speaking to it," she thought, "till its ears have come, or at least one of them." In another minute the whole head appeared, and then Alice put down her flamingo, and began an account of the game, feeling very glad she had some one to listen to her. The Cat seemed to think that there was enough of it now in sight, and no more of it appeared.

"I don't think they play at all fairly," Alice began, in rather a complaining tone, "and they all quarrel so dreadfully one ca'n't hear oneself speak—and they don't seem to have any rules in particular: at least, if there are, nobody attends to them—and you've no idea how confusing it is all the things being alive: for instance, there's the arch I've got to go through next walking about at the other end of the ground—and I should have croqueted the Queen's hedgehog just now, only it ran away when it saw mine coming!"

"How do you like the Queen?" said the Cat in a low voice.

"Not at all," said Alice: "she's so extremely—" Just then she noticed that the Queen was close behind her, listening: so she went on "—likely to win, that it's hardly worth while finishing the game."

The Queen smiled and passed on.

"Who *are* you talking to?" said the King, coming up to Alice, and looking at the Cat's head with great curiosity.

"It's a friend of mine—a Cheshire-Cat," said Alice: "allow me to introduce it."

"I don't like the look of it at all," said the King: "however, it may kiss my hand, if it likes."

"I'd rather not," the Cat remarked.

"Don't be impertinent," said the King, "and don't look at me like that!" He got behind Alice as he spoke.

"A cat may look at a king,"[8] said Alice. "I've read that in some book, but I don't remember where."

"Well, it must be removed," said the King very decidedly; and he called to the Queen, who was passing at the moment, "My dear! I wish you would have this cat removed!"

The Queen had only one way of settling all difficulties, great or small. "Off with his head!" she said without even looking round.

"I'll fetch the executioner myself," said the King eagerly, and he hurried off.

Alice thought she might as well go back and see how the game was going on, as she heard the Queen's voice in the distance, screaming with passion. She had already heard her sentence three of the players to be executed for having missed their turns, and she did not like the look of things at all, as the game was in such confusion that she never knew whether it was her turn or not. So she went off in search of her hedgehog.

The hedgehog was engaged in a fight with another hedgehog, which seemed to Alice an excellent opportunity for croqueting one of them with the other: the only difficulty was, that her flamingo was gone across to the other side of the garden, where Alice could see it trying in a helpless sort of way to fly up into a tree.

By the time she had caught the flamingo and brought it back, the fight was over, and both the hedgehogs were out of sight: "but it doesn't matter much," thought Alice, "as all the arches are gone from this side of the ground." So she tucked it away under her arm, that it might not escape again, and went back to have a little more conversation with her friend.

When she got back to the Cheshire-Cat, she was surprised to find quite a large crowd collected round it: there was a dispute going on between the executioner, the King, and the Queen, who were all talking at once, while all the rest were quite silent, and looked very uncomfortable.

The moment Alice appeared, she was appealed to by all three to settle the question, and they repeated their arguments to her, though, as they all spoke at once, she found it very hard to make out exactly what they said.

The executioner's argument was, that you couldn't cut off a head unless there was a body to cut it off from: that he had never had to do such a thing before, and he wasn't going to begin at *his* time of life.

The King's argument was that anything that had a head could be beheaded, and that you weren't to talk nonsense.

The Queen's argument was that, if something wasn't done about it in less than no time, she'd have everybody executed, all round. (It was this last remark that had made the whole party look so grave and anxious.)

Alice could think of nothing else to say but "It belongs to the Duchess: you'd better ask *her* about it."

"She's in prison," the Queen said to the executioner: "fetch her here." And the executioner went off like an arrow.

The Cat's head began fading away the moment he was gone, and, by the time he had come back with the Duchess, it had entirely disappeared: so the King and the executioner ran wildly up and down, looking for it, while the rest of the party went back to the game.

CHAPTER IX

THE MOCK TURTLE'S STORY

"You ca'n't think how glad I am to see you again, you dear old thing!" said the Duchess,[1] as she tucked her arm affectionately into Alice's, and they walked off together.

Alice was very glad to find her in such a pleasant temper, and thought to herself that perhaps it was only the pepper that had made her so savage when they met in the kitchen.

"When *I'm* a Duchess," she said to herself (not in a very hopeful tone, though), "I wo'n't have any pepper in my kitchen *at all.* Soup does very well without—Maybe it's always pepper that makes people hot-tempered," she went on, very much pleased at having found out a new kind of rule, "and vinegar that makes them sour—and camomile[2] that makes them bitter—and—and barley-sugar and such things that make children sweet-tempered. I only wish people knew *that*: then they wouldn't be so stingy about it, you know——"

She had quite forgotten the Duchess by this time, and was a little startled when she heard her voice close to her ear. "You're thinking about something, my dear, and that makes you forget to talk. I ca'n't tell you just now what the moral of that is, but I shall remember it in a bit."

"Perhaps it hasn't one," Alice ventured to remark.

"Tut, tut, child!" said the Duchess. "Every thing's got a moral, if only you can find it."[3] And she squeezed herself up closer to Alice's side as she spoke.

Alice did not much like her keeping so close to her: first, because the Duchess was *very* ugly; and secondly, because she was exactly the right height to rest her chin on Alice's shoulder, and it was an uncomfortably sharp chin. However, she did not like to be rude: so she bore it as well as she could.

"The game's going on rather better now," she said, by way of keeping up the conversation a little.

"'Tis so," said the Duchess: "and the moral of that is—'Oh, 'tis love, 'tis love, that makes the world go round!'"[4]

"Somebody said," Alice whispered, "that it's done by everybody minding their own business!"[5]

"Ah, well! It means much the same thing," said the Duchess, digging her sharp little chin into Alice's shoulder as she added "and the moral of *that* is—'Take care of the sense, and the sounds will take care of themselves.'"[6]

"How fond she is of finding morals in things!" Alice thought to herself.

"I dare say you're wondering why I don't put my arm round your waist," the Duchess said, after a pause: "the reason is, that I'm doubtful about the temper of your flamingo. Shall I try the experiment?"

"He might bite," Alice cautiously replied, not feeling at all anxious to have the experiment tried.

"Very true," said the Duchess: "flamingoes and mustard both bite. And the moral of that is—'Birds of a feather flock together.'"[7]

"Only mustard isn't a bird," Alice remarked.

"Right, as usual," said the Duchess: "what a clear way you have of putting things!"

"It's a mineral, I *think*," said Alice.

"Of course it is," said the Duchess, who seemed ready to agree to everything that Alice said: "there's a large mustard-mine near here. And the moral of that is—'The more there is of mine, the less there is of yours.'"

"Oh, I know!" exclaimed Alice, who had not attended to this last remark. "It's a vegetable. It doesn't look like one, but it is."

"I quite agree with you," said the Duchess; "and the moral of that is—'Be what you would seem to be'[8]—or, if you'd like it put more simply—'Never imagine yourself not to be otherwise than what it might appear to others that what you were or might have been was not otherwise than what you had been would have appeared to them to be otherwise.'"

"I think I should understand that better," Alice said very politely, "if I had it written down: but I ca'n't quite follow it as you say it."

"That's nothing to what I could say if I chose," the Duchess replied, in a pleased tone.

"Pray don't trouble yourself to say it any longer than that," said Alice.

"Oh, don't talk about trouble!" said the Duchess. "I make you a present of everything I've said as yet."

"A cheap sort of present!" thought Alice. "I'm glad people don't give birthday-presents like that!" But she did not venture to say it out loud.

"Thinking again?" the Duchess asked, with another dig of her sharp little chin.

"I've a right to think," said Alice sharply, for she was beginning to feel a little worried.

"Just about as much right," said the Duchess, "as pigs have to fly;[9] and the m——"

But here, to Alice's great surprise, the Duchess's voice died away, even in the middle of her favourite word 'moral,' and the arm that was linked into hers began to tremble. Alice looked up, and there stood the Queen in front of them, with her arms folded, frowning like a thunderstorm.

"A fine day, your Majesty!" the Duchess began in a low, weak voice.

"Now, I give you fair warning," shouted the Queen, stamping on the ground as she spoke; "either you or your head must be off, and that in about half no time! Take your choice!"

The Duchess took her choice, and was gone in a moment.

"Let's go on with the game," the Queen said to Alice; and Alice was too much frightened to say a word, but slowly followed her back to the croquet-ground.

The other guests had taken advantage of the Queen's absence, and were resting in the shade: however, the moment they saw her, they hurried back to the game, the Queen merely remarking that a moment's delay would cost them their lives.

All the time they were playing the Queen never left off quarreling with the other players, and shouting "Off with his head!" or "Off with her head!" Those whom she sentenced[10] were taken into custody by the soldiers, who of course had to leave off being arches to do this, so that, by the end of half an hour or so, there were no arches left, and all the players, except the King, the Queen, and Alice, were in custody and under sentence of execution.

Then the Queen left off, quite out of breath, and said to Alice "Have you seen the Mock Turtle yet?"

"No," said Alice. "I don't even know what a Mock Turtle is."

"It's the thing Mock Turtle Soup is made from,"[11] said the Queen.

"I never saw one, or heard of one," said Alice.

"Come on, then," said the Queen, "and he shall tell you his history."

As they walked off together, Alice heard the King say in a low voice, to the company generally, "You are all pardoned." "Come, *that's* a good thing!" she said to herself, for she had felt quite unhappy at the number of executions the Queen had ordered.

They very soon came upon a Gryphon,[12] lying fast asleep in the sun. (If you don't know what a Gryphon is, look at the picture.) "Up, lazy thing!" said the Queen, "and take this young lady to see the Mock Turtle, and to hear his history. I must go back and see after some executions I have ordered;" and she walked off, leaving Alice alone with the Gryphon. Alice did not quite like the look of the creature, but on the whole she thought it would be quite as safe to stay with it as to go after that savage Queen: so she waited.

The Gryphon sat up and rubbed its eyes: then it watched the Queen

till she was out of sight: then it chuckled. "What fun!" said the Gryphon, half to itself, half to Alice.

"What *is* the fun?" said Alice.

"Why, *she*," said the Gryphon. "It's all her fancy, that: they never executes nobody, you know. Come on!"

"Everybody says 'come on!' here," thought Alice, as she went slowly after it: "I never was so ordered about before, in all my life, never!"

They had not gone far before they saw the Mock Turtle in the distance, sitting sad and lonely on a little ledge of rock, and, as they came nearer, Alice could hear him sighing as if his heart would break. She pitied him deeply. "What is his sorrow?" she asked the Gryphon. And the Gryphon answered, very nearly in the same words as before, "It's all his fancy, that: he hasn't got no sorrow, you know. Come on!"

So they went up to the Mock Turtle, who looked at them with large eyes full of tears, but said nothing.

"This here young lady," said the Gryphon, "she wants for to know your history, she do."

"I'll tell it to her," said the Mock Turtle in a deep, hollow tone. "Sit down, both of you, and don't speak a word till I've finished."

So they sat down, and nobody spoke for some minutes. Alice thought to herself "I don't see how he can *ever* finish, if he doesn't begin." But she waited patiently.

"Once," said the Mock Turtle at last, with a deep sigh, "I was a real Turtle."

These words were followed by a very long silence, broken only by an occasional exclamation of "Hjckrrh!" from the Gryphon, and the constant heavy sobbing of the Mock Turtle. Alice was very nearly getting up and saying "Thank you, Sir, for your interesting story," but she could not help thinking there *must* be more to come, so she sat still and said nothing.

"When we were little," the Mock Turtle went on at last, more calmly, though still sobbing a little now and then, "we went to school in the sea. The master was an old Turtle—we used to call him Tortoise——"

"Why did you call him Tortoise, if he wasn't one?" Alice asked.

"We called him Tortoise because he taught us,"[13] said the Mock Turtle angrily. "Really you are very dull!"

"You ought to be ashamed of yourself for asking such a simple question," added the Gryphon; and then they both sat silent and looked at poor Alice, who felt ready to sink into the earth. At last the Gryphon said to the Mock Turtle "Drive on, old fellow! Don't be all day about it!", and he went on in these words:—

"Yes, we went to school in the sea,[14] though you mayn't believe it——"

"I never said I didn't!" interrupted Alice.

"You did," said the Mock Turtle.

"Hold your tongue!" added the Gryphon, before Alice could speak again. The Mock Turtle went on.

"We had the best of educations—in fact, we went to school every day——"

"*I've* been to a day-school, too," said Alice. "You needn't be so proud as all that."

"With extras?" asked the Mock Turtle, a little anxiously.

"Yes," said Alice: "we learned French and music."

"And washing?" said the Mock Turtle.

"Certainly not!" said Alice indignantly.

"Ah! Then yours wasn't a really good school," said the Mock Turtle in a tone of great relief. "Now, at *ours*, they had, at the end of the bill, 'French, music, *and washing*—extra.'"

"You couldn't have wanted it much," said Alice; "living at the bottom of the sea."

"I couldn't afford to learn it," said the Mock Turtle with a sigh. "I only took the regular course."

"What was that?" inquired Alice.

"Reeling and Writhing,[15] of course, to begin with," the Mock Turtle replied; "and then the different branches of Arithmetic—Ambition, Distraction, Uglification, and Derision."

"I never heard of 'Uglification,'" Alice ventured to say. "What is it?"

The Gryphon lifted up both its paws in surprise. "Never heard of uglifying!" it exclaimed. "You know what to beautify is, I suppose?"

"Yes," said Alice doubtfully: "it means—to—make—anything—prettier."

"Well, then," the Gryphon went on, "if you don't know what to uglify is, you *are* a simpleton."

Alice did not feel encouraged to ask any more questions about it: so she turned to the Mock Turtle, and said "What else had you to learn?"

"Well, there was Mystery," the Mock Turtle replied, counting off the subjects on his flappers,—"Mystery, ancient and modern, with Seaography: then Drawling—the Drawling-master was an old conger-eel,[16] that used to come once a week: *he* taught us Drawling, Stretching, and Fainting in Coils."

"What was *that* like?" asked Alice.

"Well, I ca'n't show it you, myself," the Mock Turtle said: "I'm too stiff. And the Gryphon never learnt it."

"Hadn't time," said the Gryphon. "I went to the Classical master, though. He was an old crab, *he* was."

"I never went to him," the Mock Turtle said with a sigh. "He taught Laughing and Grief,[17] they used to say."

"So he did, so he did," said the Gryphon, sighing in his turn; and both creatures hid their faces in their paws.

"And how many hours a day did you do lessons?" said Alice, in a hurry to change the subject.

"Ten hours the first day," said the Mock Turtle: "nine the next, and so on."

"What a curious plan!" exclaimed Alice.

"That's the reason they're called lessons," the Gryphon remarked: "because they lessen from day to day."

This was quite a new idea to Alice, and she thought it over a little before she made her next remark. "Then the eleventh day must have been a holiday?"

"Of course it was," said the Mock Turtle.

"And how did you manage on the twelfth?" Alice went on eagerly.

"That's enough about lessons," the Gryphon interrupted in a very decided tone. "Tell her something about the games now."

CHAPTER X

THE LOBSTER-QUADRILLE[1]

The Mock Turtle sighed deeply, and drew the back of one flapper across his eyes. He looked at Alice and tried to speak, but, for a minute or two, sobs choked his voice. "Same as if he had a bone in his throat," said the Gryphon; and it set to work shaking him and punching him in the back. At last the Mock Turtle recovered his voice, and, with tears running down his cheeks, he went on again:—

"You may not have lived much under the sea—" ("I haven't," said Alice)—"and perhaps you were never even introduced to a lobster—" (Alice began to say "I once tasted——" but checked herself hastily, and said "No, never") "——so you can have no idea what a delightful thing a Lobster-Quadrille is!"

"No, indeed," said Alice. "What sort of a dance is it?"

"Why," said the Gryphon, "you first form into a line along the sea-shore——"

"Two lines!" cried the Mock Turtle. "Seals, turtles, salmon, and so on: then, when you've cleared all the jelly-fish out of the way——"

"*That* generally takes some time," interrupted the Gryphon.

"—you advance twice——"

"Each with a lobster as a partner!" cried the Gryphon.

"Of course," the Mock Turtle said: "advance twice, set to partners——"

"—change lobsters, and retire in same order," continued the Gryphon.

"Then, you know," the Mock Turtle went on, "you throw the——"

"The lobsters!" shouted the Gryphon, with a bound into the air.

"—as far out to sea as you can——"

"Swim after them!" screamed the Gryphon.

"Turn a somersault in the sea!" cried the Mock Turtle, capering wildly about.

"Change lobsters again!" yelled the Gryphon at the top of its voice.

"Back to land again, and—that's all the first figure," said the Mock Turtle, suddenly dropping his voice; and the two creatures, who had been jumping about like mad things all this time, sat down again very sadly and quietly, and looked at Alice.

"It must be a very pretty dance," said Alice timidly.

"Would you like to see a little of it?" said the Mock Turtle.

"Very much indeed," said Alice.

"Come, let's try the first figure!" said the Mock Turtle to the Gryphon. "We can do it without lobsters, you know. Which shall sing?"

"Oh, *you* sing," said the Gryphon. "I've forgotten the words."

So they began solemnly dancing round and round Alice, every now and then treading on her toes when they passed too close, and waving their fore-paws to mark the time, while the Mock Turtle sang this, very slowly and sadly:—

"Will you walk a little faster?"[2] *said a whiting to a snail,*
"There's a porpoise close behind us, and he's treading on my tail.
See how eagerly the lobsters and the turtles all advance!
They are waiting on the shingle—will you come and join the dance?
Will you, wo'n't you, will you, wo'n't you, will you join the dance?
Will you, wo'n't you, will you, wo'n't you, wo'n't you join the dance?

"You can really have no notion how delightful it will be
When they take us up and throw us, with the lobsters, out to sea!"
But the snail replied "Too far, too far!", and gave a look askance—
Said he thanked the whiting kindly, but he would not join the dance.
Would not, could not, would not, could not, would not join the dance.
Would not, could not, would not, could not, could not join the dance.

"What matters it how far we go?" his scaly friend replied.
"There is another shore, you know, upon the other side.
The further off from England the nearer is to France—
Then turn not pale, beloved snail, but come and join the dance.
Will you, wo'n't you, will you, wo'n't you, will you join the dance?
Will you, wo'nt you, will you, wo'n't you, won't you join the dance?"

"Thank you, it's a very interesting dance to watch," said Alice, feeling very glad that it was over at last: "and I do so like that curious song about the whiting!"

"Oh, as to the whiting,"[3] said the Mock Turtle, "they—you've seen them, of course?"

"Yes," said Alice, "I've often seen them at dinn——" she checked herself hastily.

"I don't know where Dinn may be," said the Mock Turtle; "but, if you've seen them so often, of course you know what they're like?"

"I believe so," Alice replied thoughtfully. "They have their tails in their mouths[4]—and they're all over crumbs."

"You're wrong about the crumbs," said the Mock Turtle: "crumbs would all wash off in the sea. But they *have* their tails in their mouths; and the reason is—" here the Mock Turtle yawned and shut his eyes. "Tell her about the reason and all that," he said to the Gryphon.

"The reason is," said the Gryphon, "that they *would* go with the lobsters to the dance. So they got thrown out to sea. So they had to fall a long way. So they got their tails fast in their mouths. So they couldn't get them out again. That's all."

"Thank you," said Alice, "it's very interesting. I never knew so much about a whiting before."

"I can tell you more than that, if you like," said the Gryphon. "Do you know why it's called a whiting?"

"I never thought about it," said Alice. "Why?"

"*It does the boots and shoes*," the Gryphon replied very solemnly.

Alice was thoroughly puzzled. "Does the boots and shoes!" she repeated in a wondering tone.

"Why, what are *your* shoes done with?" said the Gryphon. "I mean, what makes them so shiny?"

Alice looked down at them, and considered a little before she gave her answer. "They're done with blacking,[5] I believe."

"Boots and shoes under the sea," the Gryphon went on in a deep voice, "are done with whiting. Now you know."

"And what are they made of?" Alice asked in a tone of great curiosity.

"Soles and eels, of course," the Gryphon replied, rather impatiently: "any shrimp could have told you that."

"If I'd been the whiting," said Alice, whose thoughts were still running on the song, "I'd have said to the porpoise 'Keep back, please! We don't want *you* with us!'"

"They were obliged to have him with them," the Mock Turtle said. "No wise fish would go anywhere without a porpoise."

"Wouldn't it, really?" said Alice, in a tone of great surprise.

"Of course not," said the Mock Turtle. "Why, if a fish came to *me*, and told me he was going a journey, I should say 'With what porpoise?'"

"Don't you mean 'purpose'?" said Alice.

"I mean what I say," the Mock Turtle replied, in an offended tone. And the Gryphon added "Come, let's hear some of *your* adventures."

"I could tell you my adventures—beginning from this morning," said Alice a little timidly; "but it's no use going back to yesterday, because I was a different person then."

"Explain all that," said the Mock Turtle.

"No, no! The adventures first," said the Gryphon in an impatient tone: "explanations take such a dreadful time."

So Alice began telling them her adventures from the time when she first saw the White Rabbit. She was a little nervous about it, just at first, the two creatures got so close to her, one on each side, and opened their eyes and mouths so *very* wide; but she gained courage as she went on. Her listeners were perfectly quiet till she got to the part about her repeating "*You are old, Father William,*" to the Caterpillar, and the words all coming different, and then the Mock Turtle drew a long breath, and said "That's very curious!"

"It's all about as curious as it can be," said the Gryphon.

"It all came different!" the Mock Turtle repeated thoughtfully. "I should like to hear her try and repeat something now. Tell her to begin." He looked at the Gryphon as if he thought it had some kind of authority over Alice.

"Stand up and repeat "*'Tis the voice of the sluggard*,'"[6] said the Gryphon.

"How the creatures order one about, and make one repeat lessons!" thought Alice. "I might just as well be at school at once." However, she got up, and began to repeat it, but her head was so full of the Lobster-Quadrille, that she hardly knew what she was saying; and the words came very queer indeed:—

> "'*Tis the voice of the Lobster:*[7] *I heard him declare*
> *'You have baked me too brown, I must sugar my hair.'*
> *As a duck with its eyelids, so he with his nose*
> *Trims his belt and his buttons, and turns out his toes.*

When the sands are all dry, he is gay as a lark,
And will talk in contemptuous tones of the Shark:
But, when the tide rises and sharks are around,
His voice has a timid and tremulous sound."

"That's different from what *I* used to say when I was a child," said the Gryphon.

"Well, *I* never heard it before," said the Mock Turtle; "but it sounds uncommon nonsense."

Alice said nothing: she had sat down with her face in her hands, wondering if anything would *ever* happen in a natural way again.

"I should like to have it explained," said the Mock Turtle.

"She ca'n't explain it," said the Gryphon hastily. "Go on with the next verse."

"But about his toes?" the Mock Turtle persisted. "How *could* he turn them out with his nose, you know?"

"It's the first position in dancing," Alice said; but she was dreadfully puzzled by the whole thing, and longed to change the subject.

"Go on with the next verse," the Gryphon repeated: "it begins '*I passed by his garden.*'"

Alice did not dare to disobey, though she felt sure it would all come wrong, and she went on in a trembling voice:—

"I passed by his garden, and marked, with one eye,
How the Owl and the Panther were sharing a pie:
The Panther took pie-crust, and gravy, and meat,
While the Owl had the dish as its share of the treat.
When the pie was all finished, the Owl, as a boon,
Was kindly permitted to pocket the spoon:
While the Panther received knife and fork with a growl,
And concluded the banquet by——"[8]

"What *is* the use of repeating all that stuff?" the Mock Turtle interrupted, "if you don't explain it as you go on? It's by far the most confusing thing *I* ever heard!"

"Yes, I think you'd better leave off," said the Gryphon, and Alice was only too glad to do so.

"Shall we try another figure of the Lobster-Quadrille?"[9] the Gryphon went on. "Or would you like the Mock Turtle to sing you another song?"

"Oh, a song, please, if the Mock Turtle would be so kind," Alice replied, so eagerly that the Gryphon said, in a rather offended tone, "Hm! No accounting for tastes! Sing her '*Turtle Soup*,'[10] will you, old fellow?"

The Mock Turtle sighed deeply, and began, in a voice choked with sobs, to sing this:—

"*Beautiful Soup,*[11] *so rich and green,*
Waiting in a hot tureen!
Who for such dainties would not stoop?
Soup of the evening, beautiful Soup!
Soup of the evening, beautiful Soup!
  Beau—ootiful Soo—oop!
  Beau—ootiful Soo—oop!
Soo—oop of the e—e—evening,
  Beautiful, beautiful Soup!

"Beautiful Soup! Who cares for fish,
Game, or any other dish?

Who would not give all else for two p
ennyworth only of beautiful Soup?
Pennyworth only of beautiful soup?
Beau—ootiful Soo—oop!
Beau—ootiful Soo—oop!
Soo—oop of the e—e—evening,
Beautiful, beauti—FUL SOUP!"

"Chorus again!" cried the Gryphon, and the Mock Turtle had just begun to repeat it, when a cry of "The trial's beginning!" was heard in the distance.

"Come on!" cried the Gryphon, and, taking Alice by the hand, it hurried off, without waiting for the end of the song.

"What trial is it?" Alice panted as she ran; but the Gryphon only answered "Come on!" and ran the faster, while more and more faintly came, carried on the breeze that followed them, the melancholy words:—

"*Soo—oop of the e—e—evening,*
Beautiful, beautiful Soup!"

CHAPTER XI

WHO STOLE THE TARTS?

The King and Queen of Hearts were seated on their throne when they arrived, with a great crowd assembled about them—all sorts of little birds and beasts, as well as the whole pack of cards: the Knave was standing before them, in chains, with a soldier on each side to guard him; and near the King was the White Rabbit, with a trumpet in one hand, and a scroll of parchment in the other. In the very middle of the court[1] was a table, with a large dish of tarts upon it: they looked so good, that it made Alice quite hungry to look at them—"I wish they'd get the trial done," she thought, "and hand round the refreshments!" But there seemed to be no chance of this; so she began looking at everything about her to pass away the time.

Alice had never been in a court of justice before,[2] but she had read about them in books, and she was quite pleased to find that she knew the name of nearly everything there. "That's the judge," she said to herself, "because of his great wig."

The judge, by the way, was the King; and, as he wore his crown over the wig (look at the frontispiece if you want to see how he did it), he did not look at all comfortable, and it was certainly not becoming.

"And that's the jury-box," thought Alice; "and those twelve creatures," (she was obliged to say "creatures," you see, because some of them were animals, and some were birds,) "I suppose they are the jurors." She said this last word two or three times over to herself, being rather proud of it: for she thought, and rightly too, that very few little girls of her age knew the meaning of it at all. However, "jurymen" would have done just as well.

The twelve jurors were all writing very busily on slates. "What are they doing?" Alice whispered to the Gryphon. "They ca'n't have anything to put down yet, before the trial's begun."

"They're putting down their names," the Gryphon whispered in reply, "for fear they should forget them before the end of the trial."

"Stupid things!" Alice began in a loud indignant voice; but she stopped herself hastily, for the White Rabbit cried out "Silence in the court!", and the King put on his spectacles and looked anxiously round, to make out who was talking.

Alice could see, as well as if she were looking over their shoulders, that all the jurors were writing down "Stupid things!" on their slates, and she could even make out that one of them didn't know how to spell "stupid," and that he had to ask his neighbour to tell him. "A nice muddle their slates'll be in, before the trial's over!" thought Alice.

One of the jurors had a pencil that squeaked. This, of course, Alice could *not* stand, and she went round the court and got behind him, and very soon found an opportunity of taking it away. She did it so quickly that the poor little juror (it was Bill, the Lizard) could not make out at all what had become of it; so, after hunting all about for it, he was obliged to write with one finger for the rest of the day; and this was of very little use, as it left no mark on the slate.

"Herald, read the accusation!" said the King.

On this the White Rabbit blew three blasts on the trumpet, and then unrolled the parchment-scroll, and read as follows:—

"The Queen of Hearts, she made some tarts,[3]
All on a summer day:
The Knave of Hearts, he stole those tarts
And took them quite away!"

"Consider your verdict,"[4] the King said to the jury.

"Not yet, not yet!" the Rabbit hastily interrupted. "There's a great deal to come before that!"

"Call the first witness," said the King; and the White Rabbit blew three blasts on the trumpet, and called out "First witness!"

The first witness was the Hatter. He came in with a teacup in one hand and a piece of bread-and-butter in the other. "I beg pardon, your Majesty," he began, "for bringing these in; but I hadn't quite finished my tea when I was sent for."

"You ought to have finished," said the King. "When did you begin?"

The Hatter looked at the March Hare, who had followed him into the court, arm-in-arm with the Dormouse. "Fourteenth of March, I *think* it was," he said.

"Fifteenth," said the March Hare.

"Sixteenth," said the Dormouse.

"Write that down," the King said to the jury; and the jury eagerly wrote down all three dates on their slates, and then added them up, and reduced the answer to shillings and pence.

"Take off your hat," the King said to the Hatter.

"It isn't mine," said the Hatter.

"*Stolen*!" the King exclaimed, turning to the jury, who instantly made a memorandum of the fact.

"I keep them to sell," the Hatter added as an explanation. "I've none of my own. I'm a hatter."

Here the Queen put on her spectacles, and began staring hard at the Hatter, who turned pale and fidgeted.

"Give your evidence," said the King; "and don't be nervous, or I'll have you executed on the spot."

This did not seem to encourage the witness at all: he kept shifting from one foot to the other, looking uneasily at the Queen, and in his confusion he bit a large piece out of his teacup instead of the bread-and-butter.

Just at this moment Alice felt a very curious sensation, which puzzled her a good deal until she made out what it was: she was beginning to grow larger again, and she thought at first she would get up and leave the court; but on second thoughts she decided to remain where she was as long as there was room for her.

"I wish you wouldn't squeeze so," said the Dormouse, who was sitting next to her. "I can hardly breathe."

"I ca'n't help it," said Alice very meekly: "I'm growing."

"You've no right to grow *here*," said the Dormouse.

"Don't talk nonsense," said Alice more boldly: "you know you're growing too."

"Yes, but *I* grow at a reasonable pace," said the Dormouse: "not in that ridiculous fashion." And he got up very sulkily and crossed over to the other side of the court.

All this time the Queen had never left off staring at the Hatter, and, just as the Dormouse crossed the court, she said, to one of the officers of the court, "Bring me the list of the singers in the last concert!" on which the wretched Hatter trembled so, that he shook off both his shoes.

"Give your evidence," the King repeated angrily, "or I'll have you executed, whether you're nervous or not."

"I'm a poor man, your Majesty," the Hatter began, in a trembling voice, "and I hadn't begun my tea—not above a week or so—and what with the bread-and-butter getting so thin—and the twinkling of the tea——"[5]

"The twinkling of *what*?" said the King.

"It *began* with the tea," the Hatter replied.

"Of course twinkling *begins* with a T!" said the King sharply. "Do you take me for a dunce? Go on!"

"I'm a poor man," the Hatter went on, "and most things twinkled after that—only the March Hare said——"

"I didn't!" the March Hare interrupted in a great hurry.

"You did!" said the Hatter.

"I deny it!" said the March Hare.

"He denies it," said the King: "leave out that part."

"Well, at any rate, the Dormouse said——" the Hatter went on, looking anxiously round to see if he would deny it too; but the Dormouse denied nothing, being fast asleep.

"After that," continued the Hatter, "I cut some more bread-and-butter——"

"But what did the Dormouse say?" one of the jury asked.

"That I ca'n't remember," said the Hatter.

"You *must* remember," remarked the King, "or I'll have you executed."

The miserable Hatter dropped his teacup and bread-and-butter, and went down on one knee. "I'm a poor man, your Majesty," he began.

"You're a *very* poor *speaker*," said the King.

Here one of the guinea-pigs cheered, and was immediately suppressed by the officers of the court. (As that is rather a hard word, I will just explain to you how it was done. They had a large canvas bag, which tied up at the mouth with strings: into this they slipped the guinea-pig, head first, and then sat upon it.)

"I'm glad I've seen that done," thought Alice. "I've so often read in the newspapers, at the end of trials, 'There was some attempt at applause, which was immediately suppressed by the officers of the court,' and I never understood what it meant till now."

"If that's all you know about it, you may stand down," continued the King.

"I ca'n't go no lower," said the Hatter: "I'm on the floor, as it is."

"Then you may *sit* down," the King replied.

Here the other guinea-pig cheered, and was suppressed.

"Come, that finishes the guinea-pigs!" thought Alice. "Now we shall get on better."

"I'd rather finish my tea," said the Hatter, with an anxious look at the Queen, who was reading the list of singers.

"You may go," said the King, and the Hatter hurriedly left the court, without even waiting to put his shoes on.

"——and just take his head off outside," the Queen added to one of the officers; but the Hatter was out of sight before the officer could get to the door.

"Call the next witness!" said the King.

The next witness was the Duchess's cook. She carried the pepper-box in her hand, and Alice guessed who it was, even before she got into the court, by the way the people near the door began sneezing all at once.

"Give your evidence," said the King.

"Sha'n't," said the cook.

The King looked anxiously at the White Rabbit, who said, in a low voice, "Your Majesty must cross-examine *this* witness."

"Well, if I must, I must," the King said with a melancholy air, and, after folding his arms and frowning at the cook till his eyes were nearly out of sight, he said, in a deep voice, "What are tarts made of?"

"Pepper, mostly," said the cook.

"Treacle," said a sleepy voice behind her.

"Collar that Dormouse!" the Queen shrieked out. "Behead that Dormouse! Turn that Dormouse out of court! Suppress him! Pinch him! Off with his whiskers!"

For some minutes the whole court was in confusion, getting the Dormouse turned out, and, by the time they had settled down again, the cook had disappeared.

"Never mind!" said the King, with an air of great relief. "Call the next witness." And, he added, in an under-tone to the Queen, "Really, my dear, *you* must cross-examine the next witness. It quite makes my forehead ache!"

Alice watched the White Rabbit as he fumbled over the list, feeling very curious to see what the next witness would be like, "—for they haven't got much evidence *yet*," she said to herself. Imagine her surprise, when the White Rabbit read out, at the top of his shrill little voice, the name "Alice!"

CHAPTER XII

ALICE'S EVIDENCE

"Here!" cried Alice, quite forgetting in the flurry of the moment how large she had grown in the last few minutes, and she jumped up in such a hurry that she tipped over the jury-box with the edge of her skirt, upsetting all the jurymen[1] on to the heads of the crowd below, and there they lay sprawling about, reminding her very much of a globe of gold-fish she had accidentally upset the week before.

"Oh, I *beg* your pardon!" she exclaimed in a tone of great dismay, and began picking them up again as quickly as she could, for the accident of the gold-fish kept running in her head, and she had a vague sort of idea that they must be collected at once and put back into the jury-box, or they would die.

"The trial cannot proceed," said the King, in a very grave voice, "until all the jurymen are back in their proper places—*all*," he repeated with great emphasis, looking hard at Alice as he said so.

Alice looked at the jury-box, and saw that, in her haste, she had put the Lizard in head downwards, and the poor little thing was waving its tail about in a melancholy way, being quite unable to move. She soon got it out again, and put it right; "not that it signifies much," she said to herself; "I should think it would be *quite* as much use in the trial one way up as the other."

As soon as the jury had a little recovered from the shock of being upset, and their slates and pencils had been found and handed back to them, they set to work very diligently to write out a history of the accident, all except the Lizard, who seemed too much overcome to do anything but sit with its mouth open, gazing up into the roof of the court.

"What do you know about this business?" the King said to Alice.

"Nothing," said Alice.

"Nothing *whatever*?" persisted the King.

"Nothing whatever," said Alice.

"That's very important," the King said, turning to the jury. They were just beginning to write this down on their slates, when the White Rabbit interrupted: "*Un*important, your Majesty means, of course," he said, in a very respectful tone, but frowning and making faces at him as he spoke.

"*Un*important, of course, I meant," the King hastily said, and went on to himself in an undertone, "important—unimportant—unimportant—important——" as if he were trying which word sounded best.

Some of the jury wrote it down "important," and some "unimportant." Alice could see this, as she was near enough to look over their slates; "but it doesn't matter a bit," she thought to herself.

At this moment the King, who had been for some time busily writing in his note-book, called out "Silence!", and read out from his book, "Rule Forty-two.[2] *All persons more than a mile high to leave the court.*"

Everybody looked at Alice.

"*I'm* not a mile high," said Alice.

"You are," said the King.

"Nearly two miles high," added the Queen.

"Well, I sha'n't go, at any rate," said Alice: "besides, that's not a regular rule: you invented it just now."

"It's the oldest rule in the book," said the King.

"Then it ought to be Number One," said Alice.

The King turned pale, and shut his note-book hastily. "Consider your verdict," he said to the jury, in a low trembling voice.

"There's more evidence to come yet, please your Majesty," said the White Rabbit, jumping up in a great hurry: "this paper has just been picked up."

"What's in it?" said the Queen.

"I haven't opened it yet," said the White Rabbit; "but it seems to be a letter, written by the prisoner to—to somebody."

"It must have been that," said the King, "unless it was written to nobody, which isn't usual, you know."

"Who is it directed to?" said one of the jurymen.

"It isn't directed at all," said the White Rabbit: "in fact, there's nothing written on the *outside*." He unfolded the paper as he spoke, and added "It isn't a letter, after all: it's a set of verses."

"Are they in the prisoner's handwriting?" asked another of the jurymen.

"No, they're not," said the White Rabbit, "and that's the queerest thing about it." (The jury all looked puzzled.)

"He must have imitated somebody else's hand," said the King. (The jury all brightened up again.)

"Please your Majesty," said the Knave, "I didn't write it, and they ca'n't prove that I did: there's no name signed at the end."

"If you didn't sign it," said the King, "that only makes the matter worse. You *must* have meant some mischief, or else you'd have signed your name like an honest man."

There was a general clapping of hands at this: it was the first really clever thing the King had said that day.

"That *proves* his guilt, of course," said the Queen: "so, off with——"

"It doesn't prove anything of the sort!" said Alice. "Why, you don't even know what they're about!"

"Read them," said the King.

The White Rabbit put on his spectacles. "Where shall I begin, please your Majesty?" he asked.

"Begin at the beginning," the King said, very gravely, "and go on till you come to the end: then stop."

There was dead silence in the court, whilst the White Rabbit read out these verses:[3]—

"They told me you had been to her,[4]
And mentioned me to him:
She gave me a good character,
But said I could not swim.

He sent them word I had not gone
(We know it to be true):
If she should push the matter on,
What would become of you?

I gave her one, they gave him two,
You gave us three or more;
They all returned from him to you,
Though they were mine before.

If I or she should chance to be
Involved in this affair,
He trusts to you to set them free,
Exactly as we were.

My notion was that you had been
(Before she had this fit)
An obstacle that came between
Him, and ourselves, and it.

Don't let him know she liked them best,
For this must ever be
A secret, kept from all the rest,
Between yourself and me."

"That's the most important piece of evidence we've heard yet," said the King, rubbing his hands; "so now let the jury——"

"If any one of them can explain it," said Alice, (she had grown so large in the last few minutes that she wasn't a bit afraid of interrupting him,) "I'll give him sixpence. *I* don't believe there's an atom of meaning in it."[5]

The jury all wrote down, on their slates, "*She* doesn't believe there's an atom of meaning in it," but none of them attempted to explain the paper.

"If there's no meaning in it," said the King, "that saves a world of trouble, you know, as we needn't try to find any. And yet I don't know," he went on, spreading out the verses on his knee, and looking at them with one eye; "I seem to see some meaning in them, after all. '*—said I could not swim—*' you ca'n't swim, can you?" he added, turning to the Knave.

The Knave shook his head sadly. "Do I look like it?" he said. (Which he certainly did *not*, being made entirely of cardboard.)

"All right, so far," said the King; and he went on muttering over the verses to himself: " '*We know it to be true*'—that's the jury, of course—'*If she should push the matter on*'—that must be the Queen—'*What would become of you?*'—What, indeed![6]—'*I gave her one, they gave him two*'—why, that must be what he did with the tarts, you know——"

"But it goes on '*they all returned from him to you,*' " said Alice.

"Why, there they are?" said the King triumphantly, pointing to the tarts on the table. "Nothing can be clearer than *that*. Then again—

'*before she had this fit*'—you never had *fits*, my dear, I think?" he said to the Queen.

"Never!" said the Queen, furiously, throwing an inkstand at the Lizard as she spoke. (The unfortunate little Bill had left off writing on his slate with one finger, as he found it made no mark; but he now hastily began again, using the ink, that was trickling down his face, as long as it lasted.)

"Then the words don't *fit* you," said the King, looking round the court with a smile. There was a dead silence.

"It's a pun!" the King added in an angry tone, and everybody laughed. "Let the jury consider their verdict,"[7] the King said, for about the twentieth time that day.

"No, no!" said the Queen. "Sentence first—verdict afterwards."

"Stuff and nonsense!" said Alice loudly. "The idea of having the sentence first!"

"Hold your tongue!" said the Queen, turning purple.

"I wo'n't!" said Alice.

"Off with her head!" the Queen shouted at the top of her voice. Nobody moved.

"Who cares for *you*?" said Alice (she had grown to her full size by this time). "You're nothing but a pack of cards!"

At this the whole pack rose up into the air, and came flying down upon her; she gave a little scream, half of fright and half of anger, and

tried to beat them off, and found herself lying on the bank, with her head in the lap of her sister, who was gently brushing away some dead leaves that had fluttered down from the trees upon her face.

"Wake up, Alice dear!" said her sister. "Why, what a long sleep you've had!"

"Oh, I've had such a curious dream!" said Alice. And she told her sister, as well as she could remember them, all these strange Adventures of hers that you have just been reading about; and, when she had finished, her sister kissed her, and said "It *was* a curious dream, dear, certainly; but now run in to your tea: it's getting late." So Alice got up and ran off, thinking while she ran, as well she might, what a wonderful dream it had been.

But her sister sat still just as she left her, leaning her head on her hand, watching the setting sun, and thinking of little Alice and all her wonderful Adventures, till she too began dreaming after a fashion, and this was her dream:—

First, she dreamed about little Alice herself:[8] once again the tiny hands were clasped upon her knee, and the bright eager eyes were looking up into hers—she could hear the very tones of her voice, and see that queer little toss of her head to keep back the wandering hair that *would* always get into her eyes—and still as she listened, or seemed to listen, the whole place around her became alive with the strange creatures of her little sister's dream.

The long grass rustled at her feet as the White Rabbit hurried by—the frightened Mouse splashed his way through the neighbouring pool—she could hear the rattle of the teacups as the March Hare and his friends shared their never-ending meal, and the shrill voice of the Queen ordering off her unfortunate guests to execution—once more the pig-baby was sneezing on the Duchess's knee, while plates and dishes crashed around it—once more the shriek of the Gryphon, the squeaking of the Lizard's slate-pencil, and the choking of the suppressed guinea-pigs, filled the air, mixed up with the distant sob of the miserable Mock Turtle.

So she sat on, with closed eyes, and half believed herself in Wonderland, though she knew she had but to open them again, and all would change to dull reality—the grass would be only rustling in the wind, and the pool rippling to the waving of the reeds—the rattling teacups would change to tinkling sheep-bells, and the Queen's shrill cries to the voice of the shepherd-boy—and the sneeze of the baby, the shriek of the Gryphon, and all the other queer noises, would change (she knew) to the confused clamour of the busy farm-yard—while the lowing of the cattle in the distance would take the place of the Mock Turtle's heavy sobs.

Lastly, she pictured to herself how this same little sister of hers[9] would, in the after-time, be herself a grown woman; and how she would keep, through all her riper years, the simple and loving heart of her childhood; and how she would gather about her other little children, and make *their* eyes bright and eager with many a strange tale, perhaps even with the dream of Wonderland of long ago; and how she would feel with all their simple sorrows, and find a pleasure in all their simple joys, remembering her own child-life, and the happy summer days.

THE END

Through the Looking-Glass,

and What Alice Found There

DRAMATIS PERSONÆ

(*As arranged before commencement of game*)

WHITE			RED	
PIECES	PAWNS		PAWNS	PIECES
Tweedledee	Daisy		Daisy	Humpty Dumpty
Unicorn	Haigha		Messenger	Carpenter
Sheep	Oyster		Oyster	Walrus
W. Queen	"Lily"		Tiger-lily	R. Queen
W. King	Fawn		Rose	R. King
Aged man	Oyster		Oyster	Crow
W. Knight	Hatta		Frog	R. Knight
Tweedledum	Daisy		Daisy	Lion

RED.

WHITE.

White pawn (Alice) to play, and win in eleven moves.

	PAGE		PAGE
1. Alice meets R. Q.	139	1. R. Q. to K. R's 4th	144
2. Alice through Q's 3d *(by railway)*	146	2. W. Q. to Q. B's 4th *(after shawl)*	170
to Q's 4th *(Tweedledum and Tweedledee)*	148		
3. Alice meets W. Q. *(with shawl)*	170	3. W. Q. to Q. B's 5th *(becomes sheep)*	174
4. Alice to Q's 5th *(shop, river, shop)*	174	4. W. Q. to K. B's 8th *(leaves egg on shelf)*	180
5. Alice to Q's 6th *(Humpty Dumpty)*	180	5. W. Q. to Q. B's 8th *(flying from R. Kt.)*	200
6. Alice to Q's 7th *(forest)*	203	6. R. Kt. to K's 2nd *(ch.)*	205
7. W. Kt. takes R. Kt.	207	7. W. Kt. to K. B's 5th	218
8. Alice to Q's 8th *(coronation)*	218	8. R. Q. to K's sq. *(examination)*	220
9. Alice becomes Queen	225	9. Queens castle	226
10. Alice castles *(feast)*	229	10. W. Q. to Q. R's 6th *(soup)*	232
11. Alice takes R. Q. & wins	235		

THROUGH THE LOOKING-GLASS,

AND WHAT ALICE FOUND THERE.

BY

LEWIS CARROLL,

AUTHOR OF "ALICE'S ADVENTURES IN WONDERLAND."

WITH FIFTY ILLUSTRATIONS

BY JOHN TENNIEL.

London:

MACMILLAN AND CO.

1872.

Child of the pure unclouded brow[1]
And dreaming eyes of wonder!
Though time be fleet, and I and thou
Are half a life asunder,
Thy loving smile will surely hail
The love-gift of a fairy-tale.

I have not seen thy sunny face,
Nor heard thy silver laughter:
No thought of me shall find a place
In thy young life's hereafter—
Enough that now thou wilt not fail
To listen to my fairy-tale.

A tale begun in other days,
When summer suns were glowing—
A simple chime, that served to time
The rhythm of our rowing—
Whose echoes live in memory yet,
Though envious years would say 'forget.'

Come, hearken then, ere voice of dread,
With bitter tidings laden,
Shall summon to unwelcome bed
A melancholy maiden!
We are but older children, dear,
Who fret to find our bedtime near.

Without, the frost, the blinding snow,
   The storm-wind's moody madness—
Within, the firelight's ruddy glow,
   And childhood's nest of gladness.
The magic words shall hold thee fast:
Thou shalt not heed the raving blast.

And, though the shadow of a sigh
   May tremble through the story,
For 'happy summer days'[2] gone by,
   And vanish'd summer glory[3]—
It shall not touch, with breath of bale,
The pleasance[4] of our fairy-tale.

CONTENTS

Chapter		Page
I	LOOKING-GLASS HOUSE	121
II	THE GARDEN OF LIVE FLOWERS	135
III	LOOKING-GLASS INSECTS	145
IV	TWEEDLEDUM AND TWEEDLEDEE	156
V	WOOL AND WATER	170
VI	HUMPTY DUMPTY	181
VII	THE LION AND THE UNICORN	194
VIII	"IT'S MY OWN INVENTION"	205
IX	QUEEN ALICE	220
X	SHAKING	235
XI	WAKING	237
XII	WHICH DREAMED IT?	238

CHAPTER I

LOOKING-GLASS HOUSE

One thing was certain, that the *white* kitten had nothing to do with it—it was the black kitten's fault entirely. For the white kitten had been having its face washed by the old cat for the last quarter of an hour (and bearing it pretty well, considering): so you see that it *couldn't* have had any hand in the mischief.

The way Dinah washed her children's faces was this: first she held the poor thing down by its ear with one paw, and then with the other paw she rubbed its face all over, the wrong way, beginning at the nose: and just now, as I said, she was hard at work on the white kitten, which was lying quite still and trying to purr—no doubt feeling that it was all meant for its good.

But the black kitten had been finished with earlier in the afternoon, and so, while Alice was sitting curled up in a corner of the great armchair, half talking to herself and half asleep, the kitten had been having a grand game of romps with the ball of worsted Alice had been trying to wind up, and had been rolling it up and down till it had all come undone again; and there it was, spread over the hearth-rug, all knots and tangles, with the kitten running after its own tail in the middle.

"Oh, you wicked wicked little thing!" cried Alice, catching up the kitten, and giving it a little kiss to make it understand that it was in disgrace. "Really, Dinah ought to have taught you better manners! You *ought*, Dinah, you know you ought!" she added, looking reproachfully at the old cat, and speaking in as cross a voice as she could manage—and then she scrambled back into the arm-chair, taking the kitten and the worsted with her, and began winding up the ball again. But she didn't get on very fast, as she was talking all the time, sometimes to the kitten, and sometimes to herself. Kitty sat very demurely on her knee, pretending to watch the progress of the winding, and now and then putting out one paw and gently touching the ball, as if it would be glad to help if it might.

"Do you know what to-morrow is, Kitty?"[1] Alice began. "You'd have guessed if you'd been up in the window with me—only Dinah was making you tidy, so you couldn't. I was watching the boys getting in sticks for the bonfire—and it wants plenty of sticks, Kitty! Only it got so cold, and it snowed so, they had to leave off. Never mind, Kitty, we'll go and see the bonfire to-morrow." Here Alice wound two or three turns of the worsted round the kitten's neck, just to see how it would look: this led to a scramble, in which the ball rolled down upon the floor, and yards and yards of it got unwound again.

"Do you know, I was so angry, Kitty," Alice went on, as soon as they were comfortably settled again, "when I saw all the mischief you had been doing, I was very nearly opening the window, and putting you out into the snow! And you'd have deserved it, you little mischievous darling! What have you got to say for yourself? Now don't interrupt me!" she went on, holding up one finger. "I'm going to tell you all your faults. Number one: you squeaked twice while Dinah was washing your face this morning. Now you ca'n't deny it, Kitty: I heard you! What's that you say?" (pretending that the kitten was speaking). "Her paw went into your eye? Well, that's *your* fault, for keeping your eyes open—if you'd shut them tight up, it wouldn't have happened. Now don't make any more excuses, but listen! Number two: you pulled

Snowdrop[2] away by the tail just as I had put down the saucer of milk before her! What, you were thirsty, were you? How do you know she wasn't thirsty too? Now for number three: you unwound every bit of the worsted while I wasn't looking!

"That's three faults, Kitty, and you've not been punished for any of them yet. You know I'm saving up all your punishments for Wednesday week—Suppose they had saved up all *my* punishments?" she went on, talking more to herself than the kitten. "What *would* they do at the end of a year? I should be sent to prison, I suppose, when the day came. Or—let me see—suppose each punishment was to be going without a dinner: then, when the miserable day came, I should have to go without fifty dinners at once! Well, I shouldn't mind *that* much! I'd far rather go without them than eat them!

"Do you hear the snow against the window-panes, Kitty? How nice and soft it sounds! Just as if some one was kissing the window all over outside. I wonder if the snow *loves* the trees and fields, that it kisses them so gently? And then it covers them up snug, you know, with a white quilt; and perhaps it says 'Go to sleep, darlings, till the summer comes again.' And when they wake up in the summer, Kitty, they dress themselves all in green, and dance about—whenever the wind blows—oh, that's very pretty!" cried Alice, dropping the ball of worsted to clap her hands. "And I do so *wish* it was true! I'm sure the woods look sleepy in the autumn, when the leaves are getting brown.

"Kitty, can you play chess?[3] Now, don't smile, my dear, I'm asking it seriously. Because, when we were playing just now, you watched just as if you understood it: and when I said 'Check!' you purred! Well, it *was* a nice check, Kitty, and really I might have won, if it hadn't been for that nasty Knight, that came wriggling down among my pieces. Kitty, dear, let's pretend——" And here I wish I could tell you half the things Alice used to say, beginning with her favourite phrase "Let's pretend." She had had quite a long argument with her sister only the day before—all because Alice had begun with "Let's pretend we're kings and queens;"[4] and her sister, who liked being very exact, had argued that they couldn't, because there were only two of them, and Alice had been reduced at last to say "Well *you* can be one of them, then, and *I'll* be all the rest." And once she had really frightened her old nurse by shouting suddenly in her ear, "Nurse! Do let's pretend that I'm a hungry hyæna, and you're a bone!"

But this is taking us away from Alice's speech to the kitten. "Let's pretend that you're the Red Queen, Kitty! Do you know, I think if you sat up and folded your arms, you'd look exactly like her. Now do try, there's a dear!" And Alice got the Red Queen off the table, and set it up before the kitten as a model for it to imitate: however, the thing didn't succeed, principally, Alice said, because the kitten wouldn't fold

its arms properly. So, to punish it, she held it up to the Looking-glass, that it might see how sulky it was, "—and if you're not good directly," she added, "I'll put you through into Looking-glass House. How would you like *that*?

"Now, if you'll only attend, Kitty, and not talk so much, I'll tell you all my ideas about Looking-glass House.[5] First, there's the room you-can see through the glass—that's just the same as our drawing-room,

only the things go the other way. I can see all of it when I get upon a chair—all but the bit just behind the fireplace. Oh! I do so wish I could see *that* bit! I want so much to know whether they've a fire in the winter: you never *can* tell, you know, unless our fire smokes, and then smoke comes up in that room too—but that may be only pretence, just to make it look as if they had a fire. Well then, the books are something like our books, only the words go the wrong way: I know *that*, because

I've held up one of our books to the glass, and then they hold up one in the other room.

"How would you like to live in Looking-glass House, Kitty? I wonder if they'd give you milk in there? Perhaps Looking-glass milk isn't good to drink—but oh, Kitty! now we come to the passage. You can just see a little *peep* of the passage in Looking-glass House, if you leave the door of our drawing-room wide open: and it's very like our passage as far as you can see, only you know it may be quite different on beyond. Oh, Kitty, how nice it would be if we could only get through into Looking-glass House! I'm sure it's got, oh! such beautiful things in it! Let's pretend there's a way of getting through into it, somehow, Kitty. Let's pretend the glass has got all soft like gauze, so that we can get through. Why, it's turning into a sort of mist now, I declare! It'll be easy enough to get through——" She was up on the chimney-piece while she said this, though she hardly knew how she had got there. And certainly the glass *was* beginning to melt away, just like a bright silvery mist.[6]

In another moment Alice was through the glass, and had jumped lightly down into the Looking-glass room. The very first thing she did was to look whether there was a fire in the fireplace, and she was quite pleased to find that there was a real one, blazing away as brightly as the one she had left behind. "So I shall be as warm here as I was in the old room," thought Alice: "warmer, in fact, because there'll be no one here to scold me away from the fire. Oh, what fun it'll be, when they see me through the glass in here, and ca'n't get at me!"

Then she began looking about, and noticed that what could be seen from the old room was quite common and uninteresting, but that all the rest was as different as possible. For instance, the pictures on the wall next the fire seemed to be all alive, and the very clock on the chimney-piece (you know you can only see the back of it in the Looking-glass) had got the face of a little old man, and grinned at her.

"They don't keep this room so tidy as the other," Alice thought to herself, as she noticed several of the chessmen down in the hearth among the cinders; but in another moment, with a little "Oh!" of surprise, she was down on her hands and knees watching them. The chessmen were walking about, two and two!

"Here are the Red King and the Red Queen," Alice said (in a whisper, for fear of frightening them), "and there are the White King and the White Queen sitting on the edge of the shovel—and here are two

Castles walking arm in arm[7]—I don't think they can hear me," she went on, as she put her head closer down, "and I'm nearly sure they ca'n't see me. I feel somehow as if I was getting invisible——"

Here something began squeaking on the table behind Alice, and made her turn her head just in time to see one of the White Pawns roll over and begin kicking: she watched it with great curiosity to see what would happen next.

"It is the voice of my child!" the White Queen cried out, as she rushed past the King, so violently that she knocked him over among the cinders. "My precious Lily! My imperial kitten!" and she began scrambling wildly up the side of the fender.

"Imperial fiddlestick!" said the King, rubbing his nose, which had been hurt by the fall. He had a right to be a *little* annoyed with the

Queen, for he was covered with ashes from head to foot.

Alice was very anxious to be of use, and, as the poor little Lily was nearly screaming herself into a fit, she hastily picked up the Queen and set her on the table by the side of her noisy little daughter.

The Queen gasped, and sat down: the rapid journey through the air had quite taken away her breath, and for a minute or two she could do nothing but hug the little Lily in silence. As soon as she had recovered her breath a little, she called out to the White King, who was sitting sulkily among the ashes, "Mind the volcano!"

"What volcano?" said the King, looking up anxiously into the fire, as if he thought that was the most likely place to find one.

"Blew—me—up," panted the Queen, who was still a little out of breath. "Mind you come up—the regular way—don't get blown up!"

Alice watched the White King as he slowly struggled up from bar to bar, till at last she said "Why, you'll be hours and hours getting to the table, at that rate. I'd far better help you, hadn't I?" But the King took no notice of the question: it was quite clear that he could neither hear her nor see her.

So Alice picked him up very gently, and lifted him across more slowly than she had lifted the Queen, that she mightn't take his breath away; but, before she put him on the table, she thought she might as well dust him a little, he was so covered with ashes.

She said afterwards that she had never seen in all her life such a face as the King made, when he found himself held in the air by an invisible hand, and being dusted: he was far too much astonished to cry out, but his eyes and his mouth went on getting larger and larger, and rounder and rounder, till her hand shook so with laughing that she nearly let him drop upon the floor.

"Oh! *please* don't make such faces, my dear!" she cried out, quite forgetting that the King couldn't hear her. "You make me laugh so that I can hardly hold you! And don't keep your mouth so wide open! All the ashes will get into it—there, now I think you're tidy enough!" she added, as she smoothed his hair, and set him upon the table near the Queen.

The King immediately fell flat on his back, and lay perfectly still; and Alice was a little alarmed at what she had done, and went round the

room to see if she could find any water to throw over him. However, she could find nothing but a bottle of ink, and when she got back with it she found he had recovered, and he and the Queen were talking together in a frightened whisper—so low, that Alice could hardly hear what they said.

The King was saying "I assure you, my dear, I turned cold to the very ends of my whiskers!"

To which the Queen replied "You haven't got any whiskers."

"The horror of that moment," the King went on, "I shall never, *never* forget!"

"You will, though," the Queen said, "if you don't make a memorandum of it."

Alice looked on with great interest as the King took an enormous memorandum-book[8] out of his pocket, and began writing. A sudden thought struck her, and she took hold of the end of the pencil, which came some way over his shoulder, and began writing for him.

The poor King looked puzzled and unhappy, and struggled with the pencil for some time without saying anything; but Alice was too strong for him, and at last he panted out "My dear! I really *must* get a thinner pencil. I ca'n't manage this one a bit: it writes all manner of things that I don't intend——"

"What manner of things?" said the Queen, looking over the book (in which Alice had put '*The White Knight is sliding down the poker. He balances very badly*'). "That's not a memorandum of *your* feelings!"[9]

There was a book lying near Alice on the table, and while she sat watching the White King (for she was still a little anxious about him, and had the ink all ready to throw over him, in case he fainted again), she turned over the leaves, to find some part that she could read, "—for it's all in some language I don't know," she said to herself.

It was like this.

JABBERWOCKY[10]

'Twas brillig, and the slithy toves
Did gyre and gimble in the wabe:
All mimsy were the borogoves,
And the mome raths outgrabe.

She puzzled over this for some time, but at last a bright thought struck her. "Why, it's a Looking-glass book, of course! And, if I hold it up to a glass, the words will all go the right way again."

This was the poem that Alice read.

JABBERWOCKY[11]

'Twas brillig, and the slithy toves[12]
Did gyre and gimble[13] *in the wabe:*
All mimsy[14] *were the borogoves,*
And the mome raths[15] *outgrabe.*[16]

"Beware the Jabberwock,[17] *my son!*
The jaws that bite, the claws that catch!
Beware the Jubjub bird,[18] *and shun*
The frumious Bandersnatch!"[19]

He took his vorpal[20] *sword in hand:*
Long time the manxome[21] *foe he sought—*
So rested he by the Tumtum tree,[22]
And stood awhile in thought.

And, as in uffish thought[23] *he stood,*
The Jabberwock, with eyes of flame,
Came whiffling through the tulgey wood,[24]
And burbled[25] *as it came!*

One, two! One, two! And through and through
The vorpal blade went snicker-snack!
He left it dead, and with its head
He went galumphing[26] *back.*

"And, hast thou slain the Jabberwock?
Come to my arms, my beamish[27] *boy!*
O frabjous day! Callooh! Callay!"[28]
He chortled[29] *in his joy.*

'Twas brillig, and the slithy toves
Did gyre and gimble in the wabe:
All mimsy were the borogoves,
And the mome raths outgrabe.

"It seems very pretty," she said when she had finished it, "but it's *rather* hard to understand!" (You see she didn't like to confess, even to herself, that she couldn't make it out at all.) "Somehow it seems to fill my head with ideas—only I don't exactly know what they are! However, *somebody* killed *something*:[30] that's clear, at any rate——"

"But oh!" thought Alice, suddenly jumping up, "if I don't make haste, I shall have to go back through the Looking-glass, before I've seen what the rest of the house is like! Let's have a look at the garden first!" She was out of the room in a moment, and ran down stairs—or, at least, it wasn't exactly running, but a new invention for getting down stairs quickly and easily, as Alice said to herself. She just kept the tips of her fingers on the hand-rail, and floated gently down without even touching the stairs with her feet: then she floated on through the hall, and would have gone straight out at the door in the same way, if she hadn't caught hold of the door-post. She was getting a little giddy with so much floating in the air, and was rather glad to find herself walking again in the natural way.

CHAPTER II

THE GARDEN OF LIVE FLOWERS

"I should see the garden[1] far better," said Alice to herself, "if I could get to the top of that hill: and here's a path that leads straight to it—at least, no, it doesn't do *that*——" (after going a few yards along the path, and turning several sharp corners), "but I suppose it will at last. But how curiously it twists! It's more like a corkscrew than a path! Well, *this* turn goes to the hill, I suppose—no, it doesn't! This goes straight back to the house! Well then, I'll try it the other way."

And so she did: wandering up and down, and trying turn after turn, but always coming back to the house, do what she would. Indeed, once, when she turned a corner rather more quickly than usual, she ran against it before she could stop herself.

"It's no use talking about it," Alice said, looking up at the house and pretending it was arguing with her. "I'm *not* going in again yet. I know I should have to get through the Looking-glass again—back into the old room—and there'd be an end of all my adventures!"

So, resolutely turning her back upon the house, she set out once more down the path, determined to keep straight on till she got to the hill. For a few minutes all went on well, and she was just saying "I really *shall* do it this time——" when the path gave a sudden twist and shook itself (as she described it afterwards), and the next moment she found herself actually walking in at the door.

"Oh, it's too bad!" she cried. "I never saw such a house for getting in the way! Never!"

However, there was the hill full in sight, so there was nothing to be done but start again. This time she came upon a large flower-bed, with a border of daisies, and a willow-tree growing in the middle.

"O Tiger-lily!"[2] said Alice, addressing herself to one that was waving gracefully about in the wind, "I *wish* you could talk!"

"We *can* talk," said the Tiger-lily, "when there's anybody worth talking to."

Alice was so astonished that she couldn't speak for a minute: it quite seemed to take her breath away. At length, as the Tiger-lily only went on waving about, she spoke again, in a timid voice—almost in a whisper. "And can *all* the flowers talk?"

"As well as *you* can," said the Tiger-lily. "And a great deal louder."

"It isn't manners for us to begin, you know," said the Rose, "and I really was wondering when you'd speak! Said I to myself, 'Her face has got *some* sense in it, though it's not a clever one!' Still you're the right colour, and that goes a long way."

"I don't care about the colour," the Tiger-lily remarked. "If only her petals curled a little more, she'd be all right."

Alice didn't like being criticized, so she began asking questions. "Aren't you sometimes frightened at being planted out here, with nobody to take care of you?"

"There's the tree in the middle," said the Rose. "What else is it good for?"

"But what could it do, if any danger came?" Alice asked.

"It could bark," said the Rose.

"It says 'Bough-wough!'" cried a Daisy. "That's why its branches are called boughs!"

"Didn't you know *that*?" cried another Daisy. And here they all began shouting together, till the air seemed quite full of little shrill voices. "Silence, every one of you!" cried the Tiger-lily, waving itself passionately from side to side, and trembling with excitement. "They know I ca'n't get at them!" it panted, bending its quivering head towards Alice, "or they wouldn't dare to do it!"

"Never mind!" Alice said in a soothing tone, and, stooping down to the daisies, who were just beginning again, she whispered "If you don't hold your tongues, I'll pick you!"

There was silence in a moment, and several of the pink daisies turned white.

"That's right!" said the Tiger-lily. "The daisies are worst of all. When one speaks, they all begin together, and it's enough to make one wither to hear the way they go on!"

"How is it you can all talk so nicely?" Alice said, hoping to get it into a better temper by a compliment. "I've been in many gardens before, but none of the flowers could talk."

"Put your hand down, and feel the ground," said the Tiger-lily. "Then you'll know why."

Alice did so. "It's very hard," she said; "but I don't see what that has to do with it."

"In most gardens," the Tiger-lily said, "they make the beds too soft—so that the flowers are always asleep."

This sounded a very good reason, and Alice was quite pleased to know it. "I never thought of that before!" she said.

"It's *my* opinion that you never think *at all*," the Rose said, in a rather severe tone.

"I never saw anybody that looked stupider," a Violet said, so suddenly, that Alice quite jumped; for it hadn't spoken before.

"Hold *your* tongue!" cried the Tiger-lily. "As if *you* ever saw anybody! You keep your head under the leaves, and snore away there, till you know no more what's going on in the world, than if you were a bud!"

"Are there any more people in the garden besides me?" Alice said, not choosing to notice the Rose's last remark.

"There's one other flower in the garden that can move about like you," said the Rose. "I wonder how you do it——" ("You're always wondering," said the Tiger-lily), "but she's more bushy than you are."

"Is she like me?" Alice asked eagerly, for the thought crossed her mind, "There's another little girl in the garden, somewhere!"

"Well, she has the same awkward shape as you," the Rose said: "but she's redder—and her petals are shorter, I think."

"They're done up close, like a dahlia," said the Tiger-lily: "not tumbled about, like yours."

"But that's not *your* fault," the Rose added kindly. "You're beginning to fade, you know—and then one ca'n't help one's petals getting a little untidy."

Alice didn't like this idea at all: so, to change the subject, she asked "Does she ever come out here?"

"I daresay you'll see her soon," said the Rose. "She's one of the kind that has nine spikes,[3] you know."

"Where does she wear them?" Alice asked with some curiosity.

"Why, all round her head, of course," the Rose replied. "I was wondering *you* hadn't got some too. I thought it was the regular rule."

"She's coming!" cried the Larkspur. "I hear her footstep, thump, thump, along the gravel-walk!"

Alice looked round eagerly and found that it was the Red Queen. "She's grown a good deal!" was her first remark. She had indeed: when Alice first found her in the ashes, she had been only three inches high—and here she was, half a head taller than Alice herself!

"It's the fresh air that does it," said the Rose: "wonderfully fine air it is, out here."

"I think I'll go and meet her," said Alice, for, though the flowers were interesting enough, she felt that it would be far grander to have a talk with a real Queen.

"You ca'n't possibly do that," said the Rose: "*I* should advise you to walk the other way."

This sounded nonsense to Alice, so she said nothing, but set off at once towards the Red Queen. To her surprise she lost sight of her in a moment, and found herself walking in at the front-door again.

A little provoked, she drew back, and, after looking everywhere for the Queen (whom she spied out at last, a long way off), she thought she would try the plan, this time, of walking in the opposite direction.

It succeeded beautifully.[4] She had not been walking a minute before she found herself face to face with the Red Queen, and full in sight of the hill she had been so long aiming at.

"Where do you come from?" said the Red Queen. "And where are you going? Look up, speak nicely,[5] and don't twiddle your fingers all the time."

Alice attended to all these directions, and explained, as well as she could, that she had lost her way.

"I don't know what you mean by *your* way," said the Queen: "all the ways about here belong to *me*—but why did you come out here at all?" she added in a kinder tone. "Curtsey while you're thinking what to say. It saves time."

Alice wondered a little at this, but she was too much in awe of the Queen to disbelieve it. "I'll try it when I go home," she thought to herself, "the next time I'm a little late for dinner."

"It's time for you to answer now," the Queen said, looking at her watch: "open your mouth a *little* wider when you speak, and always say 'your Majesty.' "

"I only wanted to see what the garden was like, your Majesty——"

"That's right," said the Queen, patting her on the head, which Alice didn't like at all: "though, when you say 'garden'—*I've* seen gardens, compared with which this would be a wilderness."

Alice didn't dare to argue the point, but went on: "—and I thought I'd try and find my way to the top of that hill——"

"When you say 'hill,'" the Queen interrupted, "*I* could show you hills, in comparison with which you'd call that a valley."

"No, I shouldn't," said Alice, surprised into contradicting her at last: "a hill *ca'n't* be a valley, you know. That would be nonsense——"

The Red Queen shook her head. "You may call it 'nonsense' if you like," she said, "but *I've* heard nonsense, compared with which that would be as sensible as a dictionary!"[6]

Alice curtseyed again, as she was afraid from the Queen's tone that she was a *little* offended: and they walked on in silence till they got to the top of the little hill.

For some minutes Alice stood without speaking, looking out in all directions over the country—and a most curious country it was. There

were a number of tiny little brooks running straight across it from side to side, and the ground between was divided up into squares by a number of little green hedges, that reached from brook to brook.

"I declare it's marked out just like a large chess-board!"[7] Alice said at last. "There ought to be some men moving about somewhere—and so there are!" she added in a tone of delight, and her heart began to beat quick with excitement as she went on. "It's a great huge game of chess that's being played[8]—all over the world—if this *is* the world at all, you know. Oh, what fun it is! How I *wish* I was one of them! I wouldn't mind being a Pawn, if only I might join—though of course I should *like* to be a Queen, best."[9]

She glanced rather shyly at the real Queen as she said this, but her companion only smiled pleasantly, and said "That's easily managed. You can be the White Queen's Pawn, if you like, as Lily's too young to play;[10] and you're in the Second Square to begin with: when you get to the Eighth Square you'll be a Queen——" Just at this moment, somehow or other, they began to run.

Alice never could quite make out, in thinking it over afterwards, how it was that they began: all she remembers is, that they were running hand in hand, and the Queen went so fast that it was all she could do to keep up with her: and still the Queen kept crying "Faster!

Faster!", but Alice felt she *could not* go faster, though she had no breath left to say so.

The most curious part of the thing was, that the trees and the other things round them never changed their places at all: however fast they went, they never seemed to pass anything. "I wonder if all the things move along with us?" thought poor puzzled Alice. And the Queen seemed to guess her thoughts, for she cried "Faster! Don't try to talk!"

Not that Alice had any idea of doing *that*. She felt as if she would never be able to talk again, she was getting so much out of breath: and still the Queen cried "Faster! Faster!", and dragged her along. "Are we nearly there?" Alice managed to pant out at last.

"Nearly there!" the Queen repeated. "Why, we passed it ten minutes ago! Faster!" And they ran on for a time in silence, with the wind whistling in Alice's ears, and almost blowing her hair off her head, she fancied.

"Now! Now!" cried the Queen. "Faster! Faster!" And they went so fast that at last they seemed to skim through the air, hardly touching the ground with their feet, till suddenly, just as Alice was getting quite exhausted, they stopped, and she found herself sitting on the ground, breathless and giddy.

The Queen propped her up against a tree, and said kindly, "You may rest a little, now."

Alice looked round her in great surprise. "Why, I do believe we've been under this tree the whole time! Everything's just as it was!"

"Of course it is," said the Queen. "What would you have it?"

"Well, in *our* country," said Alice, still panting a little, "you'd generally get to somewhere else—if you ran very fast for a long time as we've been doing."

"A slow sort of country!" said the Queen. "Now, *here*, you see, it takes all the running *you* can do, to keep in the same place. If you want to get somewhere else, you must run at least twice as fast as that!"

"I'd rather not try, please!" said Alice. "I'm quite content to stay here—only I *am* so hot and thirsty!"

"I know what *you'd* like!" the Queen said good-naturedly, taking a little box out of her pocket. "Have a biscuit?"

Alice thought it would not be civil to say "No," though it wasn't at all what she wanted. So she took it, and ate it as well as she could: and it was *very* dry: and she thought she had never been so nearly choked in all her life.

"While you're refreshing yourself," said the Queen, "I'll just take the measurements." And she took a ribbon out of her pocket, marked in inches, and began measuring the ground, and sticking little pegs in here and there.

"At the end of two yards," she said, putting in a peg to mark the distance, "I shall give you your directions—have another biscuit?"

"No, thank you," said Alice: "one's *quite* enough!"

"Thirst quenched, I hope?"[11] said the Queen.

Alice did not know what to say to this, but luckily the Queen did not wait for an answer, but went on. "At the end of *three* yards I shall repeat them—for fear of your forgetting them. At the end of *four*, I shall say good-bye. And at the end of *five*, I shall go!"

She had got all the pegs put in by this time, and Alice looked on with great interest as she returned to the tree, and then began slowly walking down the row.

At the two-yard peg she faced round, and said "A pawn goes two squares in its first move, you know. So you'll go *very* quickly through the Third Square—by railway, I should think—and you'll find yourself in the Fourth Square in no time. Well, *that* square belongs to Tweedledum and Tweedledee—the Fifth is mostly water—the Sixth belongs to Humpty Dumpty—But you make no remark?"

"I—I didn't know I had to make one—just then," Alice faltered out.

"You *should* have said," the Queen went on in a tone of grave reproof, "'It's extremely kind of you to tell me this'—however, we'll suppose it said—the Seventh Square is all forest—however, one of the Knights will show you the way—and in the Eighth Square we shall be Queens together,[12] and it's all feasting and fun!" Alice got up and curtseyed, and sat down again.

At the next peg the Queen turned again, and this time she said "Speak in French when you ca'n't think of the English for a thing—turn out your toes as you walk—and remember who you are!" She did not wait for Alice to curtsey, this time, but walked on quickly to the next peg, where she turned for a moment to say "Good-bye," and then hurried on to the last.

How it happened, Alice never knew, but exactly as she came to the last peg, she was gone. Whether she vanished into the air, or whether she ran quickly into the wood ("and she *can* run very fast!" thought Alice), there was no way of guessing, but she was gone,[13] and Alice began to remember that she was a Pawn, and that it would soon be time for her to move.

CHAPTER III

LOOKING-GLASS INSECTS

Of course the first thing to do was to make a grand survey of the country[1] she was going to travel through. "It's something very like learning geography," thought Alice, as she stood on tiptoe in hopes of being able to see a little further. "Principal rivers—there *are* none. Principal mountains—I'm on the only one, but I don't think it's got any name. Principal towns—why, what *are* those creatures, making honey down there? They ca'n't be bees—nobody ever saw bees a mile off, you know——" and for some time she stood silent, watching one of them that was bustling about among the flowers, poking its proboscis into them, "just as if it was a regular bee," thought Alice.

However, this was anything but a regular bee: in fact it was an elephant[2]—as Alice soon found out, though the idea quite took her breath away at first. "And what enormous flowers they must be!" was her next idea. "Something like cottages with the roofs taken off, and stalks put to them—and what quantities of honey they must make! I think I'll go down and—no, I wo'n't go *just* yet," she went on, checking herself just as she was beginning to run down the hill, and trying to find some excuse for turning shy so suddenly. "It'll never do to go down among them without a good long branch to brush them away—and what fun it'll be when they ask me how I liked my walk. I shall say 'Oh, I liked it well enough——' (here came the favourite little toss of the head), 'only it *was* so dusty and hot, and the elephants *did* tease so!'

"I think I'll go down the other way," she said after a pause; "and perhaps I may visit the elephants later on. Besides, I *do* so want to get into the Third Square!"

So, with this excuse, she ran down the hill, and jumped over the first of the six little brooks.[3]

*   *   *   *   *

*   *   *   *

*   *   *   *   *

"Tickets, please!" said the Guard,[4] putting his head in at the window. In a moment everybody was holding out a ticket: they were about the same size as the people, and quite seemed to fill the carriage.

"Now then! Show your ticket, child!" the Guard went on, looking angrily at Alice. And a great many voices all said together ("like the chorus of a song," thought Alice)[5] "Don't keep him waiting, child! Why, his time is worth a thousand pounds a minute!"

"I'm afraid I haven't got one," Alice said in a frightened tone: "there wasn't a ticket-office where I came from." And again the chorus of voices went on. "There wasn't room for one where she came from. The land there is worth a thousand pounds an inch!"

"Don't make excuses," said the Guard: "you should have bought one from the engine-driver." And once more the chorus of voices went on with "The man that drives the engine. Why, the smoke alone is worth a thousand pounds a puff!"

Alice thought to herself "Then there's no use in speaking." The voices didn't join in, *this* time, as she hadn't spoken, but, to her great surprise, they all *thought* in chorus (I hope you understand what *thinking in chorus* means—for I must confess that *I* don't), "Better say nothing at all. Language is worth a thousand pounds a word!"

"I shall dream about a thousand pounds to-night, I know I shall!" thought Alice.

All this time the Guard was looking at her, first through a telescope, then through a microscope, and then through an opera glass. At last he said "You're traveling the wrong way," and shut up the window, and went away.

"So young a child," said the gentleman sitting opposite to her, (he was dressed in white paper,)[6] "ought to know which way she's going, even if she doesn't know her own name!"

A Goat, that was sitting next to the gentleman in white, shut his eyes and said in a loud voice, "She ought to know her way to the ticket-office, even if she doesn't know her alphabet!"

There was a Beetle sitting next the Goat (it was a very queer

carriage-full of passengers altogether), and, as the rule seemed to be that they should all speak in turn, *he* went on with "She'll have to go back from here as luggage!"

Alice couldn't see who was sitting beyond the Beetle, but a hoarse voice spoke next. "Change engines——" it said, and there it choked and was obliged to leave off.

"It sounds like a horse," Alice thought to herself. And an extremely small voice, close to her ear, said "You might make a joke on that—something about 'horse' and 'hoarse,' you know."

Then a very gentle voice in the distance said, "She must be labeled 'Lass, with care,'[7] you know——"

And after that other voices went on ("What a number of people there are in the carriage!" thought Alice), saying "She must go by post, as she's got a head on her[8]——" "She must be sent as a message by the telegraph——" "She must draw the train herself the rest of the way——," and so on.

But the gentleman dressed in white paper leaned forwards and whispered in her ear, "Never mind what they all say, my dear, but take a return-ticket every time the train stops."

"Indeed I sha'n't!" Alice said rather impatiently. "I don't belong to this railway journey at all—I was in a wood just now—and I wish I could get back there!"

"You might make a joke on *that*," said the little voice close to her ear: "something about 'you *would* if you could,' you know."

"Don't tease so," said Alice, looking about in vain to see where the voice came from. "If you're so anxious to have a joke made, why don't you make one yourself?"

The little voice sighed deeply. It was *very* unhappy, evidently, and Alice would have said something pitying to comfort it, "if it would only sigh like other people!" she thought. But this was such a wonderfully small sigh, that she wouldn't have heard it at all, if it hadn't come *quite* close to her ear. The consequence of this was that it tickled her ear very much, and quite took off her thoughts from the unhappiness of the poor little creature.

"I know you are a friend," the little voice went on: "a dear friend, and an old friend. And you wo'n't hurt me, though I *am* an insect."

"What kind of insect?" Alice inquired, a little anxiously. What she really wanted to know was, whether it could sting or not, but she thought this wouldn't be quite a civil question to ask.

"What, then you don't——" the little voice began, when it was drowned by a shrill scream from the engine, and everybody jumped up in alarm, Alice among the rest.

The Horse, who had put his head out of the window, quietly drew it in and said "It's only a brook we have to jump over." Everybody seemed satisfied with this, though Alice felt a little nervous at the idea of trains jumping at all. "However, it'll take us into the Fourth Square, that's some comfort!" she said to herself. In another moment she felt the carriage rise straight up into the air, and in her fright she caught at the thing nearest to her hand, which happened to be the Goat's beard.[9]

*   *   *   *   *

*   *   *   *

*   *   *   *   *

But the beard seemed to melt away as she touched it, and she found herself sitting quietly under a tree—while the Gnat (for that was the insect she had been talking to) was balancing itself on a twig just over her head, and fanning her with its wings.

It certainly was a *very* large Gnat: "about the size of a chicken," Alice thought. Still, she couldn't feel nervous with it, after they had been talking together so long.

"—then you don't like *all* insects?" the Gnat went on, as quietly as if nothing had happened.

"I like them when they can talk," Alice said. "None of them ever talk, where *I* come from."

"What sort of insects do you rejoice in, where *you* come from?" the Gnat inquired.

"I don't *rejoice* in insects at all," Alice explained, "because I'm rather afraid of them—at least the large kinds. But I can tell you the names of some of them."

"Of course they answer to their names?" the Gnat remarked carelessly.

"I never knew them do it."

"What's the use of their having names,"[10] the Gnat said, "if they wo'n't answer to them?"

"No use to *them*," said Alice; "but it's useful to the people that name them, I suppose. If not, why do things have names at all?"

"I ca'n't say," the Gnat replied. "Further on, in the wood down there, they've got no names—however, go on with your list of insects: you're wasting time."

"Well, there's the Horse-fly," Alice began, counting off the names on her fingers.

"All right," said the Gnat. "Half way up that bush, you'll see a Rocking-horse-fly, if you look. It's made entirely of wood, and gets about by swinging itself from branch to branch."

"What does it live on?" Alice asked, with great curiosity.

"Sap and sawdust," said the Gnat. "Go on with the list."

Alice looked at the Rocking-horse-fly with great interest, and made up her mind that it must have been just repainted, it looked so bright and sticky; and then she went on.

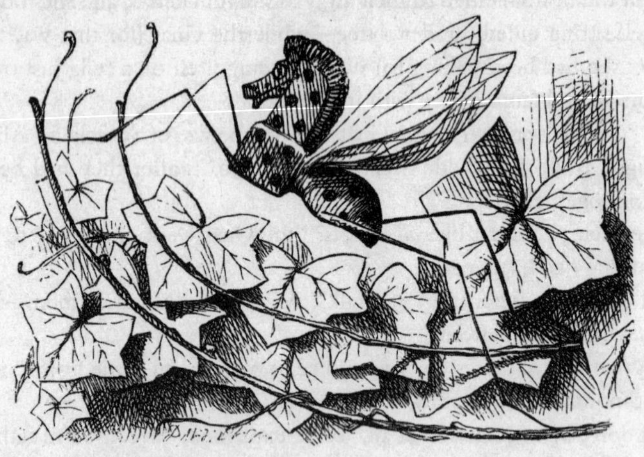

"And there's the Dragon-fly."

"Look on the branch above your head," said the Gnat, "and there you'll find a Snap-dragon-fly.[11] Its body is made of plum-pudding, its wings of holly-leaves, and its head is a raisin burning in brandy."

"And what does it live on?" Alice asked, as before.

"Frumenty and mince-pie,"[12] the Gnat replied; "and it makes its nest in a Christmas-box."

"And then there's the Butterfly," Alice went on, after she had taken a good look at the insect with its head on fire, and had thought to herself, "I wonder if that's the reason insects are so fond of flying into candles—because they want to turn into Snap-dragon-flies!"

"Crawling at your feet," said the Gnat (Alice drew her feet back in some alarm), "you may observe a Bread-and-butter-fly. Its wings are thin slices of bread-and-butter, its body is a crust, and its head is a lump of sugar."

"And what does *it* live on?"

"Weak tea with cream in it."

A new difficulty came into Alice's head. "Supposing it couldn't find any?" she suggested.

"Then it would die, of course."

"But that must happen very often," Alice remarked thoughtfully.

"It always happens," said the Gnat.

After this, Alice was silent for a minute or two, pondering. The Gnat amused itself meanwhile by humming round and round her head: at last it settled again and remarked "I suppose you don't want to lose your name?"

"No, indeed," Alice said, a little anxiously.

"And yet I don't know," the Gnat went on in a careless tone: "only think how convenient it would be if you could manage to go home without it! For instance, if the governess wanted to call you to your lessons, she would call out 'Come here——,' and there she would have to leave off, because there wouldn't be any name for her to call, and of course you wouldn't have to go, you know."

"That would never do, I'm sure," said Alice: "the governess would never think of excusing me lessons for that. If she couldn't remember my name, she'd call me 'Miss,' as the servants do."

"Well, if she said 'Miss,' and didn't say anything more," the Gnat remarked, "of course you'd miss your lessons. That's a joke. I wish *you* had made it."

"Why do you wish *I* had made it?" Alice asked. "It's a very bad one."

But the Gnat only sighed deeply, while two large tears came rolling down its cheeks.

"You shouldn't make jokes," Alice said, "if it makes you so unhappy."[13]

Then came another of those melancholy little sighs, and this time the poor Gnat really seemed to have sighed itself away, for, when Alice looked up, there was nothing whatever to be seen on the twig, and, as she was getting quite chilly with sitting still so long, she got up and walked on.

She very soon came to an open field, with a wood on the other side of it: it looked much darker than the last wood, and Alice felt a *little* timid about going into it. However, on second thoughts, she made up her mind to go on: "for I certainly won't go *back*," she thought to herself, and this was the only way to the Eighth Square.

"This must be the wood," she said thoughtfully to herself, "where things have no names. I wonder what'll become of *my* name when I go in? I shouldn't like to lose it at all——because they'd have to give me another, and it would be almost certain to be an ugly one. But then the fun would be, trying to find the creature that had got my old name! That's just like the advertisements, you know, when people lose dogs—— '*answers to the name of "Dash":*[14] *had on a brass collar*'——just fancy calling everything you met 'Alice,' till one of them answered! Only they wouldn't answer at all, if they were wise."

She was rambling on in this way when she reached the wood: it looked very cool and shady. "Well, at any rate it's a great comfort," she said as she stepped under the trees, "after being so hot, to get into the—into the—into *what*?"[15] she went on, rather surprised at not being able to think of the word. "I mean to get under the—under the—under *this*, you know!" putting her hand on the trunk of the tree. "What *does* it call itself, I wonder? I do believe it's got no name—why, to be sure it hasn't!"

She stood silent for a minute, thinking: then she suddenly began again. "Then it really *has* happened, after all! And now, who am I? I *will* remember, if I can! I'm determined to do it!" But being determined didn't help her much, and all she could say, after a great deal of puzzling, was "L, I *know* it begins with L!"[16]

Just then a Fawn came wandering by: it looked at Alice with its large gentle eyes, but didn't seem at all frightened. "Here then! Here then!" Alice said, as she held out her hand and tried to stroke it; but it only started back a little, and then stood looking at her again.

"What do you call yourself?" the Fawn said at last. Such a soft sweet voice it had!

"I wish I knew!" thought poor Alice. She answered, rather sadly, "Nothing, just now."

"Think again," it said: "that wo'n't do."

Alice thought, but nothing came of it. "Please would you tell me what *you* call yourself?" she said timidly. "I think that might help a little."

"I'll tell you, if you'll come a little further on," the Fawn said. "I ca'n't remember *here*."

So they walked on together through the wood, Alice with her arms clasped lovingly round the neck of the Fawn, till they came out into another open field, and here the Fawn gave a sudden bound into the air, and shook itself free from Alice's arm. "I'm a Fawn!" it cried out in a voice of delight. "And, dear me! you're a human child!" A sudden look of alarm came into its beautiful brown eyes, and in another moment it had darted away at full speed.

Alice stood looking after it, almost ready to cry with vexation at having lost her dear little fellow-traveler so suddenly. "However, I know my name now," she said: "that's *some* comfort. Alice—Alice—I wo'n't forget it again. And now, which of these finger-posts ought I to follow, I wonder?"

It was not a very difficult question to answer, as there was only one road through the wood, and the two finger-posts both pointed along it. "I'll settle it," Alice said to herself, "when the road divides and they point different ways."

But this did not seem likely to happen. She went on and on, a long way, but, wherever the road divided, there were sure to be two finger-posts pointing the same way, one marked 'TO TWEEDLEDUM'S HOUSE,' and the other 'TO THE HOUSE OF TWEEDLEDEE.'

"I do believe," said Alice at last, "that they live in the *same* house! I wonder I never thought of that before—But I ca'n't stay there long. I'll just call and say 'How d'ye do?' and ask them the way out of the wood. If I could only get to the Eighth Square before it gets dark!" So she wandered on, talking to herself as she went, till, on turning a sharp corner, she came upon two fat little men, so suddenly that she could not help starting back, but in another moment she recovered herself, feeling sure that they must be[17]

CHAPTER IV

TWEEDLEDUM AND TWEEDLEDEE.

They were standing under a tree,[1] each with an arm round the other's neck, and Alice knew which was which in a moment, because one of them had 'DUM' embroidered on his collar, and the other 'DEE.' "I suppose they've each got 'TWEEDLE' round at the back of the collar," she said to herself.

They stood so still that she quite forgot they were alive, and she was just going round to see if the word 'TWEEDLE' was written at the back of each collar, when she was startled by a voice coming from the one marked 'DUM.'

"If you think we're wax-works," he said, "you ought to pay, you know. Wax-works weren't made to be looked at for nothing. Nohow!"

"Contrariwise," added the one marked 'DEE,' "if you think we're alive, you ought to speak."

"I'm sure I'm very sorry," was all Alice could say; for the words of the old song[2] kept ringing through her head like the ticking of a clock, and she could hardly help saying them out loud: —

"Tweedledum and Tweedledee
Agreed to have a battle;
For Tweedledum said Tweedledee
Had spoiled his nice new rattle.

Just then flew down a monstrous crow,
As black as a tar-barrel;
Which frightened both the heroes so,
They quite forgot their quarrel."

"I know what you're thinking about," said Tweedledum; "but it isn't so, nohow."

"Contrariwise," continued Tweedledee, "if it was so, it might be; and if it were so, it would be but as it isn't, it ain't. That's logic."

"I was thinking," Alice said very politely, "which is the best way out of this wood: it's getting so dark. Would you tell me, please?"

But the fat little men only looked at each other and grinned.

They looked so exactly like a couple of great schoolboys, that Alice couldn't help pointing her finger at Tweedledum, and saying "First Boy!"

"Nohow!" Tweedledum cried out briskly, and shut his mouth up again with a snap.

"Next Boy!" said Alice, passing on to Tweedledee, though she felt quite certain he would only shout out "Contrariwise!" and so he did.

"You've begun wrong!" cried Tweedledum. "The first thing in a visit is to say 'How d'ye do?' and shake hands!" And here the two brothers gave each other a hug, and then they held out the two hands that were free, to shake hands with her.

Alice did not like shaking hands with either of them first, for fear of hurting the other one's feelings; so, as the best way out of the difficulty, she took hold of both hands at once: the next moment they were dancing round in a ring. This seemed quite natural (she remembered afterwards), and she was not even surprised to hear music playing: it seemed to come from the tree under which they were dancing, and it was done (as well as she could make it out) by the branches rubbing one across the other, like fiddles and fiddle-sticks.

"But it certainly *was* funny," (Alice said afterwards, when she was telling her sister the history of all this,) "to find myself singing '*Here we go round the mulberry bush*.'[3] I don't know when I began it, but somehow I felt as if I'd been singing it a long long time!"

The other two dancers were fat, and very soon out of breath. "Four times round is enough for one dance," Tweedledum panted out, and they left off dancing as suddenly as they had begun: the music stopped at the same moment.

Then they let go of Alice's hands, and stood looking at her for a minute: there was a rather awkward pause, as Alice didn't know how to begin a conversation with people she had just been dancing with. "It would never do to say 'How d'ye do?' *now*," she said to herself: "we seem to have got beyond that, somehow!"

"I hope you're not much tired?" she said at last.

"Nohow. And thank you *very* much for asking," said Tweedledum.

"So *much* obliged!" added Tweedledee. "You like poetry?"

"Ye-es, pretty well—*some* poetry," Alice said doubtfully. "Would you tell me which road leads out of the wood?"

"What shall I repeat to her?" said Tweedledee, looking round at Tweedledum with great solemn eyes, and not noticing Alice's question.

"'*The Walrus and the Carpenter*'[4] is the longest," Tweedledum replied, giving his brother an affectionate hug.

Tweedledee began instantly:

"The sun was shining——"

Here Alice ventured to interrupt him. "If it's *very* long," she said, as politely as she could, "would you please tell me first which road——"

Tweedledee smiled gently, and began again:

The sun was shining on the sea,
Shining with all his might:
He did his very best to make
The billows smooth and bright—
And this was odd, because it was
The middle of the night.

The moon was shining sulkily,
Because she thought the sun
Had got no business to be there
After the day was done—
'It's very rude of him,' she said,
'To come and spoil the fun!'

The sea was wet as wet could be,
The sands were dry as dry.
You could not see a cloud, because
No cloud was in the sky:
No birds were flying overhead—
There were no birds to fly.

The Walrus and the Carpenter
Were walking close at hand:[5]
They wept like anything to see
Such quantities of sand:
'If this were only cleared away,'
They said, 'it would *be grand!'*

'If seven maids with seven mops[6]
Swept it for half a year,
Do you suppose,' the Walrus said,
'That they could get it clear?'
'I doubt it,' said the Carpenter,
And shed a bitter tear.

'O Oysters, come and walk with us!'
The Walrus did beseech.
'A pleasant walk, a pleasant talk,
Along the briny beach:
We cannot do with more than four,
To give a hand to each.'

The eldest Oyster looked at him,
But never a word he said:
The eldest Oyster winked his eye,
And shook his heavy head—
Meaning to say he did not choose
To leave the oyster-bed.

But four young Oysters hurried up,
All eager for the treat:
Their coats were brushed, their faces washed,
Their shoes were clean and neat—
And this was odd, because, you know,
They hadn't any feet.

Four other oysters followed them,
And yet another four;
And thick and fast they came at last,
And more, and more, and more—
All hopping through the frothy waves,
And scrambling to the shore.

The Walrus and the Carpenter
Walked on a mile or so,
And then they rested on a rock
Conveniently low:
And all the little Oysters stood
And waited in a row.

'The time has come,' the Walrus said,
'To talk of many things:
Of shoes—and ships—and sealing-wax—
Of cabbages—and kings—
And why the sea is boiling hot—
And whether pigs have wings.'[7]

'But wait a bit,' the Oysters cried,
'Before we have our chat:
For some of us are out of breath,
And all of us are fat!'
'No hurry!' said the Carpenter.
They thanked him much for that.

'A loaf of bread,' the Walrus said,
'Is what we chiefly need:
Pepper and vinegar besides
Are very good indeed—
Now, if you're ready, Oysters dear,
We can begin to feed.'

'But not on us!' the Oysters cried,
Turning a little blue.
'After such kindness, that would be
A dismal thing to do!'
'The night is fine,' the Walrus said.
'Do you admire the view?

'It was so kind of you to come!
And you are very nice!'
The Carpenter said nothing but
'Cut us another slice.
I wish you were not quite so deaf—
I've had to ask you twice!'

'It seems a shame,' the Walrus said,
'To play them such a trick.
After we've brought them out so far,
And made them trot so quick!'
The Carpenter said nothing but
'The butter's spread too thick!'

'I weep for you,' the Walrus said:
'I deeply sympathize.'
With sobs and tears he sorted out
Those of the largest size,
Holding his pocket-handkerchief
Before his streaming eyes.

'O Oysters,' said the Carpenter,[8]
'You've had a pleasant run!
Shall we be trotting home again?'
But answer came there none—
And this was scarcely odd, because
They'd eaten every one."[9]

"I like the Walrus best," said Alice: "because he was a *little* sorry for the poor oysters."

"He ate more than the Carpenter, though," said Tweedledee. "You see he held his handkerchief in front, so that the Carpenter couldn't count how many he took: contrariwise."

"That was mean!" Alice said indignantly. "Then I like the Carpenter best—if he didn't eat so many as the Walrus."

"But he ate as many as he could get," said Tweedledum.

This was a puzzler. After a pause, Alice began, "Well! They were *both* very unpleasant characters——" Here she checked herself in some alarm, at hearing something that sounded to her like the puffing of a large steam-engine in the wood near them, though she feared it was more likely to be a wild beast. "Are there any lions or tigers about here?" she asked timidly.

"It's only the Red King snoring," said Tweedledee.

"Come and look at him!" the brothers cried, and they each took one of Alice's hands, and led her up to where the King was sleeping.

"Isn't he a *lovely* sight?" said Tweedledum.

Alice couldn't say honestly that he was. He had a tall red night-cap on, with a tassel, and he was lying crumpled up into a sort of untidy heap, and snoring loud——"fit to snore his head off!" as Tweedledum remarked.

"I'm afraid he'll catch cold with lying on the damp grass," said Alice, who was a very thoughtful little girl.

"He's dreaming now," said Tweedledee: "and what do you think he's dreaming about?"

Alice said "Nobody can guess that."

"Why, about *you*!" Tweedledee exclaimed, clapping his hands triumphantly. "And if he left off dreaming about you, where do you suppose you'd be?"

"Where I am now, of course," said Alice.

"Not you!" Tweedledee retorted contemptuously. "You'd be nowhere. Why, you're only a sort of thing in his dream!"[10]

"If that there King was to wake," added Tweedledum, "you'd go out—bang!—just like a candle!"

"I shouldn't!" Alice exclaimed indignantly. "Besides, if *I'm* only a sort of thing in his dream, what are *you*, I should like to know?"

"Ditto," said Tweedledum.

"Ditto, ditto!" cried Tweedledee.

He shouted this so loud that Alice couldn't help saying "Hush! You'll be waking him, I'm afraid, if you make so much noise."

"Well, it's no use *your* talking about waking him," said Tweedledum, "when you're only one of the things in his dream. You know very well you're not real."

"I *am* real!" said Alice, and began to cry.

"You wo'n't make yourself a bit realler by crying," Tweedledee remarked: "there's nothing to cry about."

"If I wasn't real," Alice said—half-laughing through her tears, it all seemed so ridiculous—"I shouldn't be able to cry."

"I hope you don't suppose those are *real* tears?" Tweedledum interrupted in a tone of great contempt.

"I know they're talking nonsense," Alice thought to herself: "and it's foolish to cry about it." So she brushed away her tears, and went on, as cheerfully as she could, "At any rate I'd better be getting out of the wood, for really it's coming on very dark. Do you think it's going to rain?"

Tweedledum spread a large umbrella over himself and his brother, and looked up into it. "No, I don't think it is," he said: "at least—not under *here*. Nohow."

"But it may rain *outside*?"

"It may—if it chooses," said Tweedledee: "we've no objection. Contrariwise."

"Selfish things!" thought Alice, and she was just going to say "Good-night" and leave them, when Tweedledum sprang out from under the umbrella, and seized her by the wrist.

"Do you see *that*?" he said, in a voice choking with passion, and his eyes grew large and yellow all in a moment, as he pointed with a trembling finger at a small white thing lying under the tree.

"It's only a rattle," Alice said, after a careful examination of the little white thing. "Not a rattle-*snake*, you know," she added hastily, thinking that he was frightened: "only an old rattle—quite old and broken."

"I knew it was!" cried Tweedledum, beginning to stamp about wildly and tear his hair. "It's spoilt, of course!" Here he looked at Tweedledee, who immediately sat down on the ground, and tried to hide himself under the umbrella.

Alice laid her hand upon his arm, and said, in a soothing tone, "You needn't be so angry about an old rattle."

"But it *isn't* old!" Tweedledum cried, in a greater fury than ever. "It's *new*, I tell you—I bought it yesterday—my nice NEW RATTLE!" and his voice rose to a perfect scream.

All this time Tweedledee was trying his best to fold up the umbrella, with himself in it: which was such an extraordinary thing to do, that it quite took off Alice's attention from the angry brother. But he couldn't quite succeed, and it ended in his rolling over, bundled up in the umbrella, with only his head out: and there he lay, opening and shutting his mouth and his large eyes——"looking more like a fish than anything else," Alice thought.

"Of course you agree to have a battle?" Tweedledum said in a calmer tone.

"I suppose so," the other sulkily replied, as he crawled out of the umbrella: "only *she* must help us to dress up, you know."

So the two brothers went off hand-in-hand into the wood, and returned in a minute with their arms full of things—such as bolsters, blankets, hearth-rugs, table-cloths, dish-covers, and coal-scuttles. "I hope you're a good hand at pinning and tying strings?" Tweedledum remarked. "Every one of these things has got to go on, somehow or other."

Alice said afterwards she had never seen such a fuss made about anything in all her life—the way those two bustled about—and the quantity of things they put on—and the trouble they gave her in tying strings and fastening buttons——"Really they'll be more like bundles of old clothes than anything else, by the time they're ready!" she said to herself, as she arranged a bolster round the neck of Tweedledee, "to keep his head from being cut off," as he said.

"You know," he added very gravely, "it's one of the most serious things that can possibly happen to one in a battle—to get one's head cut off."

Alice laughed loud: but she managed to turn it into a cough, for fear of hurting his feelings.

"Do I look very pale?" said Tweedledum, coming up to have his helmet tied on. (He *called* it a helmet,[11] though it certainly looked much more like a saucepan.)

"Well—yes—a *little*," Alice replied gently.

"I'm very brave, generally," he went on in a low voice: "only to-day I happen to have a headache."

"And *I've* got a toothache!" said Tweedledee, who had overheard the remark. "I'm far worse than you!"

"Then you'd better not fight to-day," said Alice, thinking it a good opportunity to make peace.

"We *must* have a bit of a fight, but I don't care about going on long," said Tweedledum. "What's the time now?"

Tweedledee looked at his watch, and said "Half-past four."

"Let's fight till six, and then have dinner," said Tweedledum.

"Very well," the other said, rather sadly: "and *she* can watch us—only you'd better not come *very* close," he added: "I generally hit every thing I can see—when I get really excited."

"And *I* hit every thing within reach," cried Tweedledum, "whether I can see it or not!"

Alice laughed. "You must hit the *trees* pretty often, I should think," she said.

Tweedledum looked round him with a satisfied smile. "I don't suppose," he said, "there'll be a tree left standing, for ever so far round, by the time we've finished!"

"And all about a rattle!" said Alice, still hoping to make them a *little* ashamed of fighting for such a trifle.

"I shouldn't have minded it so much," said Tweedledum, "if it hadn't been a new one."

"I wish the monstrous crow would come!" thought Alice.

"There's only one sword, you know," Tweedledum said to his brother: "but *you* can have the umbrella—it's quite as sharp. Only we must begin quick. It's getting as dark as it can."

"And darker," said Tweedledee.

It was getting dark so suddenly that Alice thought there must be a thunderstorm coming on. "What a thick black cloud that is!" she said. "And how fast it comes! Why, I do believe it's got wings!"

"It's the crow!" Tweedledum cried out in a shrill voice of alarm; and the two brothers took to their heels and were out of sight in a moment.

Alice ran a little way into the wood, and stopped under a large tree. "It can never get at me *here*," she thought: "it's far too large to squeeze itself in among the trees. But I wish it wouldn't flap its wings so—it makes quite a hurricane in the wood—here's somebody's shawl being blown away!"

CHAPTER V

WOOL AND WATER

She caught the shawl as she spoke, and looked about for the owner: in another moment the White Queen came running[1] wildly through the wood, with both arms stretched out wide, as if she were flying, and Alice very civilly went to meet her with the shawl.

"I'm very glad I happened to be in the way," Alice said, as she helped her to put on her shawl again.

The White Queen only looked at her in a helpless frightened sort of way, and kept repeating something in a whisper to herself that sounded like "Bread-and-butter, bread-and-butter,"[2] and Alice felt that if there was to be any conversation at all, she must manage it herself. So she began rather timidly: "Am I addressing the White Queen?"

"Well, yes, if you call that a-dressing," the Queen said. "It isn't *my* notion of the thing, at all."

Alice thought it would never do to have an argument at the very beginning of their conversation, so she smiled and said "If your Majesty will only tell me the right way to begin, I'll do it as well as I can."

"But I don't want it done at all!" groaned the poor Queen. "I've been a-dressing myself for the last two hours."

It would have been all the better, as it seemed to Alice, if she had got some one else to dress her, she was so dreadfully untidy. "Every single thing's crooked," Alice thought to herself, "and she's all over pins! ——May I put your shawl straight for you?" she added aloud.

"I don't know what's the matter with it!" the Queen said, in a melancholy voice. "It's out of temper, I think. I've pinned it here, and I've pinned it there, but there's no pleasing it!"

"It *ca'n't* go straight, you know, if you pin it all on one side," Alice said, as she gently put it right for her; "and, dear me, what a state your hair is in!"

"The brush has got entangled in it!" the Queen said with a sigh. "And I lost the comb yesterday."

Alice carefully released the brush, and did her best to get the hair into order. "Come, you look rather better now!" she said, after altering most of the pins. "But really you should have a lady's-maid!"

"I'm sure I'll take *you* with pleasure!" the Queen said. "Twopence a week, and jam every other day."

Alice couldn't help laughing, as she said "I don't want you to hire *me*—and I don't care for jam."

"It's very good jam," said the Queen.

"Well, I don't want any *to-day*, at any rate."

"You couldn't have it if you *did* want it," the Queen said. "The rule is, jam to-morrow and jam yesterday—but never jam *to-day*."[3]

"It *must* come sometimes to 'jam to-day,'" Alice objected.

"No, it ca'n't," said the Queen. "It's jam every *other* day: to-day isn't any *other* day, you know."

"I don't understand you," said Alice. "It's dreadfully confusing!"

"That's the effect of living backwards," the Queen said kindly: "it always makes one a little giddy at first——"

"Living backwards!"[4] Alice repeated in great astonishment. "I never heard of such a thing!"

"—but there's one great advantage in it, that one's memory works both ways."

"I'm sure *mine* only works one way," Alice remarked. "I ca'n't remember things before they happen."

"It's a poor sort of memory that only works backwards," the Queen remarked.

"What sort of things do *you* remember best?" Alice ventured to ask.

"Oh, things that happened the week after next," the Queen replied in a careless tone. "For instance, now," she went on, sticking a large piece of plaster on her finger as she spoke, "there's the King's Messenger. He's in prison now, being punished: and the trial doesn't even begin till next Wednesday: and of course the crime comes last of all."

"Suppose he never commits the crime?" said Alice.

"That would be all the better, wouldn't it?" the Queen said, as she bound the plaster round her finger with a bit of ribbon.

Alice felt there was no denying *that*. "Of course it would be all the better," she said: "but it wouldn't be all the better his being punished."

"You're wrong *there*, at any rate," said the Queen. "Were *you* ever punished?"

"Only for faults," said Alice.

"And you were all the better for it, I know!" the Queen said triumphantly.

"Yes, but then I *had* done the things I was punished for," said Alice: "that makes all the difference."

"But if you *hadn't* done them," the Queen said, "that would have been better still; better, and better, and better!" Her voice went higher with each "better," till it got quite to a squeak at last.

Alice was just beginning to say "There's a mistake somewhere——," when the Queen began screaming, so loud that she had to leave the sentence unfinished. "Oh, oh, oh!" shouted the Queen, shaking her hand about as if she wanted to shake it off. "My finger's bleeding! Oh, oh, oh, oh!"

Her screams were so exactly like the whistle of a steam-engine, that Alice had to hold both her hands over her ears.

"What *is* the matter?" she said, as soon as there was a chance of making herself heard. "Have you pricked your finger?"

"I haven't pricked it *yet*," the Queen said, "but I soon shall—oh, oh, oh!"

"When do you expect to do it?" Alice asked, feeling very much inclined to laugh.

"When I fasten my shawl again," the poor Queen groaned out: "the brooch will come undone directly. Oh, oh!" As she said the words the brooch flew open, and the Queen clutched wildly at it, and tried to clasp it again.

"Take care!" cried Alice. "You're holding it all crooked!" And she caught at the brooch; but it was too late: the pin had slipped, and the Queen had pricked her finger.

"That accounts for the bleeding, you see," she said to Alice with a smile. "Now you understand the way things happen here."

"But why don't you scream *now*?" Alice asked, holding her hands ready to put over her ears again.

"Why, I've done all the screaming already," said the Queen. "What would be the good of having it all over again?"

By this time it was getting light. "The crow must have flown away, I think," said Alice: "I'm so glad it's gone. I thought it was the night coming on."

"I wish *I* could manage to be glad!" the Queen said. "Only I never can remember the rule. You must be very happy, living in this wood, and being glad whenever you like!"

"Only it is so *very* lonely here!" Alice said in a melancholy voice; and, at the thought of her loneliness, two large tears came rolling down her cheeks.

"Oh, don't go on like that!" cried the poor Queen, wringing her hands in despair. "Consider what a great girl you are. Consider what a long way you've come to-day. Consider what o-clock it is. Consider anything, only don't cry!"

Alice could not help laughing at this, even in the midst of her tears. "Can *you* keep from crying by considering things?" she asked.

"That's the way it's done," the Queen said with great decision: "nobody can do two things at once, you know. Let's consider your age to begin with——how old are you?"

"I'm seven and a half, exactly."

"You needn't say 'exactually,'"[5] the Queen remarked. "I can believe it without that. Now I'll give *you* something to believe. I'm just one hundred and one, five months and a day."

"I ca'n't believe *that*!" said Alice.

"Ca'n't you?" the Queen said in a pitying tone. "Try again: draw a long breath, and shut your eyes."

Alice laughed. "There's no use trying," she said: "one *ca'n't* believe impossible things."[6]

"I daresay you haven't had much practice," said the Queen. "When I was your age, I always did it for half-an-hour a day. Why, sometimes I've believed as many as six impossible things before breakfast. There goes the shawl again!"

The brooch had come undone as she spoke, and a sudden gust of wind blew the Queen's shawl across a little brook. The Queen spread out her arms again, and went flying after it, and this time she succeeded in catching it for herself. "I've got it!" she cried in a triumphant tone. "Now you shall see me pin it on again, all by myself!"

"Then I hope your finger is better now?" Alice said very politely, as she crossed the little brook after the Queen.[7]

*　　*　　*　　*　　*

*　　*　　*　　*

*　　*　　*　　*　　*

"Oh, much better!" cried the Queen, her voice rising into a squeak as she went on. "Much be-etter! Be-e-e-etter! Be-e-ehh!" The last word ended in a long bleat, so like a sheep that Alice quite started.

She looked at the Queen, who seemed to have suddenly wrapped herself up in wool. Alice rubbed her eyes, and looked again. She couldn't make out what had happened at all. Was she in a shop? And was that really—was it really a sheep that was sitting on the other side of the counter? Rub as she would, she could make nothing more of it: she was in a little dark shop, leaning with her elbows on the counter,

and opposite to her was an old Sheep, sitting in an arm-chair, knitting, and every now and then leaving off to look at her through a great pair of spectacles.

"What is it you want to buy?" the Sheep said at last, looking up for a moment from her knitting.

"I don't *quite* know yet," Alice said very gently. "I should like to look all round me first, if I might."

"You may look in front of you, and on both sides, if you like," said the Sheep; "but you ca'n't look *all* round you—unless you've got eyes at the back of your head."

But these, as it happened, Alice had *not* got: so she contented herself with turning round, looking at the shelves as she came to them.

The shop seemed to be full of all manner of curious things[8]—but the oddest part of it all was that, whenever she looked hard at any shelf, to make out exactly what it had on it, that particular shelf was always quite empty, though the others round it were crowded as full as they could hold.

"Things flow about so here!"[9] she said at last in a plaintive tone, after she had spent a minute or so in vainly pursuing a large bright thing, that looked sometimes like a doll and sometimes like a work-box, and was always in the shelf next above the one she was looking at. "And this one is the most provoking of all—but I'll tell you what——" she added, as a sudden thought struck her. "I'll follow it up to the very top shelf of all. It'll puzzle it to go through the ceiling, I expect!"

But even this plan failed: the 'thing' went through the ceiling as quietly as possible, as if it were quite used to it.

"Are you a child or a teetotum?"[10] the Sheep said, as she took up another pair of needles. "You'll make me giddy soon, if you go on turning round like that." She was now working with fourteen pairs at once, and Alice couldn't help looking at her in great astonishment.

"How *can* she knit with so many?" the puzzled child thought to herself. "She gets more and more like a porcupine every minute!"

"Can you row?" the Sheep asked, handing her a pair of knitting-needles as she spoke.

"Yes, a little—but not on land—and not with needles——" Alice was beginning to say, when suddenly the needles turned into oars in her hands, and she found they were in a little boat, gliding along between banks: so there was nothing for it but to do her best.

"Feather!"[11] cried the Sheep, as she took up another pair of needles.

This didn't sound like a remark that needed any answer: so Alice said nothing, but pulled away. There was something very queer about the water, she thought, as every now and then the oars got fast in it, and would hardly come out again.

"Feather! Feather!" the Sheep cried again, taking more needles. "You'll be catching a crab directly."[12]

"A dear little crab!" thought Alice. "I should like that."

"Didn't you hear me say 'Feather'?" the Sheep cried angrily, taking up quite a bunch of needles.

"Indeed I did," said Alice: "you've said it very often—and very loud. Please where *are* the crabs?"

"In the water, of course!" said the Sheep, sticking some of the needles into her hair, as her hands were full. "Feather, I say!"

"*Why* do you say 'Feather' so often?" Alice asked at last, rather vexed. "I'm not a bird!"

"You are," said the Sheep: "you're a little goose."

This offended Alice a little, so there was no more conversation for a minute or two, while the boat glided gently on, sometimes among beds of weeds (which made the oars stick fast in the water, worse than ever), and sometimes under trees, but always with the same tall river-banks frowning over their heads.

"Oh please! There are some scented rushes!" Alice cried in a sudden transport of delight. "There really are—and *such* beauties!"

"You needn't say 'please' to *me* about 'em," the Sheep said, without looking up from her knitting: "I didn't put 'em there, and I'm not going to take 'em away."

"No, but I meant—please, may we wait and pick some?" Alice pleaded. "If you don't mind stopping the boat for a minute."

"How am *I* to stop it?" said the Sheep. "If you leave off rowing, it'll stop of itself."

So the boat was left to drift down the stream as it would, till it glided gently in among the waving rushes. And then the little sleeves were carefully rolled up, and the little arms were plunged in elbow-deep, to get hold of the rushes a good long way down before breaking them off—and for a while Alice forgot all about the Sheep and the knitting, as she bent over the side of the boat, with just the ends of her tangled hair dipping into the water—while with bright eager eyes she caught at one bunch after another of the darling scented rushes.[13]

"I only hope the boat won't tipple over!" she said to herself. "Oh, *what* a lovely one! Only I couldn't quite reach it." And it certainly *did* seem a little provoking ("almost as if it happened on purpose," she thought) that, though she managed to pick plenty of beautiful rushes as the boat glided by, there was always a more lovely one that she couldn't reach.

"The prettiest are always further!"[14] she said at last, with a sigh at the obstinacy of the rushes in growing so far off, as, with flushed cheeks and dripping hair and hands, she scrambled back into her place, and began to arrange her new-found treasures.

What mattered it to her just then that the rushes had begun to fade, and to lose all their scent and beauty, from the very moment that she picked them? Even real scented rushes, you know, last only a very little while—and these, being dream-rushes, melted away almost like snow, as they lay in heaps at her feet—but Alice hardly noticed this, there were so many other curious things to think about.

They hadn't gone much farther before the blade of one of the oars got fast in the water and *wouldn't* come out again (so Alice explained it afterwards), and the consequence was that the handle of it caught her under the chin, and, in spite of a series of little shrieks of "Oh, oh, oh!" from poor Alice, it swept her straight off the seat, and down among the heap of rushes.

However, she wasn't a bit hurt, and was soon up again: the Sheep went on with her knitting all the while, just as if nothing had happened. "That was a nice crab you caught!" she remarked, as Alice got back into her place, very much relieved to find herself still in the boat.

"Was it? I didn't see it," said Alice, peeping cautiously over the side of the boat into the dark water. "I wish it hadn't let go—I should so like a little crab to take home with me!" But the Sheep only laughed scornfully, and went on with her knitting.

"Are there many crabs here?" said Alice.

"Crabs, and all sorts of things," said the Sheep: "plenty of choice, only make up your mind. Now, what *do* you want to buy?"

"To buy!" Alice echoed in a tone that was half astonished and half frightened—for the oars, and the boat, and the river, had vanished all in a moment, and she was back again in the little dark shop.[15]

"I should like to buy an egg, please," she said timidly. "How do you sell them?"

"Fivepence farthing for one—twopence for two," the Sheep replied.

"Then two are cheaper than one?" Alice said in a surprised tone, taking out her purse.

"Only you *must* eat them both, if you buy two," said the Sheep.

"Then I'll have *one*, please," said Alice, as she put the money down on the counter. For she thought to herself, "They mightn't be at all nice, you know."

The Sheep took the money, and put it away in a box: then she said "I never put things into people's hands—that would never do—you must get it for yourself." And so saying, she went off to the other end of the shop, and set the egg upright on a shelf.[16]

"I wonder *why* it wouldn't do?" thought Alice, as she groped her way among the tables and chairs, for the shop was very dark towards the end. "The egg seems to get further away the more I walk towards it. Let me see, is this a chair? Why, it's got branches, I declare! How very odd to find trees growing here! And actually here's a little brook! Well, this is the very queerest shop I ever saw!"

* * * * *

* * * *

* * * * *

So she went on,[17] wondering more and more at every step, as everything turned into a tree the moment she came up to it, and she quite expected the egg to do the same.

CHAPTER VI

HUMPTY DUMPTY

However, the egg only got larger and larger, and more and more human: when she had come within a few yards of it, she saw that it had eyes and a nose and mouth; and, when she had come close to it, she saw clearly that it was HUMPTY DUMPTY himself.[1] "It ca'n't be anybody else!" she said to herself. "I'm as certain of it, as if his name were written all over his face!"

It might have been written a hundred times, easily, on that enormous face. Humpty Dumpty was sitting, with his legs crossed like a Turk, on the top of a high wall—such a narrow one that Alice quite wondered how he could keep his balance—and, as his eyes were steadily fixed in the opposite direction, and he didn't take the least notice of her, she thought he must be a stuffed figure, after all.

"And how exactly like an egg he is!" she said aloud, standing with her hands ready to catch him, for she was every moment expecting him to fall.

"It's *very* provoking," Humpty Dumpty said after a long silence, looking away from Alice as he spoke, "to be called an egg—*very*!"

"I said you *looked* like an egg, Sir," Alice gently explained. "And some eggs are very pretty, you know," she added, hoping to turn her remark into a sort of compliment.

"Some people," said Humpty Dumpty, looking away from her as usual, "have no more sense than a baby!"

Alice didn't know what to say to this: it wasn't at all like conversation, she thought, as he never said anything to *her*; in fact, his last remark was evidently addressed to a tree—so she stood and softly repeated to herself:—

"Humpty Dumpty sat on a wall:[2]
Humpty Dumpty had a great fall.
All the King's horses and all the King's men
Couldn't put Humpty Dumpty in his place again."

"That last line is much too long for the poetry," she added, almost out loud, forgetting that Humpty Dumpty would hear her.

"Don't stand chattering to yourself like that," Humpty Dumpty said, looking at her for the first time, "but tell me your name and your business."

"My *name* is Alice, but——"

"It's a stupid name enough!" Humpty Dumpty interrupted impatiently. "What does it mean?"

"*Must* a name mean something?" Alice asked doubtfully.

"Of course it must," Humpty Dumpty said with a short laugh: "*my* name means the shape I am—and a good handsome shape it is, too. With a name like yours, you might be any shape, almost."

"Why do you sit out here all alone?" said Alice, not wishing to begin an argument.

"Why, because there's nobody with me!" cried Humpty Dumpty. "Did you think I didn't know the answer to *that*? Ask another."

"Don't you think you'd be safer down on the ground?" Alice went on, not with any idea of making another riddle, but simply in her good-natured anxiety for the queer creature. "That wall is so *very* narrow!"

"What tremendously easy riddles you ask!"[3] Humpty Dumpty growled out. "Of course I don't think so! Why, if ever I *did* fall off—which there's no chance of—but *if* I did——" Here he pursed his lips, and looked so solemn and grand that Alice could hardly help laughing. "*If* I *did* fall," he went on, "*the King has promised me*—ah, you may turn pale, if you like! You didn't think I was going to say that, did you? *The King has promised me—with his very own mouth*—to—to——"

"To send all his horses and all his men," Alice interrupted, rather unwisely.

"Now I declare that's too bad!" Humpty Dumpty cried, breaking

into a sudden passion. "You've been listening at doors—and behind trees—and down chimneys—or you couldn't have known it!"

"I haven't, indeed!" Alice said very gently. "It's in a book."

"Ah, well! They may write such things in a *book*," Humpty Dumpty said in a calmer tone. "That's what you call a History of England,[4] that is. Now, take a good look at me! I'm one that has spoken to a King, *I* am: mayhap you'll never see such another: and, to show you I'm not proud, you may shake hands with me!" And he grinned almost from ear to ear, as he leant forwards (and as nearly as possible fell off the wall in doing so) and offered Alice his hand. She watched him a little anxiously as she took it. "If he smiled much more the ends of his mouth might meet behind," she thought: "and then I don't know *what* would happen to his head! I'm afraid it would come off!"

"Yes, all his horses and all his men," Humpty Dumpty went on. "They'd pick me up again in a minute, *they* would! However, this conversation is going on a little too fast: let's go back to the last remark but one."

"I'm afraid I ca'n't quite remember it," Alice said, very politely.

"In that case we start afresh," said Humpty Dumpty, "and it's my turn to choose a subject——" ("He talks about it just as if it was a game!" thought Alice.) "So here's a question for you. How old did you say you were?"

Alice made a short calculation, and said "Seven years and six months."[5]

"Wrong!" Humpty Dumpty exclaimed triumphantly. "You never said a word like it!"

"I thought you meant 'How old *are* you?'" Alice explained.

"If I'd meant that, I'd have said it," said Humpty Dumpty.

Alice didn't want to begin another argument, so she said nothing.

"Seven years and six months!" Humpty Dumpty repeated thoughtfully. "An uncomfortable sort of age. Now if you'd asked *my* advice, I'd have said 'Leave off at seven'——but it's too late now."

"I never ask advice about growing," Alice said indignantly.

"Too proud?"[6] the other enquired.

Alice felt even more indignant at this suggestion. "I mean," she said, "that one ca'n't help growing older."

"*One* ca'n't, perhaps," said Humpty Dumpty; "but *two* can.[7] With proper assistance, you might have left off at seven."

"What a beautiful belt you've got on!" Alice suddenly remarked. (They had had quite enough of the subject of age, she thought: and, if they really were to take turns in choosing subjects, it was *her* turn now.) "At least," she corrected herself on second thoughts, "a beautiful cravat, I should have said—no, a belt, I mean—I beg your pardon!" she added in dismay, for Humpty Dumpty looked thoroughly offended, and she began to wish she hadn't chosen that subject. "If only I knew," she thought to herself, "which was neck and which was waist!"

Evidently Humpty Dumpty was very angry, though he said nothing for a minute or two. When he *did* speak again, it was in a deep growl.

"It is a—*most*—*provoking*—thing," he said at last, "when a person doesn't know a cravat from a belt!"

"I know it's very ignorant of me," Alice said, in so humble a tone that Humpty Dumpty relented.

"It's a cravat, child, and a beautiful one, as you say. It's a present from the White King and Queen. There now!"

"Is it really?" said Alice, quite pleased to find that she *had* chosen a good subject, after all.

"They gave it me," Humpty Dumpty continued thoughtfully, as he crossed one knee over the other and clasped his hands round it, "they gave it me—for an un-birthday present."

"I beg your pardon?" Alice said with a puzzled air.

"I'm not offended," said Humpty Dumpty.

"I mean, what *is* an un-birthday present?"

"A present given when it isn't your birthday, of course."

Alice considered a little. "I like birthday presents best," she said at last.

"You don't know what you're talking about!" cried Humpty Dumpty. "How many days are there in a year?"

"Three hundred and sixty-five," said Alice.

"And how many birthdays have you?"

"One."

"And if you take one from three hundred and sixty-five, what remains?"

"Three hundred and sixty-four, of course."

Humpty Dumpty looked doubtful. "I'd rather see that done on paper," he said.

Alice couldn't help smiling as she took out her memorandum-book, and worked the sum for him:

$$\begin{array}{r} 365 \\ 1 \\ \hline 364 \\ \hline \end{array}$$

Humpty Dumpty took the book, and looked at it carefully. "That seems to be done right——"[8] he began.

"You're holding it upside down!" Alice interrupted.

"To be sure I was!" Humpty Dumpty said gaily, as she turned it round for him. "I thought it looked a little queer. As I was saying, that *seems* to be done right—though I haven't time to look it over thoroughly just now—and that shows that there are three hundred and sixty-four days when you might get un-birthday presents——"

"Certainly," said Alice.

"And only *one* for birthday presents, you know. There's glory for you!"

"I don't know what you mean by 'glory,'" Alice said.

Humpty Dumpty smiled contemptuously. "Of course you don't—till I tell you. I meant 'there's a nice knock-down argument for you!'"

"But 'glory' doesn't mean 'a nice knock-down argument,'" Alice objected.

"When *I* use a word," Humpty Dumpty said, in rather a scornful tone, "it means just what I choose it to mean[9] —neither more nor less."

"The question is," said Alice, "whether you *can* make words mean so many different things."

"The question is," said Humpty Dumpty, "which is to be master ——that's all."

Alice was too much puzzled to say anything; so after a minute Humpty Dumpty began again. "They've a temper, some of them—particularly verbs: they're the proudest—adjectives you can do anything with, but not verbs—however, *I* can manage the whole lot of them! Impenetrability! That's what *I* say!"

"Would you tell me, please," said Alice, "what that means?"

"Now you talk like a reasonable child," said Humpty Dumpty, looking very much pleased. "I meant by 'impenetrability' that we've had enough of that subject, and it would be just as well if you'd mention what you mean to do next, as I suppose you don't mean to stop here all the rest of your life."

"That's a great deal to make one word mean," Alice said in a thoughtful tone.

"When I make a word do a lot of work like that," said Humpty Dumpty, "I always pay it extra."

"Oh!" said Alice. She was too much puzzled to make any other remark.

"Ah, you should see 'em come round me of a Saturday night," Humpty Dumpty went on, wagging his head gravely from side to side, "for to get their wages, you know."

(Alice didn't venture to ask what he paid them with; and so you see I ca'n't tell *you*.)

"You seem very clever at explaining words, Sir," said Alice. "Would you kindly tell me the meaning of the poem called 'Jabberwocky'?"[10]

"Let's hear it," said Humpty Dumpty. "I can explain all the poems that ever were invented—and a good many that haven't been invented just yet."

This sounded very hopeful, so Alice repeated the first verse:—

"'Twas brillig, and the slithy toves
Did gyre and gimble in the wabe:
All mimsy were the borogoves,
And the mome raths outgrabe."

"That's enough to begin with," Humpty Dumpty interrupted: "there are plenty of hard words there. '*Brillig*' means four o'clock in the afternoon—the time when you begin *broiling* things for dinner."

"That'll do very well," said Alice: "and '*slithy*'?"

"Well, '*slithy*' means 'lithe and slimy.' 'Lithe' is the same as 'active.' You see it's like a portmanteau[11]—there are two meanings packed up into one word."

"I see it now," Alice remarked thoughtfully: "and what are '*toves*'?"

"Well, '*toves*' are something like badgers—they're something like lizards—and they're something like corkscrews."

"They must be very curious-looking creatures."

"They are that," said Humpty Dumpty: "also they make their nests under sun-dials—also they live on cheese."

"And what's to '*gyre*' and to '*gimble*'?"

"To '*gyre*' is to go round and round like a gyroscope. To '*gimble*' is to make holes like a gimblet."

"And '*the wabe*' is the grass-plot round a sun-dial, I suppose?" said Alice, surprised at her own ingenuity.

"Of course it is. It's called '*wabe*,' you know, because it goes a long way before it, and a long way behind it——"

"And a long way beyond it on each side," Alice added.

"Exactly so. Well then, '*mimsy*' is 'flimsy and miserable' (there's another portmanteau for you). And a '*borogove*' is a thin shabby-looking bird with its feathers sticking out all round—something like a live mop."

"And then '*mome raths*'?" said Alice. "I'm afraid I'm giving you a great deal of trouble."

"Well, a '*rath*' is a sort of green pig: but '*mome*' I'm not certain about. I think it's short for 'from home'—meaning that they'd lost their way, you know."

"And what does '*outgrabe*' mean?"

"Well, '*outgribing*' is something between bellowing and whistling, with a kind of sneeze in the middle: however, you'll hear it done, maybe—down in the wood yonder—and, when you've once heard it, you'll be *quite* content. Who's been repeating all that hard stuff to you?"

"I read it in a book," said Alice. "But I *had* some poetry repeated to me much easier than that, by—Tweedledee, I think it was."

"As to poetry, you know," said Humpty Dumpty, stretching out one of his great hands, "*I* can repeat poetry as well as other folk, if it comes to that——"

"Oh, it needn't come to that!" Alice hastily said, hoping to keep him from beginning.

"The piece I'm going to repeat," he went on without noticing her remark, "was written entirely for your amusement."

Alice felt that in that case she really *ought* to listen to it; so she sat down, and said "Thank you" rather sadly.

"In winter, when the fields are white,[12]
I sing this song for your delight——

only I don't sing it," he added, as an explanation.

"I see you don't," said Alice.

"If you can *see* whether I'm singing or not, you've sharper eyes than most," Humpty Dumpty remarked severely. Alice was silent.

"In spring, when woods are getting green,
I'll try and tell you what I mean:"

"Thank you very much," said Alice.

"In summer, when the days are long,
Perhaps you'll understand the song:

In autumn, when the leaves are brown,
Take pen and ink, and write it down."

"I will, if I can remember it so long," said Alice.

"You needn't go on making remarks like that," Humpty Dumpty said: "they're not sensible, and they put me out."

"I sent a message to the fish:
I told them 'This is what I wish.'

The little fishes of the sea,
They sent an answer back to me.

The little fishes' answer was
'We cannot do it, Sir, because——'"

"I'm afraid I don't quite understand," said Alice.

"It gets easier further on," Humpty Dumpty replied.

"I sent to them again to say
'It will be better to obey.'

The fishes answered, with a grin,
'Why, what a temper you are in!'

I told them once, I told them twice:
They would not listen to advice.

I took a kettle large and new,
Fit for the deed I had to do.

My heart went hop, my heart went thump:
I filled the kettle at the pump.

Then some one came to me and said
'The little fishes are in bed.'

I said to him, I said it plain,
'Then you must wake them up again.'

I said it very loud and clear:
I went and shouted in his ear."

Humpty Dumpty raised his voice almost to a scream as he repeated this verse, and Alice thought, with a shudder, "I wouldn't have been the messenger for *anything*!"

"But he was very stiff and proud:
He said 'You needn't shout so loud!'

And he was very proud and stiff:
He said 'I'd go and wake them, if——'

I took a corkscrew from the shelf:
I went to wake them up myself.

And when I found the door was locked,
I pulled and pushed and kicked and knocked.

And when I found the door was shut.
I tried to turn the handle, but——"[13]

There was a long pause.

"Is that all?" Alice timidly asked.

"That's all," said Humpty Dumpty. "Good-bye."

This was rather sudden, Alice thought: but, after such a *very* strong hint that she ought to be going, she felt that it would hardly be civil to stay. So she got up, and held out her hand. "Good-bye, till we meet again!" she said as cheerfully as she could.

"I shouldn't know you again if we *did* meet," Humpty Dumpty replied in a discontented tone, giving her one of his fingers to shake: "you're so exactly like other people."

"The face is what one goes by, generally," Alice remarked in a thoughtful tone.

"That's just what I complain of," said Humpty Dumpty. "Your face is the same as everybody has—the two eyes, so——" (marking their places in the air with his thumb) "nose in the middle, mouth under. It's always the same. Now if you had the two eyes on the same side of the nose, for instance—or the mouth at the top—that would be *some* help."

"It wouldn't look nice," Alice objected. But Humpty Dumpty only shut his eyes, and said "Wait till you've tried."

Alice waited a minute to see if he would speak again, but, as he never opened his eyes or took any further notice of her, she said "Good-bye!"

once more, and, getting no answer to this, she quietly walked away: but she couldn't help saying to herself, as she went, "Of all the unsatisfactory——" (she repeated this aloud, as it was a great comfort to have such a long word to say) "of all the unsatisfactory people I *ever* met——" She never finished the sentence,[14] for at this moment a heavy crash shook the forest from end to end.

CHAPTER VII

THE LION AND THE UNICORN

The next moment soldiers came running through the wood, at first in twos and threes, then ten or twenty together, and at last in such crowds that they seemed to fill the whole forest. Alice got behind a tree, for fear of being run over, and watched them go by.

She thought that in all her life she had never seen soldiers so uncertain on their feet: they were always tripping over something or other, and whenever one went down, several more always fell over him, so that the ground was soon covered with little heaps of men.

Then came the horses. Having four feet, these managed rather better than the foot-soldiers; but even *they* stumbled now and then; and it seemed to be a regular rule that, whenever a horse stumbled, the rider fell off instantly. The confusion got worse every moment, and Alice was very glad to get out of the wood into an open place, where she found the White King seated on the ground, busily writing in his memorandum-book.[1]

"I've sent them all!" the King cried in a tone of delight, on seeing Alice. "Did you happen to meet any soldiers, my dear, as you came through the wood?"

"Yes, I did," said Alice: "several thousand, I should think."

"Four thousand two hundred and seven, that's the exact number," the King said, referring to his book. "I couldn't send all the horses, you know, because two of them are wanted in the game.[2] And I haven't sent the two Messengers, either. They're both gone to the town. Just look along the road, and tell me if you can see either of them."

"I see nobody on the road," said Alice.

"I only wish *I* had such eyes," the King remarked in a fretful tone. "To be able to see Nobody! And at that distance too! Why, it's as much as *I* can do to see real people, by this light!"

All this was lost on Alice, who was still looking intently along the road, shading her eyes with one hand. "I see somebody now!" she exclaimed at last. "But he's coming very slowly—and what curious attitudes he goes into!" (For the Messenger kept skipping up and down, and wriggling like an eel, as he came along, with his great hands spread out like fans on each side.)

"Not at all," said the King. "He's an Anglo-Saxon Messenger—and those are Anglo-Saxon attitudes.[3] He only does them when he's happy. His name is Haigha."[4] (He pronounced it so as to rhyme with 'mayor.')

"I love my love with an H,"[5] Alice couldn't help beginning, "because he is Happy. I hate him with an H, because he is Hideous. I fed him with—with—with Ham-sandwiches and Hay. His name is Haigha, and he lives——"

"He lives on the Hill," the King remarked simply, without the least idea that he was joining in the game, while Alice was still hesitating for the name of a town beginning with H. "The other Messenger's called Hatta.[6] I must have *two*, you know—to come and go. One to come, and one to go."

"I beg your pardon?" said Alice.

"It isn't respectable to beg," said the King.

"I only meant that I didn't understand," said Alice. "Why one to come and one to go?"

"Don't I tell you?" the King repeated impatiently. "I must have *two*—to fetch and carry. One to fetch, and one to carry."

At this moment the Messenger arrived: he was far too much out of breath to say a word, and could only wave his hands about, and make the most fearful faces at the poor King.

"This young lady loves you with an H," the King said, introducing Alice in the hope of turning off the Messenger's attention from himself—but it was of no use—the Anglo-Saxon attitudes only got more extraordinary every moment, while the great eyes rolled wildly from side to side.

"You alarm me!" said the King. "I feel faint——Give me a ham sandwich!"

On which the Messenger, to Alice's great amusement, opened a bag that hung round his neck, and handed a sandwich to the King, who devoured it greedily.

"Another sandwich!" said the King.

"There's nothing but hay left now," the Messenger said, peeping into the bag.

"Hay, then,"[7] the King murmured in a faint whisper.

Alice was glad to see that it revived him a good deal. "There's

nothing like eating hay when you're faint," he remarked to her, as he munched away.

"I should think throwing cold water over you would be better," Alice suggested: "—or some sal-volatile."

"I didn't say there was nothing *better*," the King replied. "I said there was nothing *like* it." Which Alice did not venture to deny.

"Who did you pass on the road?" the King went on, holding out his hand to the Messenger for some more hay.

"Nobody," said the Messenger.

"Quite right," said the King: "this young lady saw him too. So of course Nobody walks slower than you."

"I do my best," the Messenger said in a sullen tone. "I'm sure nobody walks much faster than I do!"

"He ca'n't do that," said the King, "or else he'd have been here first. However, now you've got your breath, you may tell us what's happened in the town."

"I'll whisper it," said the Messenger, putting his hands to his mouth in the shape of a trumpet and stooping so as to get close to the King's ear. Alice was sorry for this, as she wanted to hear the news too. However, instead of whispering, he simply shouted, at the top of his voice, "They're at it again!"

"Do you call *that* a whisper?" cried the poor King, jumping up and shaking himself. "If you do such a thing again, I'll have you buttered! It went through and through my head like an earthquake!"

"It would have to be a very tiny earthquake!" thought Alice. "Who are at it again?" she ventured to ask.

"Why, the Lion and the Unicorn, of course," said the King.

"Fighting for the crown?"

"Yes, to be sure," said the King: "and the best of the joke is, that it's *my* crown all the while! Let's run and see them." And they trotted off, Alice repeating to herself, as she ran, the words of the old song:[8]—

"The Lion and the Unicorn were fighting for the crown:
The Lion beat the Unicorn all round the town.
Some gave them white bread, some gave them brown:
Some gave them plum-cake and drummed them out of town."

"Does——the one——that wins——get the crown?" she asked, as well as she could, for the run was putting her quite out of breath.

"Dear me, no!" said the King. "What an idea!"

'Would you—be good enough——" Alice panted out, after running a little further, "to stop a minute—just to get—one's breath again?"

"I'm *good* enough," the King said, "only I'm not *strong* enough. You see, a minute goes by so fearfully quick. You might as well try to stop a Bandersnatch!"[9]

Alice had no more breath for talking; so they trotted on in silence, till they came into sight of a great crowd, in the middle of which the Lion and Unicorn were fighting. They were in such a cloud of dust, that at first Alice could not make out which was which; but she soon managed to distinguish the Unicorn by his horn.

They placed themselves close to where Hatta, the other Messenger, was standing watching the fight, with a cup of tea in one hand and a piece of bread-and-butter in the other.

"He's only just out of prison, and he hadn't finished his tea when he was sent in," Haigha whispered to Alice: "and they only give them oyster-shells[10] in there—so you see he's very hungry and thirsty. How are you, dear child?" he went on, putting his arm affectionately round Hatta's neck.

Hatta looked round and nodded, and went on with his bread-and-butter.

"Were you happy in prison, dear child?" said Haigha.

Hatta looked round once more, and this time a tear or two trickled down his cheek; but not a word would he say.

"Speak, ca'n't you!" Haigha cried impatiently. But Hatta only munched away, and drank some more tea.

"Speak, wo'n't you!" cried the King. "How are they getting on with the fight?"

Hatta made a desperate effort, and swallowed a large piece of bread-and-butter. "They're getting on very well," he said in a choking voice: "each of them has been down about eighty-seven times."

"Then I suppose they'll soon bring the white bread and the brown?" Alice ventured to remark.

"It's waiting for 'em now," said Hatta; "this is a bit of it as I'm eating."

There was a pause in the fight just then, and the Lion and the Unicorn sat down, panting, while the King called out "Ten minutes allowed for refreshments!" Haigha and Hatta set to work at once, carrying round trays of white and brown bread. Alice took a piece to taste, but it was *very* dry.

"I don't think they'll fight any more to-day," the King said to Hatta: "go and order the drums to begin." And Hatta went bounding away like a grasshopper.

For a minute or two Alice stood silent, watching him. Suddenly she brightened up. "Look, look!" she cried, pointing eagerly. "There's the White Queen running across the country! She came flying out of the wood over yonder——How fast those Queens *can* run!"[11]

"There's some enemy after her, no doubt," the King said, without even looking round. "That wood's full of them."

"But aren't you going to run and help her?" Alice asked, very much surprised at his taking it so quietly.

"No use, no use!" said the King. "She runs so fearfully quick. You might as well try to catch a Bandersnatch! But I'll make a memorandum about her, if you like——She's a dear good creature," he repeated softly to himself, as he opened his memorandum-book. "Do you spell 'creature' with a double 'e'?"

At this moment the Unicorn sauntered by them, with his hands in his pockets. "I had the best of it this time?" he said to the King, just glancing at him as he passed.

"A little—a little," the King replied, rather nervously. "You shouldn't have run him through with your horn, you know."

"It didn't hurt him," the Unicorn said carelessly, and he was going on, when his eye happened to fall upon Alice: he turned round instantly, and stood for some time looking at her with an air of the deepest disgust.

"What—is—this?" he said at last.

"This is a child!" Haigha replied eagerly, coming in front of Alice to introduce her, and spreading out both his hands towards her in an Anglo-Saxon attitude. "We only found it to-day. It's as large as life, and twice as natural!"[12]

"I always thought they were fabulous monsters!"[13] said the Unicorn. "Is it alive?"

"It can talk," said Haigha solemnly.

The Unicorn looked dreamily at Alice, and said "Talk, child."

Alice could not help her lips curling up into a smile as she began: "Do you know, I always thought Unicorns were fabulous monsters, too? I never saw one alive before!"

"Well, now that we *have* seen each other," said the Unicorn, "if you'll believe in me, I'll believe in you. Is that a bargain?"

"Yes, if you like," said Alice.

"Come, fetch out the plum-cake, old man!" the Unicorn went on, turning from her to the King. "None of your brown bread for me!"

"Certainly—certainly!" the King muttered, and beckoned to Haigha. "Open the bag!" he whispered. "Quick! Not that one—that's full of hay!"

Haigha took a large cake out of the bag, and gave it to Alice to hold, while he got out a dish and carving-knife. How they all came out of it Alice couldn't guess. It was just like a conjuring-trick, she thought.

The Lion had joined them[14] while this was going on: he looked very tired and sleepy, and his eyes were half shut. "What's this!" he said, blinking lazily at Alice, and speaking in a deep hollow tone that sounded like the tolling of a great bell.

"Ah, what *is* it, now?" the Unicorn cried eagerly. "You'll never guess! *I* couldn't."

The Lion looked at Alice wearily. "Are you animal—or vegetable—or mineral?" he said, yawning at every other word.

"It's a fabulous monster!" the Unicorn cried out, before Alice could reply.

"Then hand round the plum-cake, Monster," the Lion said, lying down and putting his chin on his paws. "And sit down, both of you," (to the King and the Unicorn): "fair play with the cake, you know!"

The King was evidently very uncomfortable at having to sit down between the two great creatures; but there was no other place for him.

"What a fight we might have for the crown, *now*!" the Unicorn said, looking slyly up at the crown, which the poor King was nearly shaking off his head, he trembled so much.

"I should win easy," said the Lion.

"I'm not so sure of that," said the Unicorn.

"Why, I beat you all round the town, you chicken!" the Lion replied angrily, half getting up as he spoke.

Here the King interrupted, to prevent the quarrel going on: he was very nervous, and his voice quite quivered. "All round the town?" he said. "That's a good long way. Did you go by the old bridge, or the market-place? You get the best view by the old bridge."

"I'm sure I don't know," the Lion growled out as he lay down again. "There was too much dust to see anything. What a time the Monster is, cutting up that cake!"

Alice had seated herself on the bank of a little brook, with the great dish on her knees, and was sawing away diligently with the knife. "It's very provoking!" she said, in reply to the Lion (she was getting quite used to being called 'the Monster'). "I've cut several slices already, but they always join on again!"

"You don't know how to manage Looking-glass cakes," the Unicorn remarked. "Hand it round first, and cut it afterwards."

This sounded nonsense, but Alice very obediently got up, and carried the dish round, and the cake divided itself into three pieces as she did so. "*Now* cut it up," said the Lion, as she returned to her place with the empty dish.

"I say, this isn't fair!" cried the Unicorn, as Alice sat with the knife in her hand, very much puzzled how to begin. "The Monster has given the Lion twice as much as me!"[15]

"She's kept none for herself, anyhow," said the Lion. "Do you like plum-cake, Monster?"

But before Alice could answer him, the drums began.

Where the noise came from, she couldn't make out: the air seemed full of it, and it rang through and through her head till she felt quite deafened. She started to her feet and sprang across the little brook in her terror,[16]

* * * * * *

* * * * *

* * * * * *

and had just time to see the Lion and the Unicorn rise to their feet, with angry looks at being interrupted in their feast, before she dropped to her knees, and put her hands over her ears, vainly trying to shut out the dreadful uproar.

"If *that* doesn't 'drum them out of town,'" she thought to herself, "nothing ever will!"

CHAPTER VIII

"IT'S MY OWN INVENTION"

After a while the noise seemed gradually to die away, till all was dead silence, and Alice lifted up her head in some alarm. There was no one to be seen, and her first thought was that she must have been dreaming about the Lion and the Unicorn and those queer Anglo-Saxon Messengers. However, there was the great dish still lying at her feet, on which she had tried to cut the plum-cake, "So I wasn't dreaming, after all," she said to herself, "unless—unless we're all part of the same dream. Only I do hope it's *my* dream, and not the Red King's![1] I don't like belonging to another person's dream," she went on in a rather complaining tone: "I've a great mind to go and wake him, and see what happens!"

At this moment her thoughts were interrupted by a loud shouting of "Ahoy! Ahoy! Check!" and a Knight, dressed in crimson armour, came galloping[2] down upon her, brandishing a great club. Just as he reached her, the horse stopped suddenly: "You're my prisoner!" the Knight cried, as he tumbled off his horse.

Startled as she was, Alice was more frightened for him than for herself at the moment, and watched him with some anxiety as he mounted again. As soon as he was comfortably in the saddle, he began once more "You're my——" but here another voice broke in "Ahoy! Ahoy! Check!" and Alice looked round in some surprise for the new enemy.

This time it was a White Knight.[3] He drew up at Alice's side, and tumbled off his horse just as the Red Knight had done: then he got on again, and the two Knights sat and looked at each other for some time without speaking. Alice looked from one to the other in some bewilderment.

"She's *my* prisoner, you know!" the Red Knight said at last.

"Yes, but then *I* came and rescued her!" the White Knight replied.

"Well, we must fight for her, then," said the Red Knight, as he took up his helmet (which hung from the saddle, and was something the shape of a horse's head) and put it on.

"You will observe the Rules of Battle, of course?" the White Knight remarked, putting on his helmet too.

"I always do," said the Red Knight, and they began banging away at each other with such fury that Alice got behind a tree to be out of the way of the blows.

"I wonder, now, what the Rules of Battle are," she said to herself, as she watched the fight, timidly peeping out from her hiding-place. "One Rule seems to be, that if one Knight hits the other, he knocks him off his horse; and, if he misses, he tumbles off himself—and another Rule seems to be that they hold their clubs with their arms, as if

they were Punch and Judy——What a noise they make when they tumble! Just like a whole set of fire-irons falling into the fender! And how quiet the horses are! They let them get on and off them just as if they were tables!"

Another Rule of Battle, that Alice had not noticed, seemed to be that they always fell on their heads; and the battle ended with their both falling off in this way, side by side. When they got up again, they shook hands, and then the Red Knight mounted and galloped off.

"It was a glorious victory, wasn't it?"[4] said the White Knight, as he came up panting.

"I don't know," Alice said doubtfully. "I don't want to be anybody's prisoner. I want to be a Queen."

"So you will, when you've crossed the next brook,"[5] said the White Knight. "I'll see you safe to the end of the wood—and then I must go back, you know. That's the end of my move."

"Thank you very much," said Alice. "May I help you off with your helmet?" It was evidently more than he could manage by himself: however she managed to shake him out of it at last.

"Now one can breathe more easily," said the Knight, putting back his shaggy hair with both hands, and turning his gentle face and large mild eyes to Alice. She thought she had never seen such a strange-looking soldier in all her life.

He was dressed in tin armour, which seemed to fit him very badly, and he had a queer-shaped little deal box fastened across his shoulders, upside-down, and with the lid hanging open. Alice looked at it with great curiosity.

"I see you're admiring my little box," the Knight said in a friendly tone. "It's my own invention[6]—to keep clothes and sandwiches in. You see I carry it upside-down, so that the rain ca'n't get in."

"But the things can get *out*," Alice gently remarked. "Do you know the lid's open?"

"I didn't know it," the Knight said, a shade of vexation passing over his face. "Then all the things must have fallen out! And the box is no use without them." He unfastened it as he spoke, and was just going to throw it into the bushes, when a sudden thought seemed to strike him, and he hung it carefully on a tree. "Can you guess why I did that?" he said to Alice.

Alice shook her head.

"In hopes some bees may make a nest in it—then I should get the honey."

"But you've got a bee-hive—or something like one—fastened to the saddle," said Alice.

"Yes, it's a very good bee-hive," the Knight said in a discontented tone, "one of the best kind. But not a single bee has come near it yet. And the other thing is a mouse-trap. I suppose the mice keep the bees out—or the bees keep the mice out, I don't know which."

"I was wondering what the mouse-trap was for," said Alice. "It isn't very likely there would be any mice on the horse's back."

"Not very likely, perhaps," said the Knight; "but, if they *do* come, I don't choose to have them running all about."

"You see," he went on after a pause, "it's as well to be provided for *everything*. That's the reason the horse has all those anklets round his feet."

"But what are they for?" Alice asked in a tone of great curiosity.

"To guard against the bites of sharks," the Knight replied. "It's an invention of my own. And now help me on. I'll go with you to the end of the wood——What's that dish for?"

"It's meant for plum-cake," said Alice.

"We'd better take it with us," the Knight said. "It'll come in handy if we find any plum-cake. Help me to get it into this bag."

This took a long time to manage, though Alice held the bag open very carefully, because the Knight was so *very* awkward in putting in the dish: the first two or three times that he tried he fell in himself instead. "It's rather a tight fit, you see," he said, as they got it in at last; "there are so many candlesticks in the bag." And he hung it to the saddle, which was already loaded with bunches of carrots, and fire-irons, and many other things.

"I hope you've got your hair well fastened on?" he continued, as they set off.

"Only in the usual way," Alice said, smiling.

"That's hardly enough," he said, anxiously. "You see the wind is so *very* strong here. It's as strong as soup."

"Have you invented a plan for keeping the hair from being blown off?" Alice enquired.

"Not yet," said the Knight. "But I've got a plan for keeping it from *falling* off."

"I should like to hear it, very much."

"First you take an upright stick," said the Knight. "Then you make your hair creep up it, like a fruit-tree. Now the reason hair falls off is because it hangs *down*—things never fall *upwards*, you know. It's a plan of my own invention. You may try it if you like."

It didn't sound a comfortable plan, Alice thought, and for a few minutes she walked on in silence, puzzling over the idea, and every now and then stopping to help the poor Knight, who certainly was *not* a good rider.

Whenever the horse stopped (which it did very often), he fell off in front; and, whenever it went on again (which it generally did rather

suddenly), he fell off behind. Otherwise he kept on pretty well, except that he had a habit of now and then falling off sideways; and, as he generally did this on the side on which Alice was walking, she soon found that it was the best plan not to walk *quite* close to the horse.

"I'm afraid you've not had much practice in riding,"[7] she ventured to say, as she was helping him up from his fifth tumble.

The Knight looked very much surprised, and a little offended at the remark. "What makes you say that?" he asked, as he scrambled back into the saddle, keeping hold of Alice's hair with one hand, to save himself from falling over on the other side.

"Because people don't fall off quite so often, when they've had much practice."

"I've had plenty of practice," the Knight said very gravely: "plenty of practice!"

Alice could think of nothing better to say than "Indeed?" but she said it as heartily as she could. They went on a little way in silence after this, the Knight with his eyes shut, muttering to himself, and Alice watching anxiously for the next tumble.

"The great art of riding," the Knight suddenly began in a loud voice, waving his right arm as he spoke, "is to keep——" Here the sentence ended as suddenly as it had begun, as the Knight fell heavily on the top of his head exactly in the path where Alice was walking. She was quite frightened this time, and said in an anxious tone, as she picked him up, "I hope no bones are broken?"

"None to speak of," the Knight said, as if he didn't mind breaking two or three of them. "The great art of riding, as I was saying, is—to keep your balance properly. Like this, you know——"

He let go the bridle, and stretched out both his arms to show Alice what he meant, and this time he fell flat on his back, right under the horse's feet.

"Plenty of practice!" he went on repeating, all the time that Alice was getting him on his feet again. "Plenty of practice!"

"It's too ridiculous!" cried Alice, losing all her patience this time. "You ought to have a wooden horse on wheels, that you ought!"

"Does that kind go smoothly?" the Knight asked in a tone of great interest, clasping his arms round the horse's neck as he spoke, just in time to save himself from tumbling off again.

"Much more smoothly than a live horse," Alice said, with a little scream of laughter, in spite of all she could do to prevent it.

"I'll get one," the Knight said thoughtfully to himself. "One or two—several."

There was a short silence after this, and then the Knight went on again. "I'm a great hand at inventing things. Now, I daresay you noticed, the last time you picked me up, that I was looking rather thoughtful?"

"You *were* a little grave," said Alice.

"Well, just then I was inventing a new way of getting over a gate—would you like to hear it?"

"Very much indeed," Alice said politely.

"I'll tell you how I came to think of it," said the Knight. "You see, I said to myself 'The only difficulty is with the feet: the *head* is high enough already.' Now, first I put my head on the top of the gate—then the head's high enough—then I stand on my head—then the feet are high enough, you see—then I'm over, you see."

"Yes, I suppose you'd be over when that was done," Alice said thoughtfully: "but don't you think it would be rather hard?"

"I haven't tried it yet," the Knight said, gravely; "so I ca'n't tell for certain—but I'm afraid it *would* be a little hard."

He looked so vexed at the idea, that Alice changed the subject hastily. "What a curious helmet you've got!" she said cheerfully. "Is that your invention too?"

The Knight looked down proudly at his helmet, which hung from the saddle. "Yes," he said; "but I've invented a better one than that—like a sugar-loaf.[8] When I used to wear it, if I fell off the horse, it always touched the ground directly. So I had a *very* little way to fall, you see—But there *was* the danger of falling *into* it, to be sure. That happened to me once—and the worst of it was, before I could get out again, the other White Knight came and put it on. He thought it was his own helmet."

The Knight looked so solemn about it that Alice did not dare to laugh. "I'm afraid you must have hurt him," she said in a trembling voice, "being on the top of his head."

"I had to kick him, of course," the Knight said, very seriously. "And then he took the helmet off again—but it took hours and hours to get me out. I was as fast as—as lightning, you know."

"But that's a different kind of fastness," Alice objected.

The Knight shook his head. "It was all kinds of fastness with me, I can assure you!" he said. He raised his hands in some excitement as he said this, and instantly rolled out of the saddle, and fell headlong into a deep ditch.

Alice ran to the side of the ditch to look for him. She was rather startled by the fall, as for some time he had kept on very well, and she was afraid that he really *was* hurt this time. However, though she could see nothing but the soles of his feet, she was much relieved to hear that he was talking on in his usual tone. "All kinds of fastness," he repeated: "but it was careless of him to put another man's helmet on—with the man in it, too."

"How *can* you go on talking so quietly, head downwards?" Alice asked, as she dragged him out by the feet, and laid him in a heap on the bank.

The Knight looked surprised at the question. "What does it matter where my body happens to be?" he said. "My mind goes on working all the same. In fact, the more head-downwards I am, the more I keep inventing new things."

"Now the cleverest thing of the sort that I ever did," he went on after a pause, "was inventing a new pudding during the meat-course."

"In time to have it cooked for the next course?" said Alice. "Well, that *was* quick work, certainly!"

"Well, not the *next* course," the Knight said in a slow thoughtful tone: "no, certainly not the next *course*."

"Then it would have to be the next day. I suppose you wouldn't have two pudding-courses in one dinner?"

"Well, not the *next* day," the Knight repeated as before: "not the next *day*. In fact," he went on, holding his head down, and his voice getting lower and lower, "I don't believe that pudding ever *was* cooked! In fact, I don't believe that pudding ever *will* be cooked! And yet it was a very clever pudding to invent."

"What did you mean it to be made of?" Alice asked, hoping to cheer him up, for the poor Knight seemed quite low-spirited about it.

"It began with blotting-paper," the Knight answered with a groan.

"That wouldn't be very nice, I'm afraid——"

"Not very nice *alone*," he interrupted, quite eagerly: "but you've no idea what a difference it makes, mixing it with other things—such as gunpowder and sealing-wax. And here I must leave you." They had just come to the end of the wood.

Alice could only look puzzled: she was thinking of the pudding.

"You are sad," the Knight said in an anxious tone: "let me sing you a song to comfort you."

"Is it very long?" Alice asked, for she had heard a good deal of poetry that day.

"It's long," said the Knight, "but it's very, *very* beautiful. Everybody that hears me sing it—either it brings the *tears* into their eyes, or else——"

"Or else what?" said Alice, for the Knight had made a sudden pause.

"Or else it doesn't, you know. The name of the song is called '*Haddocks' Eyes*.'"[9]

"Oh, that's the name of the song, is it?" Alice said, trying to feel interested.

"No, you don't understand," the Knight said, looking a little vexed. "That's what the name is *called*. The name really *is 'The Aged Aged Man.'*"

"Then I ought to have said 'That's what the *song* is called'?" Alice corrected herself.

"No, you oughtn't: that's quite another thing! The *song* is called '*Ways And Means*': but that's only what it's *called*, you know!"

"Well, what *is* the song, then?" said Alice, who was by this time completely bewildered.

"I was coming to that," the Knight said. "The song really *is 'A-sitting On A Gate'*: and the tune's my own invention."

So saying, he stopped his horse and let the reins fall on its neck: then, slowly beating time with one hand, and with a faint smile lighting up his gentle foolish face, as if he enjoyed the music of his song, he began.

Of all the strange things that Alice saw in her journey Through The Looking-Glass, this was the one that she always remembered most clearly.[10] Years afterwards she could bring the whole scene back again, as if it had been only yesterday—the mild blue eyes and kindly smile of the Knight—the setting sun gleaming through his hair, and shining on his armour in a blaze of light that quite dazzled her—the horse quietly moving about, with the reins hanging loose on his neck, cropping the grass at her feet—and the black shadows of the forest behind—all this she took in like a picture, as, with one hand shading her eyes, she leant against a tree, watching the strange pair, and listening, in a half-dream, to the melancholy music of the song.

"But the tune *isn't* his own invention," she said to herself: "it's '*I give thee all, I can no more*.'"[11] She stood and listened very attentively, but no tears came into her eyes.

"I'll tell thee everything I can:[12]
There's little to relate.
I saw an aged aged man,
A-sitting on a gate.

'Who are you, aged man?' I said.
'And how is it you live?'
And his answer trickled through my head,
Like water through a sieve.

He said 'I look for butterflies
That sleep among the wheat:
I make them into mutton-pies,
And sell them in the street.
I sell them unto men,' he said,
'Who sail on stormy seas;
And that's the way I get my bread—
A trifle, if you please.'

But I was thinking of a plan
To dye one's whiskers green,
And always use so large a fan
That they could not be seen.
So, having no reply to give
To what the old man said,
I cried, 'Come, tell me how you live!'
And thumped him on the head.

His accents mild took up the tale:
He said 'I go my ways,
And when I find a mountain-rill,
I set it in a blaze;
And thence they make a stuff they call
Rowland's Macassar-Oil[13]*—*
Yet twopence-halfpenny is all
They give me for my toil.'

But I was thinking of a way
To feed oneself on batter,
And so go on from day to day
Getting a little fatter

I shook him well from side to side,
Until his face was blue:
'Come, tell me how you live,' I cried,
'And what it is you do!'

He said 'I hunt for haddocks' eyes
Among the heather bright,
And work them into waistcoat-buttons
In the silent night.
And these I do not sell for gold
Or coin of silvery shine,
But for a copper halfpenny,
And that will purchase nine.

'I sometimes dig for buttered rolls,
Or set limed twigs for crabs:
I sometimes search the grassy knolls
For wheels of Hansom-cabs

And that's the way' (he gave a wink)
'By which I get my wealth—
And very gladly will I drink
Your Honour's noble health.'

I heard him then, for I had just
Completed my design
To keep the Menai bridge[14] *from rust*
By boiling it in wine.
I thanked him much for telling me
The way he got his wealth,
But chiefly for his wish that he
Might drink my noble health.

And now, if e'er by chance I put
My fingers into glue,
Or madly squeeze a right-hand foot
Into a left-hand shoe,
Or if I drop upon my toe
A very heavy weight,
I weep, for it reminds me so[15]
Of that old man I used to know—
Whose look was mild, whose speech was slow,
Whose hair was whiter than the snow,
Whose face was very like a crow,
With eyes, like cinders, all aglow,
Who seemed distracted with his woe,
Who rocked his body to and fro,
And muttered mumblingly and low,
As if his mouth were full of dough,
Who snorted like a buffalo——
That summer evening long ago,
A-sitting on a gate."

As the Knight sang the last words of the ballad, he gathered up the reins, and turned his horse's head along the road by which they had come. "You've only a few yards to go," he said, "down the hill and over that little brook, and then you'll be a Queen——But you'll stay and see me off first?" he added as Alice turned with an eager look in the direction to which he pointed. "I sha'n't be long. You'll wait and wave your handkerchief when I get to that turn in the road! I think it'll encourage me, you see."

"Of course I'll wait," said Alice: "and thank you very much for coming so far—and for the song—I liked it very much."

"I hope so," the Knight said doubtfully: "but you didn't cry so much as I thought you would."

So they shook hands, and then the Knight rode slowly away into the forest. "It wo'n't take long to see him *off*, I expect," Alice said to herself, as she stood watching him. "There he goes! Right on his head as usual! However, he gets on again pretty easily—that comes of having so many things hung round the horse——" So she went on talking to herself, as she watched the horse walking leisurely along the road, and the Knight tumbling off, first on one side and then on the other. After the fourth or fifth tumble he reached the turn, and then she waved her handkerchief to him, and waited till he was out of sight.[16]

"I hope it encouraged him," she said, as she turned to run down the hill: "and now for the last brook, and to be a Queen! How grand it sounds!" A very few steps brought her to the edge of the brook.[17] "The Eighth Square at last!"[18] she cried as she bounded across,

*   *   *   *   *   *

*   *   *   *   *

*   *   *   *   *   *

and threw herself down to rest on a lawn as soft as moss, with little flower-beds dotted about it here and there. "Oh, how glad I am to get here! And what *is* this on my head?" she exclaimed in a tone of dismay, as she put her hands up to something very heavy, that fitted tight all round her head.

"But how *can* it have got there without my knowing it?" she said to herself, as she lifted it off, and set it on her lap to make out what it could possibly be.

It was a golden crown.

CHAPTER IX

QUEEN ALICE

"Well, this *is* grand!" said Alice. "I never expected I should be a Queen so soon—and I'll tell you what it is, your Majesty," she went on, in a severe tone (she was always rather fond of scolding herself), "it'll never do for you to be lolling about on the grass like that! Queens have to be dignified, you know!"[1]

So she got up and walked about—rather stiffly just at first, as she was afraid that the crown might come off: but she comforted herself with the thought that there was nobody to see her, "and if I really am a Queen," she said as she sat down again, "I shall be able to manage it quite well in time."

Everything was happening so oddly that she didn't feel a bit surprised at finding the Red Queen and the White Queen sitting close to her, one on each side:[2] she would have liked very much to ask them how they came there, but she feared it would not be quite civil. However, there would be no harm, she thought, in asking if the game was over. "Please, would you tell me——" she began, looking timidly at the Red Queen.

"Speak when you're spoken to!" the Queen sharply interrupted her.

"But if everybody obeyed that rule," said Alice, who was always ready for a little argument, "and if you only spoke when you were spoken to, and the other person always waited for *you* to begin, you see nobody would ever say anything, so that——"

"Ridiculous!" cried the Queen. "Why, don't you see, child——" here she broke off with a frown, and, after thinking for a minute, suddenly changed the subject of the conversation. "What do you mean by 'If you really are a Queen'? What right have you to call yourself so? You ca'n't be a Queen, you know, till you've passed the proper examination.[3] And the sooner we begin it, the better."

"I only said 'if'!" poor Alice pleaded in a piteous tone.

The two Queens looked at each other, and the Red Queen remarked, with a little shudder, "She *says* she only said 'if'——"

"But she said a great deal more than that!" the White Queen moaned, wringing her hands. "Oh, ever so much more than that!"

"So you did, you know," the Red Queen said to Alice. "Always speak the truth—think before you speak—and write it down afterwards."

"I'm sure I didn't mean——" Alice was beginning, but the Red Queen interrupted her impatiently.

"That's just what I complain of! You *should* have meant! What do you suppose is the use of a child without any meaning? Even a joke should have some meaning—and a child's more important than a joke, I hope. You couldn't deny that, even if you tried with both hands."

"I don't deny things with my *hands*," Alice objected.

"Nobody said you did," said the Red Queen. "I said you couldn't if you tried."

"She's in that state of mind," said the White Queen, "that she wants to deny *something*—only she doesn't know what to deny!"

"A nasty, vicious temper," the Red Queen remarked; and then there was an uncomfortable silence for a minute or two.

The Red Queen broke the silence by saying, to the White Queen, "I invite you to Alice's dinner-party this afternoon."

The White Queen smiled feebly, and said "And I invite *you*."

"I didn't know I was to have a party at all," said Alice; "but, if there *is* to be one, I think *I* ought to invite the guests."

"We gave you the opportunity of doing it," the Red Queen remarked: "but I daresay you've not had many lessons in manners yet?"

"Manners are not taught in lessons," said Alice. "Lessons teach you to do sums, and things of that sort."

"Can you do Addition?" the White Queen asked. "What's one and one and one and one and one and one and one and one and one and one?"

"I don't know," said Alice. "I lost count."

"She ca'n't do Addition," the Red Queen interrupted. "Can you do Subtraction? Take nine from eight."

"Nine from eight I ca'n't, you know," Alice replied very readily: "but——"

"She ca'n't do Substraction," said the White Queen. "Can you do Division? Divide a loaf by a knife—what's the answer to *that*?"

"I suppose——" Alice was beginning, but the Red Queen answered for her. "Bread-and-butter, of course. Try another Subtraction sum. Take a bone from a dog: what remains?"

Alice considered. "The bone wouldn't remain, of course, if I took it—and the dog wouldn't remain: it would come to bite me—and I'm sure *I* shouldn't remain!"

"Then you think nothing would remain?" said the Red Queen.

"I think that's the answer."

"Wrong, as usual," said the Red Queen: "the dog's temper would remain."

"But I don't see how——"

"Why, look here!" the Red Queen cried. "The dog would lose its temper, wouldn't it?"

"Perhaps it would," Alice replied cautiously.

"Then if the dog went away, its temper would remain!" the Queen exclaimed triumphantly.

Alice said, as gravely as she could, "They might go different ways." But she couldn't help thinking to herself "What dreadful nonsense we *are* talking!"

"She can't do sums a *bit*!" the Queens said together, with great emphasis.

"Can *you* do sums?" Alice said, turning suddenly on the White Queen, for she didn't like being found fault with so much.

The Queen gasped and shut her eyes. "I can do Addition," she said, "if you give me time—but I ca'n't do Substraction under *any* circumstances!"

"Of course you know your ABC?" said the Red Queen.

"To be sure I do," said Alice.

"So do I," the White Queen whispered: "we'll often say it over together, dear. And I'll tell you a secret—I can read words of one letter! Isn't *that* grand? However, don't be discouraged. You'll come to it in time."

Here the Red Queen began again. "Can you answer useful questions?" she said. "How is bread made?"

"I know *that*!" Alice cried eagerly. "You take some flour——"

"Where do you pick the flower?" the White Queen asked. "In a garden or in the hedges?"

"Well, it isn't *picked* at all," Alice explained: "it's *ground*——"

"How many acres of ground?" said the White Queen. "You mustn't leave out so many things."

"Fan her head!" the Red Queen anxiously interrupted. "She'll be feverish after so much thinking." So they set to work and fanned her with bunches of leaves, till she had to beg them to leave off, it blew her hair about so.

"She's all right again now," said the Red Queen. "Do you know Languages? What's the French for fiddle-de-dee?"

"Fiddle-de-dee's not English,"[4] Alice replied gravely.

"Who ever said it was?" said the Red Queen.

Alice thought she saw a way out of the difficulty, this time. "If you'll tell me what language 'fiddle-de-dee' is, I'll tell you the French for it!" she exclaimed triumphantly.

But the Red Queen drew herself up rather stiffly, and said "Queens never make bargains."

"I wish Queens never asked questions," Alice thought to herself.

"Don't let us quarrel," the White Queen said in an anxious tone. "What is the cause of lightning?"

"The cause of lightning," Alice said very decidedly, for she felt quite certain about this, "is the thunder—no, no!" she hastily corrected herself. "I meant the other way."

"It's too late to correct it," said the Red Queen: "when you've once said a thing, that fixes it, and you must take the consequences."

"Which reminds me——" the White Queen said, looking down and nervously clasping and unclasping her hands, "we had *such* a thunderstorm last Tuesday—I mean one of the last set of Tuesdays, you know."

Alice was puzzled. "In *our* country," she remarked, "there's only one day at a time."

The Red Queen said "That's a poor thin way of doing things. Now *here*, we mostly have days and nights two or three at a time, and sometimes in the winter we take as many as five nights together—for warmth, you know."

"Are five nights warmer than one night, then?" Alice ventured to ask.

"Five times as warm, of course."

"But they should be five times as *cold*, by the same rule——"

"Just so!" cried the Red Queen. "Five times as warm, *and* five times as cold—just as I'm five times as rich as you are, *and* five times as clever!"

Alice sighed and gave it up. "It's exactly like a riddle with no answer!" she thought.

"Humpty Dumpty saw it too," the White Queen went on in a low voice, more as if she were talking to herself. "He came to the door with a corkscrew in his hand——"

"What did he want?" said the Red Queen.

"He said he *would* come in," the White Queen went on, "because he was looking for a hippopotamus. Now, as it happened, there wasn't such a thing in the house, that morning."

"Is there generally?" Alice asked in an astonished tone.

"Well, only on Thursdays," said the Queen.

"I know what he came for,"[5] said Alice: "he wanted to punish the fish, because——"

Here the White Queen began again. "It was *such* a thunderstorm, you ca'n't think!" ("She *never* could, you know," said the Red Queen.) "And part of the roof came off, and ever so much thunder got in—and it went rolling round the room in great lumps—and knocking over the tables and things—till I was so frightened, I couldn't remember my own name!"

Alice thought to herself "I never should *try* to remember my name in the middle of an accident! Where would be the use of it?" but she did not say this aloud, for fear of hurting the poor Queen's feelings.

"Your Majesty must excuse her," the Red Queen said to Alice, taking one of the White Queen's hands in her own, and gently stroking it: "she means well, but she ca'n't help saying foolish things, as a general rule."

The White Queen looked timidly at Alice, who felt she *ought* to say something kind, but really couldn't think of anything at the moment.

"She never was really well brought up," the Red Queen went on: "but it's amazing how good-tempered she is! Pat her on the head, and see how pleased she'll be!" But this was more than Alice had courage to do.

"A little kindness—and putting her hair in papers—would do wonders with her——"

The White Queen gave a deep sigh, and laid her head on Alice's shoulder. "I *am* so sleepy!" she moaned.

"She's tired, poor thing!" said the Red Queen. "Smoothe her hair—lend her your nightcap—and sing her a soothing lullaby."

"I haven't got a nightcap with me," said Alice, as she tried to obey the first direction: "and I don't know any soothing lullabies."

"I must do it myself, then," said the Red Queen, and she began:—

"Hush-a-by lady,[6] *in Alice's lap!*
Till the feast's ready, we've time for a nap.
When the feast's over, we'll go to the ball—
Red Queen, and White Queen, and Alice, and all!

"And now you know the words," she added, as she put her head down on Alice's other shoulder, "just sing it through to *me*. I'm getting sleepy, too." In another moment both Queens were fast asleep, and snoring loud.

"What *am* I to do?" exclaimed Alice, looking about in great perplexity, as first one round head, and then the other, rolled down from her shoulder, and lay like a heavy lump in her lap. "I don't think it *ever* happened before, that any one had to take care of two Queens asleep at once! No, not in all the History of England[7] —it couldn't, you know, because there never was more than one Queen at a time. Do wake up, you heavy things!" she went on in an impatient tone; but there was no answer but a gentle snoring.

The snoring got more distinct every minute, and sounded more like a tune: at last she could even make out words, and she listened so eagerly that, when the two great heads suddenly vanished from her lap, she hardly missed them.

She was standing before an arched doorway, over which were the words "QUEEN ALICE" in large letters, and on each side of the arch there was a bell-handle; one was marked "Visitors' Bell," and the other "Servants' Bell."

"I'll wait till the song's over," thought Alice, "and then I'll ring the—the—*which* bell must I ring?" she went on, very much puzzled by the names. "I'm not a visitor, and I'm not a servant. There *ought* to be one marked 'Queen,' you know——"

Just then the door opened a little way, and a creature with a long beak put its head out for a moment and said "No admittance till the week after next!"[8] and shut the door again with a bang.

Alice knocked and rang in vain for a long time; but at last a very old Frog, who was sitting under a tree, got up and hobbled slowly towards her: he was dressed in bright yellow, and had enormous boots on.

"What is it, now?" the Frog said in a deep hoarse whisper.

Alice turned round, ready to find fault with anybody. "Where's the

servant whose business it is to answer the door?" she began angrily.

"Which door?" said the Frog.

Alice almost stamped with irritation at the slow drawl in which he spoke. "*This* door, of course!"

The Frog looked at the door with his large dull eyes for a minute: then he went nearer and rubbed it with his thumb, as if he were trying whether the paint would come off: then he looked at Alice.

"To answer the door?" he said. "What's it been asking of?" He was so hoarse that Alice could scarcely hear him.

"I don't know what you mean," she said.

"I speaks English, doesn't I?" the Frog went on. "Or are you deaf? What did it ask you?"

"Nothing!" Alice said impatiently. "I've been knocking at it!"

"Shouldn't do that—shouldn't do that——" the Frog muttered. "Wexes it,[9] you know." Then he went up and gave the door a kick with one of his great feet. "You let *it* alone," he panted out, as he hobbled back to his tree, "and it'll let *you* alone, you know."

At this moment the door was flung open, and a shrill voice was heard singing:—

"To the Looking-Glass world it was Alice that said[10]
'I've a sceptre in hand I've a crown on my head.
Let the Looking-Glass creatures, whatever they be
Come and dine with the Red Queen, the White Queen, and me!'"

And hundreds of voices joined in the chorus:—

"Then fill up the glasses as quick as you can,
And sprinkle the table with buttons and bran:
Put cats in the coffee, and mice in the tea—
And welcome Queen Alice with thirty-times-three!"

Then followed a confused noise of cheering, and Alice thought to herself "Thirty times three makes ninety. I wonder if any one's counting?" In a minute there was silence again, and the same voice sang another verse:—

"'Oh Looking-Glass creatures,' quoth Alice, 'draw near!
'Tis an honour to see me, a favour to hear:
'Tis a privilege high to have dinner and tea
Along with the Red Queen, the White Queen, and me!'"

Then came the chorus again:—

"Then fill up the glasses with treacle and ink,
Or anything else that is pleasant to drink:
Mix sand with the cider, and wool with the wine—
And welcome Queen Alice with ninety-times-nine!"

"Ninety times nine!" Alice repeated in despair. "Oh, that'll never be done! I'd better go in at once——" and in she went, and there was a dead silence the moment she appeared.

Alice glanced nervously along the table, as she walked up the large hall, and noticed that there were about fifty guests, of all kinds: some were animals, some birds, and there were even a few flowers among them. "I'm glad they've come without waiting to be asked," she thought: "I should never have known who were the right people to invite!"

There were three chairs at the head of the table: the Red and White Queens had already taken two of them, but the middle one was empty. Alice sat down in it, rather uncomfortable at the silence, and longing for some one to speak.

At last the Red Queen began. "You've missed the soup and fish," she said. "Put on the joint!" And the waiters set a leg of mutton before Alice, who looked at it rather anxiously, as she had never had to carve a joint before.

"You look a little shy: let me introduce you to that leg of mutton," said the Red Queen. "Alice——Mutton: Mutton——Alice." The leg of mutton got up in the dish and made a little bow to Alice: and Alice returned the bow, not knowing whether to be frightened or amused.

"May I give you a slice?" she said, taking up the knife and fork, and looking from one Queen to the other.

"Certainly not," the Red Queen said, very decidedly: "it isn't

etiquette to cut any one[11] you've been introduced to. Remove the joint!" And the waiters carried it off, and brought a large plum-pudding in its place.

"I wo'n't be introduced to the pudding, please," Alice said rather hastily, "or we shall get no dinner at all. May I give you some?"

But the Red Queen looked sulky, and growled "Pudding——Alice: Alice——Pudding. Remove the pudding!", and the waiters took it away so quickly that Alice couldn't return its bow.

However, she didn't see why the Red Queen should be the only one to give orders; so, as an experiment, she called out "Waiter! Bring back the pudding!", and there it was again in a moment, like a conjuring-trick. It was so large that she couldn't help feeling a *little* shy with it, as she had been with the mutton: however, she conquered her shyness by a great effort, and cut a slice and handed it to the Red Queen.

"What impertinence!" said the Pudding. "I wonder how you'd like it, if I were to cut a slice out of *you*, you creature!"

It spoke in a thick, suety sort of voice, and Alice hadn't a word to say in reply: she could only sit and look at it and gasp.

"Make a remark," said the Red Queen: "it's ridiculous to leave all the conversation to the pudding!"

"Do you know, I've had such a quantity of poetry repeated to me to-day," Alice began, a little frightened at finding that, the moment she opened her lips, there was dead silence, and all eyes were fixed upon her: "and it's a very curious thing, I think—every poem was about fishes in some way. Do you know why they're so fond of fishes, all about here?"

She spoke to the Red Queen, whose answer was a little wide of the mark. "As to fishes," she said, very slowly and solemnly, putting her mouth close to Alice's ear, "her White Majesty knows a lovely riddle—all in poetry—all about fishes. Shall she repeat it?"

"Her Red Majesty's very kind to mention it," the White Queen murmured into Alice's other ear, in a voice like the cooing of a pigeon. "It would be *such* a treat! May I?"

"Please do," Alice said very politely.

The White Queen laughed with delight, and stroked Alice's cheek. Then she began:

"'First, the fish must be caught.'[12]
That is easy: a baby, I think, could have caught it.
'Next, the fish must be bought.'
That is easy: a penny, I think, would have bought it.

'Now cook me the fish!'
That is easy, and will not take more than a minute.
'Let it lie in a dish!'
That is easy, because it already is in it.

'Bring it here! Let me sup!'
It is easy to set such a dish on the table.
'Take the dish-cover up!'
Ah, that *is so hard that I fear I'm unable!*

For it holds it like glue—
Holds the lid to the dish, while it lies in the middle:
Which is easiest to do,
Un-dish-cover the fish, or dishcover the riddle?"

"Take a minute to think about it, and then guess," said the Red Queen. "Meanwhile, we'll drink your health—Queen Alice's health!" she screamed at the top of her voice, and all the guests began drinking it directly, and very queerly they managed it: some of them put their glasses upon their heads like extinguishers,[13] and drank all that trickled down their faces—others upset the decanters, and drank the wine as it ran off the edges of the table—and three of them (who looked like kangaroos) scrambled into the dish of roast mutton, and began eagerly lapping up the gravy, "just like pigs in a trough!" thought Alice.

"You ought to return thanks in a neat speech," the Red Queen said, frowning at Alice as she spoke.

"We must support you, you know," the White Queen whispered, as Alice got up to do it, very obediently, but a little frightened.

"Thank you very much," she whispered in reply, "but I can do quite well without."

"That wouldn't be at all the thing," the Red Queen said very decidedly: so Alice tried to submit to it with a good grace.

("And they *did* push so!" she said afterwards, when she was telling her sister the history of the feast. "You would have thought they wanted to squeeze me flat!")

In fact it was rather difficult for her to keep in her place while she made her speech: the two Queens pushed her so, one on each side, that they nearly lifted her up into the air. "I rise to return thanks——" Alice began: and she really *did* rise as she spoke, several inches; but she got hold of the edge of the table, and managed to pull herself down again.

"Take care of yourself!" screamed the White Queen, seizing Alice's hair with both hands. "Something's going to happen!"

And then (as Alice afterwards described it) all sorts of things happened in a moment. The candles all grew up to the ceiling, looking something like a bed of rushes with fireworks at the top. As to the bottles, they each took a pair of plates, which they hastily fitted on as wings, and so, with forks for legs, went fluttering about in all directions: "and very like birds they look," Alice thought to herself, as well as she could in the dreadful confusion that was beginning.

At this moment she heard a hoarse laugh at her side, and turned to see what was the matter with the White Queen; but, instead of the Queen, there was the leg of mutton sitting in the chair. "Here I am!" cried a voice from the soup-tureen, and Alice turned again, just in time to see the Queen's broad good-natured face grinning at her for a moment over the edge of the tureen, before she disappeared into the soup.

There was not a moment to be lost. Already several of the guests were lying down in the dishes, and the soup-ladle was walking up the table towards Alice's chair, and beckoning to her impatiently to get out of its way.

"I ca'n't stand this any longer!"[14] she cried, as she

jumped up and seized the tablecloth with both hands: one good pull, and plates, dishes, guests, and candles came crashing down together in a heap on the floor.

"And as for *you*," she went on, turning fiercely upon the Red Queen,[15] whom she considered as the cause of all the mischief—but the Queen was no longer at her side—she had suddenly dwindled down to the size of a little doll, and was now on the table, merrily running round and round after her own shawl, which was trailing behind her.

At any other time, Alice would have felt surprised at this, but she was far too much excited to be surprised at anything *now*. "As for *you*," she repeated, catching hold of the little creature in the very act of jumping over a bottle which had just lighted upon the table, "I'll shake you into a kitten, that I will!"

CHAPTER X

SHAKING

She took her off the table as she spoke, and shook her backwards and forwards with all her might.

The Red Queen made no resistance whatever: only her face grew very small, and her eyes got large and green: and still, as Alice went on shaking her, she kept on growing shorter—and fatter—and softer—and rounder—and——

CHAPTER XI

WAKING

——and it really *was* a kitten, after all.

CHAPTER XII

WHICH DREAMED IT?

"Your Red Majesty shouldn't purr so loud," Alice said, rubbing her eyes, and addressing the kitten, respectfully, yet with some severity. "You woke me out of oh! such a nice dream![1] And you've been along with me, Kitty—all through the Looking-Glass world. Did you know it, dear?"

It is a very inconvenient habit of kittens (Alice had once made the remark) that, whatever you say to them, they *always* purr. "If they would only purr for 'yes,' and mew for 'no,' or any rule of that sort," she had said, "so that one could keep up a conversation! But how *can* you talk with a person if they *always* say the same thing?"

On this occasion the kitten only purred: and it was impossible to guess whether it meant 'yes' or 'no.'

So Alice hunted among the chessmen on the table till she had found the Red Queen: then she went down on her knees on the hearth-rug, and put the kitten and the Queen to look at each other. "Now, Kitty!" she cried, clapping her hands triumphantly. "Confess that was what you turned into!"

("But it wouldn't look at it," she said, when she was explaining the thing afterwards to her sister: "it turned away its head, and pretended not to see it: but it looked a *little* ashamed of itself, so I think it *must* have been the Red Queen.")

"Sit up a little more stiffly, dear!" Alice cried with merry laugh. "And curtsey while you're thinking what to—what to purr. It saves time, remember!" And she caught it up and gave it one little kiss, "just in honour of its having been a Red Queen."

"Snowdrop, my pet!" she went on, looking over her shoulder at the White Kitten, which was still patiently undergoing its toilet, "when *will* Dinah have finished with your White Majesty, I wonder? That

must be the reason you were so untidy in my dream.——Dinah! Do you know that you're scrubbing a White Queen? Really, it's most disrespectful of you!

"And what did *Dinah* turn to, I wonder?" she prattled on, as she settled comfortably down, with one elbow on the rug, and her chin in her hand, to watch the kittens. "Tell me, Dinah, did you turn to Humpty Dumpty? I *think* you did—however, you'd better not mention it to your friends just yet, for I'm not sure.

"By the way, Kitty, if only you'd been really with me in my dream, there was one thing you *would* have enjoyed——I had such a quantity of poetry said to me, all about fishes![2] To-morrow morning you shall have a real treat. All the time you're eating your breakfast, I'll repeat 'The Walrus and the Carpenter' to you; and then you can make believe it's oysters, dear!

"Now, Kitty, let's consider who it was that dreamed it all. This is a serious question, my dear, and you should *not* go on licking your paw like that—as if Dinah hadn't washed you this morning! You see, Kitty, it *must* have been either me or the Red King. He was part of my dream, of course—but then I was part of his dream, too! *Was* it the Red King, Kitty? You were his wife, my dear, so you ought to know——Oh, Kitty, *do* help to settle it! I'm sure your paw can wait!" But the provoking kitten only began on the other paw, and pretended it hadn't heard the question.

Which do *you* think it was?[3]

A boat, beneath a sunny sky[4]
Lingering onward dreamily
In an evening of July—

Children three that nestle near,
Eager eye and willing ear,
Pleased a simple tale to hear—

Long has paled that sunny sky:
Echoes fade and memories die:
Autumn frosts have slain July.

Still she haunts me, phantomwise,[5]
Alice moving under skies
Never seen by waking eyes.

Children yet, the tale to hear,
Eager eye and willing ear,
Lovingly shall nestle near.

In a Wonderland they lie,
Dreaming as the days go by,
Dreaming as the summers die:

Ever drifting down the stream—
Lingering in the golden gleam—
Life, what is it but a dream?[6]

THE END

INTRODUCTION: ALICE'S ADVENTURES UNDER GROUND

If Alice's Adventures really began on 4 July 1862 on the famous boat-trip along the River Isis, their textual life began soon afterwards when, at Alice's request, he wrote it out for her, with illustrations. As Carroll wrote later:

> The germ of *Alice* was an extensive story, told in a boat to the 3 children of Dean Liddell: it was afterwards written out for her, in MS print, with pen-and-ink pictures (such pictures!) of my own devising: without the least idea, at the time, that it would ever be published. But friends urged me to print it, so it was re-written, and enlarged, and published.[1]

The manuscript version was completed on 10 February 1863 and the pictures, which proved more recalcitrant, on 13 September the following year, 1864. Having had the completed manuscript bound, Dodgson presented it to Alice, under the title *Alice's Adventures under Ground*, on 26 November as 'A Christmas Gift to a Dear Child in Memory of a Summer Day'. As a result of her and other readers' enthusiastic reception of it, he then went on to revise and expand it (enlarging it from 12,715 words to 26,211), publishing it in 1865 with the new title of *Alice's Adventures in Wonderland*.

Though we will never know exactly what form the original 'germ' of the story took that 'Summer Day', the first hand-written and illustrated version remained in Alice Liddell's possession. Then on 1 March 1885 Dodgson approached her, to ask whether she had 'any objection to the original MS book of *Alice's Adventures* (which I suppose you still possess) being published in facsimile'; though he knows he risks being charged with 'gross egoism', he is convinced 'there must be many who would like to see the original form'.[2] She hadn't, and Macmillan duly brought out a full facsimile edition of 5,000 for Christmas 1886 (though, in respect towards Alice's wishes, without reproducing the photograph of the seven-year-old heroine at the end).[3]

Though some previous English editions of *Alice* have included extracts from *Alice's Adventures under Ground*, none have reprinted it complete in readable printed form, as here. The earlier version will never replace the fuller, revised text, but it is of considerable historical interest as the first textual incarnation of one of the classics of children's literature: it's also interesting in its own right. If not exactly *raw*, it is none the less a less *cooked* version of the story, and it tells us a lot about Dodgson's original conception as well as his secondary elaboration and development of the primary material when expanding it for publication. Like Goethe's ur-*Faust* or the 1799 draft of Wordsworth's *The Prelude*, *Alice's Adventures under Ground* is more than a pretext, it is a fascinating and distinct text in its own right. For this reason, though the bulk of the text was absorbed into the final printed text and is therefore familiar to all readers of *Alice*, the cumulative effect of the ur-*Alice* is very different. It is certainly less artfully elaborated and unified, but it has its own dreamy, associative integrity, and it's altogether more *primitive* and rooted in a world of physical transformations than the full published version.

In enlarging the book for publication in 1864–5, Dodgson not only more than doubled its length (the first version has only four chapters, the later twelve), he added some of its most memorable characters – the Mad Hatter and the March Hare, the Duchess and the Cheshire Cat; some of its most familiar songs ('Fury said to a mouse', 'Twinkle, twinkle, little bat', 'Will you walk a little faster, said a whiting to a snail?'); and some of its funniest satirical episodes, such as the extended pun-studded nostalgic duet about school performed by the Mock Turtle and the Gryphon. In revising the manuscript, he also skilfully contrived to transform the looser, picaresque dream sequence he originally created into a more architecturally conceived and consciously staged work, built around the characteristic but puzzling games with language and logic that demonstrate Dodgson's concerns as a logician. In the earlier version, the game of cards only surfaces in the last chapter, three-quarters of the way through, whereas in the final version it surfaces in Book 6, half way through. Though it takes up little more space in the final version, it provides a principle of unity which draws together the various strands and main characters. The climax too is considerably extended. The court-scene trial of the Knave of Hearts, for example, is expanded to introduce almost the entire cast list of the story, with the effect of a closing 'number' or theatrical finale, such as wound up the pantomimes and comedies Dodgson enjoyed so much. Throughout the rewrite, the improvised and casual thread of the dream was taken up into a larger scale, through-composed literary structure.

The gains in artistic effect and sophistication are evident to almost any reader, I think, but there is a shift of tonality and narrative mode that involves loss as well as gain, a shift comparable to that later between *Wonderland* and *Through the Looking-Glass*, from greater immediacy to greater control. This is most evident at the level of punctuation. *Alice's Adventures under Ground* is composed in long, straggling, improvisatory paragraphs – often one or at most two sentences long – and it's punctuated with commas and colons, with comparatively rare full stops. As to the dialogue, which provides the main thrust of the narrative, the speech of Alice and the other characters in the earlier text is riddled with exclamation marks. The overall effect is of breathlessness and headlong flow as the reader is swept along the current of the dream story, with its dizzying falls and abrupt changes of physical scale, through a world of sudden metamorphoses, exclamations and ejaculations. Dodgson's strained, primitive drawings convey something of the same dream oddity as his ur-text. Taken together, they offer the reader of *Alice's Adventures under Ground* a very different experience to *Alice's Adventures in Wonderland* – one which, though not the 'original' oral tale spun out for the Liddell children in a punt on the Isis, takes us back closer to its earliest evolution and its own strange evolutionary journey.

At the heart of the book is not the Queen of Hearts, the homicidal matriarch who presides over the last chapter, but Alice, who in answer to the pigeon's question ('"*What* are you?"') and challenge ('"I can see you're trying to invent something"') answers '"I'm a little girl"', but 'rather doubtfully, as she remembered the number of changes she had gone through'. And that of course is what the book is about, Alice's trying to invent herself as 'a little girl', in the face of the dizzying changes of size and context she undergoes underground. *Alice's*

Adventures under Ground offers a different, developmental narrative of Dodgson's invented story but also of Alice's fictional journey of growth and self-invention in a world of startling physical and biological transformations. When Dodgson arranged for its publication in 1886, he recognized that the early text, like its seven-year-old heroine, had its own identity. As we may read plural versions of Coleridge's *The Rime of the Ancient Mariner* or Wordsworth's *The Prelude*, Marlowe's *Dr Faustus* and W. H. Auden's 'Dover', so too we should be able to read the two texts of *Alice's Adventures*, as in this edition, which transcribes Dodgson's MS text and reproduces some of his pencilled illustrations.

Notes

1 Letter of 16 July 1885, *The Letters of Lewis Carroll*, ed. Morton N. Cohen, with the assistance of R. L. Green, 2 vols, Oxford, 1979, vol 1, p. 591.
2 Letter to Alice (Liddell) Hargreaves, 1 March 1885, *Letters*, vol 1, p. 560.
3 The MS *Alice's Adventures under Ground* was auctioned at Sotheby's in 1928, bought by an American collector, auctioned again in the US in 1946, and then offered to the British Library in 1948, where it is now housed. The Macmillan facsimile edition has been reprinted, notably edited by Martin Gardner (New York: Dover Publications Inc, 1965), and more recently the British Library produced another photographic facsimile edition (London: Pavilion Books Ltd in association with the British Library, 1985).

Alice's Adventures under Ground

A Christmas Gift
to
a Dear Child
in Memory
of
a Summer Day.

CHAPTER I

Alice was beginning to get very tired of sitting by her sister on the bank, and of having nothing to do: once or twice she had peeped into the book her sister was reading, but it had no pictures or conversations in it, and where is the use of a book, thought Alice, without pictures or conversations? So she was considering in her own mind, (as well as she could, for the hot day made her feel very sleepy and stupid,) whether the pleasure of making a daisy-chain was worth the trouble of getting up and picking the daisies, when a white rabbit with pink eyes ran close by her.

There was nothing very remarkable in that, nor did Alice think it so *very* much out of the way to hear the rabbit say to itself "dear, dear! I shall be too late!" (when she thought it over afterwards, it occurred to her that she ought to have wondered at this, but at the time it all seemed quite natural); but when the rabbit actually *took a watch out of its waistcoat-pocket*, looked at it, and then hurried on, Alice started to her feet, for it flashed across her mind that she had never before seen a rabbit with either a waistcoat-pocket or a watch to take out of it, and, full of curiosity, she hurried across the field after it, and was just in time to see it pop down a large rabbit-hole under the hedge. In a moment down went Alice after it, never once considering how in the world she was to get out again.

The rabbit-hole went straight on like a tunnel for some way, and then dipped suddenly down, so suddenly, that Alice had not a moment to think about stopping herself, before she found herself falling down what seemed a deep well. Either the well was very deep, or she fell very slowly, for she had plenty of time as she went down to look about her, and to wonder what would happen next. First, she tried to look down and make out what she was coming to, but it was too dark to see anything: then, she looked at the sides of the well, and noticed that they were filled with cupboards and book-shelves: here and there were maps and pictures hung on pegs. She took a jar down off one of the shelves as she passed: it was labelled "Orange Marmalade," but to her great disappointment it was empty: she did not like to drop the jar, for fear of killing somebody underneath, so managed to put it into one of the cupboards as she fell past it.

"Well!" thought Alice to herself, "after such a fall as this, I shall think nothing of tumbling down stairs! How brave they'll all think me at home! Why, I wouldn't say anything about it, even if I fell off the top of the house!" (which was most likely true.)

Down, down, down. Would the fall *never* come to an end? "I wonder how many miles I've fallen by this time?" said she aloud, "I must be getting somewhere near the centre of the earth. Let me see: that would be four thousand miles down, I think — " (for you see Alice had learnt several things of this sort in her lessons in the schoolroom, and though this was not a *very* good opportunity for showing off her knowledge, as there was no one to hear her, still it was good practice to say it over,) "yes, that's the right distance, but then what Longitude or Latitude-line shall I be in?" (Alice had no idea what Longitude was, or Latitude either, but she thought they were nice grand words to say.)

Presently she began again: "I wonder if I shall fall right *through* the earth! How funny it'll be to come out among the people that walk with their heads downwards! But I shall have to ask them what the name of the country is, you know. Please, Ma'am, is this New Zealand or Australia?" — and she tried to curtsey as she spoke, (fancy *curtseying* as you're falling through the air! do you think you could manage it?) "and what an ignorant little girl she'll think me for asking! No, it'll never do to ask: perhaps I shall see it written up somewhere."

Down, down, down: there was nothing else to do, so Alice soon began talking again. "Dinah will miss me very much tonight, I should think!" (Dinah was the cat.) "I hope they'll remember her saucer of milk at tea-time! Oh, dear Dinah, I wish I had you here! There are no mice in the air, I'm afraid, but you might catch a bat, and that's very like a mouse, you know, my dear. But do cats eat bats, I wonder?" And here Alice began to get rather sleepy, and kept on saying to herself, in a dreamy sort of way "do cats eat bats? do cats eat bats?" and sometimes, "do bats eat cats?" for, as she couldn't answer either question, it didn't much matter which way she put it. She felt that she was dozing off, and had just begun to dream that she was walking hand in hand with Dinah, and was saying to her very earnestly, "Now, Dinah, my dear, tell me the truth. Did you ever eat a bat?" when suddenly, bump! bump! down she came upon a heap of sticks and shavings, and the fall was over.

Alice was not a bit hurt, and jumped on to her feet directly: she looked up, but it was all dark overhead; before her was another long passage, and the white rabbit was still in sight, hurrying down it. There was not a moment to be lost: away went Alice like the wind, and just heard it say, as it turned a corner, "my ears and whiskers, how late it's getting!" She turned the corner after it, and instantly found herself in a long, low hall, lit up by a row of lamps which hung from the roof.

There were doors all round the hall, but they were all locked, and when Alice had been all round it, and tried them all, she walked sadly down the middle, wondering how she was ever to get out again: suddenly she came upon a little three-legged table, all made of solid glass; there was nothing lying it, but a tiny golden key, and Alice's first idea was that it might belong to one of the doors of the hall, but alas! either the locks were too large, or the key too small, but at any rate it would open none of them. However, on the second time round, she came to a low curtain, behind which was a door about eighteen inches high: she tried the little key in the keyhole, and it fitted! Alice opened the door, and looked down a small passage, not larger than a rat-hole, into the loveliest garden you ever saw. How she longed to get out of that dark hall, and wander about among those beds of bright flowers and those cool fountains, but she could not even get her head through the doorway, "and even if my head would go through," thought poor Alice, "it would be very little use without my shoulders. Oh, how I wish I could shut up like a telescope! I think I could, if I only knew how to begin." For, you see, so many out-of-the-way things had happened lately, that Alice began to think very few things indeed were really impossible.

There was nothing else to do, so she went back to the table, half hoping she might find another key on it, or at any rate a book of rules for shutting up people like telescopes: this time there was a little bottle on it — "which certainly was not there before" said Alice — and tied round the neck of the bottle was a paper label with the words DRINK ME beautifully printed on it in large letters.

It was all very well to say "drink me," "but I'll look first," said the wise little Alice, "and see whether the bottle's marked 'poison' or not," for Alice had read several nice little stories about children that got burnt, and eaten up by wild beasts, and other unpleasant things, because they *would* not remember the simple rules their friends had given them, such as, that, if you get into the fire, it will burn you, and that, if you cut your finger very deeply with a knife, it generally bleeds, and she had never forgotten that, if you drink a bottle marked "poison," it is almost certain to disagree with you, sooner or later.

However, this bottle was *not* marked poison, so Alice tasted it, and finding it very nice, (it had, in fact, a sort of mixed flavour of cherry-tart, custard, pine-apple, roast turkey, toffy, and hot buttered toast,) she very soon finished it off.

* * * * * *

"What a curious feeling!" said Alice, "I must be shutting up like a telescope."

It was so indeed: she was now only ten inches high, and her face brightened up as it occurred to her that she was now the right size for going through the little door into that lovely garden. First, however, she waited for a few minutes to see whether she was going to shrink any further: she felt a little nervous about this, "for it might end, you know," said Alice to herself, "in my going out altogether, like a candle, and what should I be like then, I wonder?" and she tried to fancy what the flame of a candle is like after the candle is blown out, for she could not remember having ever seen one. However, nothing more happened, so she decided on going into the garden at once, but, alas for poor Alice! when she got to the door, she found she had forgotten the little golden key, and when she went back to the table for the key, she found she could not possibly reach it: she could see it plainly enough through the glass, and she tried her best to climb up one of the legs of the table, but it was too slippery, and when she had tired herself out with trying, the poor little thing sat down and cried.

"Come! there's no use in crying!" said Alice to herself rather sharply, "I advise you to leave off this minute!" (she generally gave herself very good advice, and sometimes scolded herself so severely as to bring tears into her eyes, and once she remembered boxing her own ears for having been unkind to herself in a game of croquet she was playing with herself, for this curious child was very fond of pretending to be two people,) "but it's no use now," thought poor Alice, "to pretend to be two people! Why, there's hardly enough of me left to make one respectable person!"

Soon her eyes fell on a little ebony box lying under the table: she opened it, and found in it a very small cake, on which was lying a card with the words EAT ME beautifully printed on it in large letters. "I'll eat," said Alice, "and if it makes me larger, I can reach the key, and if it makes me smaller, I can creep under the door, so either way I'll get into the garden, and I don't care which happens!"

She eat a little bit, and said anxiously to herself "which way? which way?" and laid her hand on the top of her head to feel which way it was growing, and was quite surprised to find that she remained the same size: to be sure this is what generally happens when one eats cake, but Alice had got into the way of expecting nothing but out-of-the-way things to happen, and it seemed quite dull and stupid for things to go on in the common way.

So she set to work, and very soon finished off the cake.

*   *   *   *   *

"Curiouser and curiouser!" cried Alice, (she was so surprised that she quite forgot how to speak good English,) "now I'm opening out like the largest telescope that ever was! Goodbye, feet!" (for when she looked down at her feet, they seemed almost out of sight, they were getting so far off,) "oh, my poor little feet, I wonder who will put on your shoes and stockings for you now, dears? I'm sure *I* ca'n't! I shall be a great deal too far off to bother myself about you: you must manage the best way you can — but I must be kind to them," thought Alice, "or perhaps they won't walk the way I want to go! Let me see: I'll give them a new pair of boots every Christmas."

And she went on planning to herself how she would manage it: "they must go by the carrier," she thought, "and how funny it'll seem, sending presents to one's own feet! And how odd the directions will look! ALICE'S RIGHT FOOT, ESQ.

THE CARPET,

with ALICE'S LOVE.

oh dear! what nonsense I am talking!"

Just at this moment, her head struck against the roof of the hall: in fact, she was now rather more than nine feet high, and she at once took up the little golden key, and hurried off to the garden door.

Poor Alice! it was as much as she could do, lying down on one side, to look through into the garden with one eye, but to get through was more hopeless than ever: she sat down and cried again.

"You ought to be ashamed of yourself," said Alice, "a great girl like you," (she might well say this,) "to cry in this way! Stop this instant, I tell you!" But she cried on all the same, shedding gallons of tears, until there was a large pool, about four inches deep, all round her, and reaching half way across the hall. After a time, she heard a little pattering of feet in the distance, and dried her eyes to see what was coming. It was the white rabbit coming back again, splendidly dressed, with a pair of white kid gloves in one hand, and a nosegay in the other. Alice was ready to ask help of any one, she felt so desperate, and as the rabbit passed her, she said, in a low, timid voice, "If you please, Sir — " the rabbit started violently, looked up once into the roof of the hall, from which the voice seemed to come, and then dropped the nosegay and the white kid gloves, and skurried away into the darkness as hard as it could go.

Alice took up the nosegay and gloves, and found the nosegay so delicious that she kept smelling at it all the time she went on talking to herself — "dear, dear! how queer everything is today! and yesterday everything happened just as usual: I wonder if I was changed in the night? Let me think: was I the same when I got up this morning? I think I remember feeling rather different. But if I'm not the same, who in the world am I? Ah, that's the great puzzle!" And she began thinking over all the children she knew of the same age as herself, to see if she could have been changed for any of them.

"I'm sure I'm not Gertrude," she said, "for her hair goes in such long ringlets, and mine doesn't go in ringlets at all — and I'm sure I ca'n't be Florence, for I know all sorts of things, and she, oh! she knows such a very little! Besides, *she*'s she, and *I'm* I, and — oh dear! how puzzling it all is! I'll try if I know all the things I used to know. Let me see: four times five is twelve, and four times six is thirteen, and four times seven is fourteen — oh dear! I shall never get to twenty at this rate! But the Multiplication Table don't signify — let's try Geography. London is the capital of France, and Rome is the capital of Yorkshire, and Paris — oh dear! dear! *that*'s all wrong, I'm certain! I must have been changed for Florence! I'll try and say 'How doth the little,'" and she crossed her hands on her lap, and began, but her voice sounded hoarse and strange, and the words did not sound the same as they used to do:

"How doth the little crocodile
Improve its shining tail,
And pour the waters of the Nile
On every golden scale!

How cheerfully it seems to grin!
How neatly spreads its claws!
And welcomes little fishes in
With gently-smiling jaws!"

"I'm sure those are not the right words," said poor Alice, and her eyes filled with tears as she thought "I must be Florence after all, and I shall have to go and live in that poky little house, and have next to no toys to play with, and oh! ever so many lessons to learn! No! I've made up my mind about it: if I'm Florence, I'll stay down here! It'll be no use their putting their heads down and saying 'come up, dear!' I shall only look up and say 'who am I, then? answer me that first, and then, if I like being that person, I'll come up: if not, I'll stay down here till I'm somebody else — but, oh dear!" cried Alice with a sudden burst of tears, "I do wish they *would* put their heads down! I am so tired of being all alone here!"

As she said this, she looked down at her hands, and was surprised to find she had put on one of the rabbit's little gloves while she was talking. "How *can* I have done that?" thought she, "I must be growing small again." She got up and went to the table to measure herself by it, and found that, as nearly as she could guess, she was now about two feet high, and was going on shrinking rapidly: soon she found out that the reason of it was the nosegay she held in her hand: she dropped it hastily, just in time to save herself from shrinking away altogether, and found that she was now only three inches high.

"Now for the garden!" cried Alice, as she hurried back to the little door, but the little door was locked again, and the little gold key was lying on the glass table as before, and "things are worse than ever!" thought the poor little girl, "for I never was as small as this before, never! And I declare it's too bad, it is!" At this moment her foot slipped, and splash! she was up to her chin in salt water. Her first idea was that she had fallen into the sea: then she remembered that she was under ground, and she soon made out that it was the pool of tears she had wept when she was nine feet high. "I wish I hadn't cried so much!" said Alice, as she swam about, trying to find her way out, "I shall be punished for it now, I suppose, by being drowned in my own tears! Well! that'll be a queer thing, to be sure! However, every thing is queer today." Very soon she saw something splashing about in the pool near her: at first she thought it must be a walrus or a hippopotamus, but then she remembered how small she was herself, and soon made out that it was only a mouse, that had slipped in like herself.

"Would it be any use, now," thought Alice, "to speak to this mouse? The rabbit is something quite out-of-the-way, no doubt, and so have I been, ever since I came down here, but that is no reason why the mouse should not be able to talk. I think I may as well try."

So she began: "oh Mouse, do you know how to get out of this pool? I am very tired of swimming about here, oh Mouse!" The mouse looked at her rather inquisitively, and seemed to her to wink with one of its little eyes, but it said nothing.

"Perhaps it doesn't understand English," thought Alice; "I daresay it's a French mouse, come over with William the Conqueror!" (for, with all her knowledge of history, Alice had no very clear notion how long ago anything had happened,) so she began again: "où est ma chatte?" which was the first sentence out of her French lesson-book. The mouse gave a sudden jump in the pool, and seemed to quiver with fright: "oh, I beg your pardon!" cried Alice hastily, afraid that she had hurt the poor animal's feelings, "I quite forgot you didn't like cats!"

"Not like cats!" cried the mouse, in a shrill, passionate voice, "would *you* like cats if you were me?"

"Well, perhaps not," said Alice in a soothing tone, "don't be angry about it. And yet I wish I could show you our cat Dinah: I think you'd take a fancy to cats if you could only see her. She is such a dear quiet thing," said Alice, half to herself, as she swam lazily about in the pool, "she sits purring so nicely by the fire, licking her paws and washing her face: and she is such a nice soft thing to nurse, and she's such a capital one for catching mice — oh! I beg your pardon!" cried poor Alice again, for this time the mouse was bristling all over, and she felt certain that it was really offended, "have I offended you?"

"Offended indeed!" cried the mouse, who seemed to be positively trembling with rage, "our family always *hated* cats! Nasty, low, vulgar things! Don't talk to me about them any more!"

"I won't indeed!" said Alice, in a great hurry to change the conversation, "are you — are you — fond of — dogs?" The mouse did not answer, so Alice went on eagerly: "there is such a nice little dog near our house I should like to show you! A little bright-eyed terrier, you know, with oh! such long curly brown hair! And it'll fetch things when you throw them, and it'll sit up and beg for its dinner, and all sorts of things — I ca'n't remember half of them — and it belongs to a farmer, and he says it kills all the rats and — oh dear!" said Alice sadly, "I'm afraid I've offended it again!" for the mouse was swimming away from her as hard as it could go, and making quite a commotion in the pool as it went.

So she called softly after it: "mouse dear! Do come back again, and we wo'n't talk about cats and dogs any more, if you don't like them!" When the mouse heard this, it turned and swam slowly back to her: its face was quite pale, (with passion, Alice thought,) and it said in a trembling low voice "let's get to the shore, and then I'll tell you my history, and you'll understand why it is I hate cats and dogs."

It was high time to go, for the pool was getting quite full of birds and animals that had fallen into it. There was a Duck and a Dodo, a Lory and an Eaglet, and several other curious creatures. Alice led the way, and the whole party swam to the shore.

CHAPTER II

They were indeed a curious looking party that assembled on the bank — the birds with draggled feathers, the animals with their fur clinging close to them — all dripping wet, cross, and uncomfortable. The first question of course was, how to get dry: they had a consultation about this, and Alice hardly felt at all surprised at finding herself talking familiarly with the birds, as if she had known them all her life. Indeed, she had quite a long argument with the Lory, who at last turned sulky, and would only say "I am older than you, and must know best," and this Alice would not admit without knowing how old the Lory was, and as the Lory positively refused to tell its age, there was nothing more to be said.

At last the mouse, who seemed to have some authority among them, called out "sit down, all of you, and attend to me! I'll soon make you dry enough!" They all sat down at once, shivering, in a large ring, Alice in the middle, with her eyes anxiously fixed on the mouse, for she felt sure she would catch a bad cold if she did not get dry very soon.

"Ahem!" said the mouse, with a self-important air, "are you all ready? This is the driest thing I know. Silence all round, if you please!

"William the Conqueror, whose cause was favoured by the pope, was soon submitted to by the English, who wanted leaders, and had been of late much accustomed to usurpation and conquest. Edwin and Morcar, the earls of Mercia and Northumbria —"

"Ugh!" said the Lory with a shiver.

"I beg your pardon?" said the mouse, frowning, but very politely, "did you speak?"

"Not I!" said the Lory hastily.

"I thought you did," said the mouse, "I proceed. Edwin and Morcar, the earls of Mercia and Northumbria, declared for him; and even Stigand, the patriotic archbishop of Canterbury, found it advisable to go with Edgar Atheling to meet William and offer him the crown. William's conduct was at first moderate — how are you getting on now, dear?" said the mouse, turning to Alice as it spoke.

"As wet as ever," said poor Alice, "it doesn't seem to dry me at all."

"In that case," said the Dodo solemnly, rising to his feet, "I move that the meeting adjourn, for the immediate adoption of more energetic remedies —"

"Speak English!" said the Duck, "I don't know the meaning of half those long words, and what's more, I don't believe you do either!" And the Duck quacked a comfortable laugh to itself. Some of the other birds tittered audibly.

"I only meant to say," said the Dodo in a rather offended tone, "that I know of a house near here, where we could get the young lady and the rest of the party dried, and then we could listen comfortably to the story which I think you were good enough to promise to tell us," bowing gravely to the mouse.

The mouse made no objection to this, and the whole party moved along the river bank, (for the pool had by this time begun to flow out of the hall, and the edge of it was fringed with rushes and forget-me-nots,) in a slow procession, the Dodo leading the way. After a time the Dodo became impatient, and, leaving the Duck to bring up the rest of the party, moved on at a quicker pace with Alice, the Lory, and the Eaglet, and soon brought them to a little cottage, and there they sat snugly by the fire, wrapped up in blankets, until the rest of the party had arrived, and they were all dry again.

Then they all sat down again in a large ring on the bank, and begged the mouse to begin his story.

"Mine is a long and a sad tale!" said the mouse, turning to Alice, and sighing.

"It *is* a long tail, certainly," said Alice, looking down with wonder at the mouse's tail, which was coiled nearly all round the party, "but why do you call it sad?" and she went on puzzling about this as the mouse went on speaking, so that her idea of the tale was something like this:

We lived beneath the mat
Warm and snug and fat
But one woe, & that
Was the cat!
To our joys
a clog, In
our eyes a
fog, On our
hearts a log
Was the dog!
When the
cat's away,
Then
the mice
will
play,
But, alas!
one day, (So *they* say)
Came the dog and
cat, Hunting
for a
rat,
Crushed
the mice
all flat,
Each
one
as
he
sat
Underneath the mat, Warm, & snug, & fat – Thiunk of that!

"You are not attending!" said the mouse to Alice severely, "what are you thinking of?"

"I beg your pardon," said Alice very humbly, "you had got to the fifth bend, I think?"

"I had *not*!" cried the mouse, sharply and very angrily.

"A knot!" said Alice, always ready to make herself useful, and looking anxiously about her, "oh, do let me help to undo it!"

"I shall do nothing of the sort!" said the mouse, getting up and walking away from the party, "you insult me by talking such nonsense!"

"I didn't mean it!" pleaded poor Alice, "but you're so easily offended, you know."

The mouse only growled in reply.

"Please come back and finish your story!" Alice called after it, and the others all joined in chorus "yes, please do!" but the mouse only shook its ears, and walked quickly away, and was soon out of sight.

"What a pity it wouldn't stay!" sighed the Lory, and an old Crab took the opportunity of saying to its daughter "Ah, my dear! let this be a lesson to you never to lose *your* temper!" "Hold your tongue, Ma!" said the young Crab, a little snappishly, "you're enough to try the patience of an oyster!"

"I wish I had our Dinah here, I know I do!" said Alice aloud, addressing no one in particular, "*she'd* soon fetch it back!"

"And who is Dinah, if I might venture to ask the question?" said the Lory.

Alice replied eagerly, for she was always ready to talk about her pet, "Dinah's our cat. And she's such a capital one for catching mice, you ca'n't think! And oh! I wish you could see her after the birds! Why, she'll eat a little bird as soon as look at it!"

This answer caused a remarkable sensation among the party: some of the birds hurried off at once; one old magpie began wrapping itself up very carefully, remarking "I really must be getting home: the night air does not suit my throat," and a canary called out in a trembling voice to its children "come away from her, my dears, she's no fit company for you!" On various pretexts, they all moved off, and Alice was soon left alone.

She sat for some while sorrowful and silent, but she was not long before she recovered her spirits, and began talking to herself as usual: "I do wish some of them had stayed a little longer! and I was getting to be such friends with them — really the Lory and I were almost like sisters! and so was that dear little Eaglet! And then the Duck and the Dodo! How nicely the Duck sang to us as we came along through the water: and if the Dodo hadn't known the way to that nice little cottage, I don't know when we should have got dry again—" and there is no knowing how long she might have prattled on in this way, if she had not suddenly caught the sound of pattering feet.

It was the white rabbit, trotting slowly back again, and looking anxiously about it as it went, as if it had lost something, and she heard it muttering to itself "the Marchioness! the Marchioness! oh my dear paws! oh my fur and whiskers! She'll have me executed, as sure as ferrets are ferrets! Where *can* I have dropped them, I wonder?" Alice guessed in a moment that it was looking for the nosegay and the pair of white kid gloves, and she began hunting for them, but they were now nowhere to be seen — everything seemed to have changed since her swim in the pool, and her walk along the river-bank with its fringe of rushes and forget-me-nots, and the glass table and the little door had vanished.

Soon the rabbit noticed Alice, as she stood looking curiously about her, and at once said in a quick angry tone, "why, Mary Ann! what *are* you doing out here? Go home this moment, and look on my dressing-table for my gloves and nosegay, and fetch them here, as quick as you can run, do you hear?" and Alice was so much frightened that she ran off at once, without saying a word, in the direction which the rabbit had pointed out.

She soon found herself in front of a neat little house, on the door of which was a bright brass plate with the name W. RABBIT, ESQ. She went in, and hurried upstairs, for fear she should meet the real Mary Ann and be turned out of the house before she had found the gloves: she knew that one pair had been lost in the hall, "but of course," thought Alice, "it has plenty more of them in its house. How queer it seems to be going messages for a rabbit! I suppose Dinah'll be sending me messages next!" And she began fancying the sort of things that would happen: "Miss Alice! come here directly and get ready for your walk!" "Coming in a minute, nurse! but I've got to watch this mouse-hole till Dinah comes back, and see that the mouse doesn't get out —" "only I don't think," Alice went on, "that they'd let Dinah stop in the house, if it began ordering people about like that!"

By this time she had found her way into a tidy little room, with a table in the window on which was a looking-glass and, (as Alice had hoped,) two or three pairs of tiny white kid gloves: she took up a pair of gloves, and was just going to leave the room, when her eye fell upon a little bottle that stood near the looking-glass: there was no label on it this time with the words "drink me," but nevertheless she uncorked it and put it to her lips: "I know something interesting is sure to happen," she said to herself, "whenever I eat or drink anything, so I'll see what this bottle does. I do hope it'll make me grow larger, for I'm quite tired of being such a tiny little thing!"

It did so indeed, and much sooner than she expected: before she had drunk half the bottle, she found her head pressing against the ceiling, and she stooped to save her neck from being broken, and hastily put down the bottle, saying to herself "that's quite enough — I hope I sha'n't grow any more — I wish I hadn't drunk so much!"

Alas! it was too late: she went on growing and growing, and very soon had to kneel down: in another minute there was not room even for this, and she tried the effect of lying down, with one elbow against the door, and the other arm curled round her head. Still she went on growing, and as a last resource she put one arm out of the window, and one foot up the chimney, and said to herself "now I can do no more — what *will* become of me?"

Luckily for Alice, the little magic bottle had now had its full effect, and she grew no larger: still it was very uncomfortable, and as there seemed to be no sort of chance of ever getting out of the room again, no wonder she felt unhappy. "It was much pleasanter at home," thought poor Alice, "when one wasn't always growing larger and smaller, and being ordered about by mice and rabbits — I almost wish I hadn't gone down that rabbit-hole, and yet, and yet — it's rather curious, you know, this sort of life. I do wonder what *can* have happened to me! When I used to read fairy-tales, I fancied that sort of thing never

happened, and now here I am in the middle of one! There ought to be a book written about me, that there ought! and when I grow up I'll write one — but I'm grown up now" said she in a sorrowful tone, "at least there's no room to grow up any more *here*."

"But then," thought Alice, "shall I *never* get any older than I am now? That'll be a comfort, one way — never to be an old woman — but then — always to have lessons to learn! Oh, I shouldn't like *that*!"

"Oh, you foolish Alice!" she said again, "how can you learn lessons in here? Why, there's hardly room for you, and no room at all for any lesson-books!"

And so she went on, taking first one side, and then the other, and making quite a conversation of it altogether, but after a few minutes she heard a voice outside, which made her stop to listen.

"Mary Ann! Mary Ann!" said the voice, "fetch me my gloves this moment!" Then came a little pattering of feet on the stairs: Alice knew it was the rabbit coming to look for her, and she trembled till she shook the house, quite forgetting that she was now about a thousand times as large as the rabbit, and had no reason to be afraid of it. Presently the rabbit came to the door, and tried to open it, but as it opened inwards, and Alice's elbow was against it, the attempt proved a failure. Alice heard it say to itself "then I'll go round and get in at the window."

"*That* you wo'n't!" thought Alice, and, after waiting till she fancied she heard the rabbit just under the window, she suddenly spread out her hand, and made a snatch in the air. She did not get hold of anything, but she heard a little shriek and a fall and a crash of breaking glass, from which she concluded that it was just possible it had fallen into a cucumber-frame, or something of the sort.

Next came an angry voice — the rabbit's — "Pat, Pat! where are you?" And then a voice she had never heard before, "shure then I'm here! digging for apples, anyway, yer honour!"

"Digging for apples indeed!" said the rabbit angrily, "here, come and help me out of *this*!" — Sound of more breaking glass.

"Now, tell me, Pat, what is that coming out of the window?"

"Shure it's an arm, yer honour!" (He pronounced it "arrum".)

"An arm, you goose! Who ever saw an arm that size? Why, it fills the whole window, don't you see?"

"Shure, it does, yer honour, but it's an arm for all that."

"Well, it's no business there: go and take it away!"

There was a long silence after this, and Alice could only hear whispers now and then, such as "shure I don't like it, yer honour, at all at all!" "do as I tell you, you coward!" and at last she spread out her hand again and made another snatch in the air. This time there were *two* little shrieks, and more breaking glass —"what a number of cucumber-frames there must be!" thought Alice, "I wonder what they'll do next! As for pulling me out of the window, I only wish they *could*! I'm sure *I* don't want to stop in here any longer!"

She waited for some time without hearing anything more: at last came a rumbling of little cart-wheels, and the sound of a good many voices all talking together: she made out the words "where's the other ladder? — why, I hadn't to bring but one, Bill's got the other — here, put 'em up at this corner — no, tie 'em together first — they don't reach high enough yet — oh, they'll do well enough, don't be particular — here, Bill! catch hold of this rope — will the roof bear? — mind that loose slate — oh, it's coming down! heads below! —" (a loud crash) "now, who did that? — it was Bill, I fancy — who's to go down the chimney? — nay, *I* sha'n't! *you* do it! — *that* I won't then — Bill's got to go down — here, Bill! the master says you've to go down the chimney!"

"Oh, so Bill's got to come down the chimney, has he?" said Alice to herself, "why, they seem to put everything upon Bill! I wouldn't be in Bill's place for a good deal: the fireplace is a pretty tight one, but I *think* I can kick a little!"

She drew her foot as far down the chimney as she could, and waited till she heard a little animal (she couldn't guess what sort it was) scratching and scrambling in the chimney close above her: then, saying to herself "this is Bill," she gave one sharp kick, and waited again to see what would happen next.

The first thing was a general chorus of "there goes Bill!" then the rabbit's voice alone "catch him, you by the hedge!" then silence, and then another confusion of voices, "how was it, old fellow? what happened to you? tell us all about it."

Last came a little feeble squeaking voice, ("that's Bill" thought

Alice,) which said "well, I hardly know — I'm all of a fluster myself — something comes at me like a Jack-in-the-box, and the next minute up I goes like a rocket!" "And so you did, old fellow!" said the other voices.

"We must burn the house down!" said the voice of the rabbit, and Alice called out as loud as she could "if you do, I'll set Dinah at you!" This caused silence again, and while Alice was thinking "but how can I get Dinah here?" she found to her great delight that she was getting smaller: very soon she was able to get up out of the uncomfortable position in which she had been lying, and in two or three minutes more she was once more three inches high.

She ran out of the house as quick as she could, and found quite a crowd of little animals waiting outside — guinea-pigs, white mice, squirrels, and "Bill" a little green lizard, that was being supported in the arms of one of the guinea-pigs, while another was giving it something out of a bottle. They all made a rush at her the moment she appeared, but Alice ran her hardest, and soon found herself in a thick wood.

CHAPTER III

"The first thing I've got to do," said Alice to herself, as she wandered about in the wood, "is to grow to my right size, and the second thing is to find my way into that lovely garden. I think that will be the best plan."

It sounded an excellent plan, no doubt, and very neatly and simply arranged: the only difficulty was, that she had not the smallest idea how to set about it, and while she was peering anxiously among the trees round her, a little sharp bark just over her head made her look up in a great hurry.

An enormous puppy was looking down at her with large round eyes, and feebly stretching out one paw, trying to reach her: "poor thing!" said Alice in a coaxing tone, and she tried hard to whistle to it, but she was terribly alarmed all the while at the thought that it might be hungry, in which case it would probably devour her in spite of all her coaxing. Hardly knowing what she did, she picked up a little bit of stick, and held it out to the puppy: whereupon the puppy jumped into the air off all its feet at once, and with a yelp of delight rushed at the stick, and made believe to worry it: then Alice dodged behind a great thistle to keep herself from being run over, and, the moment she appeared at the other side, the puppy made another dart at the stick, and tumbled head over heels in its hurry to get hold: then Alice, thinking it was very like having a game of play with a cart-horse, and expecting every moment to be trampled under its feet, ran round the thistle again: then the puppy began a series of short charges at the stick, running a very little way forwards each time and a long way back, and barking hoarsely all the while, till at last it sat down a good way off, panting, with its tongue hanging out of its mouth, and its great eyes half shut.

This seemed to Alice a good opportunity for making her escape: she set off at once, and ran till the puppy's bark sounded quite faint in the distance, and till she was quite tired and out of breath.

"And yet what a dear little puppy it was!" said Alice, as she leant against a buttercup to rest herself, and fanned herself with her hat, "I should have liked teaching it tricks, if — if I'd only been the right size to do it! Oh! I'd nearly forgotten that I've got to grow up again! Let me see: how *is* it to be managed? I suppose I ought to eat or drink something or other, but the great question is, what?"

The great question certainly was, what? Alice looked all round her at the flowers and the blades of grass, but could not see anything that looked like the right thing to eat under the circumstances. There was a large mushroom near her, about the same height as herself, and when she had looked under it, and on both sides of it, and behind it, it occurred to her to look and see what was on the top of it.

She stretched herself up on tiptoe, and peeped over the edge of the mushroom, and her eyes immediately met those of a large blue caterpillar, which was sitting with its arms folded, quietly smoking a long hookah, and taking not the least notice of her or of anything else.

For some time they looked at each other in silence: at last the caterpillar took the hookah out of its mouth, and languidly addressed her.

"Who are you?" said the caterpillar.

This was not an encouraging opening for a conversation: Alice replied rather shyly, "I — I hardly know, sir, just at present — at least I know who I *was* when I got up this morning, but I think I must have been changed several times since that."

"What do you mean by that?" said the caterpillar, "explain yourself!"

"I ca'n't explain *myself*, I'm afraid, sir," said Alice, "because I'm not myself, you see."

"I don't see," said the caterpillar.

"I'm afraid I ca'n't put it more clearly," Alice replied very politely, "for I ca'n't understand it myself, and really to be so many different sizes in one day is very confusing."

"It isn't," said the caterpillar.

"Well, perhaps you haven't found it so yet," said Alice, "but when you have to turn into a chrysalis, you know, and then after that into a butterfly, I should think it'll feel a little queer, don't you think so?"

"Not a bit," said the caterpillar.

"All I know is," said Alice, "it would feel queer to *me*."

"*You*!" said the caterpillar contemptuously, "who are you?"

Which brought them back again to the beginning of the conversation: Alice felt a little irritated at the caterpillar making such *very* short remarks, and she drew herself up and said very gravely "I think you ought to tell me who *you* are, first."

"Why?" said the caterpillar.

Here was another puzzling question: and as Alice had no reason ready, and the caterpillar seemed to be in a *very* bad temper, she turned round and walked away.

"Come back!" the caterpillar called after her, "I've something important to say!"

This sounded promising: Alice turned and came back again.

"Keep your temper," said the caterpillar.

"Is that all?" said Alice, swallowing down her anger as well as she could.

"No," said the caterpillar.

Alice thought she might as well wait, as she had nothing else to do, and perhaps after all the caterpillar might tell her something worth hearing. For some minutes it puffed away at its hookah without speaking, but at last it unfolded its arms, took the hookah out of its mouth again, and said "so you think you're changed, do you?"

"Yes, sir," said Alice, "I ca'n't remember the things I used to know — I've tried to say 'How doth the little busy bee' and it came all different!"

"Try and repeat 'You are old, father William'," said the caterpillar.

Alice folded her hands, and began:

"You are old, father William," the young man said,
  "And your hair is exceedingly white:
And yet you incessantly stand on your head —
  Do you think, at your age, it is right?"

"In my youth," father William replied to his son,
  "I feared it *might* injure the brain:
But now that I'm perfectly sure I have none,
  Why, I do it again and again."

"You are old," said the youth, "as I mentioned before,
  And have grown most uncommonly fat:
Yet you turned a back-somersault in at the door —
  Pray what is the reason of that?"

"In my youth," said the sage, as he shook his gray locks,
  "I kept all my limbs very supple
By the use of this ointment, five shillings the box —
  Allow me to sell you a couple."

"You are old," said the youth, "and your jaws are too weak
  For anything tougher than suet:
Yet you eat all the goose, with the bones and the beak —
  Pray, how did you manage to do it?"

"In my youth," said the old man, "I took to the law,
  And argued each case with my wife,
And *the muscular strength, which it gave to my jaw*,
  Has lasted the rest of my life."

"You are old," said the youth, "one would hardly suppose
  That your eye was as steady as ever:
Yet you balanced an eel on the end of your nose —
  What made you so *awfully* clever?"

"I have answered three questions, and that is enough,"
  Said his father, "don't give yourself airs!
Do you think I can listen all day to such stuff?
  Be off, or I'll kick you down stairs!"

"That is not said right," said the caterpillar.

"Not *quite* right, I'm afraid," said Alice timidly, "some of the words have got altered."

"It is wrong from beginning to end," said the caterpillar decidedly, and there was silence for some minutes: the caterpillar was the first to speak.

"What size do you want to be?" it asked.

"Oh, I'm not particular as to size," Alice hastily replied, "only one doesn't like changing so often, you know."

"Are you content now?" said the caterpillar.

"Well, I should like to be *little* larger, sir, if you wouldn't mind," said Alice, "three inches is such a wretched height to be."

"It is a very good height indeed!" said the caterpillar loudly and angrily, rearing itself straight up as it spoke (it was exactly three inches high).

"But I'm not used to it!" pleaded poor Alice in a piteous tone, and she thought to herself "I wish the creatures wouldn't be so easily offended!"

"You'll get used to it in time," said the caterpillar, and it put the hookah into its mouth, and began smoking again.

This time Alice waited quietly until it chose to speak again: in a few minutes the caterpillar took the hookah out of its mouth, and got down off the mushroom, and crawled away into the grass, merely remarking as it went: "the top will make you grow taller, and the stalk will make you grow shorter."

"The top of *what*? the stalk of *what*?" thought Alice.

"Of the mushroom," said the caterpillar, just as if she had asked it aloud, and in another moment it was out of sight.

Alice remained looking thoughtfully at the mushroom for a minute, and then picked it and carefully broke it in two, taking the stalk in one hand, and the top in the other. "*Which* does the stalk do?" she said, and nibbled a little bit of it to try: the next moment she felt a violent blow on her chin: it had struck her foot!

She was a good deal frightened by this very sudden change, but as she did not shrink any further, and had not dropped the top of the mushroom, she did not give up hope yet. There was hardly room to open her mouth, with her chin pressing against her foot, but she did it at last, and managed to bite off a little bit of the top of the mushroom.

* * * * *

"Come! my head's free at last!" said Alice in a tone of delight, which changed into alarm in another moment, when she found that her shoulders were nowhere to be seen: she looked down upon an immense length of neck, which seemed to rise like a stalk out of a sea of green leaves that lay far below her.

"What *can* all that green stuff be?" said Alice, "and where *have* my shoulders got to? And oh! my poor hands! how is it I ca'n't see you?" She was moving them about as she spoke, but no result seemed to follow, except a little rustling among the leaves. Then she tried to bring her head down to her hands, and was delighted to find that her neck would bend about easily in every direction, like a serpent. She had just succeeded in bending it down in a beautiful zig-zag, and was going to dive in among the leaves, which she found to be the tops of the trees of the wood she had been wandering in, when a sharp hiss made her draw back: a large pigeon had flown into her face, and was violently beating her with its wings.

"Serpent!" screamed the pigeon.

"I'm *not* a serpent!" said Alice indignantly, "let me alone!"

"I've tried every way!" the pigeon said desperately, with a kind of sob: "nothing seems to suit 'em!"

"I haven't the least idea what you mean," said Alice.

"I've tried the roots of trees, and I've tried banks, and I've tried hedges," the pigeon went on without attending to her, "but them serpents! There's no pleasing 'em!"

Alice was more and more puzzled, but she thought there was no use in saying anything till the pigeon had finished.

"As if it wasn't trouble enough hatching the eggs!" said the pigeon, "without being on the look out for serpents, day and night! Why, I haven't had a wink of sleep these three weeks!"

"I'm very sorry you've been annoyed," said Alice, beginning to see its meaning.

"And just as I'd taken the highest tree in the wood," said the pigeon raising its voice to a shriek, "and was just thinking I was free of 'em at last, they must needs come down from the sky! Ugh! Serpent!"

"But I'm *not* a serpent," said Alice, "I'm a — I'm a —"

"Well! *What* are you?" said the pigeon, "I see you're trying to invent something."

"I — I'm a little girl," said Alice, rather doubtfully, as she remembered the number of changes she had gone through.

"A likely story indeed!" said the pigeon, "I've seen a good many of them in my time, but never *one* with such a neck as yours! No, you're a serpent, I know *that* well enough! I suppose you'll tell me next that you never tasted an egg!"

"I *have* tasted eggs, certainly," said Alice, who was a very truthful child, "but indeed I don't want any of yours. I don't like them raw."

"Well, be off, then!" said the pigeon, and settled down into its nest again. Alice crouched down among the trees, as well as she could, as her neck kept getting entangled among the branches, and several times she had to stop and untwist it. Soon she remembered the pieces of mushroom which she still held in her hands, and set to work very carefully, nibbling first at one and then at the other, and growing sometimes taller and sometimes shorter, until she had succeeded in bringing herself down to her usual size.

It was so long since she had been of the right size that it felt quite strange at first, but she got quite used to it in a minute or two, and began talking to herself as usual: "well! there's half my plan done now! How puzzling all these changes are! I'm never sure what I'm going to be, from one minute to another! However, I've got to my right size again: the next thing is, to get into that beautiful garden — how *is* it to be done, I wonder?"

Just as she said this, she noticed that one of the trees had a doorway leading right into it. "That's very curious!" she thought, "but everything's curious today: I may as well go in." And in she went.

Once more she found herself in the long hall, and close to the little

glass table: "now, I'll manage better this time" she said to herself, and began by taking the little golden key, and unlocking the door that led into the garden. Then she set to work eating the pieces of mushroom till she was about fifteen inches high: then she walked down the little passage: and *then* — she found herself at last in the beautiful garden, among the bright flowerbeds and the cool fountains.

CHAPTER IV

A large rose tree stood near the entrance of the garden: the roses on it were white, but there were three gardeners at it, busily painting them red. This Alice thought a very curious thing, and she went near to watch them, and just as she came up she heard one of them say "look out, Five! Don't go splashing paint over me like that!"

"I couldn't help it," said Five in a sulky tone, "Seven jogged my elbow."

On which Seven lifted up his head and said "that's right, Five! Always lay the blame on others!"

"*You'd* better not talk!" said Five, "I heard the Queen say only yesterday she thought of having you beheaded!"

"What for?" said the one who had spoken first.

"That's not your business, Two!" said Seven.

"Yes, it *is* his business!" said Five, "and I'll tell him: it was for bringing tulip-roots to the cook instead of potatoes."

Seven flung down his brush, and had just begun "well! Of all the unjust things —" when his eye fell upon Alice, and he stopped suddenly: the others looked round, and all of them took off their hats and bowed low.

"Would you tell me, please," said Alice timidly, "why you are painting those roses?"

Five and Seven looked at Two, but said nothing: Two began, in a low voice, "why, Miss, the fact is, this ought to have been a red rose tree, and we put a white one in by mistake, and if the Queen was to find it out, we should all have our heads cut off. So, you see, we're doing our best, before she comes, to —" At this moment Five, who had been looking anxiously across the garden called out "the Queen! the

Queen!" and the three gardeners instantly threw themselves flat upon their faces. There was a sound of many footsteps, and Alice looked round, eager to see the Queen.

First came ten soldiers carrying clubs: these were all shaped like the three gardeners, flat and oblong, with their hands and feet at the corners: next the ten courtiers; these were all ornamented with diamonds, and walked two and two, as the soldiers did. After these came the Royal children: there were ten of them, and the little dears came jumping merrily along, hand in hand, in couples: they were all ornamented with hearts. Next came the guests, mostly kings and queens, among whom Alice recognised the white rabbit: it was talking in a hurried nervous manner, smiling at everything that was said, and went by without noticing her. Then followed the Knave of Hearts, carrying the King's crown on a cushion, and, last of all this grand procession, came THE KING AND QUEEN OF HEARTS.

When the procession came opposite to Alice, they all stopped and looked at her, and the Queen said severely "who is this?" She said it to the Knave of Hearts, who only bowed and smiled in reply.

"Idiot!" said the Queen, turning up her nose, and asked Alice "what's your name?"

"My name is Alice, so please your Majesty," said Alice boldly, for she thought to herself "why, they're only a pack of cards! I needn't be afraid of them!"

"Who are these?" said the Queen, pointing to the three gardeners lying round the rose tree, for, as they were lying on their faces, and the pattern on their backs was the same as the rest of the pack, she could not tell whether they were gardeners, or soldiers, or courtiers, or three of her own children.

"How should *I* know?" said Alice, surprised at her own courage, "it's no business of *mine*."

The Queen turned crimson with fury, and, after glaring at her for a minute, began in a voice of thunder "off with her —"

"Nonsense!" said Alice, very loudly and decidedly, and the Queen was silent.

The King laid his hand upon her arm, and said timidly "remember, my dear! She is only a child!"

The Queen turned angrily away from him, and said to the Knave "turn them over!"

The Knave did so, very carefully, with one foot.

"Get up!" said the Queen, in a shrill loud voice, and the three gardeners instantly jumped up, and began bowing to the King, the Queen, the Royal children, and everybody else.

"Leave off that!" screamed the Queen, "you make me giddy." And then, turning to the rose tree, she went on "what *have* you been doing here?"

"May it please your Majesty," said Two very humbly, going down on one knee as he spoke, "we were trying —"

"*I* see!" said the Queen, who had meantime been examining the roses, "off with their heads!" and the procession moved on, three of the soldiers remaining behind to execute the three unfortunate gardeners, who ran to Alice for protection.

"You sha'n't be beheaded!" said Alice, and she put them into her pocket: the three soldiers marched once round her, looking for them, and then quietly marched off after the others.

"Are their heads off?" shouted the Queen.

"Their heads are gone," the soldiers shouted in reply, "if it please your Majesty!"

"That's right!" shouted the Queen, "can you play croquet?"

The soldiers were silent, and looked at Alice, as the question was evidently meant for her.

"Yes!" shouted Alice at the top of her voice.

"Come on then!" roared the Queen, and Alice joined the procession, wondering very much what would happen next.

"It's — it's a very fine day!" said a timid little voice: she was walking by the white rabbit, who was peeping anxiously into her face.

"Very," said Alice, "where's the Marchioness?"

"Hush, hush!" said the rabbit in a low voice, "she'll hear you. The Queen's the Marchioness: didn't you know that?"

"No, I didn't," said Alice, "what of?"

"Queen of Hearts," said the rabbit in a whisper, putting its mouth close to her ear, "and Marchioness of Mock Turtles."

"What are *they*?" said Alice, but there was no time for the answer, for they had reached the croquet-ground, and the game began instantly.

Alice thought she had never seen such a curious croquet-ground in all her life: it was all in ridges and furrows: the croquet-balls were live hedgehogs, the mallets live ostriches, and the soldiers had to double themselves up, and stand on their feet and hands, to make the arches.

The chief difficulty which Alice found at first was to manage her ostrich: she got its body tucked away, comfortably enough, under her arm, with its legs hanging down, but generally, just as she had got its neck straightened out nicely, and was going to give a blow with its head, it *would* twist itself round, and look up into her face, with such a puzzled expression that she could not help bursting out laughing: and when she had got its head down, and was going to begin again, it was very confusing to find that the hedgehog had unrolled itself, and was in the act of crawling away: besides all this, there was generally a ridge or a furrow in her way, wherever she wanted to send the hedgehog to, and as the doubled-up soldiers were always getting up and walking off to other parts of the ground, Alice soon came to the conclusion that it was a very difficult game indeed.

The players all played at once without waiting for turns, and quarrelled all the while at the tops of their voices, and in a very few minutes the Queen was in a furious passion, and went stamping about and shouting "off with his head!" or "off with her head!" about once in a minute. All those whom she sentenced were taken into custody by the soldiers, who of course had to leave off being arches to do this, so that, by the end of half an hour or so, there were no arches left, and all the players, except the King, the Queen, and Alice, were in custody, and under sentence of execution.

Then the Queen left off, quite out of breath, and said to Alice "have you seen the Mock Turtle?"

"No," said Alice, "I don't even know what a Mock Turtle is."

"Come on then," said the Queen, "and it shall tell you its history."

As they walked off together, Alice heard the King say in a low voice, to the company generally, "you are all pardoned."

"Come, that's a good thing!" thought Alice, who had felt quite grieved at the number of executions which the Queen had ordered.

They very soon came upon a Gryphon, which lay fast asleep in the sun: (if you don't know what a Gryphon is, look at the picture): "up, lazy thing!" said the Queen, "and take this young lady to see the Mock Turtle, and to hear its history. I must go back and see after some executions I ordered," and she walked off, leaving Alice with the Gryphon. Alice did not quite like the look of the creature, but on the whole she thought it quite as safe to stay as to go after that savage Queen: so she waited.

The Gryphon sat up and rubbed its eyes: then it watched the Queen till she was out of sight: then it chuckled. "What fun!" said the Gryphon, half to itself, half to Alice.

"What *is* the fun?" said Alice.

"Why, *she*," said the Gryphon; "it's all her fancy, that: they never executes nobody, you know: come on!"

"Everybody says 'come on!' here," thought Alice, as she walked slowly after the Gryphon; "I never was ordered about so before in all my life — never!"

They had not gone far before they saw the Mock Turtle in the distance, sitting sad and lonely on a little ledge of rock, and, as they came nearer, Alice could hear it sighing as if its heart would break. She pitied it deeply: "what is its sorrow?" she asked the Gryphon, and the Gryphon answered, very nearly in the same words as before, "it's all its fancy, that: it hasn't got no sorrow, you know: come on!"

So they went up to the Mock Turtle, who looked at them with large eyes full of tears, but said nothing.

"This here young lady" said the Gryphon, "wants for to know your history, she do."

"I'll tell it," said the Mock Turtle, in a deep hollow tone, "sit down, and don't speak till I've finished."

So they sat down, and no one spoke for some minutes: Alice thought to herself "I don't see how it can *ever* finish, if it doesn't begin," but she waited patiently.

"Once," said the Mock Turtle at last, with a deep sigh, "I was a real Turtle."

These words were followed by a very long silence, broken only by an occasional exclamation of "hjckrrh!" from the Gryphon, and the constant heavy sobbing of the Mock Turtle. Alice was very nearly getting up and saying, "thank you, sir, for your interesting story," but she could not help thinking there *must* be more to come, so she sat still and said nothing.

"When we were little," the Mock Turtle went on, more calmly, though still sobbing a little now and then, "we went to school in the sea. The master was an old Turtle — we used to call him Tortoise —"

"Why did you call him Tortoise, if he wasn't one?" asked Alice.

"We called him Tortoise because he taught us," said the Mock Turtle angrily, "really you are very dull!"

"You ought to be ashamed of yourself for asking such a simple question," added the Gryphon, and then they both sat silent and looked at poor Alice, who felt ready to sink into the earth: at last the Gryphon said to the Mock Turtle, "get on, old fellow! Don't be all day!" and the Mock Turtle went on in these words:

"You may not have lived much under the sea —" ("I haven't," said Alice,) "and perhaps you were never even introduced to a lobster—" (Alice began to say "I once tasted —" but hastily checked herself, and said "no, never," instead,) "so you can have no idea what a delightful thing a Lobster Quadrille is!"

"No, indeed," said Alice, "what sort of a thing is it?"

"Why," said the Gryphon, "you form into a line along the sea shore —"

"Two lines!" cried the Mock Turtle, "seals, turtles, salmon, and so on — advance twice —"

"Each with a lobster as partner!" cried the Gryphon.

"Of course," the Mock Turtle said, "advance twice, set to partners—"

"Change lobsters, and retire in same order —" interrupted the Gryphon.

"Then, you know," continued the Mock Turtle, "you throw the —"

"The lobsters!" shouted the Gryphon, with a bound into the air.

"As far out to sea as you can —"

"Swim after them!" screamed the Gryphon.

"Turn a somersault in the sea!" cried the Mock Turtle, capering wildly about.

"Change lobsters again!" yelled the Gryphon at the top of its voice, "and then —"

"That's all," said the Mock Turtle, suddenly dropping its voice, and the two creatures, who had been jumping about like mad things all this time, sat down again very sadly and quietly, and looked at Alice.

"It must be a very pretty dance," said Alice timidly.

"Would you like to see a little of it?" said the Mock Turtle.

"Very much indeed," said Alice.

"Come, let's try the first figure!" said the Mock Turtle to the Gryphon, "we can do it without lobsters, you know. Which shall sing?"

"Oh! *you* sing!" said the Gryphon, "I've forgotten the words."

So they began solemnly dancing round and round Alice, every now and then treading on her toes when they came too close, and waving their fore-paws to mark the time, while the Mock Turtle sang, slowly and sadly, these words:

"Beneath the waters *of* the sea
Are lobsters thick as thick can be —
They love to dance with you and me,
  My own, my gentle Salmon!"

The Gryphon joined in singing the chorus, which was:

"Salmon come up! Salmon go down!
Salmon come twist your tail around!
Of all the fishes *of* the sea
  There's none so good as Salmon!"

"Thank you," said Alice, feeling very glad that the figure was over.

"Shall we try the second figure?" said the Gryphon, "or would you prefer a song?"

"Oh, a song, please!" Alice replied, so eagerly, that the Gryphon said, in a rather offended tone, "hm! no accounting for tastes! Sing her 'Mock Turtle Soup,' will you, old fellow!"

The Mock Turtle sighed deeply, and began, in a voice sometimes choked with sobs, to sing this:

"Beautiful Soup, so rich and green,
Waiting in a hot tureen!
Who for such dainties would not stoop?
Soup of the evening, beautiful Soup!
Soup of the evening, beautiful Soup!
Beau—ootiful Soo—oop!
Beau—ootiful Soo—oop!
Soo–oop of the e–e–evening,
Beautiful beautiful Soup!

"Chorus again!" cried the Gryphon, and the Mock Turtle had just begun to repeat it, when a cry of "the trial's beginning!" was heard in the distance.

"Come on!" said the Gryphon, and, taking Alice by the hand, he hurried off, without waiting for the end of the song.

"What trial is it?" panted Alice as she ran, but the Gryphon only answered "come on!" and ran the faster, and more and more faintly came, borne on the breeze that followed them, the melancholy words:

"Soo–oop of the e–e–evening,
Beautiful beautiful Soup!"

The King and Queen were seated on their throne when they arrived, with a great crowd assembled around them: the Knave was in custody: and before the King stood the white rabbit, with a trumpet in one hand, and a scroll of parchment in the other.

"Herald! read the accusation!" said the King.

On this the white rabbit blew three blasts on the trumpet, and then unrolled the parchment scroll, and read as follows:

"The Queen of Hearts she made some tarts
All on a summer day:
The Knave of Hearts he stole those tarts,
And took them quite away!"

"Now for the evidence," said the King, "and then the sentence."

"No!" said the Queen, "first the sentence, and then the evidence!"

"Nonsense!" cried Alice, so loudly that everybody jumped, "the idea of having the sentence first!"

"Hold your tongue!" said the Queen.

"I won't!" said Alice, "you're nothing but a pack of cards! Who cares for you?"

At this the whole pack rose up into the air, and came flying down upon her: she gave a little scream of fright, and tried to beat them off, and found herself lying on the bank, with her head in the lap of her sister, who was gently brushing away some leaves that had fluttered down from the trees on to her face.

"Wake up! Alice dear!" said her sister, "what a nice long sleep you've had!"

"Oh, I've had such a curious dream!" said Alice, and she told her sister all her Adventures Under Ground, as you have read them, and when she had finished, her sister kissed her and said "it *was* a curious dream, dear, certainly! But now run in to your tea: it's getting late."

So Alice ran off, thinking while she ran (as well she might) what a wonderful dream it had been.

But her sister sat there some while longer, watching the setting sun, and thinking of little Alice and her Adventures, till she too began dreaming after a fashion, and this was her dream:

She saw an ancient city, and a quiet river winding near it along the plain, and up the stream went slowly gliding a boat with a merry party of children on board — she could hear their voices and laughter like music over the water — and among them was another little Alice, who sat listening with bright eager eyes to a tale that was being told, and she listened for the words of the tale, and lo! it was the dream of her own little sister. So the boat wound slowly along, beneath the bright summer-day, with its merry crew and its music of voices and laughter, till it passed round one of the many turnings of the stream, and she saw it no more.

Then she thought, (in a dream within the dream, as it were,) how this same little Alice would, in the after-time, be herself a grown woman: and how she would keep, through her riper years, the simple and loving heart of her childhood: and how she would gather around her other little children, and make *their* eyes bright and eager with many a wonderful tale, perhaps even with these very adventures of the little Alice of long-ago: and how she would feel with all their simple sorrows, and find a pleasure in all their simple joys, remembering her own child-life, and the happy summer days.

"ALICE" ON THE STAGE

(*The Theatre*, April, 1887)

"Look here; here's all this Judy's clothes falling to pieces again." Such were the pensive words of Mr. Thomas Codlin; and they may fitly serve as a motto for a writer who has set himself the unusual task of passing in review a set of puppets that are virtually his own—the stage embodiments of his own dream-children.

Not that the play itself is in any sense mine. The arrangements, in dramatic form, of a story written without the slightest idea that it would be so adapted, was a task that demanded powers denied to me, but possessed in an eminent degree, so far as I can judge, by Mr. Savile Clarke. I do not feel myself qualified to criticise his play, as a play; nor shall I venture on any criticism of the players as players.

What is it, then, I have set myself to do? And what possible claim have I to be heard? My answer must be that, as the writer of the two stories thus adapted, and the originator (as I believe, for at least I have not *consciously* borrowed them) of the "airy nothings" for which Mr. Saville Clarke has so skilfully provided, if not a name, at least, a "local habitation," I may without boastfulness claim to have a special knowledge of what it was I meant them to be, and so a special understanding of how far that intention has been realised. And I fancied there might be some readers of *The Theatre* who would be interested in sharing that knowledge and that understanding.

Many a day had we rowed together on that quiet stream—the three little maidens and I—and many a fairy tale had been extemporised for their benefit—whether it were at times when the narrator was "i' the vein," and fancies unsought came crowding thick upon him, or at times when the jaded Muse was goaded into action, and plodded meekly on, more because she had to say something than that she had something to say—yet none of these many tales got written down: they lived and died, like summer midges, each in its own golden afternoon until there came a day when, as it chanced, one of my little listeners petitioned that the tale might be written out for her. That was many a year ago, but I distinctly remember, now as I write, how, in a desperate attempt to strike out some new line of fairy-lore, I had sent my heroine straight down a rabbit-hole, to begin with, without the least idea what was to happen afterwards. And so, to please a child I loved (I don't remember any other motive), I printed in manuscript, and illustrated with my own crude designs—designs that rebelled against every law of Anatomy or Art (for I had never had a lesson in drawing)—the book which I have just had published in facsimile. In writing it out, I added many fresh ideas, which seemed to grow of themselves upon the original stock; and many more added themselves when, years afterwards, I wrote it all over again for publication: but (this may interest some readers of "Alice" to know) every such idea and nearly every word of the dialogue, *came of itself*. Sometimes an idea comes at night, when I have had to get up and strike a light to note it down—sometimes when out on a lonely winter walk, when I have had to stop, and with half-frozen fingers jot down a few words which should keep the new-born idea from perishing—but whenever or however it comes, *it comes of itself*. I cannot set invention going like a clock, by any voluntary winding up: nor do I believe that any *original* writing (and what other writing is worth preserving?) was ever so produced. If you sit down, unimpassioned and uninspired, and *tell* yourself to write for so many hours, you will merely produce (at least I am sure *I* should merely produce) some of that article which fills, so far as I can judge, two-thirds of most magazines—most easy to write most weary to read—men call it "padding," and it is to my mind one of the most detestable things in modern literature. "Alice" and the "Looking-Glass" are made up almost wholly of bits and scraps, single ideas which came of themselves. Poor they may have been; but at least they were the best I had to offer: and I can desire no higher praise to be written of me than the words of a Poet, written of a Poet,

> "He gave the people of his best:
> The worst he kept, the best he gave."

I have wandered from my subject, I know: yet grant me another minute to relate a little incident of my own experience. I was walking on a hillside, alone, one bright summer day, when suddenly there came into my head one line of verse—one solitary line—"For the Snark *was* a Boojum, you see." I knew not what it meant, then: I know not what it means, now; but I wrote it down: and, some time afterwards, the rest of the stanza occurred to me, that being its last line: and so by degrees, at odd moments during the next year or two, the rest of the poem pieced itself together, that being its last stanza. And since then, periodically I have received courteous letters from strangers, begging to know whether "The Hunting of the Snark" is an allegory, or contains some hidden moral, or is a political satire: and for all such questions I have but one answer, "*I don't know!*" And now I return to my text, and will wander no more.

Stand forth, then, from the shadowy past, "Alice," the child of my dreams. Full many a year has slipped away, since that "golden afternoon" that gave thee birth, but I can call it up almost as clearly as if it were yesterday—the cloudless blue above, the watery mirror below, the boat drifting idly on its way, the tinkle of the drops that fell from the oars, as they waved so sleepily to and fro, and (the one bright gleam of life in all the slumberous scene) the three eager faces, hungry for news of fairy-land, and who would not be said "nay" to: from whose lips "Tell us a story, please," had all the stern immutability of Fate!

What wert thou, dream-Alice, in thy foster-father's eyes ? How shall he picture thee? Loving, first, loving and gentle: loving as a dog (forgive the prosaic simile, but I know no earthly love so pure and perfect), and gentle as a fawn: then courteous—courteous to *all*, high or low, grand or grotesque, King or Caterpillar, even as though she were herself a King's daughter, and her clothing of wrought gold: then trustful, ready to accept the wildest impossibilities with all that utter trust that only dreamers know; and lastly, curious—wildly curious, and with the eager enjoyment of Life that comes only in the happy hours of childhood, when all is new and fair, and when Sin and Sorrow are but names—empty words signifying nothing!

And the White Rabbit, what of *him*? Was *he* framed on the " Alice" lines, or meant as a contrast? As a contrast, distinctly. For *her* "youth," "audacity," "vigour," and "swift directness of purpose," read "elderly," "timid," "feeble," and "nervously shilly-shallying," and you will get *something* of what I meant him to be. I *think* the White Rabbit should wear spectacles. I am sure his voice should quaver, and his knees quiver, and his whole air suggest a total inability to say "Bo" to a goose!

But I cannot hope to be allowed, even by the courteous Editor of *The Theatre*, half the space I should need (even if my *reader's* patience would hold out) to discuss each of my puppets one by one. Let me cull from the two books a Royal Trio—the Queen of Hearts, the Red Queen, and the White Queen. It was certainly hard on my Muse, to expect her to sing of *three* Queens, within such brief compass, and yet to give to each her own individuality. Each, of course, had to preserve, through all her eccentricities, a certain queenly *dignity. That* was essential. And for distinguishing traits, I pictured to myself the Queen of Hearts as a sort of embodiment of ungovernable passion—a blind and aimless Fury. The Red Queen I pictured as a Fury, but of another type; *her* passion must be cold and calm; she must be formal and strict, yet not unkindly; pedantic to the tenth degree, the concentrated essence of all governesses! Lastly, the White Queen seemed, to my dreaming fancy, gentle, stupid, fat and pale; helpless as an infant; and with a slow, maundering, bewildered air about her just *suggesting* imbecility, but never quite passing into it; that would be, I think, fatal to any comic effect she might otherwise produce. There is a character strangely like her in Wilkie Collins' novel "No Name": by two different converging paths we have somehow reached the same ideal, and Mrs. Wragg and the White Queen might have been twin-sisters.

As it is no part of my present purpose to find fault with any of those who have striven so zealously to make this "dream-play" a waking success, I shall but name two or three who seemed to me specially successful in realising the characters of the story.

None, I think, was better realised than the two undertaken by Mr. Sydney Harcourt, "the Hatter" and "Tweedledum." To see him enact the Hatter was a weird and uncanny thing, as though some grotesque monster, seen last night in a dream, should walk into the room in broad daylight, and quietly say "Good morning!" I need not try to describe what I meant the Hatter to be, since, so far as I can now remember, it was exactly what Mr. Harcourt has made him: and I may say nearly the same of Tweedledum: but the Hatter surprised me most—perhaps only because it came first in the play.

There were others who realised my ideas nearly as well; but I am not attempting a complete review: I will conclude with a few words about the two children who played "Alice" and "the Dormouse."

Of Miss Phoebe Carlo's performance it would be difficult to speak too highly. As a mere effort of memory, it was surely a marvellous feat for so young a child, to learn no less than two hundred and fifteen speeches—nearly three times as many as Beatrice in "Much Ado About Nothing." But what I admired most, as realising most nearly my ideal heroine, was her perfect assumption of the high spirits, and readiness to enjoy *everything*, of a child out for a holiday. I doubt if any grown actress, however experienced, could have worn this air so perfectly; *we* look before and after, and sigh for what is not; a child never does *this*: and it is only a child that can utter from her heart the words poor Margaret Fuller Ossoli so longed to make her own, "I am all happy *now*!"

And last (I may for once omit the time honoured addition "not least," for surely no tinier maiden ever yet achieved so genuine a theatrical success?) comes our dainty Dormouse. "Dainty" is the only epithet that seems to me exactly to suit her: with her beaming baby-face, the delicious crispness of her speech, and the perfect realism with which she makes herself the embodied essence of Sleep, she is surely the daintiest Dormouse that ever yet told us "I sleep when I breathe!" With the first words of that her opening speech, a sudden silence falls upon the house (at least it has been so every time *I* have been there), and the baby tones sound strangely clear in the stillness. And yet I doubt if the charm is due only to the incisive clearness of her articulation; to me there was an even greater charm in the utter self-abandonment and conscientious *thoroughness* of her acting. If Dorothy ever adopts a motto, it ought to be "thorough." I hope the time may soon come when she will have a better part than "Dormouse" to play—when some enterprising manager will revive the "Midsummer Night's Dream" and do his obvious duty to the public by securing Miss Dorothy d'Alcourt as "Puck"!

It would be well indeed for our churches if some of the clergy could take a lesson in enunciation from this little child; and better still, for "our noble selves," if *we* would lay to heart some things that she could teach us, and would learn by her example to realise, rather more than we do, the spirit of a maxim I once came across in an old book, "Whatsoever thy hand findeth to do, *do it with thy might*."

NOTES TO ALICE'S ADVENTURES IN WONDERLAND

For the sake of simplicity the notes that follow refer to the author of the Alice books by his pseudonym of Lewis Carroll throughout. They do not distinguish (as the Introduction does) between the biographical Charles Dodgson and the authorial Lewis Carroll.

NOTE ON THE TITLE

In a letter to Tom Taylor of 10 June 1864, Carroll speaks of his difficulties over finding a title for his story:

I should be very glad if you could help me in fixing on a name for my fairy-tale, which Mr Tenniel (in consequence of your kind introduction) is now illustrating . . . I first thought of 'Alice's Adventures under Ground', but that was pronounced too like a lesson-book, in which instruction about mines would be administered in the form of a grill; then I took 'Alice's Golden Hour' but that I gave up, having a dark suspicion that there is already a book called 'Lily's Golden Hours'. Here are the other names I have thought of:

<table>
<tr><td rowspan="3">Alice among the</td><td rowspan="3">elves
goblins</td><td rowspan="3">Alice's</td><td rowspan="3">doings
hours
adventures</td><td rowspan="3">in</td><td rowspan="3">elf-land
wonderland.</td></tr>
</table>

Of all these I at present prefer 'Alice's Adventures in Wonderland'. In spite of your 'morality', I want something sensational. Perhaps you can suggest a better name than any of these (*The Letters of Lewis Carroll*, ed. Morton N. Cohen, with the assistance of R. L. Green, 2 vols, London, 1979, vol 1, p. 65).

INTRODUCTORY POEM 'ALL IN THE GOLDEN AFTERNOON'

1 *All in the golden afternoon.* The brief poetic prelude (not in *AAUG*) retells the origins of 'the tale of Wonderland' on the boating expedition undertaken by Carroll, the Reverend Robinson Duckworth and the three Liddell children

(disguised as Prima, Secunda and Tertia in the poem) on the 'golden afternoon' of 4 July 1862. Carroll records the incident in his diaries for that day:

> Duckworth and I made an expedition *up* the river to Godstow with the three Liddells: we had tea on the bank there, and did not reach Christ Church again till quarter past eight, when we took them on to my rooms to see my collection of microphotographs, and restored them to the Deanery just before nine (*The Diaries of Lewis Carroll*, ed. R. L. Green, 2 vols, London, 1953, vol 2, p. 181).

The following February he added a marginal note to the entry:

> On which occasion I told them the fairy-tale of *Alice's Adventures under Ground*, which I undertook to write out for Alice, and which is now finished (as to the text) though the pictures are not yet nearly done.

He gave a much later and more elaborate account of the same occasion in '"Alice" on the Stage' in *The Theatre*, April 1887. (See pp. 293–8.) For a fuller account see 'The Genesis of Alice' in the Introduction (pp. xxx ff.).

Carroll shows his characteristic formal complexity by preceding the frame narrative of the 'childish story' with a frame poem about its origins and his friendship with the Liddell children. Compare the Introduction to Blake's *Songs of Innocence*, a book that was clearly important to Carroll, where the child commissions the poet to pipe songs for him just as the three Liddell girls 'beg a tale' from Carroll. During the course of Carroll's first meeting with the publisher of Alice's Adventures, Macmillan, he asked him to print "some of Blake's *Songs of Innocence* on large paper" (*Diaries*, vol 1, p. 206). The metre and idiom of Carroll's prelude is reminiscent of *The Lyrical Ballads* of Wordsworth and Coleridge.

2 *Like pilgrim's wither'd wreath . . . far-off land.* Pilgrims often returned with wreaths of flowers on their heads. Carroll strikes the note not only of a 'far-off land' but a far-off time here, a touch of Bunyan's dream-narrative *A Pilgrim's Progress* or Byron's *Childe Harold's Pilgrimage.*

CHAPTER I: DOWN THE RABBIT-HOLE

1 *without pictures or conversations.* The dream narrative that follows fulfils Alice's wish for a story *with* 'pictures' and 'conversations'.

2 *I must be getting somewhere near the centre of the earth.* Alice's figure is pretty accurate about the distance involved (3981.25 miles). Jules Verne's *Voyage au centre de la terre* was published in 1864, the year after Carroll's MS was written and a year before *Wonderland* first appeared in print. Carroll treats gravity with comparable levity in *Sylvie and Bruno*: in chapter 8 he demonstrates some of the problems of having tea in a falling house and in chapter 7 he speculates on the idea of an underground train with gravity as its sole means of propulsion.

3 *Dinah was the cat.* The name of the Liddell family's tabby cat, a favourite of Alice's, named after the music-hall song 'Villikins and his Dinah'. She recurs in the opening chapter of *Through the Looking-Glass.*

4 *a tiny golden key.* The scene has a curious resemblance to the 'Crystal Cabinet' of William Blake ('The Maiden caught me in the Wild,/Where I was dancing merrily;/She put me into her Cabinet/And Lock'd me up with a Golden key'). The story 'The Golden Key' by Carroll's friend George MacDonald was not published until 1867 in *Dealings with the Fairies*, but Carroll may have seen it in manuscript by 1862 and/or read MacDonald's poem 'The Golden Key' published in *Victoria Regis*, 1861.

5 *those beds of bright flowers and those cool fountains.* They have reminded some readers of the gardens of an Oxford college, such as those of Christ Church, where both Carroll and the Liddells lived. The garden is also a version of the gardens of romance, a reminder that Carroll is a contemporary of the Pre-Raphaelites and Tennyson, and that nonsense – represented here by her huge head and the idea of shutting up like a telescope – involves an absurd telescoping of romance.

6 *several nice little stories.* Carroll is poking fun at the moralistic literature for children represented by such books as Elizabeth Turner's *Cautionary Tales*, and were parodied in *Struwwelpeter* (translated into English in the 1840s). Alice would probably have been all too familiar with such stories.

7 *EAT ME.* 'Eat' or 'To be Eaten' would be more normal labels, equivalent to the spoken instruction 'Eat it'. 'Eat me' introduces a more disturbing note of animation and self-sacrifice. The threat of eating and being eaten runs through both Alice books. It is a sign of Carroll's psychological realism that Alice's dream is so preoccupied by ideas of changing size and growing, drinking and eating. According to his nephew, Carroll was 'very abstemious always', taking nothing in the middle of the day 'except a glass of wine and a biscuit', so that 'the healthy appetites of his little friends filled him with wonder, and even with alarm' (Stuart Dodgson Collingwood, *Life and Letters of Lewis Carroll*, London, 1898, p. 390).

CHAPTER II: THE POOL OF TEARS

1 *how to speak good English.* Alice, as a respectable upper-middle-class child, shares Carroll's preoccupation with 'good English'. The pleasure in transgressing the rules of language and logic in nonsense depends on belief in the conventions of linguistic correctness. Isa Bowman recalls how he 'loved correct elocution' (Isa Bowman, *Lewis Carroll as I Knew Him*, London, 1899, p. 88) and in a letter to his sister Mary written in 1892, Carroll having ticked her off for the slipshod grammar of a pamphlet she had written, affirmed:

> Good *English*, and graceful arrangement, are higher qualities, not attainable by *rule*, but only by having read much good English, and so having got a musical 'ear', so to speak . . . I think *newspapers* are largely responsible for the bad English now used in books. How few novels of the day are written in correct English! To find any such, you must go back 50 years or more. That is one reason why I like reading the *older* novels – Scott's, Miss Austen's, Miss Edgeworth's, etc. – that the *English* is so perfect (*Letters*, vol 2, p. 916).

Alice in general speaks as correctly as any of Jane Austen's heroines.

2 *what nonsense I'm talking*. The first time Alice uses the term 'nonsense' to describe what is happening (though it has cropped up in the introductory poem). According to the *Concordance*, she is the main critical user of the term in the book. Of the fifteen times 'nonsense' appears in the text, nine of them refer to Alice's judgement on the absurdity of what is being said.

3 *a pair of white kid-gloves in one hand and a large fan in the other*. The fan was originally a 'nosegay' (*Alice's Adventures under Ground*, see p. 254). The White Rabbit's fussiness about gloves was shared by Carroll who, according to one of his child friends, 'had a curious habit of always wearing, in all seasons of the year, a pair of grey and black cotton gloves' (Bowman, *Lewis Carroll as I Knew Him*, p. 9).

4 *I'm sure I'm not Ada . . . I ca'n't be Mabel*. In the original MS written out for Alice Liddell, the names were Gertrude and Florence, names of her cousins. The change later on from 'I must have been changed for Florence' to 'I must have been changed for Mabel' saved Carroll from family embarrassment but lost a nominal geographical joke.

5 *I shall never get to twenty at that rate!* Gardner explains why as follows: 'the multiplication table traditionally stops with the twelves, so if you continue this nonsense progression – 4 times 5 is 12, 4 times 6 is 13, 4 times 7 is 14, and so on – you end with 4 times 12 (the highest she can go) is 19 – just one short of twenty', *The Annotated Alice*, ed. Martin Gardner, Harmondsworth, 1965/1970, p. 38.

6 *How doth the little crocodile*. The first poem in the story, like most of those that follow, is a parody of a well-known children's poem. It parodies the first two stanzas of 'Against Idleness and Mischief' from *Divine Songs Attempted in Easy Language for the Use of Children* (1715) by the poet and divine, Isaac Watts (1674–1748):

How doth the little busy Bee
Improve each shining Hour,
And gather Honey all the Day
From ev'ry op'ning Flow'r!

How skilfully she builds her Cell!
How neat she spreads the Wax;
And labours hard to store it well
With the sweet Food she makes.

In works of labour or of skill,
I would be busy too;
For Satan finds some mischief still
For idle hands to do.

When reflecting on the French translation of *Alice* in 1867, Carroll observed: "The verses would be the great difficulty, as I fear, if the originals are not known in France, the parodies would be unintelligible", *Lewis Carroll and the House of Macmillan* ed. Morton N. Cohen and Anita Gandolfo, Cambridge, 1987, p. 50.

7 *Alice had been to the seaside once in her life.* The references to the seaside and railway were not part of *AAUG*. They may refer to Alice Liddell's visit to Llandudno for a summer holiday in 1861. *Bathing-machines*: horse-drawn changing rooms on wheels, a feature of the most popular Victorian seaside resorts, and a monument to the era's rather public cult of privacy. One of the 'five unmistakable marks' of a Snark is its taste for them:

The fourth is its fondness for bathing-machines,
Which it constantly carries about,
And believes that they add to the beauty of scenes—
A sentiment open to doubt.

Seaside resorts played a large part in the annual rituals of Victorian families like the Liddells – as they did for the bachelor Lewis Carroll in cultivating his friendships with little girls like Alice. Carroll regularly spent his holidays by the sea, first at Whitby, then on the Isle of Wight and latterly at Eastbourne.

8 *her brother's Latin Grammar.* Presumably a reference to Harry Liddell (1847–1911), Alice's brother, a pupil of Carroll's for a short period. The Latin Grammar in question would probably be Kennedy's, later known as *The Public School Latin Primer.* Though like most Victorian girls Alice does not learn Latin herself, her reflexes are always towards 'the right way' of addressing those she meets – as in this evocatively punctilious vocative, 'O Mouse!'

9 *the first sentence in her French lesson-book.* It is indeed the first sentence of the first lesson of the often reprinted *La Bagatelle: Intended to introduce children of three or four years old to some knowledge of the French Language*, 1804. Alice's recourse to it during her conversation with the Mouse is a sad index of the difficulty of applying text-book French to the real world.

10 *afraid that she had hurt the poor animal's feelings.* Compare Carroll's letter to Mrs Blakemore:

It is curious how apt one is, sometimes, to say just *the* thing the most mal-à-propos. I was calling not long ago on a lady, whose husband suffers from periodic attacks of madness – so that one would wish to avoid *all* allusion to so painful a subject: and before I knew what I was saying, I found myself in the middle of a comic story about a madman! (quoted in Jeffrey Stern, 'Lewis Carroll and Mrs Blakemore – an Unpublished Correspondence', *Jabberwocky*, vol 10, no 3, Summer 1981, p. 69).

11 *there was a Duck and a Dodo, a Lory and an Eaglet, and several other curious creatures.* The whole episode is a disguised allusion to an 'Expedition to Nuneham' recorded in Carroll's diary for 17 June 1862 (*Diaries*, vol 1, p. 178). This took the form of a boating-party involving Carroll, Duckworth and the Liddell girls, during which they all got thoroughly 'drenched'. The Duck is the Reverend Duckworth, the Dodo is Lewis Carroll himself (with his stutter he would often pronounce his name 'Do-do-Dodgson'). The Lory (a brightly coloured Australian parrot) is Lorina Liddell, the Eaglet Edith Liddell. The other 'curious creatures' in this 'queer-looking party' refer to Carroll's aunt Lucy Lutwidge and his sisters Frances and Elizabeth Dodgson. When Carroll published the facsimile of the original manuscript of *Alice* in 1886 he inscribed Duckworth's copy, 'The Duck, from the Dodo'. 'The Dodo' is an apt disguise for a conservative bachelor don, but the success of the Alice books has ensured that Dodgson/Carroll's name is not extinct.

CHAPTER III: A CAUCUS-RACE AND A LONG TALE

1 *William the Conqueror, whose cause was favoured by the pope.* A quotation from Havilland Chepmell, *A Short Course of History*, 1862, pp. 143–4, a book studied by the Liddell children. Compare Humpty Dumpty's 'That's what you call a History of England, that is' (*TLG*, chapter 6).

2 *Speak English.* At the beginning of the previous chapter Alice forgot 'how to speak good English'. The Dodo here *is* speaking English, despite the Eaglet's impatience – not 'good English' exactly but a good imitation of the English spoken by committees. In 'The Pool of Tears' Alice translates Latin grammar and speaks French to the Mouse (on the assumption 'it's a French mouse, come over with William the Conqueror'); in 'A Caucus-Race and a Long Tale', she hears an account of the Norman Conquest and the twilight of Anglo-Saxon England. This means that the Eaglet's tetchy appeal to the Dodo to "Speak English!" occurs in a context in which the Latin, Norman and Anglo-Saxon roots of current English are invoked via Alice's textbooks. 'Jabberwocky' had originally been offered as a 'Stanza of Anglo-Saxon Poetry' (see *TLG*, chapter 1, note 11).

3 *a Caucus-race.* The *OED* defines a 'caucus' as 1. In USA: A private or preliminary meeting of members of a political party, to select candidates for office ... 2. In England: a committee popularly elected for the purposes of securing concerted political action in a constituency; as a term of abuse, an organization seeking to manage an election and dictate to the constituencies (1878). Carroll self-mockingly portrays the Dodo as prone to political pomposity, no doubt learned at Oxford. In his near contemporary satire 'The Elections to the Hebdomadal Council', Carroll wrote: 'To save beloved Oxford from the yoke,/ For this majority's beyond a joke,/ We must combine, aye! hold a *caucus*-meeting,/ Unless we want to get another beating.' A note to this topical squib quotes a letter of 1866 by Godwin Smith to the Senior Censor of Christ Church: 'Caucus-holding and wire-pulling would still be almost inevitably carried on to some extent' and 'I never go to a *caucus* without reluctance.' (*The Lewis Carroll Picture Book*, pp. 82–83.) The idea of a 'caucus race' undermines the whole idea of a caucus as well as that of a race. The caucus race was added to the original manuscript, *AAUG*, replacing a dry narrative about how the original party managed to get dry, recorded in Carroll's diary. It ended as follows:

> After a time the Dodo became impatient, and, leaving the Duck to bring up the rest of the party, moved on at a quicker pace with Alice, the Lory and the Eaglet, and soon brought them to a little cottage, and there they sat snugly by the fire, wrapped up in blankets, until the rest of the party had arrived, and they were all dry again (*AAUG*, see p. 261).

The prosy snugness of this is alien to the frictional Wonderland of the final version.

4 *the position in which you usually see Shakespeare.* Carroll refers to this again as the 'approved Shakespeare attitude' (*Letters*, vol 1, p. 456) elsewhere, but none of the 'usual' images of Shakespeare show him in this position. The influential sculptures of the poet by Schumaker in Westminster Abbey and by Roubiliac show him with his hand under his chin rather than on his forehead.

5 *it is a long tail, certainly.* Carroll uses a similar pun to similar effect in a letter to Gertrude Chataway, one of his child friends: 'Why is a pig that has lost its tail like a girl on the sea-shore? Because it says, "I should like another Tale, please!"' (*Letters*, vol 1, p. 236).

6 *Fury said to a mouse.* 'The Mouse's Tale' is a kind of visual pun, a mirror of the verbal pun in its title, and one of the most famous 'figured poems' in English (see John Hollander, 'The Poem in the Eye', *Vision and Resonance*, New York: OUP, 1975, pp. 245–87). The idea of the poetic tale included in Alice's dream may have been sparked off by a dream of the Poet Laureate's. In a letter of 1859 Carroll describes a visit to Tennyson at Freshwater in which the poet spoke of dreaming 'long passages of poetry'; he particularly recalled 'an enormously long one on fairies, where the lines from being very long at first, gradually got shorter and shorter, till it ended with 50 or 60 lines of 2 syllables each!' (*Letters*, vol 1, p. 37). The mouse's tale is shorter, has nothing to do with fairies, and ends, like so many of the poems and jokes in the Alice books, in the threat of 'death' (Old Fury is one of the grimmest of the many tyrannical authority-figures who haunt the book). Jeffrey Stern suggests that Carroll's poem echoes 'Trial by Jury', a poem about a fairy trial that appeared a little later in *Poems Written for a Child* published by his cousin Menella Bute Smedley in 1868: it includes such lines as 'They all refuse to be jury/ They all desire to be judge:/ They all strut about in a fury,/ Each oweing the other a grudge' and has a judge putting on his 'black cap/ In a death-condemning speed' (*Jabberwocky*, vol 12, no. 1, Winter 1982, pp. 9–11). The tail-shaped poem recited by the mouse in the original *AAUG*, though weaker, has more bearing on its 'history' and 'why it is [it] hates cats and dogs' (see p. 262).

CHAPTER IV: THE RABBIT SENDS IN A LITTLE BILL

1 *The Duchess.* Originally 'The Marchioness', *AAUG* (see p. 265). The Rabbit's fears of execution come hard on the heels of Cunning Old Fury's intemperate death sentence and prepare the ground for the Queen of Hearts' general recourse to the death penalty as a solution to all difficulties.

2 *When I used to read fairy tales.* Alice's historical period witnessed a spectacular renaissance of the fairy tale. The publication of Taylor's translation of Grimms' *German Popular Tales* (1823–6) first opened the way for a 'literary' acceptance of fairy tales and the first of many English translations of Hans Christian Andersen in 1846 helped popularize the idea of a modern fantastic literature for children. The Victorian period saw the development of a consciously invented children's literature based around the 'fairy tale' exemplified by writers such as John Ruskin (*The King of the Golden River*, 1841), Charles Dickens (*A Christmas Carol*, 1843), William Makepeace Thackeray (*The Rose and the*

Ring, 1845), Christina Rossetti (*Goblin Market*, 1862), Charles Kingsley (*The Water-Babies*, 1863), George MacDonald (*At the Back of the North Wind*, 1871, *The Princess and the Goblin*, 1872). Carroll occasionally refers to *AAIW* as a 'fairy tale', as in the letter to Tom Taylor of 1864 about 'fixing a name for my fairy tale', but in the same letter he notes that though the heroine meets 'various birds, beasts, etc ... endowed with speech', there are '*no* fairies' (*Letters*, vol 1, p. 65). It is part of the originality of Carroll's tale that, unlike MacDonald's, it avoids all reference to the supernatural and 'fairy' dimensions of children's stories.

3 *digging for apples yer honour*. By the gardener's stage Irish accent, this must be an Irish 'bull' – though a Frenchman might well dig for 'apples of the earth' or 'pommes de terre' (i.e. potatoes).

4 *a crowd of little animals*. Originally more specific: 'guinea-pigs, white mice, squirrels, and "Bill" a little green lizard, that was being supported in the arms of one of the guinea-pigs, while another was giving it something out of a bottle' (*AAUG*, p. 270).

5 *Safe in a thick wood*. Originally this was the close of chapter 2, *AAUG*.

CHAPTER V: ADVICE FROM A CATERPILLAR

1 *You are old, Father William*. The first line of 'The Old Man's Comforts and How He Gained Them' by Robert Southey (1774–1843), first published in *The Annual Anthology*, i, 1799. Southey's poetry had been satirized as early as 'The Knife Grinder' in *The Anti-Jacobin Review* of 1797 (and Carroll's library included both Southey's poems and selections from *The Anti-Jacobin Review*). Like the earlier parody of Isaac Watts's hymn, Carroll's 'You are old, Father William' is a parody of the earlier poet's *faux-naïf* didacticism:

> 'You are old, father William,' the young man cried,
> 'The few locks which are left you are grey;
> You are hale, father William, a hearty old man;
> Now tell me the reason, I pray.'
>
> 'In the days of my youth', father William replied,
> 'I remember that youth would fly fast,
> And abus'd not my health and my vigour at first,
> That I never might need them at last.'

The youth puts two further variants on the same question and receives two further variants of the same reply, the last being as follows:

'You are old, father William,' the young man cried,
'And life must be hast'ning away;
You are cheerful and love to converse upon death;
Now tell me the reason, I pray.'

'I am cheerful, young man,' father William replied,
'Let the cause thy attention engage;
In the days of my youth I remembered my God!
And He hath not forgotten my age.'

Carroll's parody undermines the pious didacticism of Southey's dialogue and gives Father William an eccentric vitality that rebounds upon his idiot questioner. The poem clearly bears upon the conversational preoccupations of Alice and the Caterpillar – who are both concerned with growing up and growing old.

2 *one side . . . the other side.* Originally 'the top . . . the stalk' (*AAUG*, p. 275).

3 *Well! What are you?* A version of Alice's recurrent question, 'Who am I?' The pigeon's apparently nonsensical classification of Alice as a 'serpent' makes sense in terms of its definition of a 'serpent' as something which eats its eggs. 'The next thing is to get back to that beautiful garden', Alice decides at the close of the chapter and behind this scene may stand the first 'beautiful garden' and its 'serpent', as described in the book of Genesis: Alice finds herself treated as a serpent in the trees by a version of the *sacré pigeon*, who understandably sees her as a predator. 'I've seen a good many little girls in my time, but never *one* with a neck like that!', the bird notes, and William Empson remarks that the whole episode gives Alice a strangely phallic role and appearance. The pigeon is concerned with her eggs, and the following chapter takes up the idea of babies.

4 *As she said this.* In *AAUG* this led straight into the opening of the penultimate paragraph of what is now chapter 7 (see p. 277). Chapters 6 and 7, which tell of 'Pig and Pepper' and 'The Mad Hatter's Tea-Party' were added during revision and played no part in the first version of the story.

CHAPTER VI: PIG AND PEPPER

1 *The Frog-Footman.* Tenniel's drawing is clearly modelled on a caricature by the great French illustrator Grandville.

2 *the Duchess was sitting.* Tenniel has modelled his portrait of the Duchess on a painting now in the National Gallery, London, *A Grotesque Old Woman* by Quentin Massys or an imitator, possibly modelled on a grotesque drawing attributed to Leonardo.

3 *whether it was good manners.* Alice is characteristically conscious of her manners at all times. Carroll praised his sister-in-law for bringing up her family to "have the high spirits of children with the good manners of grown-up people", *Letters*, vol 2, p. 676.

4 *It's a Cheshire-Cat.* 'To grin like a Cheshire cat' is a proverbial expression, the origin of which was extensively discussed in *Notes and Queries*, no. 55, 16 November 1850, and no. 130, 24 April 1852. It was suggested that the expression referred either to the fact that 1) Cheshire was a county Palatine and 2) some Cheshire cheese was produced in cat-shaped moulds or 3) some painted inn-signs in Cheshire notoriously looked more like grinning cats than growling lions. Carroll, who was born in Cheshire, was a regular subscriber to *Notes and Queries* and may well have grinned at these linguistic speculations.

5 *Speak roughly to your little boy.* The Duchess's 'sort of a lullaby' is a parody of a poem, 'Speak Gently', by David Bates, published in *The Eolian* in 1849 and in his *Collected Works* (1870). The first four of its nine stanzas go as follows:

Speak gently! It is better far
To rule by love than fear;
Speak gently; let no harsh words mar
The good we might do here!

Speak gently! Love doth whisper low
The vows that true hearts bind;
And gently Friendship's accents flow;
Affection's voice is kind.

Speak gently to the little child!
Its love be sure to gain;
Teach it in accents soft and mild;
It may not long remain.

Speak gently to the young, for they
Will have enough to bear;
Pass through this life as best they may,
'Tis full of anxious care.

The Duchess's version of this long, sentimental piece of advice is the literary equivalent of a short sharp shock – a burlesque of conventional lullabies and accepted views of child-rearing.

6 *neither more nor less than a pig.* If the whole scene travesties nurses and babies, it may also reflect Carroll's attitude towards little boys. In a letter of 1860 he wrote '(parenthetically, I hate babies, but that is irrelevant)' (*Letters*, vol 1, p.

392) and in one of 1882 'Boys are not in my line: I think they are a mistake: girls are less objectionable' (*Letters*, vol 1, p. 455). In *Sylvie and Bruno Concluded*, a character called Uggug is described as 'a hideous fat boy . . . with the expression of a prize pig'; *he* eventually turns into a porcupine.

7 *they're both mad.* 'Mad as a hatter' and 'mad as a March hare' are proverbial English expressions. Correspondents in *Notes and Queries* disagreed over the origin of the first of these: it may have been a corruption of 'mad as an adder' or have owed its currency to the fact that hatters were indeed liable to madness due to the side-effects of the mercury used in curing felt. 'Mad as a March hare' alludes to the acrobatic capering of hares in the mating season in March. Alice reflects that 'as this is May it won't be raving mad', but the eccentricity of the March Hare in Wonderland has nothing to do with the mating season. Carroll's near contemporary at Rugby Thomas Hughes in *Tom Brown's Schooldays* makes a reference to 'a very good fellow, but mad as a hatter' (1857). The hare's pedigree may be more ancient. John Skelton, for example, has 'Thou madde Marche hare' (1529) and *The Two Noble Kinsmen* refers to a woman 'as mad as a March hare' (III.v.73).

8 *we're all mad here.* Compare the Cheshire-Cat's observation with an entry in Carroll's diary for 9 February 1856:

> Query: when we are dreaming, and as often happens, have a dim consciousness of the fact and try to wake, do we not say and do things which in waking life would be insane? May we not then sometimes define insanity as an inability to distinguish which is the waking and which the sleeping life? We often dream without the least suspicion of unreality: 'Sleep hath its own world', and it is often as lifelike as the other. (*Diaries*, vol 1, p. 76).

Freud would no doubt have found confirmation for his views in Carroll's remarks on the relation of dreams and madness. The 'dream realism' of the Alice books depends on it.

CHAPTER VII: A MAD TEA-PARTY

1 *the Hatter.* Tenniel's drawing of the Hatter is reputed to have been based on an eccentric Oxford character called Theophilus Carter, known as the Mad Hatter because he always wore a top hat ('Tenniel was brought down to Oxford by the author to see him. The likeness was unmistakable', H. W. Greene in a letter to *The Times*, 13 March 1931). In '"Alice" on the Stage' Carroll describes Sydney Harcourt's impersonation of him: 'To see him enact the Hatter was a weird and uncanny thing, as though some grotesque monster, seen last night in a dream, should walk into the room in broad daylight, and quietly say "Good morning!" I need not describe what I meant the Hatter to be, since, as far as I can now remember, it was exactly what Mr Harcourt has made him' (see pp. 296–7).

2 *having tea at it.* Isa Bowman records the mild eccentricity of Carroll's tea parties at Christ Church:

> He was very particular about his tea, which he always made himself, and in order that it should draw properly he would walk about the room swinging the tea-pot from side to side for exactly ten minutes. The idea of the grave professor promenading his book-lined study and carefully waving a teapot to and fro may seem ridiculous, but all the minutiae of life received an extreme attention at his hands (*Lewis Carroll as I Knew Him*, pp. 36–7).

3 *a Dormouse.* According to the *OED*, 'a small rodent of a family intermediate between the squirrels and the mice; espec. the British species *Myoxus avellanarius*, noted for its hibernation'; also, in a transferred sense, 'a sleepy or dozing person', as in Milton's 'swashbuckler against the Pope, and a dormouse against the Devil' (1641). *Some Reminiscences of William Michael Rossetti*, 1906, informs us that the dormouse may have been modelled on Dante Gabriel Rossetti's pet wombat, which used to sleep on the table. Carroll certainly knew the Rossettis well and had visited and photographed them.

4 *Why is a raven like a writing-desk?* In his preface to the 1896 edition Carroll wrote:

> Enquiries have so often been addressed to me, as to whether any answer to the Hatter's Riddle can be imagined, that I may as well put on record here what seems to me to be a fairly appropriate answer, viz. 'Because it can produce a few notes, though they are *very* flat; and it is never put with the wrong end in front!' This, however, is merely an afterthought; the Riddle, as originally invented, had no answer at all.

5 *I'm glad they've begun asking riddles.* Lewis Carroll's letters to girl correspondents are literally riddled with riddles. See *Letters*, vol 1 pp. 157, 158, 221, 236, 292, 320, 323, 367, 384, and vol 2, p. 942.

6 *The fourth.* Since Alice noted it was May in the previous chapter (p. 58), this makes the date of her adventures 4 May, Alice Liddell's birthday. Alice Liddell was born on 4 May 1852, making her ten on that 'golden afternoon' of July 1862; however, the photograph Carroll affixed to the original manuscript of *Alice's Adventures under Ground* shows her aged seven and in *Through the Looking-Glass* she says her age is 'seven and a half, exactly' (p. 174), so that Carroll's fictional Alice in Wonderland is probably seven exactly, which is three years younger than her real-life counterpart on the date he told her story. In fictional time, then, the story is set in 1859 at the latest – during the period for which the Carroll diaries have not survived (though they were available to his biographer in 1897).

7 *Two days wrong.* A. L. Taylor notes: 'it would be possible to measure time by the phases of the moon, and this is the principle of the Mad Hatter's watch . . . on that day, 4 May 1862, there were exactly two days' difference between the two ways of reckoning the date. As the amount varies with every month and year, there can be no doubt that Dodgson consulted an almanac and based his calculations upon it' (A. L. Taylor, *The White Knight: A Study of C. L. Dodgson*, Edinburgh, 1952, p. 57).

8 *Twinkle, twinkle, little bat!* A parody of the first verse of the famous nursery song by Jane Taylor (1783–1824), first published in *Rhymes for the Nursery* by A. and J. Taylor, 1806.

> Twinkle, twinkle, little star,
> How I wonder what you are!
> Up above the world so high,
> Like a diamond in the sky.

Alice remembered it as one of the 'songs popular at the time' they sang on their picnics on the river.

9 *It's always six o'clock . . . it's always tea-time.* In 'Alice's Recollections of Carrollian Days' (*Cornhill Magazine*, 73, July 1932, reprinted in *Lewis Carroll: Interviews and Recollections*, ed. Morton N. Cohen, London, 1989) she remembers: 'We never went to tea with him, nor did he come to tea with us. In any case, five-o'clock tea had not become an established practice in those days . . . At the time when we first went to Oxford, my parents, having had luncheon at one o'clock, did not have another meal until dinner, which they took at 6.30 p.m.' However, in his *Diaries*, Carroll records that in 1863, on 4 July, the Liddells had 'tea on the bank' of the river, and on 9 June he had 'tea with the three in the schoolroom'; again on 19 December 'at five went over to the Deanery, where I stayed till eight, making a sort of dinner at their tea'.

In *The Blank Cheque: A Fable* (1874) he remarks on 'five o'clock tea' is a phrase our 'rude forefathers, even of the last generation, would not have understood, so completely is it a thing of today' (*The Lewis Carroll Picture Book*, ed. Stuart Dodgson Collingwood, London, 1889, p. 150).

10 *Once upon a time there were three little sisters.* Isa Bowman recalls Carroll saying:

> 'Tell me a story, and mind you begin with "once upon a time". A story which does not begin with "once upon a time" can't possibly be a good story. It's *most* important' (*Lewis Carroll as I Knew Him*, p. 71).

11 *their names were Elsie, Lacie, and Tillie.* The 'three little sisters' are an allusion to the 'three Liddell sisters': 'Elsie' is a punning reference to Lorina (or L. C. Liddell), 'Lacie' an anagram of Alice, and 'Tillie' an abbreviation of Matilda, a nickname given to Edith. They are the Prima, Secunda and Tertia of the opening poem.

12 *It was a treacle-well.* Alice understandably says 'there's no such thing' but medicinal springs in Oxfordshire seem sometimes to have been known as 'treacle-wells' (R. L. Green ed. *AAIW and TLG*, Oxford, 1982, p. 259). Ironically eating the treacle from the *well* makes the sisters *ill*.

13 *'much of a muchness'.* Nowadays the word 'muchness' only survives in the idiomatic phrase 'much of a muchness', meaning 'very much the same or alike', but 'muchness' is recorded by the *OED* as earlier meaning magnitude or greatness as in Hylton's 'The endles mochenes of the loue of God' (1494) and current as late as William James 'We have relations of muchness and littleness between times . . . as well as places' (1887).

14 *Just as she said this.* At this point, after completing the two new episodes of 'Pig and Pepper' and 'A Mad Tea-Party', Carroll returns to the original storyline of *AAUG*.

CHAPTER VIII: THE QUEEN'S CROQUET-GROUND

1 *last of all this grand procession, came THE KING AND THE QUEEN OF HEARTS.* Alice soon notices they are 'only a pack of cards' (p. 71) but in animating it Carroll has dealt out the pack with care. Spades are gardeners, clubs are soldiers, diamonds are courtiers, hearts are the royal children and the court cards are the titled members of the court. The Queen of Hearts comes last as the most powerful in Carroll's 'grand procession'. Wonderland, like the chess world of *Through the Looking-Glass*, is a matriarchal society. In '"Alice" on the Stage' Carroll wrote: 'I pictured to myself the Queen of Hearts as a sort of embodiment of ungovernable passion – a blind and aimless Fury' (see p. 296). Christina Rossetti published a poem called 'The Queen of Hearts' in *The Prince's Progress* (1866), which suggests another kind of 'passion':

> How comes it, Flora, that, whenever we
> Play cards together, you invariably,
>   However the pack parts,
>   Still hold the Queen of Hearts?

Carroll's interest in cards began in 1858, as he records in the *Diaries*: 'Bought Hoyle's *Games*: I have taken to learning cards in the last few days, for the first time in my life' (*Diaries*, vol 1, p. 138). In 1858 he invented a new game he called 'Court Circular', the rules of which he printed out for the Liddells in 1860 and again in 1862. See *The Complete Works of Lewis Carroll*, ed. Alexander Woollcott, London, 1939, reprinted Harmondsworth, 1985, pp. 1140–43.

2 *Alice was rather doubtful.* This paragraph was added to the original manuscript account of the Croquet-Game in *AAUG*.

3 *Off with her head!* An allusion to *Richard III*, where the future king cries 'Off with his head. Now, by Saint Paul I swear,/ I will not dine until I see the same' (3.4. 76–7). Carroll joked on the same phrase in a letter of 1889 to his stage Alice, Isa Bowman, after she had appeared as the Duke of York in a production of Shakespeare's play: 'I do not wonder that your excellent Uncle Richard should say "off with his head!" as a hint to the photographer to print it off' (*Letters*, vol 2, p. 735).

4 *Can you play croquet?* The Liddell children all played croquet and Carroll often took part in their games. In his diary for 26 May 1862, six weeks before the first version of *Alice*, he records rowing with the three Liddell children: 'Afterwards we went in and had a game of croquet with them in the Deanery garden.' (*Diaries*, vol 1, p. 176). He invented his own variant for them, the rules of which he outlined in *Croquet Castles*, originally written down in Oxford on Alice Liddell's birthday, 4 May 1863, and reprinted in *The Lewis Carroll Picture Book*, 1899, p. 271 (*The Complete Works*, pp. 1143–45).

5 *Where's the Duchess?* In *AAUG*, 'Where's the Marchioness?'. Alice's brief exchange with the Rabbit originally suggested a less violent but more confusing political situation:

> "Hush, hush!" said the Rabbit in a low voice, "she'll hear you. The Queen's the Marchioness: didn't you know that?"
>
> "No, I didn't, said Alice, "what of?"
>
> "Queen of Hearts," said Rabbit in a whisper, putting its mouth close to her ear, "and Marchioness of Mock Turtles" (*AAUG*, see p. 282).

6 *live flamingoes*. Originally 'live ostriches'. Tenniel's picture of Alice with her flamingo seems to be closely modelled on Carroll's original sketch in *AAUG*, one of the relatively few instances where the artist seems to have worked from one of the author's drawings.

7 *Alice began to feel very uneasy*. From this point Carroll diverges from the text of *AAUG* until half way through the next chapter, where he resumes the original story with 'those whom she sentenced were taken into custody by soldiers'. Alice's conversations with the Cheshire-Cat and the Duchess weren't in the first version.

8 *"A cat may look at a king," said Alice*. This proverb is recorded as early as J. Heywood's *Dialogue of Proverbs* (1546). In Robert Greene's *Never Too Late* (1590) we find: 'A Cat may look at a King, and a swaynes eye hath as high a reach as a Lords looke'. Carroll's library at his death included H. G. Bohn, *A Handbook of Proverbs* (1855).

CHAPTER IX: THE MOCK TURTLE'S STORY

1 *the Duchess.* The long dialogue with the Duchess is added to *AAUG* and adds a very different dimension to the Croquet Game.

2 *camomile.* Still used to make herb tea, this was a common herbal medicine taken by Victorian children.

3 *Everything's got a moral, if only you can find it.* The Ugly Duchess here embodies the ugly moralism of much earlier nineteenth-century children's literature. She offers a complementary (though uncomplimentary) image of education to the Mock Turtle later in the chapter.

Compare Carroll's anonymously published *The New Belfry of Christ Church, Oxford* (1872), a satirical pamphlet attacking Dean Liddell's architectural innovations: 'Everything has a moral, if you choose to look for it. In Wordsworth, a good half of every poem is devoted to the Moral: in Byron, a smaller proportion: in Tupper the whole' (*Lewis Carroll Picture Book*, p. 117).

4 *Oh, 'tis love, 'tis love, that makes the world go round.* Perhaps a reference to Ségur's *Chansons nationales et populaires* (1851) which includes 'C'est l'amour, l'amour,/ Qui fait le monde/ A la ronde'. In Carroll's *Sylvie and Bruno Concluded*, the two children sing a pious song that spells out much the same claim:

> Say whose is the skill that paints valley and hill,
> Like a picture so fair to the sight?
> That flecks the green meadow with sunshine and shadow,
> Till the little lambs leap with delight?
>
> 'Tis a secret untold to hearts cruel and cold,
> Though 'tis sung, by the angels above,
> In notes that ring clear for the ears that can hear—
> And the name of the secret is Love!
>
> For I think it is Love,
> For I feel it is Love
> For I'm sure it is nothing but Love!
>
> (*The Complete Works*, p. 626)

5 *Somebody said . . . it's done by everyone minding their own business.* I.e. the Duchess herself in chapter 6.

6 *Take care of the sense, and the sounds will take care of themselves.* A play on the proverb 'Take care of the pence and the pounds will take care of themselves' ('Old Mr Lowndes, the famous Secretary of the Treasury, used to say . . . Take care of the pence and the pounds will take care of themselves', Lord Chesterfield, *Letters*). The Duchess's advice also evokes Pope's famous formula from *The Essay on Criticism*, I, 365: 'The sound must seem an echo to the sense'.

7 *Birds of a feather flock together.* In 1600 Secker referred to 'Our English Proverb . . . That birds of a feather will flocke together. To be intimate with sinners is to intimate that you are sinners'. See also Ray, *Collection of English Proverbs*, 1678, p. 101. In this and the previous chapter proverbs flock together.

8 *Be what you would seem to be.* Another proverbial phrase, going back as far as Langland's *Piers Plowman*: G. Herbert's *Outlandish Proverbs* of 1640 has 'Be what thou wouldst seeme to be'. The Duchess's subsequent commentary *seems* to be an elucidation of this, but isn't.

9 *as pigs have to fly.* Withals in his dictionary defines *terra volet* as 'pigs flie in the ayre with their tayles forward'. 'When pigs fly' is a slang idiom meaning 'never', just as 'pigs might fly' means 'perhaps' (Partridge, *A Dictionary of Historical Slang*, London, 1937). One of the 'many things' of which the Walrus in 'The Walrus and the Carpenter' desires to speak is 'Whether pigs have wings' (See p. 161).

10 *Those whom she sentenced.* At this point the narrative resumes that of *AAUG*.

11 *It's the thing Mock Turtle Soup is made from.* Mock Turtle is 'Calf's head dressed with sauces and condiments so as to resemble turtle' (*OED*). Mock-turtle soup was usually made from calf's head, which is why Tenniel gives the Mock Turtle a turtle's shell but a calf's head and feet. This is more plausible than Carroll's drawing of a Mock Turtle which shows a pathetic nondescript sort of creature like an earless rabbit in badly fitting armour.

12 *a Gryphon.* A fabulous composite creature, of more respectable ancestry than the Mock Turtle: in classical mythology 'a fabulous animal having the head and wings of an eagle and the body and hindquarters of a lion' (*OED*). It survives in heraldry (for example in the emblem of Trinity College, Oxford) as well as poetry (for example in Milton's 'As when a Gryphon through the wilderness . . . Pursues the Arimaspian', *Paradise Lost* 2, 943).

13 *We called him Tortoise because he taught us.* Carroll resorts to the same pun in 'What the Tortoise said to Achilles', a philosophical article he contributed to *Mind* in 1895. The tortoise refers there to 'a pun that my cousin the Mock Turtle will make . . . Taught us'. Turtles are of course marine tortoises and so the Mock Turtle and the Tortoise are indeed cousins.

14 *Yes, we went to school in the sea.* The account of the Mock Turtle's schooldays that follows is an insertion into the original manuscript story, *AAUG* (see

p. 286). The original storyline is resumed again in the second paragraph of the next chapter, 'The Lobster-Quadrille' (p. 87). In 1857 Thomas Hughes published *Tom Brown's Schooldays*, based on his education at Thomas Arnold's Rugby School, the public school where Carroll was educated (1846–50). In 1863 Charles Kingsley, an acquaintance, published *The Water-Babies* about the watery education of a boy. The Mock Turtle's account might be seen as a comic conflation of the two.

15 *Reeling and Writhing*. The Mock Turtle's school subjects are all puns, i.e. mock subjects: reading, writing, addition, subtraction, multiplication, division, history, geography, drawing, sketching, painting in oils, Latin and Greek. His curriculum reads as a satire on Victorian education. The Mock Turtle is a composite creature, fathered by an ambiguity in language, so it is appropriate that he should speak a dialect largely composed of puns – a kind of speech based on the possibilities of double meaning in language. Addison thought them a sign of false humour: 'There is no kind of false Wit which has been so recommended by the Practice of all Ages, as that which consists in a Jingle of Words, and is comprehended under the general Name of *Punning*'. Nevertheless he concedes that 'The Seeds of Punning are in the Minds of all Men, and tho' they may be subdued by reason, Reflection and good Sense, they will be very apt to shoot up in the greatest Genius, that is not broken and cultivated by the Rules of Art' (*Spectator*, No 61).

16 *the Drawling-master was an old conger-eel*. The Liddell children had a particularly distinguished drawing-master at this time, John Ruskin, who was to claim that Henry Liddell 'first showed (him) the difference between classic and common art'. He taught Alice drawing in the deanery, lending her paintings of Turner to copy, assuring her that a child could copy them. Alice later enrolled in Ruskin's Art School and won a prize for one of her sketches in 1870. (See Colin Gordon, *Beyond the Looking-Glass: Reflections of Alice and her Family*, London, 1982, pp. 98–107.)

17 *Laughing and Grief*. The crabby 'Classical master' teaches Laughing and Grief rather than Latin and Greek, but the Greeks taught us Laughing and Grief too in the shape of Comedy and Tragedy (Aristotle wrote treatises on both, though only the second survives). The Mock Turtle is especially prone to Grief, though his puns inspire Laughter. Alice's father, Dr Liddell, was a classicist too and editor, with Dr Scott, of the famous Greek lexicon, first published in 1843, used in all public schools and universities. The Mock Turtle and the Gryphon are travesties of the new public-school ethos of the time.

CHAPTER X: THE LOBSTER-QUADRILLE

1 *Quadrille.* A fashionable ballroom dance, known to the Liddell children through their dancing lessons. Alice's grandmother reported on their progress, "I hope five or six lessons more will make them dance a quadrille and polka" (quoted in Gordon, *Beyond the Looking-Glass*, p. 111).
2 *Will you walk a little faster?* The song is a parody of Mary Howett's famous nursery song 'The Spider and the Fly', published in her *Sketches of Natural History*, 1834. It begins as follows:

'Will you walk into my parlour?' said the spider to the fly,
''Tis the prettiest little parlour that ever you did spy.
The way into my parlour is up a winding stair,
And I've got many curious things to show when you are there.'
'Oh no, no,' said the little fly, 'to ask me is in vain,
For who goes up your winding stair can ne'er go down again.'

The dance provides an interesting commentary on the predatory invitation of Howett's spider. In *AAUG* the Mock Turtle sings a different but equally fishy dancing-song:

Beneath the waters *of* the sea
Are lobsters thick as thick can be—
They love to dance with you and me,
My own, my gentle Salmon!
CHORUS:
Salmon come up! Salmon go down!
Salmon come twist your tail around!
Of all the fishes *of* the sea
There's none so good as Salmon!
(*AAUG*, p. 288)

This was a parody of the Nigger Minstrel Song 'Sally Come Up' by T. Ramsey and E. W. Mackney which Carroll had heard the three Liddell girls sing at the Deanery the day before the river trip on which he improvised the first version of *Alice* (*Diaries*, vol 1, p. 181).
3 *as to the whiting.* The dialogue on the next three or four pages represents an addition to *AAUG*; the original version is resumed when the Gryphon asks 'Shall we try another figure' and they sing 'Beautiful Soup' (p. 93).
4 *they have their tails in their mouths.* Carroll is later reported to have said: 'When I wrote that, I believed whiting really did have their tails in their mouths, but I have since been told that fishmongers put the tail through the eye, not in the

mouth at all' (Collingwood, *Life*, p. 402). Alice's natural history here is influenced by the fact that her main acquaintance with much of the marine world has been at the dinner table.

5 *blacking*. A now archaic term for black shoe polish.

6 *'Tis the voice of the sluggard*. The first line of 'The Sluggard' from *Divine Songs for Children*, 1715, by Isaac Watts. Watts's song opens:

> 'Tis the voice of the *Sluggard*; I hear him complain,
> *You have wak'd me too soon, I must slumber again.*
> As the Door on its Hinges, so he on his Bed,
> Turns his Sides and his Shoulders and his heavy Head.

Its ending conforms perfectly to the Duchess's view that everything should have a moral:

> Said I to my Heart, 'Here's a Lesson for me,'
> This man's but a Picture of what I might be:
> But thanks to my Friends for their Care in my Breeding,
> Who taught me betimes to love Working and Reading.

7 *'Tis the voice of the Lobster.* A parody of Watts's moral nursery poem. Until 1886 this consisted only of the first four lines of the first stanza and the first two of the second. An additional two lines were added to the second stanza for William Boyd's *Songs from Alice in Wonderland*, 1870, so that it read:

> I passed by his garden, and marked with one eye,
> How the owl and the oyster were sharing a pie,
> While the duck and the Dodo, the lizard and cat,
> Were swimming in milk round the brim of a hat.

Carroll then enlarged the poem to the present sixteen lines for Savile Clarke's stage version of *Alice* at the Prince of Wales Theatre, London, in 1886. Subsequent editions of *Alice* – both the 6s and People's Editions – print this expanded version thereafter.

8 *And concluded the banquet by——*. The withheld conclusion featured in the 1886 edition of Savile Clarke's musical *Alice*: 'eating the owl'.

9 *Shall we try another figure of the Lobster-Quadrille?* At this point the story returns to the original manuscript of *AAUG*.

10 *Turtle Soup*. Originally 'Mock Turtle Soup', *AAUG*, p. 288. During this chapter Alice continually tries to avoid mentioning eating fish out of sensitivity to the Mock Turtle, but it ends with his mournful celebration of the beauties of Turtle Soup. Perhaps as a Mock Turtle he has no qualms about soup made out of real turtles.

11 *Beautiful Soup*. A parody of 'Star of the Evening' by James M. Sayles, a song Carroll records hearing Alice and Edith Liddell sing on 1 August 1862 (*Diaries*, vol 1, p.185).

Beautiful star in heav'n so bright,
Softly falls thy silv'ry light,
As thou movest from earth so far,
Star of the evening, beautiful star.

CHORUS

Beautiful Star,
Beautiful Star,
Star of the evening,
Beautiful, beautiful star.

Only the first verse of Carroll's parody appeared in *AAUG*. With 'Twinkle, twinkle, little bat', this makes two anti-stellar spoofs.

CHAPTER XI: WHO STOLE THE TARTS?

1 *In the very middle of the court*. The court scene, now two chapters long, occupied a mere page of the original manuscript (*AAUG* pp. 289–90). The careful setting of the scene is all added. We take up the original again with 'Herald, read the accusation'.

2 *Alice had never been in a court of justice before*. Carroll visited the Assize Court on 13 July 1863, after he had completed *AAUG*. He recorded that he'd seen 'some very petty cases, but they were interesting to me, as I have seen so little of trials' (*Diaries*, vol 1, p. 199).

3 *The Queen of Hearts, she made some tarts*. This is first recorded in the *European Magazine*, April 1782, as part of a much longer poem about a pack of cards, but it may have been, as the Opies suggest, a traditional nursery rhyme well beforehand (*Oxford Dictionary of Nursery Rhymes*, 1951, p. 360). It was included in James Orchard Halliwell, *The Nursery Rhymes of England* (1844) and formed the basis of *The New Story of the Queen of Hearts*, illustrated by George Cruikshank *c.* 1860. It is the only bona fide 'nursery rhyme' in *Wonderland*. *Through the Looking-Glass* makes systematic use of nursery rhymes throughout.

4 *Consider your verdict*. The entire text from the end of the song to the King's final command to the jury at the close of the trial (p. 107) represents new material added to the original manuscript of *AAUG*.

5 *the twinkling of the tea*. The Hatter is getting mixed up about the line 'Like a tea-tray in the sky, from 'Twinkle, twinkle little bat' which he had sung for the Queen's last concert.

CHAPTER XII: ALICE'S EVIDENCE

1 *upsetting all the jurymen.* In *The Nursery 'Alice'* Carroll remarks on the fact that Tenniel's illustration includes all twelve assorted jurymen.
2 *Rule Forty-two.* There is also a 'Rule 42' mentioned in the Preface to *The Hunting of the Snark*, of equally obscure significance: *'No one shall speak to the Man at the Helm . . . and the Man at the Helm shall speak to no one'* (*The Complete Works of Lewis Carroll*, pp. 677–8).
3 *whilst the White Rabbit read out these verses.* This sentence was added in Carroll's final revision of 1897, replacing the flatly factual 'These were the verses the White Rabbit read' which had appeared in all previous editions.
4 *They told me you had been to her.* A revised and shortened version of Carroll's 'She's All My Fancy Painted Him', first published in *The Comic Times*, 1855. This affecting fragment started as a parody of 'Alice Gray' by William Mee, a popular love song of the day which he was to parody once again in 'Disillusioned' (*The Works of Lewis Carroll*, pp. 826–7). Mee's original poem began:

She's all my fancy painted her,
She's lovely, she's divine,
But her heart it is another's,
She never can be mine.

Carroll's parody took off from here:

She's all my fancy painted him
(I make no idle boast)
If he or you had lost a limb,
Which would have suffered most?

But then it took its own way:

He said that you had been to her,
And seen me here before;
But, in another character,
She was the same of yore.

There was not one that spoke to us,
Of all that thronged the street:
So he sadly got into a 'bus,
And pattered with his feet.

They sent him word I had not gone
(We know it to be true);
If she should push the matter on,
What would become of you?

They gave her one, they gave me two,
They gave us three or more;
They all returned from him to you,
Though they were mine before.

If I or she should chance to be
Involved in this affair,
He trusts to you to set them free,
Exactly as we were.

It seemed to me that you had been
(Before she had this fit)
An obstacle, that came between
Him, and ourselves, and it.

Don't let him know she liked them best,
For this must ever be
A secret, kept from all the rest,
Between yourself and me.

In the song being parodied the speaker says he loved 'as man never loved,/ A love without decay,/ O my heart, my heart is breaking/ For the love of Alice Gray.' Carroll's love for another Alice may be 'a secret' encoded in this parody.

For *Wonderland* Carroll tightened up five of the original eight stanzas and added a final twist in a new final stanza. The result is a nonsense poem quite unlike any of the others, based on a phenomenal pronominal comedy of errors.

5 *I don't believe there's an atom of meaning in it.* The accusation which launches the trial is an absurd nursery rhyme and the main evidence produced in it is a nonsense poem of Carroll's invention. Alice's dream explodes soon after these items of nonsense language are put on trial and subjected to elaborate judicial interpretation.

6 *If she should push the matter on . . . What indeed.* Carroll added these four phrases in his revision for the final 1897 edition.

7 *Let the jury consider their verdict.* At this point the text reverts to the original *AAUG* (p. 290), with variations.

8 *First she dreamed about little Alice herself.* This and the following two paragraphs are an elaboration of the original dream frame of *AAUG* (pp. 290–91).

9 *this same little sister of hers. AAUG* reads 'this same little Alice'. In the MS, the phrase 'perhaps even with the dream of Wonderland of long ago' read 'even with these very adventures of the little Alice of long-ago' and the whole book which Carroll sent to Alice in November 1864 ends with a photograph of 'little Alice', aged seven. When, in 1976, this was removed, a small drawing of Alice by Carroll was found concealed beneath it. In preparing the book for publication, Carroll removed the picture of Oxford, the dream's setting, and generalized his heroine a little, preferring to recapitulate the dramatis personae of the 'dream of Wonderland' than build it all around Alice Liddell herself. *AAUG*, unlike the published book, is a love-gift to its heroine, with whose image it closes.

NOTES TO THROUGH THE LOOKING-GLASS

NOTE ON THE TITLE

As with the earlier book, Carroll had problems in settling on a title for the second Alice book. When he sent off the first chapter to Macmillan's in 1869 he referred to it as *Behind the Looking-Glass and what Alice found there* (*The Diaries of Lewis Carroll*, ed. R. L. Green, 1953, vol 1, p. 279). It later became *Looking-Glass House and what Alice saw there*. The actual title was decided very late in the day as proofs survive in the Huntingdon Library (Los Angeles) with the title *Looking-Glass House and what Alice saw there*, dated 1870 (reproduced in *The Lewis Carroll Handbook*, Plate VII). The proofs also show that the book as originally envisaged was to have forty-two illustrations (like *Wonderland*) rather than the fifty afterwards included in the first edition, and eleven chapters (though Collingwood in the *Life* says thirteen) rather than the current twelve (which mirror the twelve chapters of *Wonderland*).

NOTE ON DRAMATIS PERSONAE

As in 1872, but omitted in 1897 and later editions except the People's Edition. It may be that Carroll deliberately omitted the Dramatis Personae on the grounds that it only confused a rather confusing chess game further. This could equally be grounds for retaining it, as I have here.

NOTE ON THE CHESS GAME

Opinions vary about the plausibility of the chess game. In *The Lewis Carroll Handbook*, S. H. Williams and Falconer Madan, pronounce a particularly severe verdict on the game, despite Carroll's explanation in the Preface (see Appendix II):

> . . . in spite of this explanation the chess framework is full of absurdities and impossibilities, and it is unfortunate that Dodgson did not display his usual dexterity by bringing the game, as a game, up to chess standard. He is known to have been a chess-player . . . He might have searched for a printed problem to suit his story, or have made one. But he allows the White side to make nine consecutive moves(!): he allows Alice (a white

pawn) and Alice becoming a Queen, to be two separate moves: he allows the White King to be checked without either side taking any notice of the fact: he allows two Queens to castle(!): he allows the White Queen to fly from the Red Knight, when she should take it. Hardly a move has a sane purpose, from the point of view of chess (*The Lewis Carroll Handbook*, originally published 1931, revised edition, 1979, p. 66).

Such a view of the game played out in *Through the Looking-Glass* ignores two fundamental facts. 1. This is not a conventional game of chess. It is a game played on the other side of the mirror (where, as Alice notes, 'they don't keep the room so tidy as the other') – and in a dream. 2. It is dramatized from Alice's point of view. The heroine of the book is a mere pawn in the game and the progress of the game is seen through her eyes – unlike most conventional accounts of chess which see it through the eyes of either players or spectators. In *Through the Looking-Glass* Carroll has used his dexterity not to bring the game 'up to chess standard' but to represent a dream of a pawn's-eye view of a looking-glass game of chess.

NOTE ON THE FRONTISPIECE

The frontispiece shows Alice in conversation with the White Knight whom she meets in chapter 8: 'It's My Own Invention'. It is clearly a parody of one of the most famous Pre-Raphaelite paintings of the time, *Sir Isumbras at the Ford* by John Everett Millais, first exhibited in 1857 under the title *A Dream of the Past* (now in the Lady Lever Art Gallery, Port Sunlight). Millais's painting represents an elaborately armoured medieval knight on a beautifully armoured horse bestriding a river while bearing two children (a rather Alice-like girl and a small boy with a bundle of sticks). In Tenniel's drawing the chivalresque armour becomes household furniture, the sword a toy wooden sword, and the bundle of sticks a bundle of carrots and turnips. The noble figure of the knight becomes a walrus-moustached and rather anxious-looking dodderer. Carroll had originally intended the illustration to 'Jabberwocky' to stand as frontispiece, but when the parents to whom he showed it confirmed it was 'too terrible a monster', he opted instead for the altogether less disturbing picture of the Knight (see *Diaries*, vol 1, pp. 162–3).

INTRODUCTORY POEM
'CHILD OF THE PURE UNCLOUDED BROW'

1 *Child of the pure unclouded brow.* The introductory poem strikes a darker note than that of *Wonderland*, giving a vivid sense of time and distance. On 13 March

1863, Carroll noted: 'I began a poem the other day in which I mean to embody something about Alice (if I can at all please myself by any description of her) and which I mean to call "Life's Pleasance"' (*Diaries*, vol 1, p. 194). Soon afterwards Mrs Liddell effectively cut off relations between Carroll and her daughters for reasons we do not know. On 19 December Carroll noted: 'It is nearly six months [25 June] since I have seen anything of them, to speak of' (*Diaries*, vol 1, p. 208). The Alice he is addressing here then is a remembered figure, almost a figure of memory, rather than the current companion she had been in the earlier book, and the poem looks back nostalgically not only to her but 'the tale begun in other days/When summer suns were glowing'. We are in a world of 'echoes' that 'live in memory' and that is haunted by a coming 'voice of dread'. The poet speaks from a climate of 'the frost, the blinding snow,/The storm-wind's moody madness' – and it is this world which the 'magic words' of the tale have to hold at bay. The climate of *Through the Looking-Glass* is altogether colder than that of *Wonderland*.

Carroll made five handwritten alterations to the 1870 proofs, substituting 'Melancholy' in verse four for 'Wilful weary', and in verse five substituting 'frost the blinding' for 'whirling wind and' and 'the storm wind's moody' for 'that lash themselves'.

2 *happy summer days*. The last words of *Alice's Adventures in Wonderland*.

3 *vanish'd summer glory*. The word 'glory' calls up Wordsworth's ode 'There was a time', with its question: 'Whither is fled the visionary gleam?/Where is it now the glory and the dream?'. The question underlies the whole of Carroll's brief elegiac poetic prelude on the passing of childhood.

4 *The pleasance*. In the 1870 proofs this read 'pleasures'. This is one of Carroll's numerous poetic plays upon the names of his child friends; 'Pleasance' was Alice Liddell's middle name. It is also an archaic poetic word for 'delight, pleasure, joy' (as in Chaucer's 'Thus is the quyen in plesaunce & in Ioye'), or for a 'pleasure-giving quality' (as in Spenser's 'With plesaunce of the breathing fields'), and in Carroll's day it could be used to describe 'a pleasure ground, usually attached to a mansion' (as in 'The Poet's Pleasaunce or Garden of all sorts of pleasant Flowers' from 1847).

CHAPTER I: LOOKING-GLASS HOUSE

1 *Do you know what to-morrow is Kitty?* The sticks for the bonfire suggest 'tomorrow' is 5 November, Guy Fawkes Day. This would make the date 4 November, exactly six months after the fictional trip to Wonderland on 4 May, which was Alice Liddell's birthday. Alice tells the White Queen she is 'seven and a half, exactly' (p. 174) which is therefore exactly right. Six years passed between the publication of *Alice's Adventures* (1865) and *Through the Looking-Glass* (1871, though dated 1872), but only six months of Alice's fictional time. As the first book of adventures has a warm spring-time setting, the second has a cold wintry background of autumn leaves and snow.

2 *Snowdrop.* Probably named after a kitten belonging to another of Carroll's child friends, George MacDonald's daughter Mary. MacDonald (1824–1905) was the author of *At the Back of the North Wind* (1871) and *The Princess and the Goblin* (1872). 'Snowdrop' was named after a fairy tale of that name included in Mrs MacDonald's *Chamber Dramas for Children* (1870).

3 *Kitty, can you play chess?* Alice Liddell records that much of the book was based on stories 'to do with chessmen' that Carroll made up when the Liddell children were learning to play chess ('Alice's Recollections of Carrollian Days', *Cornhill Magazine*, 73, July 1932, reprinted in *Lewis Carroll: Interviews and Recollections*, ed. Morton N. Cohen, London, 1989, p. 5).

4 *Let's pretend we're kings and queens.* This suggests that Alice's 'Let's pretend' games are the origins of her dream adventures, and like them a clue to her fantasies. The fantasy of adult power, of being 'kings and queens', is important to *Wonderland* but Alice's desire to be Queen is given greater force in *TLG*. Freud suggests that kings and queens in dreams typically symbolize someone's parents (*Interpretation of Dreams*, trans. James Strachey, London, 1954, p. 353).

5 *my ideas about Looking-glass House.* Carroll's ideas about Looking-glass House owe something to a meeting with another girl called Alice – 'I'm very fond of Alices' he told her – Alice Raikes, whom he met in the gardens of Onslow Square in 1868 when staying with his uncle Skeffington Lutwidge. See Introduction, p. xxxviii.

This suggests that the idea of a story about the looking-glass came *after* the ones 'to do with chessmen' recalled by Alice Liddell (see note 3 above).

6 *just like a bright silvery mist.* Carroll took a number of photos of girls with mirrors in their hands, but significantly Alice does not look at or see herself in the mirror in either the text or illustration. The dissolving mirror is also used as a gateway into fantasy in George MacDonald's *Phantastes* (1858). In *Philosophy and the Mirror of Nature*, Richard Rorty gives an account of the influence of mirror-models of perception, truth and language in Western philosophy. In sending his dreaming Alice *through* the mirror, Carroll offers a commentary on one of the founding dreams of Western philosophy – that philosophy (and art) can, in Hamlet's words, 'hold, as 'twere, the mirror up to nature'.

7 *two Castles walking arm in arm.* Tenniel's illustration of the chess-pieces shows the strolling Castles alongside the Knights, King and Queen who all figure in the story, but it also shows some bishops, one of whom is reading a newspaper. This draws attention to the fact that Carroll – presumably out of deference to the clergy and the Church – punctiliously excludes all reference to bishops in his book's curiously secular game of chess. We never find out what nonsense the bishop is reading.

8 *memorandum-book*. A portable notebook, perhaps like that mentioned in a letter of Jane Carlisle in 1843 which speaks of 'a pretty memorandum-book in my reticule'.

9 *That's not a memorandum of your feelings*. Elizabeth Sewell gives the poor King's memo as an example of the 'insulation against emotion and dream' which she sees as characteristic of all nonsense, 'which will . . . treat matters of emotion according to its own rules, emphasizing words rather than their supposed content, the verbal rather than the real, and will keep as close to things as possible' (*The Field of Nonsense*, London, 1952, pp. 132–5).

10 YꓘƆOWЯƎBBAႱ. In January 1868 Carroll wrote to his publisher Macmillan with the question: 'Have you any means, or can you find any, for printing a page or two, in the next volume of Alice, in *reverse*?' This suggests that he originally wanted the whole poem – or something comparable – to be printed in mirror-writing. Macmillan assured him there was no technical problem involved in producing wood-blocks in reverse script but warned it would cost 'a good deal'. (See *Lewis Carroll and the House of Macmillan*, ed. Morton N. Cohen and Anita Gandolfo, London, 1987, p. 59). Perhaps it was the cost that restricted the author to one stanza in mirror-writing.

11 *Jabberwocky*. The first stanza appeared in 1855 in 'Misch-Masch', one of the private handwritten magazines Carroll produced for his brothers and sisters. It was presented in a mock-scholarly way 'as a curious fragment' under the heading of a 'Stanza of Anglo-Saxon poetry' and accompanied by a set of pseudo-philological notes and a 'translation':

BRYLLYG (derived from the verb to BRYL or BROIL), 'the time of broiling dinner, i.e. the close of the afternoon.'

SLITHY (compounded of SLIMY and LITHE). 'Smooth and active.'

TOVE. A species of Badger. They had smooth white hair, long hind legs, and short horns like a stag: lived chiefly on cheese.

GYRE, verb (derived from GYAOUR or GIAOUR, 'a dog'). To scratch like a dog.

GYMBLE (whence GIMBLET). 'To screw out holes in anything.'

WABE (derived from the verb to SWAB or SOAK). 'The side of a hill' (from its being soaked by the rain).

MIMSY (whence MIMSERABLE and MISERABLE). 'Unhappy.'

BOROGOVE. An extinct kind of parrot. They had no wings, beaks turned up, and made their nests under sun-dials: lived on veal.

MOME (hence SOMEOME, SOLEMONE and SOLEMN). 'Grave.'

RATH. A species of land turtle. Head erect: mouth like a shark: forelegs curved out so that the animal walked on its knees: smooth green body: lived on swallows and oysters.

OUTGRABE, past tense of the verb to OUTGRIBE. (It is connected with the old verb to GRIKE, or SHRIKE, from which are derived 'shriek' and 'creak'.) 'Squeaked.'

Hence the literal English of the passage is: 'it was evening, and the smooth active badgers were scratching and boring holes in the hill-side; all unhappy were the parrots; and the grave turtles squeaked out.'

There were probably sundials on top of the hill, and the 'borogoves' were afraid that their nests would be undermined. The hill was probably full of the nests of the 'raths', which ran out, squeaking with fear, on hearing the 'toves' scratching outside. This is an obscure, but yet deeply affecting, relic of ancient Poetry (*The Lewis Carroll Picture Book*, ed. Stuart Dodgson Collingwood, 1899, pp. 37–8).

'Jabberwocky' therefore began as a parody of current philological scholarship and the nineteenth-century revival of early English texts. Five new stanzas are added to it in *Through the Looking-Glass* where the original stanza is now used to begin and end what appears to be another obscure 'relic of ancient poetry', a quasi-heroic narrative poem in which, as in *Beowulf*, a fabulous monster is slain.

The most authoritative commentator on the idiom of the poem as a whole is probably Humpty Dumpty in chapter 6 (pp. 187–9), but given the eccentricity of his apparently authoritative definition of the word 'glory' in the same chapter, readers should perhaps be wary of his linguistic exegesis of the nonsense lexicon of 'Jabberwocky' though it often coincides with that given in 'Misch-Masch'. The notes on the poem that follow are supplements to the explanations given by Carroll in 'Misch-Masch' (quoted above) and by Humpty Dumpty in chapter 6.

12 *slithy toves*. Carroll gives some information on pronunciation in the preface to *The Hunting of the Snark*:

The 'i' in 'slithy' is long, as in 'writhe'; and 'toves' is pronounced so as to rhyme with 'groves'. Again, the first 'o' in 'borogoves' is pronounced like the 'o' in 'borrow'. I have heard people try to give it the sound of the 'o' in 'worry'. Such is human perversity.

The *OED* gives 'slithy' as an obsolete variant of 'sleathy' meaning 'slovenly', as in W. Whately's *God's Husbandry*: 'We make no great matter of the lower degrees of sinne, and so grow slithy' (1622). Humpty Dumpty on the other hand defines it as a 'portmanteau word' combining 'lithe' and 'slimy' (p. 187).

13 *gyre and gimble*. Humpty Dumpty defines them respectively as 'to go round and round like a gyroscope' and 'to make holes like a gimlet'. *OED* gives 'gyre' as a poetic term for 'to turn round, revolve, whirl, gyrate', in use from as early as the fifteenth century, and gives 'gimbal' as a noun meaning a joint or ring in various specialized contexts. 'Gimble' here is clearly a verb, and might suggest gambolling under the influence of gin as well as 'making holes like a gimblet'. In Tenniel's illustration to the first stanza in chapter 6, the toves are indeed like badgers, lizards and corkscrews, as Humpty Dumpty says they are, and are clearly perfectly-equipped for gyring and gimbling.

14 *mimsy*. *OED* gives this as 'Prim, prudish, contemptible' – though the first instance is dated 1880 and both its examples post-date Carroll's poem. Humpty Dumpty explains it as a portmanteau word meaning 'flimsy and miserable'. It reappears in *The Hunting of the Snark*, 'And chanted with mimsiest tones' (fit 7, verse 9).

15 *mome raths*. *OED* has 'mome' as a noun meaning a 'blockhead' or 'carping critic' (from Latin *momus*), and as a dialect adjective meaning 'soft'. 'Rath' is an Irish word for an archaic fortified enclosure, as in R. C. Hoare's *Tour of Ireland* (1807), 'one of those raised earthworks the Irish writers call raths'. Humpty Dumpty's dubious explanation of 'rath' as a 'green pig' (p. 189) may therefore be a garbled reference to Irish history. Uncharacteristically he is 'uncertain' about 'mome' but thinks it is short for 'from home', i.e. 'lost'.

16 *outgrabe*. Compare *The Hunting of the Snark*, Fit 5, verse 10: 'But it fairly lost heart, and outgrabe in despair'. Though there are obvious English analogies for this verb form, such as 'outgrew', its closest kinship is to German *ausgraben*, meaning 'to dig out, unearth, exhume, disinter, excavate'. In 1872 under the pseudonym of Thomas Chatterton, Robert Scott, Dean Liddell's collaborator in the Greek lexicon, published an article entitled 'The Jabberwock Traced to its True Source' in which he argued, on the evidence of a seance, that Carroll's poem is a translation of an old German ballad 'Der Jammerwoch' which begins as follows:

Es brillig war. Die schlichte Toven
  Wirrten und wimmelten in Waben;
Und aller-mümsige Burrgoven
  Die mohmen Räth' ausgraben
(*Macmillan's Magazine*, February 1872).

Carroll subsequently wrote to Scott thanking him for his interest 'in the origin and history of my little ballad' and enclosing 'an attempt to trace it into a yet more remote antiquity', his uncle Hassard Dodgson's Latin translation (27 February 1872, *Letters*, vol 1, p. 172). Scott went on to speculate that the ultimate original 'may be discovered in Sanscrit' – he postulated a *Iabrivokaveda* – and that 'the Saga of Jabberwocky is one of the universal heirlooms which the Aryan race in its dispersion carried with it from the great cradle of the family' (quoted in Stuart Dodgson Collingwood, *The Life and Letters of Lewis Carroll*, London, 1898, p.143).

17 *Jabberwock.* Asked by girls from a Boston girls' school whether they could name a magazine *Jabberwock*, Carroll in giving permission also furnished some commentary on the word itself:

the Anglo-Saxon word 'wocer' or 'wocor' signifies 'offspring' or 'fruit'. Taking 'jabber' in its ordinary acceptation of 'excited and voluble discussion', this would give the meaning of 'the result of much excited and voluble discussion' (3 February 1888, *Letters*, vol 2, p. 695).

OED defines 'jabber' as an onomatopoeic word meaning 'to talk volubly and with little sense, to chatter, gabble, prattle'; to 'chatter' or 'gibber' like monkeys or other animals; and 'to speak (a foreign language) with the implication it is unintelligible to the hearer'. 'Woce' is an obsolete form of 'voice' while 'woch' is an alternative form of 'vouch' and 'woke' an early form of 'weak'. Carroll's own etymological explanation in the letter could be alternatively (and less flatteringly) construed as meaning 'gibbering children'.

18 *Jubjub bird.* 'Jub' is an obsolete word for a jerkin or a dialect word for the trot of a horse (*OED*). Carroll's bird is more likely to be related to the nightingale whose call is traditionally rendered as 'jug jug', i.e. the *nightingale* is a *Jugjug* bird. The Jubjub bird may be a 'jabbering' cousin. It rates several mentions in *The Hunting of the Snark* where it is described in some detail in the Beaver's 'Lesson in Natural History' (Fit 5, verse 21):

As to temper the Jubjub's a desperate bird.
Since it lives in perpetual passion:
Its taste in costume is entirely absurd –
It is ages ahead of the fashion.

19 *frumious Bandersnatch.* A 'bander', according to the *OED*, is 'one who leads or leagues', such as the 'banders of the West' in Scott's *Abbotsford*; a 'Bandersnatch' might therefore be a beast that specializes in snatching banders. Later, in chapter 7, the King compares the passage of time to the momentum of the Bandersnatch (p. 198). It reappears in *The Hunting of the Snark*, Fit 7, where the Bandersnatch terrifies the Banker by grabbing him with his 'frumious jaws'. In his preface to the *Snark* Carroll comments on the adjective:

take the two words 'fuming' and 'furious'. Make up your mind that you will say both words, but leave it unsettled which you will say first. Now open your mouth and speak. If your thoughts incline ever so little towards 'fuming', you will say 'fuming-furious'; if they turn, by even a hair's breadth, towards 'furious', you will say 'furious-fuming'; but if you have that rarest of gifts, a perfectly balanced mind, you will say 'frumious' (*Complete Works of Lewis Carroll*, ed. Alexander Woollcott, London, 1939, p. 678).

20 *vorpal.* In a letter to a child friend Carroll wrote: 'I'm afraid I can't explain "vorpal blade" for you – nor yet "tulgey wood"' (18 December 1877, *Letters*, vol 1. p. 293). It might, in this nonsense poem where the pen is mightier than the sword, be a warped German-sounding amalgam of 'verbal' and 'warble'.

21 *manxome.* There may be a suggestion of 'manx' provenance here, 'manx' being a reference to the inhabitants of the Isle of Man or 'the Celtic language spoken on the Isle of Man' (their 'manx home'). But the obsolete Scottish word 'mank', from Latin *mancus* and French *manque*, can be an adjective meaning 'maimed, mutilated, defective' or a verb meaning 'to maim, mangle, mutilate'; 'manxome' might on this version be an adjective composed on the model of 'fearsome' or 'awesome'. Mangled language is the essence of 'Jabberwocky'.

22 *Tumtum tree.* *OED* gives three quite different meanings: 1. an imitation of a musical sound (as in 'a nightmare of "tum-tum-tiddy-tum" and waltzes', 1859); 2. an Anglo-Indian dog-cart; and 3. an abbreviation for 'tummy' (as in W. S. Gilbert's 'The pain is in my little tum', 1868). Thinking musically, the 'Tumtum tree' might well be the natural habitat of the 'Jubjub bird'; thinking physiologically it might be a Freudian complement of the 'vorpal sword'.

23 *uffish thought.* Compare *The Hunting of the Snark*: 'The Bellman looked uffish and wrinkled his brow' (Fit 4, verse 1). In a letter Carroll gives an 'explanation': 'It seems to suggest a state of mind when the voice is gruffish, the manner roughish, and the temper huffish' (18 December 1877, *Letters*, vol 1, p. 293).

24 *whiffling through the tulgey wood.* According to *OED* a 'whiffle' is a 'trifle' and 'to whiffle' is 'to blow in puffs or slight gusts', 'to flutter in the wind', 'to talk idly' or 'to make a light whistling sound'. Carroll said he couldn't explain 'tulgey wood' (*Letters*, vol 1, p. 293).

25 *burbled.* In the same letter Carroll explained: 'if you take the three verbs "*b*leat", "m*ur*mur", and "war*ble*", and select the bits I have underlined, it certainly makes "burble"; though I'm afraid I can't distinctly remember having made it in that way' (*Letters*, vol 1, p. 293). *OED* gives 'burble' as a verb meaning 'to form bubbles', 'to gurgle' (as in 'burbling brook'); and 'to perplex, confuse, muddle' (as in a letter of Jane Carlyle, 'his external life fallen into a horribly burbled state').

26 *galumphing.* Compare *The Hunting of the Snark*: 'The Beaver went simply galumphing about' (Fit 4, verse 17). *OED* describes this as 'invented by L. Carroll (perhaps with some reminiscence of gallop, triumphant)'. There may also be a suggestion of 'lumping' and 'laughing'.

27 *beamish*. Compare *The Hunting of the Snark*: 'But oh Beamish nephew, beware of the day' (Fit 3, verse 10). Though it sounds Carrollian, *OED* gives it as a sixteenth-century word meaning 'radiant, shining brightly'.

28 *O frabjous day! Callooh! Callay! OED* defines 'frab' as a dialect verb meaning 'to harass, worry' and 'frabble' as 'confused wrangling', but 'frabjous' as 'a nonsense word invented by L. Carroll', with the suggestion of 'fair' and 'joyous'. There may be a touch of the 'fabulous' too. 'Callooh' is an arctic duck known in Scotland, but may have suggestions of Greek *kalos* meaning 'beautiful'.

29 *chortled*. Defined by the *OED* as 'A factitious word introduced by the author of *Through the Looking-Glass*, and jocularly used by others after him, with some suggestion of *chuckle* and of *snort*'. It is appropriate that Carroll's nonsensical philological play earned his book a place in the greatest monument of nineteenth-century philology.

30 *somebody killed something*. Alice's confusion is a model for the disorientating effects of all nonsense. But, though she is confused by the semantic references, she nevertheless understands the murderous shape of the plot. Tenniel's picture makes the knightly Pre-Raphaelite hero of the tale very like Alice but turns the monster s/he kills into a senile waistcoated hybrid, with dragon wings, fish face, spider talons, and a lizard's feet and tail – a creature as archaic and composite as the language of the tale itself. The picture was to have been the frontispiece of the book but faced with the suggestion that it was 'too terrible a monster, and likely to alarm nervous and imaginative children', Carroll had second thoughts. He asked mothers to try the picture out on their children and eventually had it transferred 'to its proper place in the book (where the ballad occurs which it is intended to illustrate)' (*Letters*, vol 1, p. 163).

CHAPTER II: THE GARDEN OF LIVE FLOWERS

1 *the garden*. At the opening of *Wonderland* Alice sees 'the loveliest garden you ever saw' (p. 12) and eventually gets there in chapter 7. While the desire to see a garden plays a part in the opening of both books, it is easier to get into in the second book. Once again, though, it is not long before pastoral nonsense dissolves back into a world of social contradictions.

2 *O Tiger-lily!* In *Wonderland* Alice addresses her second interlocutor with equal poetic formality as 'O Mouse' (p. 21). Here Alice enters a version of pastoral reminiscent of Marvell's 'The Garden' – Little Alice in a prospect of flowers – or Blake's *Book of Thel* but clearly modelled on a more contemporary poem. Alice's conversation with the flowers alludes to that in section 22 of Tennyson's *Maud* (1855), especially the talking flowers of stanza 10:

There has fallen a splendid tear
From the passion-flower at the gate.
She is coming, my dove, my dear;
She is coming, my life, my fate;
The red rose cries, 'She is near, she is near;'
And the white rose weeps, 'She is late;'
The larkspur listens, 'I hear, I hear;'
And the lily whispers, 'I wait.'

Most of the flowers mentioned in the episode crop up in the Tennyson too – rose, lily, violet, larkspur. 'In the original manuscript', according to Stuart Dodgson Collingwood, 'the bad-tempered flower was the passion-flower' corresponding to Tennyson's 'passion-flower at the gate'; 'the sacred origin of the name never struck him, until it was pointed out to him by a friend, when he at once changed it into a tiger-lily' (Collingwood, *Life and Letters of Lewis Carroll*, p. 127).

3 *one of the kind that has nine spikes*. Until 1897, this read 'She's one of the thorny kind' – possibly an allusion to Alice's governess Miss Prickett or 'Pricks' as she was called (see also note 5 below). Alice refers directly to her governess later in the chapter (p. 152).

4 *It succeeded beautifully*. This works of course because it represents a mirror inversion of the normal situation.

5 *Look up, speak nicely*. In '"Alice" on the Stage' Carroll sketched her portrait as follows:

> The Red Queen I pictured as a Fury, but of another type; *her* passion must be cold and calm; she must be formal and strict, yet not unkindly; pedantic to the tenth degree, the concentrated essence of all governesses (see p. 296).

6 *as sensible as a dictionary*. The Queen's comparativist positions are enunciated with all the positive trenchancy of an absolutist, though they absolutely dissolve any fundamental distinction between sense and nonsense. Carroll's career in Oxford coincided with work on what was to become the *OED*. Though not completed until 1928, it began with the appearance in 1858 of 'A Proposal for the Publication of a New English Dictionary by the Philological Society'. The proposed dictionary was to 'contain every word occurring in the literature of the language' and adopt 'the historical principle' in the treatment of individual words. This 'sensible' dictionary was very much in the air, particularly in Oxford, when Carroll was writing *Through the Looking-Glass*. Its primary definition of nonsense is 'That which is not sense; spoken or written words which make no sense or convey absurd ideas; also, absurd or senseless action'. Carroll's library at his death contained a large collection of different dictionaries – such as Johnson's, Bailey's, Webster's, a Slang Dictionary and Skeat's *Etymological Dictionary of the English Language.*

7 *just like a large chess-board.* Though Alice had encountered small actual chess pieces in the first chapter, this is the first recognition of chess as a narrative principle of the book. Tenniel's illustration is like a parody of Renaissance Perspective, the basis of so many mirror-theories of art.

8 *It's a great huge game of chess that's being played.* Compare T. H. Huxley:

> The chess-board is the world; the pieces are the phenomena of the universe; the rules of the game are what we call the laws of Nature. The player on the other side is hidden from us. We know that his play is always fair, just, and patient (*Lay Sermons, etc*, iii, *A Liberal Education*).

9 *I should like to be a Queen, best.* Alice's aspirations to power conform to the conventions of chess and also to those of fairy tales. They also represent a plausible psychological reality for the child. Compare chapter 1: 'Let's pretend we're kings and queens', p. 124).

10 *Lily's too young to play.* The White Queen's daughter Lily is mentioned in the previous chapter. The name relates the 'live flowers' to the chess game. It may also be a reference to one of Carroll's child friends, Lily MacDonald, the eldest daughter of George MacDonald, often photographed by Carroll.

11 *Thirst quenched, I hope?* The thirst-quenching biscuit is another looking-glass inversion.

12 *in the Eighth Square we shall be Queens together.* Like a prophecy in fairy tales, the Queen's words map out the future course of the narrative – and the game. When it reaches the eighth square a pawn in chess becomes a Queen.

13 *she was gone.* Alice (the white pawn) and the Red Queen have been side by side, but with this first move of the game, the Queen moves to KR4 (see the introductory diagram). Being a pawn inside the game, Alice doesn't yet understand what is going on.

CHAPTER III: LOOKING-GLASS INSECTS

1 *a grand survey of the country.* In wanting to make such a geographical survey Alice is very much a Victorian traveller.

2 *in fact, it was an elephant.* A rare touch of geographical exoticism in Carroll's work; the country Alice surveys momentarily takes on the contours of imperial India or Africa. Compare the gardener's song, 'He thought he saw an Elephant,/That practised on a fife;/He looked again, and found it was/A letter from his wife' (*Sylvie and Bruno*, *The Complete Works*, ed. Alexander Woollcott, London, 1939, reprinted Harmondsworth, 1988, p. 296).

3 *the first of the six little brooks.* The six little brooks (and the six rows of stars in the text which indicate them) represent the six boundaries on the chess board which Alice must cross in order to become a queen.

4 *"Tickets, please!" said the Guard.* As anticipated earlier by the Red Queen (p. 144), Alice travels quickly through the third square 'by railway'. Carroll's 'fairy tale' is set squarely in the technological world of its time and this particular episode is packed with references to the ways Alice could be transported passively through all manner of Victorian communication systems – not only by railway, but by telegraph, post and parcel post. Carroll travelled by train with Alice and her sisters at various times, as recorded for example in his diary for 25 June 1863: 'Ina, Alice, Edith and I (*mirabile dictu*!) walked down to Abingdon Road Station, and so home by railway: a pleasant expedition, with a *very* pleasant conclusion' (*Diaries*, vol 1, p.199).

5 *"like the chorus of a song," thought Alice.* This looks like an allusion to a popular song of the time, but if so it hasn't been traced. More to the point, Alice in the railway carriage has to hold her own against a chorus of bullying voices for whom 'language is worth a thousand pounds a word'. Perhaps this is related to the gentleman 'dressed in white paper', the world of politics and newspapers. At any rate it suggests the degree to which Alice in this episode is treated as a mere item in a system of social exchange through which she is travelling.

6 *he was dressed in white paper.* In Tenniel's illustration the man in the white suit bears a striking resemblance to Benjamin Disraeli (and in particular to Tenniel's cartoons of Disraeli in *Punch*). Perhaps his being dressed in paper reminded Tenniel of Disraeli's constant presence in the newspapers (including *Punch*); 'Disraeli dressed in newspapers' reminded William Empson of 'the new man who gets on by self-advertisement, the newspaper-fed man who believes in progress' (*Some Versions of Pastoral*, London, 1935, p. 256). From Victorian times to the present some readers have thought the goat beside him resembled Gladstone. The depiction of Alice on the other hand seems to be based on John Everett Millais's painting, *My First Sermon*, which Carroll mentions when describing a visit to Millais in 1864 (*Diaries*, vol 1, p. 213).

7 *Lass, with care.* As breakable parcels would be labelled 'Glass, with care'. It is characteristic of Carroll to find the lass in glass – through the looking-glass in fact.

8 *she must go by post, as she's got a head on her.* A reference to the queen's head on Victorian stamps. Alice of course wants to be a queen herself.

9 *which happened to be the Goat's beard.* In an earlier version this happened to be an old lady's hair and it was Tenniel (in a letter of 1 June 1870, which discusses this illustration in detail) who suggested that Carroll 'might make Alice lay hold of the Goat's *beard* as the nearest thing to her hand' (Collingwood, *Life and Letters of Lewis Carroll*, pp. 147–9).

Since Tenniel's suggestion was made in a letter also alluding to the omitted 'Wasp in a Wig' chapter, it used to be assumed that that missing chapter followed on here (e.g. Oxford's World Classics *Alice*, ed. R. L. Green, Oxford, 1971, and the *Annotated Alice*, ed. Martin Gardner, Harmondsworth, 1970). When what were apparently the galley proofs of the original cancelled text were sold at Sotheby's in 1974 and then published as *The Wasp in a Wig*, ed. Martin Gardner, in 1977, the new evidence suggested that 'The Wasp in a Wig' episode actually formed part of chapter 8 'It's All My Own Invention', rather than this chapter (see chapter 8, note 17). This remains a matter of conjecture; 'The Wasp in a Wig' may be someone else's invention.

10 *What's the use of their having names*. The Gnat on names evinces the nit-picking precisionism of Carroll the logician and philosopher. In *Symbolic Logic* Carroll calls 'classification' an 'entirely *Mental*' process and in chapter 4, 'On Names', writes as follows:

> The word 'Thing', which conveys the idea of a Thing, *without* any idea of an Adjunct, represents *any* single Thing. Any other word (or phrase), which conveys the idea of a Thing, *with* the idea of an Adjunct represents *any* Thing which possesses that Adjunct; i.e., it represents any Member of the Class to which that Adjunct is *peculiar*.
>
> Such a word (or phrase) is called a *Name*; and, if there be an existing Thing which it represents, it is said to be a Name of that Thing . . . Just as a Class is said to be *Real*, or *Unreal*, according as there *is*, or is *not*, an existing Thing in it, so also a Name is said to be *Real*, or *Unreal*, according as there *is*, or *is not*, an existing Thing represented by it . . . Every Name is either a Substantive only, or else a phrase consisting of a Substantive and one or more Adjectives (or phrases used as Adjectives) (*Lewis Carroll's Symbolic Logic*, ed. William Warren Bartley, III, Brighton, 1977, pp. 63–4).

This chapter, 'Looking-Glass Insects', might as well be named 'On Names' too. It sets real and unreal names side by side, and creates imaginary insects by adding a second adjective or substantive to a name that is already compounded of a substantive and an adjective (or substantive). Carroll's prose is always studded with hyphenated compounds, but here they come into their own to create new species. Nonsense etymology and nonsense entomology meet. Compare the nonsense flora and fauna of Edward Lear.

11 *a Snap-dragon-fly*. 'Snap-dragon' was 'a game or amusement (usually held at Christmas) consisting of snatching raisins out of a bowl or dish of burning brandy or other spirit and eating them whilst alight' (*OED*).

12 *Frumenty and mince-pie*. 'Frumenty' is 'a dish made of hulled wheat boiled in milk, and seasoned with cinnamon, sugar etc' (*OED*). Like the references to plum-puddings and snap-dragon, mince-pies are in keeping with the wintry tonality of the book as a whole.

13 *You shouldn't make jokes . . . if it makes you so unhappy.* Another looking-glass inversion, but it is also a reflection of the interplay between jokes and unhappiness represented by Beckett's 'nothing is funnier than unhappiness, I grant you that' (*Endgame*, London, 1958, p. 20) and the currency of the 'sad comedian'.

14 *answers to the name of 'Dash'.* 'Dash' is a name, but could also be a sign for a blank where a name might be '—' (as earlier in "Come here——," p. 152).

15 *into the—into what?* Nearly everything in the chapter hinges on names and naming – like the Gnat's penchant for puns – but here Alice suffers from what is now called nominal aphasia, the inability to remember names. Though frightening, this also enables a quasi-Wordsworthian communion between the human and natural worlds which is unlike anything else in the Alice books.

16 *L, I know it begins with L.* Alice's 'L' is for 'Liddell', though when she recovers her name it is 'Alice' not 'Liddell'.

17 *they must be.* The chapter ends without a full stop which indicates that this last sentence should continue into the title of the following chapter, to make the rhyming couplet:

> Feeling sure that they must be
> Tweedledum and Tweedledee.

In fact an erroneous stop crept into the 1897 edition, later removed. A chapter about losing names (and coining names through bad puns) ends with a signpost towards a chapter coined out of traditional nonsense names.

CHAPTER IV: TWEEDLEDUM AND TWEEDLEDEE.

1 *They were standing under a tree.* In Tenniel's illustration, the brothers, standing as rigidly as wax-work schoolboys, are very evidently identical twins. The only difference between them is in the last syllable of their names, as written on their collars. Their names hark back to John Byrom's rhyme on the quarrels between Handel and Bononcini in 1725:

> Some say compared to Bononcini
> That mynheer Handel's but a ninny;
> Others aver that he to Handel
> Is scarcely fit to hold a candle,
> Strange all this Difference should be
> 'Twixt Tweedle-dum and Tweedle-dee.

Twins are a special case of looking-glass doubling and Tenniel's illustration shows them as mirror-images of each other. Their penchant for 'Contrariwise' conversation represents a different kind of mirror effect, inversion.

2 *the words of the old song*. The nursery rhyme Alice quotes is first recorded in *Original Ditties for the Nursery* of 1805 or so, and was included in *The Nursery Rhymes of England* edited by J. O. Halliwell, 1853. In *The Oxford Dictionary of Nursery Rhymes* the Opies suggest the rhyme might have either preceded Byrom's satirical verses (see above) or developed out of them. Carroll's version differs marginally from Halliwell's, so he is probably quoting from memory. The Tweedles are the first of several characters in *Through the Looking-Glass* to owe their existence, like the Queen and Knave of Hearts in *Wonderland*, to the words of an 'old song'.

3 *Here we go round the mulberry bush*. This is another 'old song', and given by J. O. Halliwell as an example of a children's 'Game Rhyme' or 'ring-dance imitation-play' in *Popular Rhymes and Nursery Tales*, 1849.

4 *The Walrus and the Carpenter*. A rare instance of a nonsense poem in the Alice books which is not a parody. In a letter to his uncle Hassard Dodgson of 1872, Carroll wrote:

> In writing 'The Walrus and the Carpenter', I had no particular poem in my mind. The metre is a common one, and I don't think 'Eugene Aram' suggested it more than the many other poems I have read in the same metre (*Letters*, vol 1, p. 177).

'The Dream of Eugene Aram, the Murderer' (1829) by Thomas Hood (1799–1845), is indeed written in the same metre and begins:

> 'Twas in the prime of summer time,
>   An evening calm and cool,
> And four and twenty happy boys
>   Came bounding out of school:
> There were some that ran and some that leapt
>   Like troutlets in a pool.

The opening of Carroll's poem may also recall the nonsensical close of Wordsworth's 'The Idiot Boy' from *Lyrical Ballads* (1798): 'The cocks did crow to-whoo, to-whoo,/And the sun did shine so cold'. 'The Walrus and the Carpenter' is also a lyrical ballad.

According to another of Carroll's illustrators, Harry Furniss, Carroll told him that Tenniel 'remonstrated against the walrus and the carpenter as a hopeless combination, and begged to have the "Carpenter" abolished – I remember offering "baronet" and "butterfly" . . . but he finally chose "Carpenter"' (Dorothy Furniss, 'New Lewis Carroll Letters', *Pearson's Magazine*, December

1930, pp. 635–6). Had Tenniel decided otherwise, we might have known this grimly carnivorous nonsense masterpiece as 'The Walrus and the Butterfly' or 'The Walrus and the Baronet'. In Tenniel's illustrations the Walrus has the air of a down-at-heel Baronet beside the mean and clean-faced Carpenter, suggesting an alliance of grandee and artisan in taking advantage of the neat and well-trained oysters. The Carpenter's hat is the standard paper cap of the mid-Victorian workman comparable to those in various Tenniel cartoons for *Punch* (see Michael Hancher, *The Tenniel Illustrations to the 'Alice' Books*, Columbus, Ohio, 1986, chapter 1).

5 *Were walking close at hand.* As Carroll explained in a later letter, this had originally read 'The Walrus and the Carpenter/Were walking hand-in-hand' but this 'was altered to suit the artist' (*Letters*, vol 1, p. 222). The suggestion that they might be a homosexual couple would certainly alter the implications of their appetite for young oysters. If 'Oysters' were a nonsense word, it might suggest some blend of 'boys', 'choristers' and 'ostlers'. The oysters behave like a party of excessively well brought-up schoolboys, and it brings them to a sticky end.

6 *If seven maids with seven mops.* This is oddly reminiscent of the nursery rhyme 'As I was going to St Ives,/I met a man with seven wives,/Each wife had seven sacks,/Each sack had seven cats,' etc. It reads as a parody of a kind of mathematical exam question no doubt familiar to Carroll.

7 *And whether pigs have wings.* Perhaps an allusion to the expression 'when pigs fly' meaning 'never' (see note 9, chapter 9, *AAIW*). The Walrus's 'many things' make up one of the most celebrated agendas in the history of nonsense literature as well as one of the most memorable lists in poetry (which loves lists).

8 *'O Oysters,' said the Carpenter.* As Michael Hancher has pointed out, Tenniel's illustration of the oyster-eating Carpenter here is very close to a cartoon he had done earlier in *Punch* on 'Law and Lunacy, Or, A Glorious Oyster Season for the Lawyers' (1862), a cartoon based on the proverb 'The oyster is the lawyer's fee'. Hancher suggests Carroll may have had in mind another later *Punch* squib illustrated by Tenniel during the time he was illustrating *Wonderland*, 'The Proverb Reversed'. This tells of oysters protesting to the Lord Chancellor against the greed of lawyers, while 'edging away from the Cayenne', and ends:

> 'Henceforth the rhyme that carries smart
> To my poor Oyster's oozy heart,
> Shall in another fashion run,
> And thus be passed from sire to son:
> "The Oyster where it ought to be,
> And shell and shell the lawyer's fee."'

Again he smiled, so says the fable,
And drew his chair up near the table,
When all the oysters, seen and hid,
Cried, 'Eat and welcome.' And he did.
(Michael Hancher, *The Tenniel Illustrations*, 1986, pp. 15–20)

9 *They'd eaten every one*. Carroll's seaside ballad has a characteristically grim ending. In the stage version of *Alice*, however, Carroll added a kind of moral coda:

The Carpenter he ceased to sob;
The Walrus ceased to weep;
They'd finished all the oysters;
And they laid them down to sleep—
And of their craft and cruelty
The punishment to reap.

In this stage version the ghosts of two of the oysters go on to sing mazurkas while stamping on their consumers' chests, singing 'O woeful, weeping Walrus, your tears are all a sham!/You're greedier for oysters than children are for jam,' etc. Such moral quittance may have seemed appropriate for the stage, but luckily Carroll did not modify the poem in subsequent editions of the book (as he incorporated the additional verses of 'The Owl and the Panther' he had devised for the musical *Alice* into later editions of *Wonderland*). The only moral from the story as it stands would be, 'Beware of strangers at the seaside and be on your guard when people talk of admiring the view', or 'Don't be too neat or too keen to please and be pleased, you might do better to follow the example of the eldest oyster and stay in bed.'

10 *only a sort of thing in his dream*. This idea bothers Alice and recurs at the opening of chapter 8 (p. 205) and the final paragraphs of the book (pp. 239–40). Martin Gardner compares Bishop Berkeley's idealist proposition that the material world is the dream of God. Problems about dreams and existence and the existence of dreams recur in *Symbolic Logic*:

By 'existence' I mean of course whatever kind of existence suits its nature. The two Propositions, '*dreams* exist' and '*drums* exist', denote two totally different kinds of 'existence'. A *dream* is an aggregate of ideas, and exists only in the *mind of a dreamer*; whereas a *drum* is an aggregate of wood and parchment, and exists in the *hands of a drummer* (*Lewis Carroll's Symbolic Logic*, ed. William Warren Bartley, III, Brighton, 1977, pp. 232–3).

11 *He called it a helmet*. In text and illustration the Tweedles dress up as travestied schoolboy versions of the medieval knights of Mallory and Tennyson – as well as of the chess knights of chapter 8.

CHAPTER V: WOOL AND WATER

1 *the White Queen came running.* Carroll gives a retrospective account of his idea of the Queen in '"Alice" on the Stage', where he describes her as 'helpless as an infant; and with a slow, maundering, bewildered air about her just *suggesting* imbecility, but never quite passing into it' (see p. 296).
2 *bread-and-butter.* Alice helps herself to bread-and-butter, that staple of Victorian tea parties, in 'A Mad Tea-Party' (*AAIW*, chapter 7), the Hatter complains bread-and-butter is 'getting so thin' in the Trial (*AAIW*, chapter 11) and there is a 'bread-and-butter-fly' in 'Looking-Glass Insects' (*TLG*, chapter 3). Though it is not, as the Hatter says, 'always tea-time', tea-time is never very far away.
3 *The rule is, jam to-morrow and jam yesterday—but never jam to-day.* Now proverbial, the phrase originates here. The Queen's preoccupation with 'jam' fits in with her mutterings about 'bread-and-butter' earlier.
4 *Living backwards.* Another looking-glass inversion. The Queen later claims her remarkable two-way memory is 'the way things happen here', but in fact she is the only character to lay claim to prospective memory of this kind.
5 *exactually.* This is actually a conflation of 'actually' and 'exactly'. Alice's exact age makes her six months older than she had been during her adventures in Wonderland (see chapter 1, note 1).
6 *one ca'n't believe impossible things.* Gardner compares Carroll's letter of 23 May 1864 to Mary MacDonald in which he tells her 'not to be in such a hurry to believe' his tall stories next time:

> If you set to work to believe everything, you will tire out the believing-muscles of your mind, and then you'll be so weak you won't be able to believe the simplest true things. Only last week a friend of mine set to work to believe Jack-the-giant-killer. He managed to do it, but he was so exhausted by it that when I told him it was raining (which was true) he *couldn't* believe it, but rushed out into the street without his hat or umbrella, the consequence of which was his hair got seriously damp' (*Letters*, vol 1, p. 64).

Questions of 'belief' preoccupied Carroll all his life but he had 'a deep dread of arguments on religious topics', as he told Edith Rix in 1886, telling her she could 'do more good . . . by showing . . . what a Christian *is* than by telling . . . what a Christian *believes*' (*Letters*, vol 2, p. 618). Tertullian of course had asserted of Christian belief *certum est quia impossible est*, 'it is certain because it is impossible' (*De Carne Christi*). To Daniel Biddle, Carroll wrote on 16 July 1885: 'We cannot conceive how a point, moving from "0" to "1", through this infinite series of steps, ever reaches "1": but a thing is not *impossible*, merely because it is *inconceivable*. The human reason has very definite limits' (*Letters*, vol 1, p. 589).

7 *as she crossed the little brook after the Queen*. The White Queen has moved one square forward to QB5 while Alice advances to Q5 beside her.

8 *The shop seemed to be full of all manner of curious things*. Tenniel's illustration of the shop appears to be based on an Oxford grocery shop of the time at 83 St Aldate's Street (Williams and Madan, *Handbook of the Literature of the Rev. C. L. Dodgson*, 1931). In a letter of 22 December 1887 Carroll compares Memory to a world of shelves: 'What an odd thing Memory is! It consists . . . of odd corners and shelves, which are apt to get out of sight; and on one of these shelves (just getting a *little* dusty from neglect) I observe the name of a little girl I used to meet up and down Eastbourne in the Middle Ages' (*Letters*, vol 2, p. 688). Memory is very much at issue with the White Queen around.

9 *Things flow about so here*. Alice's words recall the Pre-Socratic Greek philosopher Heraclitus' *panta rei*, 'everything flows'. Almost everything in this chapter turns upon an almost vertiginous fluidity.

10 *a teetotum*. A popular traditional toy or spinning top, originally square and with letters on its four sides; Defoe speaks of a 'T totum, as children call it', the name combining the initial letter and then the Latin word *totum* meaning all the whole'. It can also mean a tiny person or something very unsteady.

11 *Feather*. A technical rowing term, meaning turning the oar as it leaves the water at the end of a stroke, so that it passes through the air edgeways. This rowing scene is reminiscent of Carroll's various river-trips with Alice and her sisters, such as the one on which the 'Alice' story was first conceived, recalled in the opening poem with its reference to 'The rhythm of our rowing'.

12 *You'll be catching a crab directly*. Another ambiguous rowing term. It means 'making a faulty stroke in rowing whereby the oar becomes jammed in the water'. The *OED* suggests 'the phrase probably originated in the humorous suggestion that the rower had caught a crab, which was holding his oar down under the water'.

13 *the darling scented rushes*. This is a rare instance of Carroll's Pre-Raphaelite pictorial taste shaping the narrative, and framing his heroine as viewed from outside ('the little sleeves were rolled up', etc.).

14 *The prettiest are always further!* Alice's remark recalls such proverbial expressions as 'the grass is always greener on the other side' and 'distance lends enchantment to the view'. This is a chapter of visual tantalizations.

15 *The oars, and the boat, and the river, had vanished . . . the little dark shop*. Tenniel's illustration captures the elided moment of metamorphosis from boat to shop, as Alice 'half astonished and half frightened' rows back to the scene of the previous illustration.

16 *set the egg upright on the shelf.* This sets the scene for the following chapter, which features a famously precarious egg.

17 *So she went on.* The asterisks indicate Alice has crossed the brook and moved to Q6 – after the Sheep, who has 'gone off to the other end of the shop', has moved to KB8.

CHAPTER VI: HUMPTY DUMPTY

1 *HUMPTY DUMPTY himself.* The nursery rhyme of Humpty Dumpty is not, according to the *Oxford Dictionary of Nursery Rhymes* (*ODNR*), recorded until *Mother Goose's Melody* in 1803 and in full printed form until *Gammer Gurton's Garland* (1810). Nevertheless folklorists believe that the riddle rhyme, which is found in different forms in most European countries, probably goes back into the remote past. In Halliwell's *Nursery Rhymes of England* (1846), it is classed as a 'riddle' meaning an 'egg'.

2 *Humpty Dumpty sat on a wall.* The last line of Carroll's version differs from the most familiar modern form of the rhyme ('Couldn't put Humpty together again') and also from the two variants in *Halliwell's Nursery Rhymes of England.* Pre-Carrollian versions of 'Humpty Dumpty' recorded in *ODNR* all differ and Carroll's is probably from oral memory – though Alice claims to have read it 'in a book'.

3 *What tremendously easy riddles you ask.* Humpty Dumpty owes his existence to a riddle, so his taste for riddles – a taste he shares with his creator – is ironically appropriate.

4 *a History of England.* Collectors such as Halliwell (who classified some nursery rhymes such as 'Old King Cole' as 'Historical') thought of nursery rhymes as 'popular remnants of the ancient Scandinavian nursery literature' (Preface to the fifth edn, 1853). Dickens had written *A Child's History of England* (1851–3). Humpty snobbishly prefers history to nursery rhymes and dwells on his associations with kings rather than vulnerable children and eggs. The poems of *TLG* evoke monarchs, battles, falls and quarrels quite as much as histories of England do.

5 *Seven years and six months.* See chapter 1, note 1.

6 *Too proud?* His constant harping on 'pride' in his precarious situation suggests the proverbial 'pride comes before a fall'.

7 *but two can.* The pun introduces a murderous innuendo, one of the darkest of the book's jokes about death. It also reverts to the play on 'one' and 'two' eggs in the previous chapter (p. 179).

8 *that seems to be done right.* Elizabeth Sewell in *The Field of Nonsense* comments that 'it is important to Nonsense that numbers and arithmetic should work properly'. Compare chapter 3, where Alice thinks to herself, 'Thirty times three makes ninety. I wonder if anyone's counting'.

9 *it means just what I choose it to mean.* Gardner points out the affinity between Humpty Dumpty's nominalist philosophy of language and Carroll's *Symbolic Logic* (1896) in which the author outlines his opposition to the conventional position adopted by writers and editors of 'Logical text-books':

> They speak of the Copula of a Proposition 'with bated breath', almost as if it were a living, conscious Entity, capable of declaring for itself what it chose to mean, and that we, poor human creatures, had nothing to do but to ascertain *what* was its sovereign will and pleasure, and submit to it.
>
> In opposition to this view, I maintain that any writer of a book is fully authorised in attaching any meaning he likes to a word or phrase he intends to use. If I find an author saying, at the beginning of his book, 'Let it be understood that by the word "*black*" I shall always mean "*white*", and by the word "*white*" I shall always mean "*black*", I meekly accept his ruling, however injudicious I think it" (*Lewis Carroll's Symbolic Logic*, ed. William Warren Bartley, III, Brighton, 1977, p. 232).

The *OED*'s primary (though obsolete) definition of 'glory' is peculiarly appropriate to Humpty Dumpty: 'glory' is 'the disposition to claim honour for oneself; boastful spirit'. In a letter of 21 June 1876, touching on the death of two children (one of whom was Alice's sister Edith), Dodgson used the word in one of its more usual honorific and religious senses: 'the world, even at its brightest, is not worthy to be compared to the glory that shall be revealed' (*Letters*, vol 1, p. 254). It is one of the key terms in Wordsworth's 'Ode on the Intimations of Immortality' ('trailing clouds of glory', 'where is it now the glory and the dream?'), a poem that profoundly influenced Carroll's vision of lost childhood innocence. Humpty's reductively anti-Romantic definition corresponds to his argumentative and downright character, as well as anticipating his eventual 'knock-me-down' fate.

10 *'Jabberwocky'*. The first piece of language she encounters beyond the looking-glass in chapter 1 (see note 11, chapter 1). Humpty Dumpty treats it, like everything else, as a kind of riddle. Though his subsequent 'explanation' of the poem is often linguistically extremely plausible, both his highly arbitrary attitude towards language and his intellectual over-confidence may make him a suspect guide to its meaning.

11 *it's like a portmanteau.* In the preface to *The Hunting of the Snark* Carroll says of his nonsense coinages that 'Humpty Dumpty's theory, of two meanings packed into one word like a portmanteau, seems to me the right explanation for all'. 'Portmanteau word' has now become a standard technical term for such coinages, coinages which Freud identified as a common feature of dreams and Joyce made the basis of his literary idiom in *Finnegans Wake*.

12 *In winter, when the fields are white*. An instance of a Carrollian lyric without a known parodic model or source. The poem, though as equally resistant to 'sensible' explanation as 'Jabberwocky', is quite unlike it; its *vocabulary* is pellucid, only its *reference* is comparably problematic. Humpty Dumpty finds a corkscrew in both.

13 *I tried to turn the handle but——*. Humpty earlier claims to have no problems with adjectives and to be proud of his skills in mastering otherwise fractious verbs, but the difficulties of his poem turn upon conjunctions – such as that final 'but'.

14 *She never finished the sentence*. In this respect, she repeats the 'unsatisfactory' structure of Humpty's poem, which is also marked by unfinished sentences.

CHAPTER VII: THE LION AND THE UNICORN

1 *busily writing in his memorandum-book*. As in chapter 1, note 8. The Knight in chapter 1 'balances very badly' as do all the knights in this scene (and later the White Knight); the world of the chivalrous Middle Ages is constantly spoofed. Tenniel's illustration evokes Uccello's *Battle of San Romano* in the National Gallery, London.

2 *two of them are wanted in the game*. A reference to the two horses needed for the two white knights in the game of chess.

3 *Anglo-Saxon attitudes*. 'Jabberwocky' was originally satirically introduced as a 'Stanza of Anglo-Saxon Poetry', and this too plays on the academic interest in the Anglo-Saxons in the later nineteenth century – punningly identifying their cultural and racial 'attitudes' with physical postures such as those adopted by the wriggling Messenger.

4 *Haigha*. A pseudo-Anglo-Saxon spelling of 'Hare'; from Tenniel's illustration he is clearly identifiable as the March Hare of *AAIW*.

5 *I love my love with an H*. Alice slips into the popular Victorian alphabetical game 'I love my love with an A'. In *The Nursery Rhymes of England* (1846) J. O. Halliwell classifies this as a 'scholastic' rhyme and gives the following sample for 'A': 'I love my love with an A, because he's Agreeable;/I hate him because he's Avaricious./He took me to the sign of the Acorn,/And treated me with Apples./His name's Andrew,/And he lives in Arlington'. See Edward Lear's *Nonsense Alphabets* for comparable contemporary alphabetical nonsense.

6 *Hatta*. A pseudo-Anglo-Saxon spelling of 'Hatter'; from the illustration later in the chapter (and the earlier one of the imprisoned messenger in chapter 5) he is clearly the Mad Hatter from *AAIW*. Apart from Alice herself, the hare and hatter are the only survivors or interlopers from the earlier book.

7 *Hay, then.* The 'ham sandwich' and 'hay' the King prescribes continue the sequence of H's set off by Alice's rhyme. On 2 September 1885, Carroll wrote: 'One of the deepest motives (as you are aware) in the human breast (so deep that many have failed to detect it) is Alliteration' (*Letters*, vol 1, p. 601).

8 *the words of the old song.* First recorded in *Useful Transactions in Philosophy* (1708–10) and included in Halliwell's *The Nursery Rhymes of England*. In this case, the rhyme is precisely in Humpty Dumpty's sense a 'History of England' (p. 183). According to the *Oxford Dictionary of Nursery Rhymes* 'The Lion and the Unicorn' may refer to the amalgamation of the royal arms of Scotland with those of England when James VI of Scotland was crowned James I of England; at that time one of the unicorns of the Scottish coat of arms was crowned and combined with the British lion. After the Hanoverian succession the unicorn's crown was removed and 'strife between England and Scotland resumed'. The royal rhyme fits cleverly into the chess context elaborated by Carroll, since chess too is based around the conflict for a crown.

9 *a Bandersnatch.* See chapter 1, note 19. The King must be familiar with the creature from his reading of 'Jabberwocky'.

10 *oyster-shells.* A strange reminiscence of 'The Walrus and the Carpenter' (pp. 159–63).

11 *How fast those Queens can run.* Queens have greater mobility than any other chess pieces of course. The White Queen appears to have moved to QB8, perhaps as a result of (unnecessary) fear of the Red Knight by her side.

12 *It's as large as life, and twice as natural.* A play on the phrase, usually used about representation in art, 'as large as life and quite as natural'. The *OED* gives a contemporary example from C. Bede's *Verdant Green* (1853): 'An imposing-looking Don, as large as life and quite as natural'. When he saw W. B. Richmond's painting of the Liddell children, *The Sisters*, in 1865, Carroll thought 'Alice very lovely, but not *quite* natural' (*Diaries*, vol 1, p. 228). Carroll's version has subsequently become a catch-phrase.

13 *I always thought they were fabulous monsters!* The Unicorn, as a fabulous monster himself, sees the human child as one – one of the most beautiful of the looking-glass's inversions.

14 *The Lion had joined them.* Tenniel's illustration bears a resemblance to a cartoon drawn for *Punch* twenty years earlier, also showing the Lion (complete with spectacles) and the Unicorn (though without his goatee beard) confronting each other; it accompanied a letter from 'The British Lion' to the lord responsible for the royal coat of arms remonstrating about the Scottish unicorn (*Punch*, Jan–June 1853). See Hancher, '*Punch* and *Alice*' in *Lewis Carroll:*

A Celebration, ed. E. Guiliano, New York, 1982. Since Tenniel was the quasi-official political cartoonist of *Punch*, contemporaries saw in Tenniel's *Looking-Glass* illustration of the Lion and Unicorn an allusion to the two great prime-ministerial rivals of the time – the leonine Gladstone (who represented Oxford as MP for eighteen years) and the dapperly bearded Disraeli. Carroll produced a satirical anagram of 'William Ewart Gladstone' – 'Wild agitator, Means well' – but thought Disraeli 'the greatest statesman of our time' (*Letters*, vol 1, p. 423). They too were perpetually fighting for power.

15 *the Lion twice as much as me*. Presumably an allusion to the proverbial phrase 'the lion's share'.

16 *she . . . sprang across the little brook in her terror.* Alice moves on to Q7. The terrifying drums are the aural equivalent of the comparably rhyme-derived shadow of the 'monstrous crow' in chapter 4 and the crash of Humpty Dumpty in chapter 6. Alice's progress is shadowed by violent forces, and during these episodes she experiences 'terror', 'alarm' and 'anxiety'. Tenniel's empty plate and knife, the drums and drumsticks without drummers capture this brilliantly.

CHAPTER VIII: "IT'S MY OWN INVENTION"

1 *Only I do hope it's my dream, and not the Red King's.* Alice is still preoccupied by the Tweedle brothers' claims in chapter 4 (see p. 165). Whether *Through the Looking-Glass* is her dream alone or 'another person's dream' (her author's, for example) is a moot point.

2 *a Knight, dressed in crimson armour, came galloping*. The Red Knight moves to K2, checking the White King and attacking the White Queen.

3 *This time it was a White Knight*. The White Knight moves to the square occupied by the Red Knight (next to Alice) and hence (after the battle) 'takes' him. His initial cry of 'Check' is quite inappropriate, since he would be checking only his own King, not the opposing Red King. This is a travesty of chess – and of Spenserean romance. The White Knight's peculiar status is reflected in his appearance in the frontispiece to the story.

4 *It was a glorious victory, wasn't it?* Compare Southey's *The Battle of Blenheim* (1798): '"And everybody praised the Duke,/Who this great fight did win"/"But what good came of it at last?"/Quoth little Peterkin./"Why that I cannot tell," said he/"But 'twas a famous victory"'.

5 *when you've crossed the next brook*. On her next move in the chess game (to Q8), Alice, still a mere pawn, will automatically become a Queen.

6 *It's my own invention*. Many readers have seen in this gentle and eccentric inventor a self-portrait of Carroll (though Tenniel's amiable buffer with a walrus-moustache appears to be a self-portrait of Tenniel). Carroll was, like the

Knight, an 'upside-down' inventor, a collector of strange toys to amuse his child friends and an inveterate deviser of games and gadgets – such as his Nyctograph to help writing at night, a chess game with letters, and *The Wonderland Stamp Case* (which he had manufactured in 1888, *Diaries*, vol 2, p. 465). Alice's encounter with the Knight has an almost wistful tonality that is very different to anything else in either Alice book and may suggest something of the author's elegiac feelings towards his 'dream child'. A. L. Taylor called his biography *The White Knight: A Study of Lewis Carroll* (Edinburgh, 1952).

7 *practice in riding*. The Liddell children had had riding lessons, as Carroll's diary confirms: 'Went over for the last time to Charlton Kings, and walked in to Cheltenham with Alice, Edith and Miss Prickett, and left them at the Riding School' (7 April 1863, *Diaries*, vol 1, p. 195).

8 *like a sugar-loaf*. Now unfamiliar, this was 'a moulded conical mass of hard refined sugar' (*OED*).

9 *the name of the song is called 'Haddocks' Eyes'*. For a philosophical discussion of the issues of naming involved here, see Roger Holmes, 'The Philosopher's Alice in Wonderland', *Antioch Review*, Summer 1959. For a discussion of literary titles based on the White Knight's fastidious differentiations, see John Hollander, '"Haddocks' Eyes" A Note on the Theory of Titles', in *Vision and Resonance*, 1975. Carroll has some remarks on names in book 1 chapter 4 of *Symbolic Logic* (1896) and as a professional logician shared some of the Knight's pernickety rigour.

10 *this was the one that she always remembered most clearly*. This sudden time-shift to a mood of anticipated retrospection indicates that this incident has an exceptional status in the text. Alice's final image of the Knight is consciously elegiac and 'picturesque' – it is 'like a picture' indeed – in a way almost nothing else in either book seems to be. The tonality is close to that of the introductory poem and the 'picture' is an instance of Victorian, even Pre-Raphaelite, medievalism. Tenniel's frontispiece, a parody of Millais's *A Dream of the Past* or *Sir Isumbras at the Ford*, is loosely based on this scene. Millais's painting has a little girl sitting on the horse in front of the venerable knight.

11 *'I give thee all, I can no more.'* The first line of 'My Heart and Lute' by Thomas Moore, a song set to music by Sir Henry Rowley Bishop and the metrical model of the White Knight's poem. The first stanza reads:

> I give thee all – I can give no more –
>   Though poor the offering be;
> My heart and lute are all the store
>   That I can bring to thee.

A lute whose gentle song reveals
The soul of love full well;
And, better far, a heart that feels
Much more than lute could tell

The lyric which gives the poem its tune may not be the Knight's 'own invention', as he claims, but its original words reveal 'the soul of love' far better than the Carrollian Knight's nonsense lyric can tell.

12 *I'll tell thee everything I can.* The poem is a revised and extended version of 'Upon the Lonely Moor', a poem Carroll had originally published anonymously in *The Train* in 1856 (*The Complete Works of Lewis Carroll*, ed. Alexander Woollcott, London, 1939, pp. 727–30). If it takes its metre from Thomas Moore, it takes its parodic target from another Romantic poet, as he tells his uncle in a letter of 14 May 1872:

> 'Sitting on a Gate' *is* a parody, though not as to style or metre – but its plot is borrowed from Wordsworth's 'Resolution and Independence', a poem that has always amused me a good deal (though it is by no means a comic poem) by the absurd way in which the poet goes on questioning the poor old leech-gatherer, making him tell his history over and over again, and never attending to what he says. Wordsworth ends with a moral – an example I have *not* followed. (Letter to Hassard Dodgson, *Letters*, vol 1, p. 177).

Wordsworth's 'Resolution and Independence', first published in *Poems* (1807), is a poem dramatizing the poet's encounter on a remote moor with an old leech-gatherer ('The oldest man he seemed who ever wore grey hairs') and is one of Wordsworth's many poems about dejection and ageing ('We poets in our youth begin in gladness;/But thereof come in the end despondency and madness'). Though Carroll parodies it, such concerns make it apt for the White Knight; as Carroll wrote, 'the character of the White Knight was meant to suit the speaker in the poem'.

13 *Rowland's Macassar-Oil.* The most popular and widely advertised hair-oil of the nineteenth century. Compare Byron, *Don Juan*, Canto 1, stanza 17: 'In virtues nothing earthly could surpass her,/Save thine "incomparable oil," Macassar!'

14 *the Menai bridge.* Telford's iron suspension bridge, completed in 1826, joining Anglesey and North Wales.

15 *I weep, for it reminds me so.* A parody of Wordsworth's poetry of 'emotion recollected in tranquillity', as embodied in the close of 'Resolution and Independence' ('"God", said I, "be my help and stay secure;/I'll think of the leech-gatherer on the lonely moor"') and 'Tintern Abbey'.

16 *till he was out of sight.* The White Knight returns to KB5, as before he met Alice.

17 *the edge of the brook.* It may have been at this point that the omitted 'The Wasp in a Wig' episode, mentioned in Collingwood's *Life* (p. 146), was to be inserted. What purported to be the cancelled galley proofs of the missing chapter were sold in London in 1974 and published as *The Wasp in a Wig: A 'Suppressed' Episode of Through the Looking-Glass*, with a Preface, Introduction and Notes by Martin Gardner in 1977. That edition notionally inserts the four or so galley pages of the episode between these two sentences, so that 'A very few steps brought her to the edge of the brook' is immediately followed by '. . . and she was just going to spring over, when she heard a deep sigh, which seemed to come from the wood behind her.' The authenticity of the cancelled 'Wasp in a Wig' episode is questionable: for further details, see special issue of *Jabberwocky*, vol 7, no. 3, Summer 1978.
18 *The Eighth Square at last.* In the chess game Alice has moved to Q8 and thus become a Queen. In Tenniel's illustration her crown, with its characteristic bobble in the middle, is unmistakably a *chess* crown.

CHAPTER IX: QUEEN ALICE

1 *Queens have to be dignified, you know.* In his influential 'Of Queens' Gardens' (1864) in *Sesame and Lilies* (1865) John Ruskin, at one time Alice's drawing-master and a man whom Dodgson described as 'numbering among my friends' (*Letters*, vol 1, p. 326), enjoined queenliness (which he called 'the highest dignity') on all women: 'Queens you must always be: queens to your lovers; queens to your husbands and your sons; queens of higher mystery to the world beyond, which bows itself, and will for ever bow, before the myrtle crown and the stainless sceptre of womanhood'. Though Alice has earlier said she would like 'to be a Queen best', her brief reign as a chess queen is taken up with a tedious conversation with two other Queens and a very frustrating banquet. However 'dignified' it may be, her experience doesn't make Ruskin's contemporary mythologization of femininity, also written 'to please one girl' (as he wrote in his 1871 Preface), a very appealing prospect for a girl like Alice (Ruskin incidentally makes a glancing allusion to the 'Dean of Christ Church', Alice's father, in the same lecture).
2 *one on each side.* The Red Queen has moved to K1 beside Alice, who is herself beside the White Queen. As Gardner points out, 'the White King is placed in check by this move, but neither side seems to notice it'. Alice had last met the Red Queen in chapter 2 where, amid a torrent of other advice, the Queen had explained the rules of chess to her.
3 *the proper examination.* The education of women was very much a live issue at this time; in 1847 Tennyson identified 'the higher education of women' as one

of the major issues of the day and explored it in *The Princess*, while Ruskin discussed it in his 1864 lecture 'Of Queens' Gardens' (see note 1 above). The first college for women, significantly called Queen's College, was founded in 1848, to be followed by Bedford College, which was incorporated into the University of London in 1869, the year the University of Cambridge instituted a Higher Local examination for women over eighteen years (just before *TLG*). There were no degrees open to women as yet, but in the coming years Newnham College, Cambridge (1875), and Somerville College and Lady Margaret Hall, Oxford (1879), were opened. Writing in the 1890s about the issue of 'granting university degrees to women', Dodgson opposed there being 'resident women-students' at Oxford University and argued instead for a separate 'Women's University' ('Resident Women Students', *The Complete Works*, pp. 1068–9). In the pages that follow here the Red Queen submits Alice to a prolonged travesty of an academic examination, comparable to the travesty of school education in the Mock Turtle's story (*AAIW*, chapter 9).

4 *Fiddle-de-dee's not English.* It is, however, found in English dictionaries as an interjection meaning 'nonsense' and a noun meaning 'an absurdity'. *OED* quotes an earlier lexicographer, Dr Johnson, exclaiming 'All he said was "Fiddle-de-dee, my dear"' (Boswell, *Life of Johnson*, 1784). It also forms the first line of a nursery rhyme included in Halliwell's *Nursery Rhymes of England*, 'Fiddle-de-dee, fiddle-de-dee,/The fly shall marry the bumble-bee'. The recent French translation of *Alice* does not really resolve the Queen's difficult translation question. It translates the question itself as '"Comment dit-on 'turlututu' en javanais?"' and gives Alice's answer as '"Turlututu n'est pas anglais"' (Lewis Carroll, *Oeuvres*, 1, p. 350).

5 *I know what he came for.* Alice knows because she remembers Humpty Dumpty's song from chapter 6, 'In winter, when the fields are white' (also a 'riddle with no answer'). The corkscrew, door and fish are all alluded to there (in fact Humpty Dumpty has twice already been associated with corkscrews, see chapter 6, note 12).

6 *Hush-a-by-lady.* A play on the nursery rhyme 'Hush-a-bye baby on the tree top', in Halliwell's *Nursery Rhymes of England*, one of the best-known lullabies in England and America. The Queen's lullaby for her fellow Queen infantilizes Alice's new queenly status but is notably gentler than the virulent lullaby sung by the Duchess in *AAIW*, chapter 6 ('Speak roughly to your little boy').

7 *not in all the History of England.* Alice here adopts Humpty Dumpty's grand historical scale ('That's what you call a History of England, that is', chapter 6) and reverts to the 'dry' matter of national history recalled in the Mouse's reading in *AAIW*, chapter 3. Tenniel's illustration gives the door marked 'Queen Alice' an appropriate historical aura – a Norman archway, Gothic lettering –

identifying Alice with that history too. In a preliminary pencil sketch for it Tenniel gave Queen Alice a balloon-crinoline dress, but Carroll objected.

8 *No admittance till the week after next.* Rude this may be, but it may also be an index of Looking-Glass time, as defined by the White Queen earlier (chapter 5). Asked by Alice '"What sort of things do you remember best?"' she replied, '"Oh, things that happened the week after next"'.

9 *Wexes it.* Cockney, 'vexes it'. Earlier the Frog equally demotically says, '"I speaks English, doesn't I?"' recalling Alice's forgetting how to speak 'good English' earlier in her dream adventures (see *AAIW*, chapter 2, note 1) and her concern as to whether 'fiddle-de-dee' is or is not English in this chapter.

10 *To the Looking-Glass world it was Alice that said.* A burlesque of Sir Walter Scott's 'Bonny Dundee' which begins: 'To the Lords of Convention, 'twas Claver'se who spoke./"Ere the King's crown shall fall there are crowns to be broke;/So let each Cavalier who loves honour and me,/Come follow the bonnet of Bonny Dundee"'. The chorus goes: 'Come fill up my cup, come fill up my can,/Come saddle your horses, and call up your men;/Come open the West Port, and let me gang free,/And it's room for the bonnets of Bonny Dundee!'. As with the 'Lion and the Unicorn' and the rhyme of the battling brothers Tweedle, the echo of Scott's poem conjures up an earlier fight for the crown in 'The History of England'.

11 *it isn't etiquette to cut any one.* The Red Queen, like the author, is a stickler for etiquette throughout (as we see from her earlier reference to 'lessons in manners'). This cutting joke depends on the pun on 'cut' meaning 'to affect not to see or know (a person) on meeting or passing him' (*OED*). As a campaigning anti-vivisectionist, Carroll was particularly concerned about 'cutting' live creatures.

12 *First, the fish must be caught.* The answer to the Queen's 'lovely riddle' is 'An oyster'. In 1878 the magazine *Fun* published an answer to the riddle written in the same metre that had been submitted to Carroll and polished up by him. It went: 'Get an oyster-knife strong,/Insert it 'twixt cover and dish in the middle;/Then you shall before long/Un-dish-cover the OYSTERS – dish-cover the riddle!' Oysters had figured prominently in the earlier, equally fishy 'The Walrus and the Carpenter'.

13 *like extinguishers.* Conical candle extinguishers.

14 *I can't stand this any longer.* Alice's cry of exasperation mirrors that at the equally anarchic close of *AAIW*: 'You're nothing but a pack of cards' (chapter 12). Tenniel's illustration faithfully records the 'dreadful confusion' described in the text. In one image he captures Alice's decisive gesture of dismissal, the final metamorphoses of the chess pieces – the White Queen disappearing into the tureen, for example – and the phantasmagoric dissolution of the banquet.

The bottles with wings of plates look like chess pawns, the upended pudding like a bishop, the tureen like a Queen, and Alice herself like a chess piece.

15 *turning fiercely upon the Red Queen.* The Red Queen represents the most powerful of the opposing forces in the game of chess (she is the most aggressive in character). At this point Alice takes the Red Queen and simultaneously checkmates the Red King, who has succeeded in sleeping throughout the entire game without moving. In the Preface to the Sixty-First Thousand Carroll notes that the 'final "checkmate" of the Red King will be found to be strictly in accordance with the laws of the game' (see Appendix II). Alice has made her winning move and brought the game to an end.

CHAPTER XII: WHICH DREAMED IT?

1 *such a nice dream.* The book's dream structure mirrors that of *AAIW*. As the earlier story comes full circle, so this one ends where it began in chapter 1 with Alice talking to her cat Dinah and the two kittens, Kitty and Snowdrop.

2 *all about fishes.* There's something fishy about Alice's recollection of the poetry she's heard. Of the poems in *AAIW*, one concerns a crocodile that eats fishes, another a mock turtle (an artificial marine reptile), and another a lobster; of those in *TLG*, 'The Walrus and the Carpenter' figures oysters and Humpty Dumpty's song does mention fishes, but, though the White Knight's ballad is mysteriously named 'Haddocks' Eyes', it isn't 'about fishes' in any obvious sense and neither are 'Jabberwocky' or the final drinking-song 'Queen Alice'.

3 *Which do you think it was?* This direct address to the reader shifts the narrative direction, ending the book with an unexpected questioning note, comparable to that at the close of Keats's 'To the Nightingale' ('Do I wake or sleep?'). Alice's question ('who do you think dreamed it all?') refers back to Tweedledee's contemptuous remark, 'why you're only a sort of thing in his [the Red King's] dream' (chapter 4).

4 *A boat, beneath a sunny sky.* The final poem is an acrostic; the initial letters of each line spell out Alice's full name, ALICE PLEASANCE LIDDELL. It returns to the 'golden afternoon' of the introductory poem of *AAIW* and the genesis of the original narrative, now viewed through the perspective of old age and passing time, in tone with the more sombre key of this second book.

5 *Still she haunts me, phantomwise.* If this was the case in 1871 when *TLG* was published, it remained so till the end of Carroll's life (see, for example, the account in '"Alice" on the Stage', pp. 293–5). When he met Alice's husband for the first time in 1888, he noted: 'It was not easy to link in one's mind the new face with the older memory – the stranger with the so intimately known and loved "Alice", whom I shall always remember as an entirely fascinating seven-year-old maiden' (*Diaries*, vol 2, p. 465). Inviting her to tea in 1891, he wrote to her as 'one I can scarcely picture to myself, even now, as more than seven years old' (*Letters*, vol 2, p. 465). To Mrs Liddell he wrote the same year: 'It seems but yesterday when the Dean and you arrived: yet I was hardly more than a boy, then; and many of the pleasantest memories of those early years – that foolish time when it seemed as if it would last for ever – are bound up with the names of yourself and your children' (*Letters*, vol 2, p. 870). In the two Alice books, as in some of his early photos, she does indeed 'last for ever' as a phantom of that 'seven-year-old maiden'.

6 *Life, what is it but a dream?* The final line is a variant of a familiar literary and philosophical trope. Compare Shakespeare, 'We are such stuff/As dreams are made on' (*The Tempest*, iv.1.146); Shelley, 'He is awakened from the dream of life' (*Adonais*, 1.344); Tennyson, 'Dreams are true while they last, and do we not live in dreams?' (*The Higher Pantheism*, 4). The rhyme of 'dream' and 'gleam', like the 'summer glory' of the opening poem, also echoes Wordsworth's 'Immortality Ode': 'Whither is fled the visionary gleam?/ Where is it now, the glory and the dream?'

APPENDIX I:

Preface to the Eighty-sixth Thousand of the 6/- Edition of Alice's Adventures in Wonderland

Enquiries have been so often addressed to me, as to whether any answer to the Hatter's riddle (see p. 60) can be imagined, that I may as well put on record here what seems to be a fairly appropriate answer, viz. "Because it can produce a few notes, though they are *very* flat; and it is never put with the wrong end in front!" This, however, is merely an after-thought: the Riddle, as originally invented, had no answer at all.

For this eighty-sixth thousand, fresh electrotypes have been taken from the wood-blocks (which, never having been used for printing from, are in as good condition as when first cut in 1865), and the whole book has been set up afresh with new type. If the artistic qualities of this re-issue fall short, in any particular, of those possessed by the original issue, it will not be for want of painstaking on the part of author, publisher or printer.

I take this opportunity of announcing that the Nursery "Alice," hitherto priced at four shillings, net, is now to be had on the same terms as the ordinary shilling picture-books—although I feel sure that it is, in every quality (except the *text* itself, on which I am not qualified to pronounce), greatly superior to them. Four shillings was a perfectly reasonable price to charge, considering the very heavy initial outlay I had incurred: still, as the Public have practically said "We will *not* give more than a shilling for a picture-book, however artistically got-up", I am content to reckon my outlay on the book as so much dead loss, and, rather than let the little ones, for whom it was written, go without it, I am selling it at a price which is, to me, much the same thing as *giving* it away.

Christmas, 1896.

APPENDIX II:

Preface to the Sixty-first Thousand Edition of Through the Looking-Glass

As the chess-problem, given on a previous page, has puzzled some of my readers, it may be well to explain that it is correctly worked out, so far as the moves are concerned. The *alternation* of Red and White is perhaps not so strictly observed as it might be, and the "castling" of the three Queens is merely a way of saying that they entered the palace: but the "check" of the White King at move 6, the capture of the Red Knight at move 7, and the final "checkmate" of the Red King, will be found, by any one who will take the trouble to set the pieces and play the moves as directed, to be strictly in accordance with the laws of the game.

The new words, in the poem "Jabberwocky" (see p. 132), have given rise to some differences of opinion as to their pronunciation: so it may be well to give instructions on *that* point also. Pronounce "slithy" as if it were the two words "sly, the": make the 'g' *hard* in "gyre" and "gimble": and pronounce "rath" to rhyme with "bath."

For this sixty-first thousand, fresh electrotypes have been taken from the wood-blocks (which, never having been used for printing from, are in as good condition as when first cut in 1871), and the whole book has been set up afresh with new type. If the artistic qualities of this re-issue fall short, in any particular, of those possessed by the original issue, it will not be for want of painstaking on the part of author, publisher, or printer.

I take this opportunity of announcing that the Nursery "Alice," hitherto priced at four shillings, net, is now to be had on the same terms as the ordinary shilling picture-books—although I feel sure that it is, in every quality (except the *text* itself, on which I am not qualified to pronounce), greatly superior to them. Four shillings was a perfectly reasonable price to charge, considering the very heavy initial outlay I had incurred: still, as the Public have practically said "We will *not* give more than a shilling for a picture-book, however artistically got-up," I am content to reckon my outlay on the book as so much dead loss, and, rather than let the little ones, for whom it was written, go without it, I am selling it at a price which is, to me, much the same thing as *giving* it away.

Christmas, 1896.

READ MORE IN PENGUIN

READ MORE IN PENGUIN

A CHOICE OF CLASSICS

Matthew Arnold	**Selected Prose**
Jane Austen	**Emma**
	Lady Susan/The Watsons/Sanditon
	Mansfield Park
	Northanger Abbey
	Persuasion
	Pride and Prejudice
	Sense and Sensibility
William Barnes	**Selected Poems**
Mary Braddon	**Lady Audley's Secret**
Anne Brontë	**Agnes Grey**
	The Tenant of Wildfell Hall
Charlotte Brontë	**Jane Eyre**
	Juvenilia: 1829–35
	The Professor
	Shirley
	Villette
Emily Brontë	**Complete Poems**
	Wuthering Heights
Samuel Butler	**Erewhon**
	The Way of All Flesh
Lord Byron	**Don Juan**
	Selected Poems
Lewis Carroll	**Alice's Adventures in Wonderland**
	The Hunting of the Snark
Thomas Carlyle	**Selected Writings**
Arthur Hugh Clough	**Selected Poems**
Wilkie Collins	**Armadale**
	The Law and the Lady
	The Moonstone
	No Name
	The Woman in White
Charles Darwin	**The Origin of Species**
	Voyage of the Beagle
Benjamin Disraeli	**Coningsby**
	Sybil

READ MORE IN PENGUIN

A CHOICE OF CLASSICS

Charles Dickens	**American Notes for General Circulation**
	Barnaby Rudge
	Bleak House
	The Christmas Books (in two volumes)
	David Copperfield
	Dombey and Son
	Great Expectations
	Hard Times
	Little Dorrit
	Martin Chuzzlewit
	The Mystery of Edwin Drood
	Nicholas Nickleby
	The Old Curiosity Shop
	Oliver Twist
	Our Mutual Friend
	The Pickwick Papers
	Pictures from Italy
	Selected Journalism 1850–1870
	Selected Short Fiction
	Sketches by Boz
	A Tale of Two Cities
George Eliot	**Adam Bede**
	Daniel Deronda
	Felix Holt
	Middlemarch
	The Mill on the Floss
	Romola
	Scenes of Clerical Life
	Silas Marner
Fanny Fern	**Ruth Hall**
Elizabeth Gaskell	**Cranford/Cousin Phillis**
	The Life of Charlotte Brontë
	Mary Barton
	North and South
	Ruth
	Sylvia's Lovers
	Wives and Daughters

READ MORE IN PENGUIN

A CHOICE OF CLASSICS

Walter Scott	**The Antiquary**
	Heart of Mid-Lothian
	Ivanhoe
	Kenilworth
	The Tale of Old Mortality
	Rob Roy
	Waverley
Robert Louis Stevenson	**Kidnapped**
	Dr Jekyll and Mr Hyde and Other Stories
	In the South Seas
	The Master of Ballantrae
	Selected Poems
	Weir of Hermiston
William Makepeace Thackeray	**The History of Henry Esmond**
	The History of Pendennis
	The Newcomes
	Vanity Fair
Anthony Trollope	**Barchester Towers**
	Can You Forgive Her?
	Doctor Thorne
	The Eustace Diamonds
	Framley Parsonage
	He Knew He Was Right
	The Last Chronicle of Barset
	Phineas Finn
	The Prime Minister
	The Small House at Allington
	The Warden
	The Way We Live Now
Oscar Wilde	**Complete Short Fiction**
Mary Wollstonecraft	**A Vindication of the Rights of Woman**
	Mary and Maria (includes Mary Shelley's **Matilda**)
Dorothy and William Wordsworth	**Home at Grasmere**